Book 1 of The Lost Children Series

Forgiveness

A Novel by

Joseph J. R. Johnson

1ˢᵗ edition

ISBN-13: 978-1-7346310-0-5

Cover art by Joseph Johnson

Email the author: jjohnson.johnson66@gmail.com

This work was previously published as *Forgiveness* by Thrak Farrelle.

Contents

Map of Eastern Usmer

 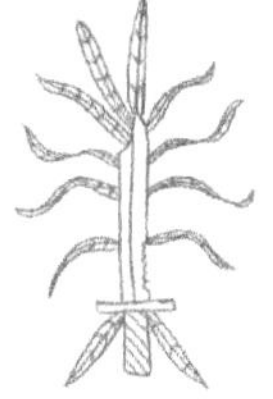 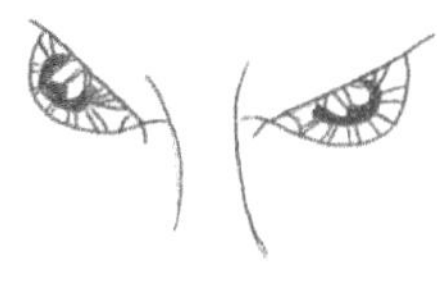

Chapter 1
Nom's Tale

The boy gazed out at the Sundering. His black skin onyx against the the Sundering's steam clouds. The great greyness of the Sundering Wall seethed up from the steely waters of the sea. He wondered what was out there. What could go through that wall of vapor, and land on the shores of what was his family's fishing village? There was no village there now. The boy was the last of that.

"Nom Carver? You are summoned to see the King at the castle."

The boy, Nom Carver, turned around in the swing he sat upon. Behind him, down the hill, was a courier from the castle's court. The courier's armor was covered in white and green feathers of local birds. Nom Carver nodded to the courier and hopped off the lonely swing tied to the lonely tree. The courier quickly turned and left Nom. Nom, hardly noticing the courier's leave, began trekking down the slope of the hill towards the castle town of Puntacan, the capital city of the Kingdom of New Keys.

*****

<u>2</u>

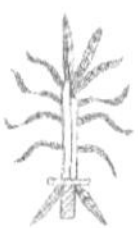

Nom Carver passed the brightly adorned guards at the entrance to the castle's courtyard. Behind the walls of the castle, the world quieted. The bright sun shone into the yard. Carver blinked up at the blue sky. His house was on the eastern shore of the island, under the tall presence of The Sundering. The sun was hidden behind the billowing wall of steam until just before noon every day. If the wind blew from the east, the sun wouldn't come out until late in the afternoon, as the winds tore the clouds from The Sundering, covering the sky.

The boy meandered his way towards the castle, the largest structure on the island. It always took Nom's breath away with wonder when he saw it. It was three stories tall and flared outward in a gentle slope from the ground floor. The building was shaped like an arrowhead with the tip pointing at the castle gate. The sun reflected blindingly off the white surface of the castle. Nom Carver approached the staircase that led inside. It was a thin stair that went into the castle's second floor. Rumor had it that the castle was built such that when the great flood would someday sweep the land, the castle would float away upon the sea. That's why the ground floor was never built with a door, because it would someday be submerged under the waves and the second floor entrance would be at water level.

The guard at the base of the stairs looked at Carver and asked somewhat unkindly, "Que?"

"The king called for me?"

The guard looked down his nose at the thirteen-year-old boy. The sun beat down on the two of them. Sweat dripped out from the helmet on the man's head. Nom Carver had to blink as the sun caught on the armor of the guard, who was adorned from head to foot in the bright plumage of tropical birds. Red feathers gave way to green, then orange, and then purple, all spiraling and shifting over the woven armor. The light reflected off the feathers in all directions, like little needles of bright glass, and Nom Carver could not look long at the guard. The guard sneered as the boy blinked and looked away. Either because he was bored of messing with Nom, or because he thought he had intimidated Nom enough; the guard stepped aside. Nom hurried up the stairs.

Nom came out of the inside of the castle and onto the flat roof. The top of the castle was perfectly flat with wooden barriers, painted white, lining the outside edge. A large canopy covered the castle from the arrow point to the center of the triangle. Under the canopy sat the king's throne. Nom Carver slowly walked towards the throne. The top of the castle was made with the same material as the building's walls. The material was strangely smooth, like metal but not metal, and sturdy. The roof was also painted a blindingly bright white. Nom scuffled his feet on the strange surface.

Under the canopy sat were three people: King Jin and two strangers. One of the strangers was a woman with long, straight, brown hair and olive skin. There seemed to be a shadow under the canopy where she sat, and a breeze played with her hair. The other stranger was a man in full armor. This was not the woven armor of the islanders but scale armor. Nom had sometimes seen this armor worn by the foreign merchants' bodyguards at the docks. This armor looked different though. It was a deep red, like the setting sun just before it lowers below the edge of the earth. The metal used for the scales looked different as well, newer, or at least better taken care of. Nom had asked a fisherman about scale armor and the fisherman had explained that the metal scales used in the armor were usually fashioned using scrap metal from the Forbears' broken artifacts. The man wore a dark purple cloak over his armor with the hood cascading down his upper back. The helmet on his head was the strangest part about the man. Nom knew when he saw the helmet that he would most likely never see such a thing again. The helmet was dark red like the scale armor. There were two golden eyes with horizontal slits of dark glass. Over the eye slits sat a golden crown with the face of a white fox and two horns curving upwards above the helmet. In the center of the forehead of both the mask and the fox were two black stones with gold U's in their centers. Leaning on the chair was a large golden war hammer with a scythe-like blade on the backside.

Nom Carver looked away from the strangers and bowed before King Jin. The King looked at Nom and said, "Hello, Nom. How is your house holding up? Is Esmira bringing you enough allowance and helping to keep the house in order?"

Nom stood up and stated, "Yes, the house is fine, and I get enough food, your highness."

"Good, good," the king waved the conversation away. Then he looked at the strange man while saying, "Morsmani and Lady Amy here are scholars from the continent. They came after hearing about what happened to your village. They claim that they can help explain what happened and may even have a solution."

Nom perked up at the mention of his childhood village and quickly glanced at the strangers. He blurted out, "What were those monsters that attacked my village? Where did they come from?" and then with a slight tremor in his voice the boy asked, "Will they come back?"

The woman, Lady Amy, gave Nom a concerned look and then turned to her companion.

The companion nodded at Nom and explained, "We think we know what they were. But before we fully decide what happened, I think it best if we hear your tale." The man paused, then began speaking in a gentle tone to Nom. "What happened? Take your time. I know it must be a horrible memory and I'm sorry to ask you to recount it, but it is necessary. I would hate to give the wrong advice to the most… hospitable King Jin." The strange man gave a curt nod to the king.

The boy's shoulders slumped. Didn't they hear the story from the king? Why did he have to retell it again? Nom's mouth opened, and then one word after another, his tale unfolded.

*****

"I was sitting on a branch of a black mangrove tree, fishing. The tree grew where the river hit the ocean. I saw movement at the end of the river," The boy paused and looked up at the adults watching.

He continued, addressing the ground again. "There were people coming out of the sea. They walked out from the waves, in the direction of my village. It was strange. They did not breathe deep like people finishing a swim. They were fully clothed. Some even in armor. I was scared, so I pulled in my line and crept back along the branch to where I could not see them anymore. Then I heard a scream. So, I climbed the mangrove."

Here the boy's voice wavered, "Th-the tree was. My dad called it 'the old man'. Cause it was an old *mang*rove tree and it was big. Cause of how old it was. So, I climbed the tree to see. I was too scared to leave the tree.

"When I got to the top, I could see the village. It was on fire. The people who came out of the ocean were slowly walking around the village with torches. They were silent. They threw a torch onto the palm thatch roof of the Maderas's house. Old Man Maderas ran out of the house. He hit one of the people from the sea with an oar. The sea person stabbed him."

Nom paused, then continued, "My parent's house went up next. It was large. My father was the chief. No one came out. I think they…my parents…were caught in the fire, the smoke. The people from the sea walked from hut to hut with their torches. There were, I think, twenty of them.

"The villagers. They ran for the shore. They were all screaming. There was one, a baby, Elisif. She would be turning three right about now. She stood outside her house and wailed. I could see the tracks her tears made on her soot covered face from the tree. She was grabbed and thrown back into the fires. I, I…I still hear how her screams changed when she began…began to burn. The villagers ran out of their houses. They ran towards the shore. To get on their ships, I think. The people from the sea that were already in the village ignored most of the running villagers, but there were more in the water. As soon as the villagers got into the boats, the boats were turned over and the villagers dragged into the water. It was, it was scary. I could not move. The rest of the villagers were killed. I saw. I could not look away.

"I snuck into the village that night. The people from the sea had left. They walked back into the ocean. I do not think they swim. They just walked slowly into the waves until the water was above their heads. Nothing was left of the village. Everything was burnt. One of the people from the sea had dropped a knife on the ground. I took it and went to the capital."

The boy looked up at the adults. The woman, Lady Amy, was watching Morsmani.

"Is the knife here?" Morsmani asked. His voice was deep and gravelly. Somehow both calming in its deepness and menacing in its gravel.

The king nodded, stating, "Si, yes, of course. We took it off the boy when he showed up here. Would not want a child, especially one who went through such an ordeal, having a weapon now would we?" The king asked with a simpering smile. He waved his hand at one of the guards. "Go get the knife. Hurry, vamos!" The guard bowed and left.

"Can you describe the people from the sea a little more, Nom?" Morsmani asked. "Can I call you Nom, or do you prefer Carver? Did these strangers jerk when they walked? Did they seem vacant? Like they weren't paying attention, or lost?"

Nom Carver thought about it then answered, "You can call me Carver or Nom. I don't care. My friends called me Nom. And si, yes, they seemed kind of lost and they did jerk a lot. They shivered too. And they dry heaved. I figured that was because they breathed in too much smoke, but maybe not."

The guard returned with the silver knife and handed it to Morsmani. He turned the knife over in his hands and ran a red, leather gloved finger over the edge of the knife. It was a strange knife. The handle was shaped with grooves to fit easily in one's hand and made of a hard material not found on the islands. The one-sided blade extended eight inches past the handle. It was made of bright steel that faded to a golden colored metal at the blade's edge. The blade was serrated for two inches along its base.

Morsmani grunted and handed the knife to Amy. He then stated, "That's a good knife. Good steel and a strong sharp edge. That knife confirms it." The last statement sounded almost like a question and Morsmani looked at Amy. Amy, not looking up from the knife, nodded.

"This attack was the work of the Terrestrial," the cloaked man explained. "The jerky movements and vacant expression are indicative of thralls. The Terrestrial is a hive mind. A being who controls the minds and wills of his followers and turns them into what we call thralls. This knife is made from manufacturing techniques that were known to the Forbears but have been lost since their fall. The handle is made of Kevlar. The blade, steel. Very good steel, even by Forbear standards. The edge is the interesting part. The golden material is tungsten carbide. Very hard to make and very expensive. Common on Forbear tools, but they never used it for a knife edge. They had no need for that. So, this was made after the fall of the Forbears."

"How do you know it was the terraristial person?" Nom Carver asked.

"The Terrestrial," Amy corrected. "He's the only person who has the knowledge and means to make something like this. Not even the Tommy Knockers can make tungsten carbide. It's a lost art,"

The king looked at the boy and said, "Thank you, Nom. You can leave now."

Nom bowed to King Jin and left the canopy. His head was buzzing with the new knowledge of what had happened to his small fishing village hidden in the mangroves.

*****

Down at Shipwright Dock the next day there was a slight commotion. Nom Carver weaved his way inbetween the sailors. The shipwright docks were Nom's favorite place to go in the capital city of New Keys, Puntacan. There was always activity and noise. He liked looking at the strange ships from foreign lands and seeing the oddly dressed merchants. This was the only port that foreigners were allowed to dock at in all of New Keys, making it the most exotic place in the kingdom.

The commotion came from the south side of the dock. There was a chanting from down there that was unusual, and a crowd was gathering. Nom made his way down the dock to see what was happening. He remembered that last time he was in the city there were a few people constructing a new building at the end of the wooden walkway. Over the heads of the onlookers, the boy could see a few stone pillars jutting towards the sky.

"Our eyes have opened…"

"And we see not as many, but as one…"

"Our thoughts were clouded…"

"But the many, combined, shine like the sun…"

The chanting became clearer as Nom came to the back of the crowd. He elbowed his way to the front. One man gave a sharp "Hey!" But when he saw that it was Nom, he quickly scowled and looked away, desperate to not be noticed as the person who yelled.

The chanters were comprised of twenty men and women who were moving and carving stones with pickaxes and chisels. They were making obelisks. There were two circles of gray obelisks. The outer most circle was half finished with five obelisks, each ten feet tall, the inner circle was complete with eleven, fifteen-foot-tall obelisks, and in the center was a single thirty foot tall obsidian obelisk polished to a mirror finish.

"As One we will conquer the cosmos…"

"As One we will throw back Chaos…"

"As many we are chaff in the wind…"

"As many we are bringers of Chaos…"

Someone sidled up behind the boy and said in his ear, "That's quite a pillar they have there, isn't it?"

Nom jumped and looked behind him. It was Lady Amy. He nodded his head and answered, "I suppose so." Then he stopped and asked, "What are you doing here?"

"Well, Morsmani and I had to make arrangements with the shipwrights for transport back to the mainland. Also, we heard about this little construction project and thought it might be interesting to see how it was going."

Nom's eyes widened. They were sailing on a shipwright's ship? Nom could only dream of that. He looked back at the pillars and asked Amy, "How is the construction going?"

"Good, it seems. Which is bad for me, and for my husband," Amy replied. Seeing the questioning look on Nom Carver's face she quickly explained, "Morsmani is my husband."

"Oh… but why is this construction bad for you?"

"Hmm? Oh, well, I'll have to tell you another time. I see Morsmani waving to me. It was nice meeting you, Nom. If I never see you again, I hope you become a successful person and have a large, happy family."

Amy quickly turned and hurried away. Nom watched her push her way out of the crowd. She did not have to push much; people seemed to darken and shy away from Amy when she came close. The boy wondered why Amy said that she will explain it later when she probably will never come back to the island. He shrugged and made his own way through the crowd, which also dispersed before Nom Carver.

*****

Nom was sitting on the swing next to his little hut. It was a lonely hut and a lonely swing. After his village was destroyed the king had given Nom the hut. It was a half hour walk out of town and under the shadow of The Sundering. Because of the view, no one wanted or used the hut before Nom. The last owners had been potters who were worshippers of Shinigorath, god of death, and thus had been run out of the capital.

Nom swung back and forth looking up at The Sundering. The sun was about to break over the top of the immeasurably tall wall of steam and vapor. The upper edge of The Sundering was a shining silver and in bright contrast with the black-grey steam.

"It has a certain beauty to it, doesn't it?"

Nom jumped and whipped around in his swing. No one ever came up here except Esmira to give him his weekly allowance of money. It was Morsmani.

"Hi. What are you doing out here?" asked Nom Carver.

"I wanted to look at The Sundering. I haven't seen it in years and I might not see it again. After all, it is the greatest manmade wall."

"Oh. Are you leaving soon?"

Morsmani tilted his head at Nom Carver and queried, "So anxious to see me leave?"

Nom turned red and answered, "No – I just, I saw Lady Amy yesterday and she said you were leaving soon. She was talking to the shipwrights about passage to the continent."

"Ah yes. She said she saw you at the new Monument of Order," Morsmani tailed off the statement and looked up at the wall. The sun now peaked over the edge, turning the side of The Sundering from steel boulders to wispy pillows.

Nom looked at Morsmani. He was a strange man with his red scale armor and weird red helmet. Nom wondered what his face looked like under that helmet. The golden war hammer was strapped onto the foreigner's back and a tomahawk was slung across his chest. Two long knives were slipped through his belt on his right side and on his left was a pouch. Nom wondered why a scholar would need so many weapons. He decided that travelling must be dangerous business.

Morsmani's head turned to look at the boy. Nom quickly looked away. "I also came here to talk to you. I feel that you should have an accounting of what happened to your village. It's only fair. King Jin was against it. Something about keeping innocence or some other hullabaloo," Morsmani began, "Ah what a good word. Hullabaloo. You ever hear that word before?"

Nom Carver shook his head and stared at the strange man. What more could this man tell him about the attack?

Morsmani continued, "Well anyway, you know that it was agents, well slaves, more like appendages really, of the Terrestrial that attacked your village. These thralls of the Terrestrial were a scouting party. They were sent to determine the defenses of these islands for their master."

"Are they going to attack more than just my village?" a wide eyed Nom Carver asked.

Morsmani nodded his head slowly. "Yes. They will attack and conquer these islands and then go after the continent. The Terrestrial is an evil being that was locked in the south by Klart Bumble and the silver folken after the Red Gold Conflict many, many years ago. He wants out now. He wants more lands and more slaves. If he manages to leave his lands, whether through these islands, or through the silver folks' lands, everything will fall under his hands. That's why Amy and I came here."

Nom Carver looked out at the shore moving forward and backward across the sand at the foot of the hill to the east. The boy then asked in a small voice, "So what are we supposed to do then?"

"Defend your lands. Prepare for the Terrestrial's assault. I will not remain here, however. I have a plan. There is a weapon, the Star of Isen, that could defeat the Terrestrial. It is in the stronghold of the silver people. Do you want to join us in finding this star? Us, as in Amy and I. We were wondering."

This surprised the boy. Ever since his village was destroyed, no one had asked Nom to do anything with them. The villagers viewed the child as someone touched by demons. They would never have anything to do with him.

Nom asked, "What about New Keys? Should I not help them?"

"If they are attacked, they won't survive. Plus, if they wanted your help, I don't think they would have put you out here in this lonely house all by yourself. Oh, I almost forgot, here's your knife back. I told Jin I wanted it for research. I thought you could use it better than he could."

Morsmani pulled the knife with the golden edge out of the pouch on his left side and held it out to Nom. The boy grabbed the knife. Looking at the keen edge reminded Nom of that day, and how he had hidden in the mangrove, terrified, as he listened to the screams and the roaring of the fire. He remembered the lifeless eyes of the attackers, how they did not seem to care or notice the fishermen they slew and the houses they burned. Nom gripped the handle of the knife and screwed up his eyes.

His hands shook as he exclaimed, "I will go with you. If I can stop them from destroying even one village, even if it is the last free village, I will!"

Morsmani looked down on the boy and said kindly, "Revenge is not the first reason to go? Good. Tonight, pack. Tomorrow meet us in Shipwright Dock."

Morsmani patted the boy on the shoulder and, turning his back on The Sundering, left, never to see the wall of mist again.

*****

Nom stared at his bowl of tostones. The fried plantains were stale and smelled of fish. He had eaten all of his fish for the week last night and had dipped the stale tostones in the thin broth he had cooked the fish in. Doing so had not made the tostones any less stale. It had only made them mushy and unappetizing. Tonight, all he had were the dry, stale tostones.

He remembered when he had first been moved here. He had been scared and the sense of loneliness had crushed him like a thousand feet of water. He was given an allowance with which he could buy food and supplies. Nom was a child, however, and spent his money on toys. He bought trinkets to distract himself and fill his time so that he did not have to think of the fire. He went hungry that first week.

When Esmira came again with his weekly allowance, Nom complained. Esmira ignored him, as most people did, and left. Nom bought food that week, and the next and the next. The food began to pile up and rot. Nom could not throw any of it out, however. He was scared that another week would come with no food. Some days he would fish off the shore near his hut, but the fish here were no good. They came up with extra eyes and fins, and they smelled of decay and mutation. The fish caught here at the edge of the world were inedible. They were strange creatures twisted by Shinigorath's Burning which raged on forever on the other side of The Sundering. Nom was forced to buy his fish from the market.

The food piled up and smelled. It rotted and caused mold. Nom could not throw it out. Finally, soldiers came. Nom assumed Esmira had told the king about the smell. The soldiers took away the food. They dumped the rotting edibles into the ocean, and when Nom had tried to stop them, they beat him. Nom went hungry again that week.

Nom stared at his tostones, assessing the green mold that had begun flourishing on their outer edges. Nom knew he should throw them out, but he could not. Esmira was not due for three days, and he was out of food. This singular bowl of tostones was the last of his stock. He sighed.

Outside a storm brewed. Lightning flashed on the other side of The Sundering. The wall of steam lit up in blue streaks. Denser areas of vapor made dark contrasts to the thin mist around them. Nom watched the lightning rage, feeling like an animal in a cage. He wished to see what was out there. He wanted to run through the storm. He wanted to feel the soft caress of the water drops on his face, the thunder booming over his head, the exhilaration as he ran, knowing that at any moment lightning could arc down and there would be nothing.

He stared at the bowl of tostones. The stale crust on the chips, cloying with salt and dust, was uninviting and dry. He picked up the bowl and stood. He would throw out the tostones and go hungry for three days. Unless he went with Amy and Morsmani, they may have food. As he stood his foot caught on the rug underneath him. It shifted, partially revealing a door. Nom had never noticed this door before.

Still holding the bowl, he knelt and brushed off the rug and the dirt, looking for a handle. There was none. He pried open the door with his fingernails. Under the trap door was blackness. Nom peered into the dark for some time before standing up. The darkness frightened him. He wanted to close the door, but he could not. He had to know what was down there. He grabbed a candle, lit it, and lowered it into the darkness. He could see nothing but a wooden ladder descending down. He put one foot on the ladder and descended.

The trip down was quick. The ladder only had eight rungs. Nom stood at the base of the ladder. He waited for his eyesight to adjust to the dark. When he could finally see, he began exploring. The room was tiny; only five feet by five feet. The walls were earthen and slowly falling apart in the damp air. Opposite the ladder was a strange shrine. Nom approached and then jumped back.

The shrine consisted of a stone square about waist high. On the stone was a statue to Shinigorath, the god of death, madness, and chaos. The statue was Shinigorath's symbol, a golden eye with a U-shaped pupil surrounded by fire. Nom knew the previous owners of this hut had been worshippers of Shinigorath. They had made their house so close to The Sundering in order to be closer to the world Shinigorath had burned. They had wanted to see his power. Eventually, the previous owners had been run out, and the house given to Nom.

Nom stood by the ladder and was prepared to rush back up and slam the door on the evil statue below, but he hesitated. He could not let such an object remain in his house. He crept across the room and snatched the statue. Standing still, his eyes shut, he waited for his punishment for moving a shrine of the gods. Nothing happened. Nom opened his eyes and scrambled up the ladder.

The boy ran out of his one room hut and down the beach. When the water rose to his knees he stopped and hurled the statue into the waves and then flung the tostones after it. He stood panting in the cool water. Stray tostones swayed on the waves all around him. He stared now at the wall of mist, the great barrier erected by the silver folken to protect the people of Usmer from Shinigorath's Burning. The lightning raged on behind it. The top of the wall leaned over Nom. The rising steam combining with the thunder heads caused the wall's top to flare out over the boy and stretch over the islands behind him.

Something brushed Nom's legs causing the boy to jump. The statue had returned. A turtle was pushing the statue back to shore and had accidentally hit Nom. The turtle bit into the wooden statue in order to grip it better and continued on his mission. When the statue was safely on shore the turtle turned to look at Nom with reproach.

"Que?" Nom asked. "I do not want it in my home."

The turtle trundled back into the waves. Nom walked to the statue. The turtle's beak had gouged large grooves into the wood. In the room under Nom's house the statue had seemed menacing, terrifying. On the beach, however, the statue seemed small and insignificant. A small water-logged trinket with large gouges.

Nom looked at the ocean and said to himself, "The ocean did not want the statue, so they put it on the edge of their world, the beach. King Jin does not want me around so he put me on the edge of his world, the beach. The statue can not leave, but I can, and I will. Maybe I will find friends out there."

Nom went back inside and packed what few belongings he had. Ready for a journey to stop the beast that destroyed his village.

*****

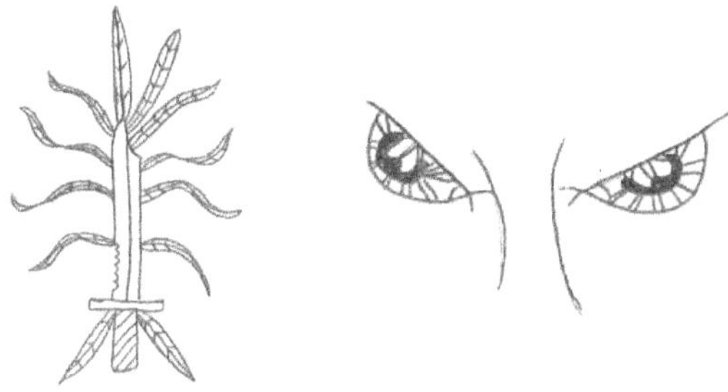

Chapter 2
The Tragedy of the Bumbles

Down at the docks, Nom Carver wandered inbetween the legs of bustling sailors. The morning heat was sweltering. Nom was sweating through his thin shirt and wished he could run through the shade of the jungle on the west side of Puntacan. He tapped a passing sailor and asked if he had seen a man in red armor. The sailor nodded and pointed Nom to the left along the docks. Nom wandered to where the sailor had suggested and sure enough, there was Morsmani on a shipwright ship.

The boy made his way up the gang way onto the deck of the ancient ship. He trembled with excitement. He was finally on a shipwright ship! The shipwrights owned the largest, strongest, and fastest ships in the world. The iconic, large, grey boats were two to five times bigger than even the largest of the wooden ships of New Keys. Even King Jin's castle paled in size to the shipwrights' ships. That is not what amazed Nom however, he wanted to see the shipwright magic. These ships did not use sails. They sailed without a breeze, and without oars. Morsmani looked over his shoulder and saw the boy.

"Hey Nom! Good to see you came. Move out of the way of the plank though, would you?" Morsmani called over.

Nom looked behind him and saw a man in blue leather armor trudging up the ramp to the deck. Nom jumped out of his way and walked over to Morsmani.

"When are we leaving?" Nom asked.

"In an hour, I think. Maybe. I'm no good with time. Soon though. We leave soon," answered the man.

An old man wandered up to Morsmani. Nom Carver ignored the man so that he could look around the old metal ship. His father had told Nom that no one knew how to make metal ships anymore. All anyone could do was maintain them; that's what the shipwrights' job was.

Someone tapped Nom on the shoulder, causing Nom to jump.

"Excuse me, Nom Carver?" the old man asked. His head was all white hair and leathered skin. Nom couldn't tell if he was fifty or eighty. He decided fifty. White hair was uncommon that young, usually, but the man seemed too fit to be older. Nom nodded his head at the old man.

"The King sent me to give parting gifts. He says that you are to be an emissary from these islands. A man who will show the world what it means to be a citizen of New Keys and make an impression on the world. He is gifting you a set of armor. The armor will adjust as you grow taller and bigger. The helmet is quite nice, quetzal feathers," The old man paused and nodded his head in wonderment. "Very fancy. Also, I brought some food for your journey and a large flask. Your companion seems to always forget these things." At that, the old man shot a mean look at Morsmani. Morsmani tilted his helmeted head back and seemed not to notice.

"Um, thank you sir. Please thank his highness for me and tell him that I will make New Keys proud." Nom stated, taking the package out of the man's hands.

The old man nodded and then said to Morsmani, "And for you, old friend, I brought a box of caff. I hope it takes you back to the days when you wandered the world without a care."

19

Morsmani let out a yelp and grabbed the box offered to him. He hugged the old man and walked with him to the gang way.

*****

It was evening. Food had been served in the ship's dining room. It was nothing special; oranges, mangos, pork, and rice. The fruit had to be eaten early before it spoiled. Nom sat next to Amy. She had been with Nom all that day. When the four cylindrical pillars of the ship started turning and the ship tore away from the pier, Amy had come up beside Nom. They stood, watching the city recede.

"Will you miss it?" she asked.

Nom looked at the shore, with the squat, single story wooden buildings with palm trees and flowers swaying lazily in the heat. The flamboyant trees were in full bloom covering the landscape in bright red.

"Maybe," the boy replied. He thought to himself, *'No one will miss me, so I will not miss it.'* Deeper down, however, his heart flung itself out to the black mangroves of his childhood home, and to the lonely swing on the lonely hill of his most recent house.

Nom grabbed a fork and knife and began cutting his pork. It was well done and tough, not the way he liked his meat cooked, but he would not complain. Food is food; eat it when you get it.

Further down the table, the sailors were talking to Morsmani and the man in blue leather. "So, you are a scholar then?"

"Yep, sure am," answered Morsmani. Nom had watched anxiously when Morsmani sat down at the table to see if he would take off the helmet. To his surprise Morsmani kept the mask on. He wasn't eating.

"And what do you do?" the sailors fielded towards the stranger.

The stranger smiled and answered, "I am a courier. I send letters and packages to people all over the world. I delivered a letter to a man named Goram and am returning with his reply."

The sailors nodded and turned back to Morsmani. "Since you ain't eating why not give us a tale? Bet you know a few, being a scholar and all." a sailor from the far west said.

The other sailors looked at the westerner in reproach. The request itself wasn't rude, just the way in which it was asked.

Morsmani looked at the sailor for a few seconds. Then quick as a snake, he lunged. The chair fell out behind Morsmani at the same time as the sailor hit the metal floor. Morsmani had only stood up. The sailors let out an uproarious laugh at their startled colleague.

"What tale would you like? Adventure? Mystery? Ancient stories of the Prometheans?" Morsmani asked through his own chuckles.

Nom hoped for tales of the Prometheans, but one sailor spoke up first. "May we have a tale of love?"

The sailors rounded on the man whose face turned red. He sunk into his plumed cloak as the sailors berated him for being a wuss. Morsmani waved his hand and everyone quieted.

"A tale of love then. Wonderful! There isn't much like a story of two star crossed lovers to put a tear in your eye, and make even the hardest of sailors wish for the soft caress of land. I have just the thing! I hope. It's also a tale of the Prometheans…"

Nom perked up, still cutting up his pork. His mouth twisted into the slightest smile, as he thought, *Maybe this adventure will be fun after all.*

*****

Morsmani spoke, "You probably know of the Bumbles. Klart Bumble, married to Beatrice Bumble, leader of the Golden Council, King of the Prometheans, The Great Prophet. Beatrice Bumble, wife of Klart Bumble, mother of dragons, savior of scags, the Incarnate. And their son, John Bumble, strongest of scags. You know these names as legendary figures of lore. They were not always so. The Bumbles were once humble. Like all heroes and villains, gods and demons, they began simply as people.

"Klart Bumble was an unfortunate man. He was not particularly smart; often he was considered dumb and ugly. It was a lonely life for Klart. After he dropped out of school he worked in restaurants. A woman came into the restaurant he waited. She was beautiful. A petite woman with porcelain skin and hair a burnished red, like copper in the sunset. Klart fell in love with her and found out her name was Beatrice.

"Beatrice was a school teacher. She loved to teach. She felt that she was a protector for her kids. She protected them both from ignorance and the cruelty of the world. Whenever she saw a child being bullied, she would always step in to help the victim. This often meant punishing bullies. This made her rather unpopular amongst the bullies' parents, many of whom were also bullies. She didn't care though. She hated to see meanness for the sake of meanness. On Tuesday nights, she would go to a restaurant that sold chicken wings with her friends and play games of trivia. At this restaurant was a timid waiter who was very friendly, but forgettable. That is until one night.

"On that night Klart was standing in at the host station helping sit people at tables. This was a big night for the restaurant, for the restaurant was hosting a very popular show. A large group came in and wanted to be seated. Unfortunately for everyone involved there were no tables available. Klart politely asked the group to wait for a table to open. The group grumbled but complied and sat on a bench next to the host stand. The restaurant did not clear. No one left. Which was reasonable, since the show was quite popular. The waiting group became louder, and louder in their grumblings and glarings.

"Beatrice watched from her table as the group of men scowled at Klart. She felt sorry for the host, who had to stand those glowers. Then a table opened, a dirty table. A table covered in chicken bones, spilt sauce, and puddles of beer. The waiter for that section was busy with another table, and Klart, the host, was talking to a customer who had just come in. They couldn't clean the table just yet. The leader of the waiting group stood up and approached Klart. Beatrice could not hear what was said, but the group leader gestured at the empty table, and Klart answered with a face of servility. The leader became angrier and spit hit Klart's face, and Klart walked away to the back. The owner of the restaurant came out of the back as the waiter began cleaning the table. The manager gestured at the group and stomped, and the group left the restaurant. Klart went back to his station and smiled. He was used to customers like that. They came every day. He figured that people were at their meanest when they were at their hungriest.

"Klart's shift ended soon after this and he left the restaurant. Beatrice left at the same time. Not purposefully, just coincidentally. When she left the building, she heard commotion. The group had waited for Klart Bumble. They yelled at him and surrounded him. He protested and asked to leave. They laughed and closed in. He tried walking forward, and was met by a stiff hand, which brushed him back. And then a fist hit him in the ribs. He went down. Beatrice saw this and her blood boiled. She ran at the group with her weapon, an old potion of the Forbear's, a bottle of hot peppers and poison gasses. She sprayed the group of men, hitting two of them. They immediately fell to the ground clawing their faces, tears streaming down their cheeks. Beatrice helped up the fallen Klart and pushed him toward her carriage as the rest of the group ran away.

"Klart was cut up and purpled. Beatrice went inside and grabbed tissues to help Klart clean up and stop the bleeding. And that is how the two fated lovers met. They married a few years later, and a few more after that, they had a child named John.

"Everything was perfect. Klart had married the most beautiful and intelligent woman, and Beatrice had married, in her opinion, the kindest man. They were content. Until Beatrice lost her job. False rumors had begun circulating from the bullies and eventually those rumors reached the rest of the school. Concerned parents and staff members forced Beatrice to quit. Klart could not support the family. He could not hope to make enough money. So, he got a second job as a drug tester."

"What's that?" Interrupted a sailor from the far end of the room.

Morsmani turned his head sideways and said, "A drug tester was someone who tested drugs. Drugs were medicines that were made by the Forbears before the Red Gold Conflict. Drug testers would be given these drugs and then observed to see what happens. Generally, to see any unforeseen side effects of the medicine."

The sailor sat back saying, "Oh, I get it. So, side effects like that time Louis over there gave me a headache medicine that made me see stars in sunlight?"

"Precisely. You may not want to take that medicine of Louis's anymore. Now, Klart got a side job as a drug tester. Some may know this part of the story, so I'll go fast here. The drug was made by the Maker, a leader amongst the titanic Forbears, and the creator of the Prometheans. Klart was monitored and when he began showing signs of being more than human he and his family were kidnapped. Klart was told by the Maker's people that his family was dead, and he was experimented on. Klart despaired. His world turned to grey and blue. He did not know where he was, who he was, or why he was. All he knew was that his love was dead. In the few moments of clarity in those dark days Klart remembered his old life. He remembered his wonderful wife and child. He despaired in those moments and closed his mind. Until, that is, he met his neighbors in the Maker's palace, The Tormented, now known as the god of fear, and Shinigorath, the god of death and madness. The three came up with an escape plan. The Tormented distracted the guards, allowing Shinigorath to control one of his thralls in the palace guard's ranks to open all the prison cell doors. Klart escaped in the prison break.

"After this escape Red, the assassin of the Forbears, came after the refugees. For safety the Golden Council was formed led by a great Promethean warrior, Gold the god of war, and Klart. Klart was still broken though. He was still sad. He was still angry."

"Wait! I thought Beatrice survives this part?" exclaimed a sailor.

"Quiet! She does. As the kind gentleman in the back mentioned, Beatrice and John actually survived. They also were experimented on by the Maker. Beatrice was turned into a dragon, and John was made into a blue haired buffscag. They too escaped during the jail break. They too led their own people. Beatrice led the dragons. John led the scags. The conflict ran on. The world of the Forbears slowly crumbled in constant warring, and plague.

"Beatrice rejoined Klart. They met after a great battle and rejoiced. The world was new again. They saw not the destruction of war, the ravages of plague, the fear from the warring hive minds. They saw blue skies and tranquil waters. They were happy again. Joyfully and wonderfully happy again, except on the days when they remembered their lost son, who they did not know had survived. John, likewise, was unaware of his parents' survival.

"Shinigorath burned the world. The Sundering was erected as a wall to protect the continent we now live on from the burning. Klart and Beatrice were worried, but happy in each other's presence. Nothing could hurt them now. Nothing. But, the war raged on even after such an apocalypse.

"Red met the Golden Council on the Field of Fallen Arms. This was to be the final battle of the Red Gold Conflict. The battle to decide if the demon Red would rule the world as an iron fisted monarch, or if the Golden Council would ascend to the position of rulers and help the new world grow. The armies squared up. Red and his armies of tyrors, scags, and men. The Golden Council and their armies of silver folken, dragons, and men. The battle was great. Many a hero died on both sides. The dragons flew above spewing fire onto the scags. Tyrors ran through the ranks burning and freezing the battlefield with ice and fire. Beescags and chocobscags took wing to topple dragons. Kajscags leapt forward to fight silver folk. Silver folk lead groups of golems to crush foes. And man fought man with shouts and glory.

"Gold was winning. Red's tyrors turned upon one another as their wont is. The scags quailed against the dragon onslaught. Then Klart's world was again split open and shattered. A buffscag riding on the insect winged back of a beescag jumped from the green carapace of his ally onto the golden red scales of the dragon Beatrice. Beatrice twisted in the air, trying to rid herself of the hairy buffscag. The scag held. With one hand around the dragon's horns he raised his other hand. In one fluid movement he brought his arm, covered in blue fur, down on Beatrice's head at the base of the neck. She crumpled in the air; her spine severed. She tumbled down, turning back to her human form. The scag lifted his hand again and was picked up by another beescag before hitting the ground.

"Klart yelled as he watched his love crumple into the dust of the field. The battle froze. Everything stopped as Klart moved towards his wife. The wind blew through the frozen combatants. The arrows and bullets hung in the air as dust swirled underneath them. The eyes of the fighters turned in their sockets watching Klart pass, as they could not turn their heads. They were paralyzed by Klart's powers. He came upon the body of his wife and fell to the ground. He screamed.

In his anguish he scanned the battlefield. He spotted the buffscag. The perpetrator of this deed. Klart jumped in the air to where the scag was, and, suspended there, he ripped the offender's head from his neck. Klart fell to the ground. The head landed next to him and rolled out of its helmet. Even with the fur and fangs and horns it was a face Klart knew. A face Klart loved. The face of his son, John.

The battle was released from Klart's spell and continued on around him. The Golden Council won, Red was vanquished, and Klart vowed to never fight again."

*****

Two days into the voyage, Nom Carver sat with his back against the barrier around the rear cylinder of the ship. The cylinder whirred away behind him as it spun. Before Carver, was the vast sea rushing away from him and his fishing line. The line of Nom's fishing pole pierced the waves like a needle. Little ridges of water trailed out diagonally from it, mirroring the wakes from the ship. Nom wanted to see what kind of fish were this far out to sea. The fishermen and women in his old fishing village always stayed within sight of shore. Out here there was no shore, there was only the vast flatness as blue water fused to blue sky. Nom imagined himself pulling up a great monster from the depths. He would pull back his line and the water would break as a great eye rose out of the salty sea. Tentacles would grab the line and pull the pole towards the horizon. Nom would plant his feet and resist the tug of the beast. After a long struggle, Nom would eventually be able to pull in the monster of the depths and the crew would be well fed and famous.

"How goes the fishing? The most peaceful of hunts."

Nom knew from the deep voice that Morsmani had found him. The boy shrugged.

Morsmani sat down next to Nom and set his leather flask next to him and pulled out a strawberry from his pouch. "Not too well then?"

Nom looked sideways at the man and said, "No, but something will bite the line. I know how to use this pole. I want to see what is out there."

"Lots of things are out there. Sunfish, tuna, manta, whale, kraken."

Nom sat up straighter at the mention of kraken. Morsmani was fiddling with his helmet and after a moment, the bottom piece of the helmet, the section that covered his mouth and chin, fell away.

Morsmani mentioned, "I don't think your pole could handle a kraken, though. A little too big, the kraken would be, I mean. A small tuna you might catch with that, though."

"What about a marlin? Could I catch one of those?" Nom asked wide eyed.

Morsmani's mouth frowned a little in thought and he replied, "Probably not. You definitely need to be strapped on board. Especially someone as small as you. Also, your pole might not be strong enough."

Nom sighed and looked back out at the ocean. The man took a bite out of his strawberry.

"Mm shiny," sighed Morsmani.

"What?"

"The strawberry's really sweet. It's good."

"You said shiny."

"Oh? I meant sweet. Do you want any caff?" Morsmani offered the flask to Nom. Caff is a dark brown, bitter drink drank by sailors and people who woke early in the mornings. The boy had tried a sip once when he was younger. The taste still sat poorly in his mouth all these years later. He took the flask and sipped to see if the taste had changed. The taste of roasted dirt filled his mouth and Nom gagged.

Smiling Morsmani took back the flask saying, "There might be a reason younger people don't drink this. I love this stuff. Gives me energy, wakes me up! Love it. I miss having it available in the north."

"Are you from the north?" Nom asked.

The man nodded and stated, "I was born in the Red Dust City, but most of my time the past few years has been in the north east. I prefer it up there. It's cold in the winter. And it snows. The never-ending summer of this area isn't my favorite."

Nom imagined snow. He had heard from sailors that snow was like cold white rain. He figured his imaginings of snow were far from the truth, but it is difficult to imagine something you have never experienced.

There was a tug on the line. The pole bent into a parabola for a second and then sprung back up. Then again. Finally, on the third tug the pole stayed bent, the line stayed taut. Nom stood up and began pulling the pole back. The pole bent more sharply, but it was holding. Nom let go of the pole with one hand and grabbed the line. There was no reel on his pole. In order to draw in a fish, the line must be pulled in by hand. He wrapped his fingers around the line and brought the line back slowly. His back muscles were tight; his breathing increased. This was a large fish. Carver imagined tentacles coming out of the water. The creature tugged the line causing Nom to step forward. Morsmani reattached the lower part of his mask, hiding his ginger whiskers, and stood up. Nom was leaning far back, away from the edge of the ship. He could not drag his prey in by force. This was a waiting game now. Either the fish would tire, and the boy would drag it in, or the boy would tire, and have to cut the line.

"Or the fish may drag you in," Morsmani offered, having seemingly read Nom's mind.

Nom's eyes got wide in momentary fear at the thought. Then, the fish tugged again and continued pulling away from the ship. Nom's feet slipped forward. He slid towards the edge of the ship. Morsmani quickly grabbed the boy around the waist. The sliding stopped. The line went to the left. Then the right. Then the pole bent more drastically as the sea creature tried swimming down. The man and boy began sliding again. The edge came closer and closer. Morsmani pulled out his war hammer and swung it back at the barrier around the ship's cylinder. The curved scythe on the back of the hammer went over the barrier and then caught and held. Their forward movement stopped.

They stayed like that for an hour. The fish moved sometimes. A crowd gathered around the fisherman's son and the scholar. At first, they cried out to cut the line and let go of the pole. Then, they exclaimed at the strength of the man for holding onto the long hammer handle for so long under such great stress. And finally, the boy was praised for holding the pole against the pull of the fish and how someone so young could be so strong and have such stamina. Another hour passed. Then another.

Then the pole's tip came up slightly, and then it came up further. The line loosened. Morsmani let go of the boy and Nom dropped to his feet on the deck and reached out for the line. He grabbed the line with shaking hands and pulled towards himself. He transferred hands and grabbed the line with his other hand and quickly brought back more line. He continued reeling in large sections of line until finally out of the water poked a long, grey lance. The sailors jumped forward to help pull the monster aboard. Behind the sword came the fish's nose, and mouth, and bluish upper body. A great purple fin furled itself out of the water as the fish came up the side of the ship.

When the fish came to rest its white underside on the metal deck, Nom fell into a sitting position. Morsmani tousled the boy's hair and said, "You caught a marlin. That's something many a sailor dreams of and a grand achievement even for the most experienced fisherman."

The captain, a short burly man, asked if Nom would allow the crew to cook and eat the fish. Nom nodded yes, and the fish was dragged away.

That night, marlin was served to the crew and Nom got four helpings and a toast to his name. Nom's beaming smile turned to tears of joy when he was presented with the fish's sword, which the captain had sawed off himself.

*****

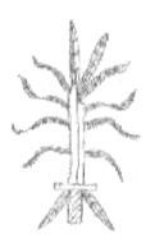

A few days later, Nom was with Amy and the shipwright in the bowels of the vessel. The shipwright was a short man with a ponytail and a large tattoo of his ship running up his right forearm. Morsmani had told Nom that on the continent most people had their professions tattooed on their right arm and any crimes on their left arm. The shipwright was giving the two passengers a tour of his ship. They had gone through the passenger cabins, crew cabins, decks, and holding rooms. The shipwright explained that the ship made most of its money by transporting goods. Amy mentioned that since the ship was so big, and needed so little crew, the profits must be fairly large. The shipwright agreed.

They were now in what the shipwright called the reactor room. It did not seem all that special to Nom. A bunch of pipes and a few large cylinders sat in the middle of the room. The pipes looked like the other pipes that ran around the ship. When Nom had first boarded, the pipes fascinated him. He had only ever seen pipes in King Jin's castle, and those no longer worked. These pipes were larger, more numerous, and most of them worked. After a few days on board however, Nom had gotten used to the pipes. The tanks were interesting. They were so large that if three Nom Carvers stood on top of each other, he would still not be able to reach the top of the tanks.

"Are these the tanks that hold the magic potion?" Nom yelled over the noise in the room.

"What?" The shipwright yelled back.

"Are these the tanks that hold your potion that makes the ship run?"

The shipwright smiled, tilted his head back, and laughed. Then he replied, "Sort of, I guess. These tanks are where the reaction occurs that creates the power to spin the cylinders above deck and the propeller below the water. It's not magic. Just old technology of the Forbears."

"How does it work then?" Amy asked.

"I don't know," the shipwright shrugged. "That knowledge is lost. All the shipwrights know how to do is maintain the reactors and the ships. We can't make any new ones and we don't know how they really work. If you want that answer, I'd go to the Tommy Knockers. Although they don't usually hand out information to foreigners."

"So, you do not know how the ship runs?" Nom asked, slightly disappointed.

"Oh no. I know how it runs. The reactor makes steam, which turns those cylinders there. That creates power. That power is then used to turn the cylinders above ship and the propeller. The propeller and cylinders then push the ship forward. I just don't know how the reactor makes the steam or how the power is transmitted. I do know how to fix those things when they break, though."

"How can cylinders push a ship forward?" Nom asked.

This time Amy answered, "When the cylinders turn while air is moving around the cylinders it creates a pressure gradient, or well, a difference in air pressure, around the cylinder. The cylinder then is pushed or pulled from the area of high pressure to the area of low pressure. Since the cylinders move, so does the ship, since they are attached to one another."

Nom nodded his head. He did not understand any of that, but he would look at the cylinders later and mull it over. The shipwright waved them forward explaining, as they left the room, that his job was mostly maintenance. The captain controlled the men and made the business transactions.

As they approached the deck, Amy bent down next to Nom and asked, "Do you want training from Morsmani and I?"

Nom looked at Amy and replied, "Training in what?"

"Combat, math, science, writing, whatever. Mostly combat though."

"Why?"

"We're on this trip to fight the Terrestrial. He has an army and there most likely will be a war. For your safety we think that you should know how to defend yourself. This will not be a safe journey. So, what do you say? Do you need some time to think about it?"

Nom looked at the ground and then back at Amy. He nodded, "Yeah, I'd like to learn how to fight. Is Morsmani a good fighter?"

Amy smiled and answered, "Yes. He is an excellent fighter. One of the best I've ever seen."

*****

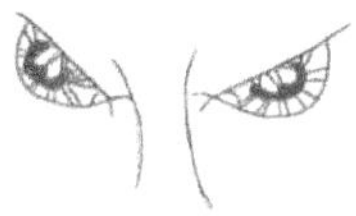

Morsmani leaned against the railing of the ship, staring at the sky. His golden war hammer leaned on the rail beside him. The hammer's head peeked over the railing and above the water. The back side of the war hammer's head, the long curving scythe, pointed towards the center of the ship. In all, the hammer was about four feet high. The bottom was a square that contained a large gold nugget.

Nom Carver came onto the deck from inside the ship. He was wearing his island armor. The armor was tough woven cotton with feathers covering the entire outside. Nom's helmet was leather underneath metal underneath green and red tropical feathers. Running from the top of the helmet were ten, three-foot-long quetzal tail feathers, which fell down the boy's back and fluttered in the wind. The sun caught his armor as he came onto the deck and the boy shone iridescent green and red.

Morsmani turned around. He was not wearing his purple cloak or his pouch today. He unsheathed a short sword and held the hilt out to Nom. Nom looked at the sword and then at the hammer, and asked, "I do not get to practice with the war hammer?"

Morsmani shook his head. "The hammer is too heavy and big for you. It's too much for even Amy to use. I'm going to train you how to use knives and swords first. This is a short sword. It is shorter than a normal sword. This means it is very good in close combat. It is also a little lighter and faster, which I think will help you. Now take the sword and attack me."

Taking the sword handle, Nom weighed the sword in his hand. Then he gripped the handle harder and swung at Morsmani. Morsmani unsheathed his other bastard sword, and blocked Nom's swing with such force that Nom lost his grip.

"Don't choke the handle. Loosen your grip a little. And swing like you mean it." Morsmani mentioned as Nom scooped up his blade.

"I do not want to hurt you though."

Morsmani looked at the boy and stated simply, "You won't. Come."

Nom swung again at Morsmani's midsection. Morsmani blocked the swing and thrust foreward at Nom. The tip of Morsmani's sword poked Nom in the neck and Nom froze.

"Good swing. It had conviction. Now I will show you form."

For the next half hour Nom copied the technique of the strange scholar. They then switched to learning the basics of blocking. Amy came up from below deck and sat down, watching the two train. She smiled to herself as she watched. She remembered when she and Morsmani learned to fight. They were so young and restless. Their teacher was a powerful young man with golden skin. Amy shivered at the memory of her old burly teacher. She had always been scared of him.

The trainer and trainee took a break. Morsmani was explaining to Nom where the power of the sword came from. He showed that the strength came not from the arms but from the core of the body. The back and chest muscles created the force of the sword. The boy listened closely. Amy found Nom interesting. He was quiet and observant, very observant. She wondered how smart the boy really was. After the tour yesterday, she had found Nom staring at one of the cylinders. He reached out a hand that hovered just next to the rotating metal. Then the boy ran around to the other side and did the same thing. When asked what he was doing he simply stated he was checking the air pressure around the cylinder.

Morsmani left Nom to practice his swing by himself. He came over to Amy and said, "I challenge you to a duel."

Amy smiled and, using her black spear, stood up. "I accept. Go pick up your hammer, boy."

Morsmani grabbed his war hammer and Amy held up her spear. Nom stopped practicing and watched the married couple circle each other. Amy held her spear in front of her with the point directed at Morsmani. She feinted a thrust at Morsmani's chest. Morsmani flinched back. Amy jumped forward incredibly quickly. The spear point shot up at Morsmani's mask. Morsmani twitched his head to the side while bringing up the butt of the hammer. The spear passed by the side of Morsmani's head as the hammer's bottom crashed into Amy's stomach. She stumbled back and Morsmani swung down with the hammer. Amy twisted out of the way of the hammer head yelling, "Too slow!" as she swept Morsmani's feet with her spear. Morsmani fell. He caught himself as he fell and rolled backwards. He sprung up out of the roll and jumped towards Amy. Amy blocked his next attack and thrust three times. Each thrust was blocked, and the final thrust was caught by Morsmani's right hand. He pulled the spear towards him. Amy let go of her weapon and charged Morsmani. She hit Morsmani with both palms in the chest. He left the ground and landed on his back. He twisted up and came at Amy. Their hands worked fast. They moved so fast that Nom could no longer keep track. A few seconds went by and then Morsmani landed a blow to Amy's stomach. Her feet left the ground and she flew back a foot. When she hit the ground, she rolled three times and then lay still. Nom Carver yelled and ran towards Amy. Before he reached her, however, black, shadowy smoke engulfed the prone woman. The smoke swirled around her midsection and then disappeared into her black clothing. Amy got up and shook her husband's hand, smiling.

Morsmani tousled Nom's helmet and said, "Lesson's over for today. Keep practicing that swinging motion. We'll continue tomorrow, same time, same place."

Nom nodded and held the short sword out to Morsmani. Morsmani shook his head, "Keep it. Good job today."

The scholarly couple left the deck holding hands.

*****

Dark clouds rolled in. The roiling, boiling masses of dark lightning and thunderous bellows raced across the dome of the sky. The ship cylinders were shut off as the gale increased. Sailors came out on deck, prepared for the storm. Amy stood at the edge of the ship with her husband. Her dark hair fluttering around her head as usual. Morsmani's cloak flew back like a tattered flag in the wind. Nom stood back watching the clouds. In his village the boats would be heading to shore, but out here there was no land in sight, nowhere to run. A sense of fear permeated the air and a shiver ran down Nom's back. The clouds moved in; faster than any clouds Nom had ever seen. Lightning arced from cloud to cloud and lit the ship in stark contrasts of purple shadow and brilliant luminescence. The captain began yelling orders and the crew ran in all directions.

Then the rain came down. It ran up to the ship in a wall of beaded tears and struck with the cold force of a scorned woman. Nom crouched as the wind buffeted his body and the rain pelted him from the side. The scholars stood strong, staring into the storm, like statues of forgotten kings and queens. Amy's hair flew in all directions, Morsmani pulled his war hammer off his back, and the air around the two darkened.

The fourth passenger of the ship, the messenger in leather, came onto the deck, and yelling above the storm, said, "There is something out there isn't there? I feel something."

Nom stumbled, as the ship tilted back, and was caught by the messenger.

The captain suddenly yelled, "Hold on to something, you worthless ingrates!"

The water in front of the ship rose up. Above the top of the cylinders, a wall of black water rose, its trembling top coalescing with the rolling blackness of clouds above it. The messenger, still holding Nom, ran to the edge of the ship next to Amy. He held the railing and Nom followed suit as the ship traveled up the mountain of water. Salty spray covered the sailors as the ship cut into the great wave and chilling rain fell upon their heads. Lightning flashed behind the wall, turning the black water into a clear green. The ship tilted further back as the tip of the wave came near.

Morsmani's booming voice came above the storm, "Hold tight. Brace yourself for the fall on the other side. Only death waits for those who go into this water."

The bow rose up into the air above the water. Slowly it fell forward as the ship crested the wave. For a moment the ship lay flat, balanced on the knife edge of the wave. Ahead and all around, the world was broken and churned up into waves just as large as the one they were riding. The ocean had turned from a calm rocking blue, into a jagged mass of demon teeth. The ship lurched forward and rushed with incredible speed down the back of the wave. So much spray came up around the ship Nom could not see. They were in the valley. A mountain of water rose behind and a wall rose in front. The world was a crack in a tumultuous sea and could be snuffed out by the uncaring, frigid water. Nom could imagine the ship being swallowed like a fly in the waves, gone in an instant and slowly floating down into the depths like a forgotten leaf left to fall from a tree. Silent and dead and weightless they would float down into suffocating blackness. They would slip from the black water to black death silently and unknowingly; just a few more drops in the all consuming sea.

As they crested the next goliath wave there was light in the distance. The messenger yelled out, "The eye! The eye of the storm!" Nom held tighter as the ship continued sailing.

Lightning struck a cylinder in an excruciating blast of sound and light as the ship sailed into the eye. The water was calm and sunlight from the circle of sky above shone down. Amy nudged Nom. Nom looked up at the lady, her hair still fluttering in the non-existent breeze. She pulled out her black spear and pointed at Nom's knife and short sword. Nom unsheathed his sword and knife, holding the knife in his right hand and his sword in his left.

The glassy water fifty feet in front of the passengers began rising in a dome. Something gray appeared under the water, rising up from the depths. Nom tightened his grip on the sword. Beside him the messenger flipped open a pouch on his hip and pulled out a kunai knife. The dome of water broke open and ran down the sides of a great whale. On the whale stood a man in a grass skirt. Large tentacles rose beside the whale and the water boiled with swarming fish and sharks.

The man on the whale held up a short spear with a long, barbed tip and shouted, "Namer, you dare come into my waters? The sea is mine and I will not tolerate your evil in my domain!"

Morsmani put a foot on the railing of the ship, and leaning forward, replied, "I didn't mean to be caught out here. Let us go, or do you wish to destroy this ancient ship and its innocent crew? How did you find me by the way, Backbone? No one went to your shrines."

"I wouldn't have found you if you had not taken control of a marlin. You must have known that I'd see that. No normal mortal can control a beast like that. Not even a lesser Promethean has the power to command such a powerful creature to bite a fishing line and succumb to death. So, I found you. And I will now kill you and this crew who harbors fugitives."

Nom looked from Morsmani to Backbone. He could not believe it. This was Backbone, member of the Golden Council, god of the oceans, and one of the Prometheans in the pantheon of gods. How could Morsmani, a simple scholar, hope to fight a god and win?

Amy stepped up onto the ship's railing, and balancing there, looked at her husband. She pointed her spear at him. "If I lose…"

Morsmani nodded.

Amy raised her arms. Tendrils of inky smoke came out of her back and then quickly jutted forward towards the whale. The smoke, now looking like solid black webs, stuck to the whale's skin and launched Amy forward through the air. She soared in a graceful arc, the smoke evaporated as she landed in front of Backbone.

Backbone smiled and opened his mouth. Before he could say anything, Amy swung her spear at his feet. He jumped over the black spear and immediately thrust his own short spear at her. She slapped the point of Backbone's spear away from her with her left hand and brought her spear around in another arc with her right arm. They thrust and parried in an amazing display of grace, speed, and power. Then the ship shook.

Nom peered over the side of the shipwright ship. The water in front of him boiled with swarms of fish. The fish swam around and on top of each other in a frenzy. They squirmed and fretted and then in an instant they stopped. They calmed and swam away from the ship. Then, some distance away, the fish, sharks, and dolphins turned and rushed back. The creatures of the ocean slammed the side of the ship, which shuddered, but did not move. The boat was too large. No amount of fish could move the boat. No amount of fish could slam holes in the metal siding.

Morsmani pulled away from the railing and yelled, "Kraken!" Tentacles rose up from the depths. Swaying in the air above the ship, they wrapped themselves around the cylinders, grabbing the railing to either side of Nom Carver. Nom fell back in horror. The tentacles pulled the ship forward as the fish rammed the bottom again. The ship rocked to the side almost imperceptibly. Then again. And again.

Someone yelled, "Cut the tentacles!" Nom saw the crew, brandishing swords and axes, cut away at the kraken's appendages. Three northmen worked together to hack at a large tentacle holding one of the cylinders. The tentacle recoiled, covered in gashes, spilling blue blood across the deck. The tentacle rose, and then in a pendulous arc swept away the great metal cylinder. The cylinder crashed across the deck, crushing one man and pinning another. Morsmani rushed to the pinned man and, screaming from exertion, lifted the cylinder. The man crawled out from the trap, his leg a mass of blood. Nom looked away, feeling queasy. He saw another sailor lifted into the air by a tentacle. The man screamed in terror. A small kunai knife appeared in the tentacle holding the man. The tentacle released its prisoner, who fell onto the deck and scrambled away. The fish rammed the ship rhythmically while this went on. The boat rocked side to side. Another cylinder was ripped out and slammed onto the deck repeatedly. After smashing the deck with the cylinder, the kraken lifted the metal shaft off the ship and slammed the side of the boat in time with the swarm of fish. The ship rocked further. The last two cylinders were taken, crew being swept aside as they tried to stop the massive tentacles. Morsmani wielded his war hammer like a demon, smashing through kraken tentacles faster than anyone. Tentacles that were so large two men had to work together to hurt them, were taken out in one swing by the golden hammer.

A trembling boom sounded from the back of ship. Nom turned and rising, dripping, out of the ocean, came the propeller. The metal leaves, each the length of four men and the width of two, shone in the sun of the eye of the storm. The metal flower hung in the air. A testament to the Forbears strength, it was held high by the kraken. The shipwright fell to his knees and screamed. The propeller rose up and then sharply down. The petals of burnished grey cut into the ship from deck to water and then fell to the waves. Water rushed into the gash, frothing white with the promise of death.

The ship tilted slowly. Amy, seeing the ship's mortality, turned and yelled. Backbone took his chance and thrust. His point pierced Amy's side and she fell forward onto one knee. Backbone thrust again, but his spear was knocked to the side by a well thrown kunai knife from the messenger. Amy rolled into the sea. Nom rushed to the edge of the sinking ship and stared into the water. Amy rose to the surface of the waves. Her eyes were closed, her arms hung to the side, relaxed, and her hair splayed out around her head, a black pool. She sank. Nom screamed and put his hands on the rail, preparing to jump after her. Someone grabbed Nom and threw him back. Nom crashed onto the deck and immediately scrambled up. He rushed towards the railing again, and was again stopped by a red gloved hand. Morsmani held the boy in one arm and yelled, "Stop!" Nom stopped and lay limp in the man's arms. Tears appeared on the boy's cheek.

"Hold him. Do not go in the water."

Nom was transferred to the messenger. There was no fight left in the boy. The messenger simply held Nom's shoulders and watched the scholar, whom Backbone had called Namer, slip off his red gloves. Through a film of tears Nom saw there were black tattoos running up each of Morsmani's fingers in spirals. Morsmani ran his right thumb along the edge of the scythe on his hammer. Red berries of blood appeared along the cut. He swiped his thumb along the inside of his left index finger and slammed his open left palm onto the deck of the ship.

Nothing happened. Then, crawling out of the walls and floors came shadowy figures. They were gaunt, their hair and tattered clothes fluttered about them. Smoke seemed to seep from their skin, and they stared with red eyes at Morsmani.

Morsmani stood and addressed the newcomers. "I have given you a taste of this world's sweet air. A few more moments of life. Help us. Save us. Take us to shore in exchange for the few seconds away from torment I have given you all."

With a shuddering, rattling breath the crowd sighed, "So be it."

Morsmani nodded and then ran his thumb along his left pinky and slammed his palm again onto the deck. Redness flowed out over the water from where the ship met the sea. The fish retreated leaving some of their brethren floating belly up in the waves. The tentacles quickly retracted into the ocean. The ship was left slowly sinking into the dark red waters.

Backbone, still on the whale, yelled, "What did you do? What is this?"

Nom whispered, "Red tide."

Morsmani yelled back at Backbone, "Death!"

More and more fish rose up to the surface to float dead, belly up, as the redness spread out. A crew member slipped on the wet deck and slid along the incline into the water. The man came up coughing and spluttering, his skin covered in welts and beginning to blister. He screamed in pain and began coughing, unable to breathe. Backbone's whale swam backwards and disappeared into the waves as the redness crept closer. The ship was alone. The ship was sinking. The water was red and filled with the dead.

Morsmani turned to the shadowy crowd and the few remaining of the crew. "Come. Follow the shades." The shadowy figures jumped from the deck en masse. In the water they held one another forming a human raft. More shades jumped down onto the raft and formed another layer; laying on top of the first people. Morsmani then jumped down onto the makeshift raft. The crew stared at the man in red scale armor and smiling mask. The messenger jumped, holding Nom in front of him, and the crew quickly followed suit. More shadowy figures began crawling out of the side of the ship and falling onto the raft. The raft moved away from the sinking ship. The captain and shipwright, refusing to leave their vessel, watched from the deck, doomed, as the raft left.

Nom sat for an hour staring back at the horizon where the ship had been. The storm clouds had dispersed as the raft approached the edge of the storm's eye. Backbone no longer controlled the area. They had left the red tide and many shades behind. The shades on the raft slowly replaced the shades who made up the raft, but the raft slowly became smaller and smaller. As the danger began to seem less and less Nom leaned onto Morsmani, who put his arm around the boy. Nom fell asleep from exhaustion and sorrow.

*****

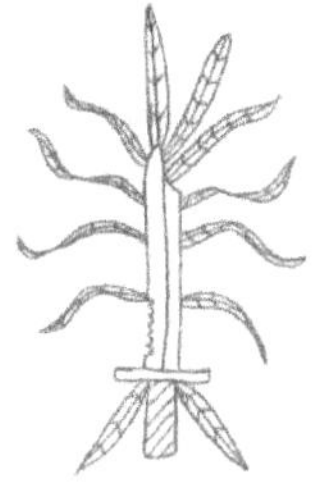 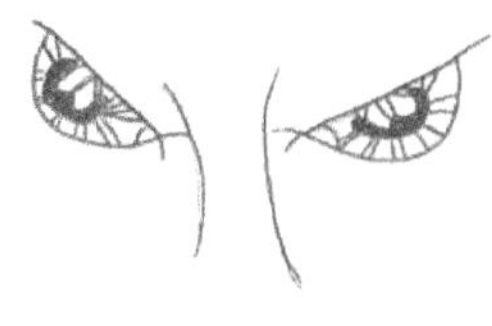

Chapter 3
A Few Choice Answers (Island of Peace)

The floor was hewn stone, hard and moist in the tropic heat. Light slanted in putrid, yellow shafts into the room. The boy sat up, rubbing his eyes, in the thick air. There were three other people in the room with him, the messenger, Amy, and Morsmani. Nom gasped and jumped up to hug Amy but was stopped short by a chain and manacle around his right wrist. He grabbed at the manacle and tried to slide it over his hand.

"Don't. You'll only make yourself bleed. And I don't think these people will heal you if you get infected." The messenger advised.

Nom stopped fretting with his manacle and looked at the messenger, then Morsmani, and finally Amy. The messenger lay on the floor, watching the boy with a tired, bored expression. His leather armor and pouch were gone. In their place were dark blue cotton pants. His left arm was covered in black tattoos from his wrist up to his shoulder. Many of the tattoos were also raised welts, like they had been burned on. Nom remembered that tattoos on the left arm usually were the markings of a convicted criminal. A tattoo ran around his right wrist like a bracelet. The tattoo on his wrist had a pattern of large, four legged, horned beasts being hunted by people with bows and spears. The messenger's black eyes watched Nom with lazy interest.

Nom turned to Morsmani. The scholar was manacled on both feet and hands, with chains so short that Morsmani could not move his limbs. He was asleep. His head rested on his shoulder. The helmet and scale armor were gone. In place of the armor were pink woolen pants and shirt and his purple cloak. Nom did a double take. Morsmani had never taken off his helmet, only the bottom part ever came off. Nom thought, *'So this is how Morsmani looks.'* It was not the prettiest of sights. Most of the man's face was covered in bright red hair that sprouted out in an unkempt tangle from his lip and chin and cheek. From the top of his head fiery hair was thrown out in a wild bush that fell down to his shoulders. Inbetween the barbed hair was a nose, eyes, and face that were chopped away and hardened by scars. His skin almost looked like the white bark of an aspen. White scars crossed over one another in a hectic, jarring mess across his entire face. His nose twisted to the side from being broken once or thrice and then ended in a flat wall where at some point the tip of his nose had been cut off. Nom shivered, wondering what could have caused such scarring.

"Not the most handsome man, eh?" The messenger asked, seeing Nom shiver. Nom shrugged and looked at Amy. Amy sat against the wall with an expression of sadness. When Nom's blue eyes locked Amy's red eyes, her expression immediately changed to that of happiness. Nom noted the change and decided to think about it later. He would hate if one of the leaders of the mission was depressed. She was dressed in the same long, flowing black tunic as before.

She smiled from her shadowy corner and asked, "How are you feeling Nom? You've been asleep for a while."

Nom sat down, noticing his armor was gone too. "I am fine," he replied.

Amy's eyes bored into the boy and she stated, "That's good."

Then Nom stared directly at Amy and said, "Actually, I have a few questions."

Amy glanced at the messenger and then back at Nom. "Okay. I can probably answer them. What are you wondering?"

"You died?"

Amy smiled. "A little bit of water can't get rid of me. I washed up on shore and was captured by the inhabitants of this island."

Nom didn't believe her but decided to drop it. Instead he said, "Okay. Who is he?" Nom nodded towards the sleeping Morsmani. "And you? What are you two? The two of you took on a member of the Golden Council and won in his own realm."

"What do you think we are, Nom?"

Nom thought about that. He figured they had to be Prometheans, but he had never heard of Amy and Morsmani before. That meant they were lesser Prometheans, weaker Prometheans. If that was the case, they could not have hoped to win against Backbone.

Nom looked at Morsmani with a frown, and answered, "Prometheans. But you two are not part of the Council. How could you defeat a council member?"

The messenger interjected by saying, "Nom, do not mistake fame with power. The members of the Golden Council are seen as the most powerful beings, the most powerful gods, in this world. And some of them are; like Klart Bumble, Gold, and Shinigorath. But there are beings out there as powerful as, or more powerful, than some members of the council. They just are not as famous."

"Like who?" Nom queried.

The messenger looked at the ceiling in thought and answered, "Like Ruhk, the Terrestrial, Tatanka and the other spirits of the land. I assume Morsmani and Amy are one of these hidden powers. Am I right?" The messenger directed at Amy.

Amy smiled and nodded. "You're right. My husband is a Promethean. A product of the Forbears created by the Maker. I am simply a shadow bender."

"A shadow bender?" Nom asked.

Amy lifted her hand and in the middle of her palm a black smoke coalesced and spread upwards like a flame. The shadow dissipated, and Amy closed her hand into a fist. "I can manipulate shadows. I can make them solid. It's why my clothes are black, it's what my spear is made from. The guards have me poisoned right now to keep the shadows at bay."

The messenger quickly asked, "Wait, you're not Amy Miliken, are you? Goddess of shadow."

Amy nodded. "I am. Goddess may be too strong of a term. Now, enough of that. What else is on your mind, Nom?"

"Those things that came out of the ship. Who were they? Morsmani called them shades."

Amy leaned back against the wall and chuckled. "Yes, those were shades. They are the shadows of dead warriors. Morsmani can summon them from their graves to fight for him. Same with the red tide he summoned. I notice, messenger, you have a summoning ring on you also."

The messenger glanced down and began scratching the tattoo on his right wrist. He stated, "Yes, I do. I can summon buffkin. I have a contract with Tatanka."

Amy nodded. "That's a good contract. Now, I imagine your next question, Nom, is, where are we?"

Nom nodded.

"We are on an island. I really don't know much else. I have not seen the rest of the crew. The inhabitants of this island locked us up and have kept us drugged to lessen my powers and to keep Morsmani asleep. I assume they did that because they know how powerful he is."

There was scratching at the door then. Amy lifted a finger to her mouth and the messenger sat up. The door to the cell slowly slid open, pushing the dry threshes on the floor to the side. Three men stepped in. They wore leather skirts covered in strange symbols. Their heads were covered by wooden masks carved into grotesque human faces with multiple pairs of eyes. They went to Amy immediately upon entering the room. Two of the men held

Amy down and the third pulled out a small, stone flask. The room darkened as Amy struggled against the islanders. The man with the flask quickly tilted the flask's contents into Amy's mouth and the room returned to the dull yellow light. Amy lay back, her hair fallen onto her face and shoulders like dark curtains.

The flask disappeared into a pocket on the man's skirt as he yelled, "Aqui! Rapido!" out towards the hallway. Another man rushed into the room holding a tray with cups of water and fruit on it. He distributed the cups and fruit to the prisoners. Morsmani was not given any food or drink.

When the man was serving Nom, Nom politely said, "Hola."

All four men reeled back, glanced at one another, and quickly left. The door slammed shut and the sound of a bar falling across the other side of the door could be heard.

The messenger strained forward in his shackles and asked, "You speak their language? How?"

Nom's face turned red as he replied, "They speak the royal tongue of New Keys. My father was the village chief, so he taught me the royal tongue for when I would become chief. Now that cannot happen though. The people of New Keys think I made a deal with demons and the village is gone."

The messenger leaned back. "Don't be so hard on yourself. You are no longer in New Keys. There is a whole new world out there for you to discover. You may yet use your dad's training."

"Maybe. By the way, what is your name?"

The messenger answered, "Skalla."

*****

The yellow bars of light from the window traveled across the floor, crawling over dry threshes. The light crept up the wall and eventually disappeared as night fell upon the world. The door slid open and two islanders stepped in. They carried obsidian tipped spears. They quickly crossed the room to Amy and Skalla. They brandished the spears at the two adults. Nom tried to stand as a third person entered the prison. The newcomer was a short woman, bent with age. She wore a leather cloak and a black wooden mask with a single glowing, green eye. The woman came over to Nom and looked down at the boy. Nom looked at the mask. There were no eye holes or mouth holes or nose holes. It was a flat black mask with that single glowing eye in its center.

The woman knelt and placed her hands on Nom's cheeks. A soft green glow came from her hands and the eye became brighter. Nom stayed perfectly still. After a few minutes of this, the woman stood up.

She stated in the royal tongue of New Keys, "The boy has no special power. He is mundane. A simple human. He does not read minds. Boy! How do you speak to us?"

Nom stared at the lady in thought. Then the boy methodically answered, "I come from the kingdom of New Keys. You speak in the royal tongue of New Keys."

The woman nodded, "No mind reading from this one. Pity. The lower people can take his power. I will absorb those two myself." She pointed at Morsmani and Amy.

She turned and left the room, followed by her guards. As the door was closing Nom yelled out, "What are you going to do with us?"

The woman turned around and the eye shone forth. "Eat you, so as to gain your power."

*****

The travelers were brought out into the bright sun. It had been a week since the battle against Backbone. The companions were led down the steep dirt path of the island village. On both sides of the path stood villagers, their faces covered by wooden masks, chanting. Each villager threw powders at the travelers and fell in step behind them. Nom was hit in the face by a red powder. His nose immediately became irritated and he sneezed. His eyes watered at the strong smell of cinnamon.

They were dragged forward through the town. The village sat on a steep hill that spilled into a small bay, protected by cliffs on either side. The wooden shacks of the islanders leaned back, straining against gravity so as to not slide down to the shore. At every turn in the switchback path were ghastly poles. Human skulls topped the poles, which were lined from base to top with vertebra. Amy kept her eyes to the ground. Nom shivered and held back more sneezing as more spices were thrown at him. Skalla observed everything on the way down with an open curiosity. He stared at the skulls as he passed. He looked up at the trees as if seeing them anew. He peered at the masks of the villagers through the multicolored clouds of spice.

Nom whispered, "Why are you so happy?"

Skalla laughed and replied, "These may be my last minutes before joining the shadow. I can either enjoy them and soak in this beautiful day, or mope and die miserable. The world is as happy or sad as you observe it to be. Don't let the last view of the world be through the shadow of fear and pain. One should try to live each moment as fully as one can until there are no more moments to live."

A man came next to Skalla and hit the messenger. "No hables!" the man barked at Skalla. Nom looked at the ground. The red dirt blurred through Nom's tears, which were no longer just from irritation. A vision of his father flashed before his eyes. His father stood proud on his small reed kayak, holding up a fish in each hand. Nom smiled at the memory, but the smile did nothing to allay the fear that grew with each drop of elevation.

The path opened up at the base of the hill and the travelers were led out onto the beach. The villagers followed and formed a half circle around a large pile of wood. A line of stone columns stood in the pile's center. A stretcher with Morsmani laid upon it was placed underneath the columns. The old lady with the green eye mask stood in front of the wood, facing the villagers.

Skalla leaned over to Nom and said, "Not the kind of funeral pyre I wanted." He was immediately hit by a villager standing behind him.

The matron of the village raised her arms. The villagers quieted immediately. She spoke out in the villagers' tongue, "The dirt of this island is red. It is red with the blood of countless battles and wars fought by the people outside this village. In strange lands long ago, a war broke out and the world was lost in bloodshed. In those days your ancestors held aloft the ideals of peace and refused to help in the war. All around this island, the world died, and the soil soaked up the blood of the fallen. But the war never touched here. Here, there was peace. Until one day, when a ship sank just off these shores.

"Wounded men washed up here in this very bay and they were healed here in this very village. Our ancestors, who left us this island as our birthright, nursed the wounded outsiders to health. And when the men were healed, they stayed for a time. They reveled in our halls, they drank our drink, and ate their fill of our food.

"Then, in their revelry, they fought. For the outside world is ruled by war, ruled by death, ruled by chaos. Those who come from the outside are tainted by the evil of the men and the gods of that world. For though there was peace here they brought conflict. The old village burned just as the rest of the world burned. My great ancestor, the first matron, punished the outsiders and adorned the new great hall that she built with their skulls. The dirt turned red as the village was rebuilt."

The matron turned her face upwards, looking up at the top of the hill, where trees spilled over onto the tops of wooden buildings. Then she jerked her head down and continued with fervor, "The earth wept, and still weeps red tears for the loss of a village of peace and healing. And so, when outsiders come anew upon our shores they are not allowed to leave. They are offered as appeasement to the earth, as healing to the earth. For humans burned the world. Humans made the world bleed. And that pain, that damage to the earth, can be seen in the soil of our land. And so, we offer the earth the healing power of dead men and in return we get the living power, the magic, inherent to men!"

The villagers shouted and called at the outsiders. Torches were lit and Nom, Skalla, and Amy were led to the wood pile. Their ankles were tied to long ropes attached to the tops of the stone columns. They were hoisted up so that they hung upside down above the wood. Amy sighed, and a shadow rose from her. The villagers quieted as the shadow traveled over to Morsmani and became the shape of a woman. The shadowy woman leaned down over the unconscious man and laid her head upon his heart. Nom looked from the shadow to Amy and saw that she was crying. Tears sprang from the corners of her eyes and rolled down the sides of her temples before turning to steam, evaporating off her face.

A torch was thrown. It arced forward, creating a swirling spiral of red flame as it rushed through the air. Nom heard it come in the short silence as the crowd inhaled together. It sounded like the wings of birds flying through the trees. A thrush, thrush of rustling feathers and a soft scrape of the leaves below. And then, with a clunk of loud finality the torch landed on the wood pile. A deep sigh. Then, without a further sound, the flames sprang forth into the fallen wood. A million snakes and worms of yellow, red, and white hate thrust forward from the brand. The villagers let out their breath in a wild shout and chant. Fire ran between the fingers of wood like water between rocks, rushing forward toward Nom and the others. Amy's tears flowed, Morsmani slept, Nom watched in frozen wonder, and Skalla smiled in wonderment at the fledgling blaze.

A few torch bearing villagers stepped forward and deposited their fiery brands onto the pyre. One man came close to Skalla who quickly kicked outward from the post with his feet. He sprang directly at the man, grasping at the man's waist. The villager fell back and Skalla slammed into the column with his hands free of the rope. He bent upwards and, with a quick jerk of the knife newly stolen from the villager, Skalla fell from the rope holding his feet, onto the wood. He rolled forward. Sparks shot up around him. He walked over to Nom. Nom's rope was cut and the boy was caught by the man and thrown to the far side of the fire. The pyre was starting to burn. The outside pieces of wood were still brown and untarnished by heat, but the layers below shone red. The wood split, cracking like a sail caught in a fresh gale. The villagers surged forward, yelling in anger. They could not reach Skalla. He stood atop the blazing wood, too light to sink into the fire burning lower in the would-be pyre. He cut Amy's rope and she fell. She sprang up. Her black tunic ablaze at its fringes. The tunic seemed to grow and twist in anguish as she rushed over to her husband and lifted his limp form from the blazing stretcher. She leapt out of the fire and joined Nom.

Skalla jumped to the edge of the wood closest to the matron of the village. He grabbed her by the waist and pulled her into the flames. Tendrils of fire encroached upon the man's feet and sparks showered him from behind as he lifted the obsidian knife to the woman's throat.

He shouted out, "Bring our things to the beach! Load them into one of your boats. Bring water and food as well! Quickly! Do this and I let her go. Refuse and she dies! Take too long and we will both burn to ash!"

The villagers stood stunned for a moment. Then a child wailed. With a collective jerk the villagers ran to their huts and the beach. They brought out the traveler's lost goods and placed them in a boat. Skalla jumped backwards out of the flames. He backed quickly down the beach; knife held ready. Nom pushed the boat out into the waves. Skalla pushed the matron away from him. The matron fell into the sand and was overtaken by the villagers charging towards the outsiders. Nom felt the boat slip on its own over the last bit of sand and leave the solid ground for the uncertain waters of the ocean. He and Amy grabbed oars and rowed out as Skalla fell into the boat. Villagers splashed into the water behind them, screaming and yelling. The matron stood, a silhouette against the now ablaze funeral pyre. The green eye of her mask shone out unnaturally in the dying light.

*****

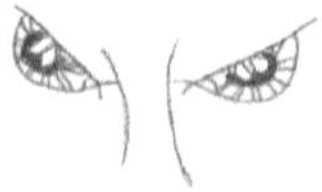

The quetzal feathers fell from Nom's helmet, green on gold, onto the sand of the shore. Three days had passed since the events on the island. The four companions had been traveling quickly along the coast lines of islands, never straying far into the deep ocean, and never stopping for fear of the possibility of the masked islanders chasing them. This morning however, their waterskins ran out and Amy made the decision to come to shore to collect more fresh water. Nom was lying on his back. He stretched out his arms and legs, adorned in the feathered armor of New Keys, and marveled at how much room there was on shore. The canoe they escaped in fit everyone and their possessions, but just barely. After three days of taking turns rowing and sleeping in the fetal position in the bottom of the boat, the travelers were immensely glad to be ashore and stretch their legs.

Nom thought about the last few weeks as he stared at a cloud traversing the sky. He was tired but happy. His time in Puntacan was a boring and sad time. Nom did not miss it. He was safer back then and never had to work. One of King Jin's servants, Esmira, came by his hut once a week with money, but she was the only person that ever came. So, Nom went into the city often to subdue his loneliness. The city was filled with wonders and Nom enjoyed walking along the docks with foreign ships and along the main market street lined with palm trees. After a time, however, Nom realized that people shied away from him. They ignored him and when they could not ignore him any longer, they acknowledged him only with short, curt phrases and commands. They did not want him around. Soon the city made Nom feel lonelier than the lonesome hut the king had given him. Nom stayed home. He took to swinging on his swing and watching the swirls of steam in The Sundering. He wandered through the thick jungle around the capital and observed the bright birds and beetles. But then Morsmani and Amy had come, and he had left with them. The journey had been dangerous so far, and his fitful sleeps were filled with visions of red water and green eyes, but he was happy. Amy and Skalla were kind to him, they cared for him. Morsmani was still asleep, but Nom knew that he was the one who had made it possible for him to leave New Keys.

Nom wondered why Morsmani had wanted him to come. So far Nom had done nothing to help anyone on this journey and he did not see how he could be of much use in the future. Morsmani was a Promethean and could probably complete the entire journey on his own, if the ancient stories of the Prometheans were true. Amy and Skalla were incredible fighters, probably better than any of the soldiers in New Keys and could obviously fend for themselves. Amy herself was apparently a goddess of some sort. Nom sighed and stood up. All he could do right now was simple tasks for the adults, and maybe that's why he was taken along for the journey. Maybe Morsmani wanted a servant for his adventures to the Terrestrial's lands.

Amy looked up from the small stream that ran tumbling over rocks under the trees and then fanned out to run thinly over the sandy shore to join the salty sea. She beckoned Nom over to her and instructed him to start filling flasks with clear water. Nom gladly filled flask after flask, happy to be of use. He looked up at Amy and said, "You should go rest. I have not seen you sleep since we left the island."

Amy opened her mouth, but before she could say anything, Skalla came out of the forest carrying mangos. He said, "You haven't slept while Nom rowed? You always row when I row. I figured you slept while Nom rowed." Skalla took a bite of a peeled mango and then pensively added, "Now that I think about it, that seems rather cruel to make young Nom row alone. Not that I don't think you're capable Nom. You did catch a marlin. In the north that would make you a master fisherman."

"I rowed with both of you. I don't need the sleep." Amy explained. Skalla made a face at Nom, and Nom stifled a giggle.

Amy quickly added, "Really! I don't. I don't need as much sleep as you people to be well rested. Anyway, let's finish getting this water and continue. Once we reach the coastal swamps, we can take more breaks."

Nom handed the filled flasks to Skalla, who took them to the canoe while Amy and Nom finished filling the rest. A shout came from the canoe and Nom and Amy looked up. Skalla had fallen and was scrambling back, away from the canoe. Amy rushed towards the fallen man. Nom followed quickly behind. Out of the canoe rose Morsmani. He was back in his red and gold armor, purple cloak and red, horned mask. The Promethean held aloft his tomahawk and, stepping out of the canoe, strode towards the messenger. A shadow flowed out behind him and Nom saw flashes of fire in his home village. The air smelt of blood. Amy held out her arm to stop Nom.

"Who are you?" Morsmani asked Skalla. "Why did you ride with us in Shipwright Erek's ship? You are no messenger. You have a contract with Tatanka, you are much too handy with your weapons for your chosen trade, and your bag is filled with potions of death."

Skalla looked back at Amy with wide eyes. Her gaze never left her husband. She stood still like a startled deer listening for another sound, ready to flee should danger appear. Nom felt nauseous. The beach was too bright, and the tropical birds too loud. His chest constricted as he felt a band close around his head, hurting his skull.

Skalla saw no help there, and so he turned around pleading, "I don't know what you're trying to say. I have helped you all this time. I saved them," he waved at the woman and child behind him, "from the cannibals. I saved you too. I only want to help you and reach civilization whole. I mean you no harm. I am just a humble messenger. The – the contract and fighting… I was in the Hatten army. A spy. I learned to fight and used summoned buffkin to escape when needed. That's all! Really!"

Morsmani threw a piece of dark cloth on the ground and said in a voice like mortar and pestle grinding down bone meal, "Then why do you have a raven's cowl? Why can I not see your mind? Your clothes are dyed blue to hide you at night. Your kunai knives are fashioned to pass as farming tools. You are an assassin from the Carrion Feeders. Is your contract to kill me? Kill Amy? Kill the boy?"

The questions hung in the bright air. Skalla mouthed words but no sound came from him. Nom was having trouble breathing. Morsmani growled and raised his axe higher for the final blow.

Before the tomahawk could come down, Amy stepped forward and yelled, "No, Mors! Stop this! Skalla has helped us. Skalla saved us. Why would he wait for you to wake up before killing us? He can't hope to win in a fight against you. You're being paranoid. You're scaring Nom. Stop this, let the man speak. Please."

The axe came down. It twirled once in the air as it descended downward and then stuck in the sand next to the assassin. Skalla rolled to the side and got on a knee.

Looking up at the armored man he said, "I am a Raven's Beak of the Carrion Feeders. My mission to New Keys was to kill the exiled Lord Goram. I have his ring as proof. I am to deliver that to Prince Bairne upon my return to the north. A message that loose ends collect dirt. That's why I said I was a courier. It was simply coincidence that I chose the same ship as you. I wanted a comfortable travel home, and I had the money for a shipwright ship."

Morsmani loomed over the kneeling man and the shadow around him faded. Nom could breathe freely again. The scent of blood dissipated. The beach was back to normal. Morsmani nodded once and then laughed.

"You should have told us that first!" Morsmani boomed. "I have many enemies, and between me and you I'm sometimes a little paranoid. If you were a Crow's Talon, I'd still be worried, since they're usually just crazy, but the Raven Order is where the smart killers go. Well then come along. Let's get a move on."

Skalla tried to stand up but fell on his butt. Morsmani laughed good naturedly and grabbed the man under the arm and pulled him to his feet. Morsmani then walked briskly to Amy and hugged her, whispering thank you. Nom carried the water flasks to the canoe and got in in front of Skalla. Amy entered the canoe next and Morsmani followed her after picking up a large sand dollar and placing it in a pocket of his cloak.

They sailed on, staying close to the shoreline and hopping from one island to the next. As they chased the setting sun over the next few days, the journeyers talked. Morsmani and Amy told tales of ancient times when the Forbears created false stars on the earth and flew across the whole world, even to the moon that hung in the night sky. Skalla discussed the political intrigue of the northern kingdoms and the Tommy Knockers in the Spine Mountains. He told them about how Prince Bairne was raising armies and had already conquered many of his neighbors, and about how the Tommy Knockers were constructing more dams in the mountains and closing trade to and from the east and west of the continent. Nom Carver did not understand much of these talks. New Keys had always kept its distance from mainland affairs. King Jin was often heard saying how the continent was filled with the evil wiles of sorcerers and witches and that the island people were better off working amongst themselves where all was natural.

As they approached the swamps that bordered the continent Nom began asking Morsmani about the mission they were on. He didn't expect many answers from the Promethean but, to his surprise, Morsmani was more than willing to answer them.

"What is the Terrestrial?" Nom asked as Morsmani rowed and Nom ate a fish he had caught earlier that day.

Morsmani thought, and finally answered, "The Terrestrial is a being not from this world. He came to Usmer just before the

Maker began creating the first Prometheans. I was just a child at the time. I think it was around four hundred years ago, maybe three, I don't remember. Actually, it might be five…four and a half? It's hard to keep track, you know? As you get older decades begin feeling like years and years like months. Anyway, he isn't from this world. But ever since he came here he has been trying to take over everything. He is a hive mind, meaning he takes control of people's minds and adds their brain power to his own. Kind of like how someone would add thatch to their roof or a new reed to their boat. The Terrestrial takes over the minds of his subjects and they are no longer themselves. They are nothing more than appendages of the Terrestrial, like your fingers or toes."

"What stopped him from taking over?"

"Shinigorath did."

"The god of death and madness? The god who burned the world of the Forbears and caused the apocalypse?" Nom quickly interjected.

Morsmani nodded. "Yes, the same one. There are only three other hive minds besides the Terrestrial known to us. The Tormented, Shinigorath, and Klart Bumble. Klart refuses to use his power to control others but can see much with his power. The Tormented has locked himself away to save humanity from his fearful mind. Shinigorath used his power for control. His subjects, however, were not easily controlled. They were not obedient slaves like the Terrestrial's. They were hateful beings that projected Shinigorath's wrath. They were terrifying zombies that killed anything they saw and Shinigorath could barely control them. After all, Shinigorath, the god of madness, could barely control his own turbulent mind."

"How did he stop the Terrestrial then?" Nom was leaning forward. None of the tales told in New Keys discussed this aspect of the most feared and hated god.

"He didn't. He only stalled him. At first it was a race between the two minds to control as many people as possible. The Terrestrial was winning. He was a master of his craft, and much more experienced. So Shinigorath turned to the other gods, the Golden Council, for help. They ignored him. They did not trust the mad god, for he was tricky and turbulent, and they were in the midst of fighting Red's claim of kingship over the world and the overthrow of the Forbears. They were busy and did not see the impending doom from the Terrestrial. Actually, many didn't believe the Terrestrial even existed; they thought he was a hallucination of Shinigorath's. And so, the Terrestrial silently took over more than half the world, which at that time was a million times the number of people alive today, while Shinigorath fought fruitlessly both against the Terrestrial and his own mind.

"Finally, Shinigorath burned the world. He released a power that killed almost everyone and everything on the planet. Where this great power touched the earth, nothing could live or set foot in for hundreds of years. Great clouds of death rolled across the heavens, sending the world into an ice age and horribly mutating in all living things for generations. To protect Usmer the silver folken pooled their powers together and erected the great wall of water and steam, the Sundering, to protect us from the poison clouds. It's not fully known why Shinigorath burned the world. He may have done it in a fit of mad rage, or it may have been a calculated move. He may have just been testing his own powers, or trying, in one fell swoop, to conquer the world. The end result of the burning, however, was that almost all of the Terrestrial's followers were dead, as was pretty much everyone. In fact, more people died on that one day than have been born since or will be born for the next few thousand years. The Terrestrial's power was put to a halt for the moment, and the end of the Red Gold Conflict was catalyzed by the event. After Red was defeated by Gold, Klart put up Isen's Wall."

"Isen's Wall?" Nom asked.

"Isen's Wall is what keeps the Terrestrial at bay. It marks the boundary of Usmer and the Terrestrial's lands. Anyone who passes through the light of Isen's Wall will lose any magical ability they have, or any spells placed upon them. If the Terrestrial tried to lead his forces through the wall, his hold on the hive would be gone immediately.”

“So how can he attack us now?”

“Good question! He's planning on going around Isen's Wall. The wall only extends from coast to coast. It's a massive wall, but you can travel around it by going far enough south. That's why he sent a scouting party to New Keys. Also, he can set up listening posts that allow him to extend his influence around the posts. You saw one in New Keys. The ring of standing stones around a central obelisk. With those in place the Terrestrial can see, hear and influence things around the listening post. As long as you stay outside the outer ring of stones, though, you're safe. Those who enter, however, may become thralls to the Terrestrial.”

Nom looked down at the bottom of the boat. Water had seeped through the reeds and splashed at the bottom of the canoe. Nom grabbed a large scoop shaped shell and began throwing the water out of the boat. After some time, the boy asked, “Why are we going to the continent if the Terrestrial is attacking the islands? Would it not have been better if we had stayed and fought him at New Keys?”

Morsmani sighed, “We aren't running away. If the Terrestrial attacks the islands he will win. There is nothing we can do to stop him once he passes by Isen's Wall. He does not know this, however. He thinks that attacking by sea would be an incredibly difficult and long campaign. He would prefer to attack by land. We have to ensure that he does just that. There is a chance we can beat him at Isen's Wall with the strength of the silver folken, scags, and hopefully some armies of the northern kingdoms. And our best chance is at the capital of the silver folkens' lands, Urbe.”

Nom screwed up his face in a perplexed look. “But how can we do that? He cannot attack Isen's Wall. You just said that.”

“We have to bring down the wall first. The banishing light of Isen's Wall is powered by The Star of Isen. A familiar stone that fell from heaven long ago. It is a great jewel that can be used to banish spells, curses, and turn the supernatural back to natural. We will remove the jewel from its holder, thus removing the light. Isen's Wall will only be a stone wall at that point, no magic in it. It will still be a formidable obstacle for the Terrestrial, but he will prefer attacking that over a conquest through the islands and swamps. Once we have removed Isen's Star we can use it as a weapon instead of a shield. Hopefully we can draw out the Terrestrial himself, and using the familiar stone, nullify the Terrestrial's powers. At that point we win!"

"It will not be that easy though, will it?"

Morsmani shook his head, "No. The silver folk will not like this plan. And it's doubtful if the Terrestrial will go on the battlefield. He never has before. It's our only shot though. If he gets past the wall the world will fall. We will all be his slaves. Every living thing will be indistinguishable from the Terrestrial. This plan, I think, is our only chance." Morsmani looked up at the stars beginning to peak out in the dying light as the sun set. Nom did not ask any more questions and the boat sailed onward.

Islands came and went as the days passed. Finally, the horizon turned from a flat blue plane to a brown shadow. The shadow slowly solidified into a line of tall trees that rose out of the water. There was no shore, but Nom could see the ocean floor rise up closer to the bottom of the boat as the trees approached, until they hit a line in the water. At the line the water turned from blue to brown and the boat passed into the coastal swamps that marked the edge of south eastern Usmer. The great mangrove trees hung their moss-covered limbs over the travelers as they slipped into the quiet wetlands. Birds fluttered in the canopy and creatures splashed in the water.

The boat followed a twisting path deep into the swamp. There was no horizon any longer, just a maze of trunks that stood like the thin legs of herons. Often the overhanging branches and vegetation blocked the sun entirely.

That night Amy directed the boat to a tussock of dirt that poked its hairy head out of the algae crusted waters and tied the boat to an overhanging branch. The travelers clambered onshore. Skalla splashed out of the boat, still not used to sailing. A fire was made, and they sat around the fire eating in silence. The thick vegetation pressed in upon them, stifling the night into an inky pool filled with cracking and splashing. The swamp felt oppressive, even to Nom, who had spent his childhood wandering amongst the wetlands and jungles of his homeland. They were far from the main shipping lanes of the merchants that traveled to and from New Keys. Here they knew there were monsters, beasts that lurked in the sludge, serpents that slithered amongst the trees, malevolent spirits that wandered the ever-shifting mists of the bayous. Nom Carver climbed to the treetops and marked where the group was from the stars. He was invisible amongst the leaves and moss in his green feathered armor, and he stayed, breathing in the cool air that flew over the humid swamp below.

*****

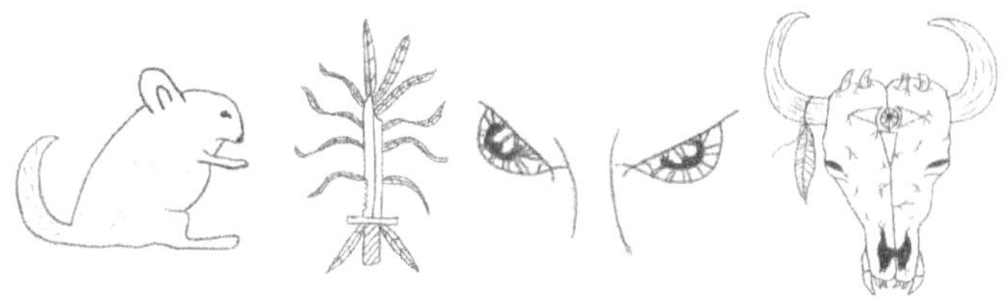

Chapter 4

City of the Chinchillas

A brown wedge flowed from behind the reed craft as it sliced the green algae blooms in twain. Shafts of light dappled down through the trees. Morsmani sat near the back of the boat carving his sand dollar into a tiny rectangle. Nom Carver sat facing backwards. He leaned against Morsmani's back as the boy lazily let his fishing line trail behind the boat. He had been very excited earlier that morning when he caught a fish that was not native to New Keys. Amy and Skalla rowed the boat forward.

They were passing through an area where small walkways crossed from tree to tree high in the branches and little windows could be seen carved into the tree trunks. Skalla stared at these as they passed, while Amy and Morsmani all but ignored them. There was a soft scurrying amongst the branches and soft splashes. In an instant, the trees, logs, and mounds of dirt were covered with small humanoid figures. Their webbed hands and feet were large, relative to their height. Their skin was mottled green and brown, and they were completely hairless. Some of the creatures were no larger than squirrels and others were as tall as three and a half feet. They watched the travelers pass, letting out clicks and buzzing their lips, which covered two rows of small, needle-sharp teeth.

"What are they?" asked an apprehensive Nom.

"They're zorscags. The scags that live in water. They won't attack us as long as we keep moving." Amy answered.

"What is that sound they're making?" Skalla queried.

Amy laughed and answered, "That's just them talking. That's their language. I hear clicks travel better underwater than words. They're asking each other if we're a threat to them."

"And what do they think?" Skalla asked.

"They think we might be but that we are much too big to attack. They also agree that Morsmani and I smell terrible. You and Nom smell really good though."

Skalla scratched his head and replied, "Well I always try to impress."

"Oh, they also agree you two humans would probably taste excellent," chimed in Morsmani.

Nom pulled in his fishing line, deciding that maybe now was not the best time to fish. Instead he watched the zorscags around the boat. They looked like human frogs. The crowds on the shores and branches slowly dwindled as the travelers rowed on. Eventually all signs of humanoid civilization faded into the soft green of the swamp. The water ways slowly shrank and became less like flat bogs and more like streams winding between muddy tussocks. In some places the water even moved, making the water blue and clear instead of brackish and brown. The bird song became more diverse as they went further inland, as did the flora.

As the light shafts began to slant toward the sailors, and the sun fell to the west, the trees opened up. The boat entered a wide, fast moving current. The adults in the boat knew that this was the Coastal Key River, the main artery leading from the ocean through the coastal swamps. This river was the path used by merchants and travelers who wished to reach the great mound city Chinchaplas by boat. The Coastal Key River was the way in which Nom Carver and his strange companions finally arrived at that great trading hub, which sat at the very corner of civilization.

The mound on which the city sat, rose out of the water as the travelers neared the swamp's edge. The sun was half fallen behind the man-made mountain, turning the city into a giant black silhouette. Small lights began to dot the eastern side of the mound as fires were lit to hold the coming night at bay. Nom was in awe. When he was a young boy, his father had once taken him to the great mountains that rose from New Keys's center. Although those mountains were all larger, none were half as impressive as the mound city of Chinchaplas. The city rose in levels with steep slopes between. With the sun behind it, the city appeared like a serrated spearhead thrust out of the swamp. A small mountain that somehow migrated out to stand sentinel over the flat lands. As they approached, the city's beacon was lit. The swamp shone out in red and yellow light, reflecting the bonfire that replaced the fallen sun upon the mound's summit.

The boat was docked and Skalla and Nom followed the Prometheans through the twilit streets to a restaurant on the lowest level of the city. A green glass lamp sat upon a tall metal post outside the restaurant. Illuminated above was a sign hanging above the door that read Green Light Brewery and Inn. A few people played a friendly game of hammerschlagen outside. Amy ducked into the inn and the rest followed suit. The inside of the brewery was alight with noise and laughter. Long wooden tables and benches lined the outside of the rectangular dining room while a large rectangular fire roared in the center. Amy walked across the dining room to the counter.

The young man on the other side of the counter looked at the travelers curiously and asked, "What can I do for you today?"

Amy smiled and replied, "We would like a room for the night and menus."

While the adults dealt with paying for the room, Nom scanned the dining room. In one corner, a group of men in muddy clothes played dice. In the opposite corner, a man and woman played a game with tiles. Nom tried to see the tiles. He had brought along his set of dominoes and was curious to see if mainlanders also played. The people were too far away and the table too tall for Nom to see. Having finished paying for rooms, the adults walked to the middle of one of the long tables. Nom followed. He gave a side eyed glance at the play tiles and saw that the tiles had carved designs of flowers and animals. No dominoes. Nom was disappointed, he used to play with his father all the time and had not played since his father died. They sat down and opened their menus. As they read through the items, which mostly consisted of rice dishes and seafood, a couple walked up to the table next to them.

"Lady Amy? Morsmani?" the woman asked.

Amy and Morsmani looked up and immediately jumped from their seats. They embraced the pair who were named Francis and Annie Duluth. The couple sat down, and the group was introduced to them. The two newcomers owned of brewery and inn as well as the textile shop next door. Francis insisted that Annie really owned those, he simply married in to the family business. The young man from the counter had come over and was standing anxiously behind his bosses.

"Can I get you anything to eat or drink?" he asked.

"Now, Quentin, you forgot to introduce yourself first. You'll get larger tips if your patrons feel like they know you." Francis admonished.

Quentin nodded and said, "Right, sorry Dad." Quentin Duluth swallowed and said to the group, "Hello, I'm Quentin. I will be your server tonight. Can I get you anything to eat or drink, or do you need more time to decide?"

Francis smiled and nodded to his son.

Morsmani raised his hand and said, "Yes, I'll have a pint of the Mad Dog Ale and a plate of the red rice please."

The young man nodded, and the rest all ordered. Skalla and Amy ordered sake with their meals, since sake was the specialty drink of Chinchaplas and Green Light was known to be the best brewery of sake as well as the best beer brewer in

Chinchaplas. Nom ordered the same red rice dish as Morsmani because Nom knew none of the other items on the menu. Even the fish dishes were foreign to him. While they waited, the owners began a conversation with the travelers.

"So, what brings you to Chinchiplas? It's been awhile Morsmani, Amy."

Morsmani and Amy looked at one another, unsure how to answer. Before they could say anything, Skalla spoke up, "I followed these guys here after our ship sank. This is just where I ended up."

The owners stared at the tan skinned Skalla wide eyed, and then Morsmani let out a booming laugh. After the laughter subsided Morsmani spoke in a deep, calming voice, "We aren't here on accident. Skalla wasn't part of our original crew. But Amy, Nom, and I intended to come here on our way south. We have to talk to King Deneth."

"Oh, political intrigue as usual with you two. You know people still aren't happy about the last time you came through here. You should visit Guy. He'd appreciate it," Francis stated.

Annie piped in, "Morsmani, you can take that ugly mask off. You don't have any enemies in here."

Morsmani turned to Amy, who nodded. Morsmani lifted first the crown piece, which contained the horns and fox face, and then the red helmet, off his head. Nom stared at the man. He had only seen Morsmani without the helmet on when he was drugged in the prison. The mane of red hair sprung out behind Morsmani as before, and the bushy beard covered most of his scarred face. The nearly missing nose was the same ghastly sight Nom remembered, but what Nom really noticed, now that Morsmani was awake, was the Promethean's eyes. They were golden with bright blue lines tracing out from the strange pupils. The pupils were not human. They were shaped in a U. There were no whites in his eyes either, the golden irises stretched to the edges of the eye. Nom thought to himself, *'Cuttlefish eyes.'*

The food was brought out and complimented by the travelers. Nom had never had anything like this rice. It was spicy. His mouth felt on fire as he ate it and his eyes watered. The food was good, but shocking. As Nom rubbed the sweat off his brow something furry rubbed against his hand. Nom cried out and quickly stood up. There was a small creature holding some of the boy's rice in its front paws. The creature had brown speckled white fur, ears like a mouse and a curled tail similar to a squirrels. It sat up on rabbit like hind legs and stared at Nom as if questioning why the boy yelled.

Annie laughed and shooed away the rodent saying, "Beatrice go away. That food isn't for you."

Nom looked wildly around and noticed that three other furry critters snuck around the long tables.

"What are those?" the boy asked.

"Chinchillas. Small creatures that like trees. They can only be found in Chinchiplas unless you go south of Isen's Wall," Morsmani answered.

"Why are they here?"

Annie put down her fork and stated, "They're our pets and main export. The chinchillas made this city and my family's fortune."

Nom sat down. "How did they make your fortune?" he queried.

Annie smiled. This was her favorite tale, for it spoke of her family's history, wealth, wisdom, and connection to the gods. She began the origin story of Chinchiplas.

*****

"Long, long ago, before the swamp's waters lapped against the great pyramid of Chinchiplas, indeed even before men began building this mound, Green Light stood. This bar, in which you now sit, lay next to a run down, ancient road of the recently fallen Forbears. It was surrounded by dusty flat lands for miles. My ancestor, Allison, made a small living here by owning the Green Light Bar and Inn. She was a beautiful woman with golden hair that shone like the sun, marble skin, and a figure so elegant that none of the artists of the day could capture her in their paintings or sculptures, though they traveled from far to try. She owned this bar and made a good living selling the beer brewed in the brewery down the road. The villagers from the nearby town of Kahoke came every night and reveled in her hall.

"Nearly all of the men propositioned her for marriage, and all she refused, for none were even a quarter as handsome as she was beautiful. Princes from northern kingdoms offered her jewels and estates for her hand in marriage. She refused them, for none of their jewels were half as bright as her radiance. Scag chieftains came from their hunting grounds and offered her buffkin steeds, entire tribes of scags to rule, and large tracts of verdant land to hold. She refused them, for all their lands and peoples were no match for her visage. Heads of Tommy Knocker houses traveled from their mountain homes to offer her their hands in exchange for incredible lost technologies and thrones of stone in the hearts of mountains. She refused, for the miracles of the Forbears were nothing next to the miracle of herself.

"Dusty days and years went by when two travelers stopped on their way south to visit the silver folken. These travelers you may know of, they were Shinigorath, and Gold, god of death and madness, and god of war. They came into the dusty tavern and ordered beer. Gold took no notice of Allison, whose skin shone more brightly than the golden light emitted by the warrior god. Gold was busy pondering the journey through the Sundering he was about to partake in. Shinigorath on the other hand, noticed the beauty of the inn keeper. He quickly changed his skin to make himself more handsome than any man in Usmer. The god of death approached Allison and offered his hand in marriage, which came with it the promise of immortality and magical powers that would rival any of the Promethean's.

"Allison looked the Promethean unflinchingly in the eyes and said, 'Your offer is an incredible one. But what would eternity be without a man as perfect as I? What use would being raised up as a goddess be if I had to marry a man as handsome as you?'

"Shinigorath bowed low with a twinkle in his eye and returned to his table. After his beer was drained and his buffkin ribs eaten, the mad god stepped outside. Next to the green lamp post which stands to this day there was once a lone tree. It had withered and died many years before this tale and stood as a stark skeleton, barren as the world was in those days after the fall of the Forbears. Shinigorath broke off a long, straight branch. That night he forewent sleep to carve a twisted staff with a hand of elegance holding a bleeding heart upon the top.

"The next morning, the Prometheans ate a breakfast of grits and drank a glass of kolsch. They left and were saddling their horses when Allison saw that Shinigorath had left his new staff behind. She grabbed the staff and ran out the door.

"When offered the staff Shinigorath stated from atop his steed, 'It is yours if you wish it my lady. May it hold you in your old age when you wither, and your radiance is lost to the dust.'

"He kicked his horse, and Shinigorath and Gold rode away south.

"Allison placed the staff above her mantle in the dining area of the tavern. No customers came in that day and Allison fell asleep early. The next morning, she awoke to a horrendous smell. She got up and looked for the source of the stench and found nothing. Throughout the day the stench never went away. The patrons of the bar came and wrinkled their noses as they quickly drank their drinks and left even more quickly. That night, Allison heard scrabbling in her bedroom as if mice played under her bed. She saw nothing when she looked.

"The smell pervaded her quarters again the next day. She closed the bar for the day and went to town to buy food. The smell went with her. The townsfolk of nearby Kahoke wrinkled their noses as Allison passed and whispered behind handkerchiefs. Allison was upset but her pride would not let her turn around. At the bakery she ordered bread, and as she waited, a strange creature darted out from under her skirt. The disgusting rodent jumped onto the counter and gave the baker a fright. The baker kicked out Allison saying that he couldn't have someone come into his store, stinking up the place and attracting rodents. Allison rushed home, feeling the glares of the townsfolk on her as she passed. The chinchilla, for that is what the creature was, followed Allison home. That night, Allison killed the animal.

"The next morning dawned bright and hot. Allison awoke to find dirt covering her bed and two chinchillas playing in the corner of her room. She screamed and killed both rodents. The pungent smell still ran rank around her. Few people came to the bar that day. Those that did quickly left, complaining about a horrid smell and lack of bread. As Allison prepared for bed, she spotted another of the smelly rodents running through the kitchen. She chased the chinchilla out of the bar yelling and crying in exasperation. She came back in to find the pest she had ran out staring in through her bedroom window and three more asleep on her pillow. She let in the offended creature and then killed all four of the new rodents.

"That night, she woke up to the sound of thirty-two small paws pattering around her room. She could not fall asleep, and so, she killed all eight animals when she rose with the sun. No one came to the bar that day.

"Sixteen chinchillas died at Allison's hands the day after, and she was refused service at the fruit stand and vegetable stall. The bar stood open, but empty. There was no longer any food for her fallen customer base, and even if there was, they wouldn't be able to taste the food over the smell that filled the air. The townsfolk spoke of her smell and how disgusting it was. They said she must be witch. That is how she was so pretty, and now her magic must be running out, causing the smell, they claimed. She was rotting away, and the ugliness of her witch soul must be coming out. Allison hid herself in her room. The only company she had was the thirty-two chinchillas.

"After a week of hiding, a young man came to the bar. He was the son of the brewer who sold Allison his beer. The brewer and his son were worried. Allison had not come that week to buy beer and they were far enough away from town to not hear the nasty rumors circulating about the Green Light's owner. He knocked on the door and Allison ignored him. After some time, the young man left.

"He came back the next day and was again ignored, for Allison could not bring herself in front of others. She smelled terribly and was now rail thin, with dark bruises under her eyes, from lack of sleep. She thought herself too ugly now to be seen by others. He tried again the next day, and the day after that, and the day after that. Finally, on the fifth day, the door opened for the young man. Allison had not opened the door. The chinchillas had. There were now sixty-two chinchillas roaming the house, for the thirty-two had all died from a lack of water and food. The man wandered up to Allison's room and saw her lying in bed. She was weak from a lack of sleep and food, and in utter despair. For how could she live in such ugliness and squalor?

"The young man gave Allison his lunch and filled bowls full of water for the chinchillas. Allison asked him why he helped the pests and he explained he thought they were cute. He left, promising to come again tomorrow with more food. After he was gone, Allison got out of bed and, grabbing the staff fashioned by Shinigorath, went outside. She burned the staff in the middle of the road. As the dry, dead wood went up in red flame so too did the sixty-four rodents. They screamed and cried and disappeared into ash. Allison fell asleep in her quiet house for the first time in many days. She was happy at the prospect of peace and her returning beauty. The curse, she thought, was broken.

"A crash from downstairs in the bar woke Allison up. She hurried downstairs, reinvigorated by her long sleep. When she got to the bottom of the stairs, all her new found energy and hope fled from her. One hundred and twenty-four rodents played in her abode and their stench filled Allison's nose. She cried and cried. Her knotted, unkempt hair falling over her wasting shoulders. Her hands, once elegant and statuesque, were now covered in dirt and cracked skin. Her radiance was gone, her beauty wasted. She stayed on the bottom stair crying until the young man from the brewery came. He had brought her a lunch, dinner, and a breakfast for the next day. He asked her what was wrong.

"'Can't you see? I've lost everything. I smell, and all my beauty is gone! I've lost everything.'

"'You still have the bar and inn. I don't know about the smell for I cannot smell anything, but your beauty isn't gone.'

"Allison looked up. Tears carving tracks through the dirt on her face, like veins of white gold traced through harsh brown stone. 'What?' she asked.

"'Your beauty is not gone. Your hair can be washed, your skin cleaned. But that's not why so many came here to see you. Those things you think made you more beautiful than the sun, but they are only fleeting superficial features. Why do you think the artists could never capture your beauty in their paintings and sculptures?'

"'Because their paints could never match the radiance of my skin or the shine of my poor golden hair. Their marble could never be shaped in such an elegant fashion as my body naturally was born in.'

"'No. They could, and they did do those things. I know, for I saw their paintings and sculptures. No, they never captured your soul, your strength of will, your serenity and peace. They never captured you, Allison.'

"Allison's breath caught in her throat and her tears stopped. Then she smiled. And lo, the young man was right. Allison's beauty was reclaimed in that single smile. Her skin still covered in grime, her hair still lusterless and clumped, but she was beautiful.

"Allison stood and, staring at the floor, said, 'Please forgive me. I don't know your name. I know we've met many times before, but I never bothered to remember you, a plain boy. I thought you were beneath me, but I don't think you are anymore.'

"The boy smiled and answered, 'I'm Louis. Nice to officially meet you.'

"They cleaned the bar, inn, and Allison's quarters that day. After Allison washed and ate dinner, she offered food and water to the chinchillas. They accepted her hospitality and that night slept quietly. Allison woke up in the morning refreshed. The smell was gone and above the mantle was Shinigorath's staff, now polished and straight, not twisted like before Allison burnt it. The chinchillas were kind to Allison and helped her run the bar, which she reopened a few days later. Louis, the brewer's son, opened a shop next to the bar where he made fine clothes out of the chinchillas' fur. Two years later, Allison and Louis married, and a small community formed around the prosperous textile shop and tavern. Louis took over his father's brewery and moved it to The Green Light Tavern and Inn. Allison lived happily for the rest of her days, using Shinigorath's curse as a lesson and means of prosperity.

*****

The next morning, Nom awoke to find himself alone in his room. Morsmani and Amy must have gotten up earlier. They couldn't have gotten much sleep, since they were up discussing errands when Nom fell to dreaming. Nom went down to the dining room of the Green Light Inn, where he saw the rest of his group and the young man who had served them yesterday. As Nom ate his breakfast of honey on toast, he found out the young man was the owners' son and named Quentin Duluth. The team was splitting up that day to each run their own errands. Morsmani wanted Nom to come with him and bring the marlin's spear with them. Quentin would be accompanying them; Nom did not know why. Nom noticed that the shell Morsmani had been carving sat on the table next to them. It looked finished. It was carved into an opalescent, rectangular based pyramid. The shell piece was about as big as one of Nom's teeth, which is what Morsmani modeled the carving off of, not that Nom was aware of this. Nom finished his breakfast; the others seemed to have already finished and were just waiting for the boy.

Outside of the tavern, the sun shone out across the tops of the trees of the swamp. The day was bright and warm and the limestone paved streets of Chinchiplas were inviting. Skalla went off in the direction of the docks to find the hideout of the Carrion Feeders. Amy hurried off to the second level of Chinchiplas, the bazaar level, to buy supplies for their journey. Morsmani strolled away with Nom anxiously following. Quentin walked behind Nom, curiously watching Morsmani. The three went up, up, up to the twelfth level of the city.

"How many levels are there in Chinchiplas?" Nom asked, as he looked sideways at a stall where two men were measuring gold coins with scales.

"Fifteen. The sixteenth will be completed in three years," Quentin answered.

Nom nodded and asked Morsmani, "Why is the waiter with us? Is he joining our adventure?"

Morsmani looked at Nom and said, "It's rude to talk about people in front of them and not include them in the conversation. You should have asked Quentin that. Quentin is here to keep you company and show you about the city. I have to meet with Skalla around noon, so you two will be left alone. Also, I figured you might want to try to make friends while you're here."

Nom looked back at Quentin. Quentin was two years older than Nom and much taller. He looked almost like an adult. Nom could not imagine how he could be friends with someone like that. They continued along the twelfth level of the city.

Quentin talked about Chinchiplas as they wound their way along the edge of the pyramid. He explained that the twelfth level of the city was for the bankers and rich foreign merchants. The city was designed in a way such that the lower levels were for the poorer people and small merchants, and as you went upwards the people, wares, and businesses became richer and richer. The top level was reserved for the military and had dormitories and training grounds, as well as a square for people to relax in. As a level was added, the richer inhabitants of a level moved up one level and the poorer remained. This gave the people some incentive to put in their state mandated one hundred hours of work towards the new level every year. They packed clay into brick molds with the hopes of moving upwards.

Morsmani turned into one of the many tunnels in the side of the man-made mountain. The teenagers followed. Nom stared at the brick work and torches that lined the tunnel. Quentin explained that every level at one point had been the top level of the city and open to the air. When new levels are made, many of the buildings and streets of the previous top level are filled in to provide structural support, but many buildings and streets are left open as tunnels and rooms in the mountain. A person could leave their house in the morning and conduct all of their business for the day without ever stepping outside, even if they travel to different levels.

The multicolored, brick-lined tunnels branched out in twists and turns that were quickly lost on Nom as he listened to Quentin chatter on. Quentin's monologue about his home would be irritating if it wasn't so informative and if Quentin didn't seem so genuinely keen on the subject. Listening to Quentin talk about Chinchiplas was like listening to the fishermen in Nom's old village talk about fish. They loved the subject.

After a while of torch lit wanderings, Morsmani suddenly stopped in front of a door. Nom ran into the back of the Promethean, who's helmeted head turned to look at the boy. Nom muttered an apology and the eyes of the fox face on the crown piece of the helmet seemed to twinkle in mirth. They had stopped in front of a store that had displays of armor and weapons on either side of the stone door and runes carved into the head jamb.

"This is the best weapon and armor smith in Chinchiplas. It's owned by a Tommy Knocker and named 'Her Lady's Steel Light' after the guardian deity of the Tommy Knockers. Do not say anything rude about the Tommy Knockers while we are in here, especially, do not refer to the owner or the Tommy Knockers as dwarrows. That term is very rude," Morsmani explained. Nom and Quentin nodded.

Morsmani reached for the door and then stopped and stated, "Oh, also he will make fun of your feathered armor, Nom. Do not take offense. Tommy Knockers are proud, and this smith is one of the proudest I know."

Morsmani opened the door and stepped in. The weapon smith's shop was small with a waiting area on one side and a large circular furnace on the other. In the back room, Nom could see a bed and kitchen area. A pale, short man came out of the back and when he spotted the customers, he nodded his head and said, "Morsmani, Quentin Duluth."

Morsmani nodded back saying, "Lichtenfrumph." and held out his hand.

The Tommy Knocker grasped Morsmani's forearm and then the men butted heads with a sharp click. Nom's head hurt at the prospect.

Luckily, he didn't have to, because the smith turned and asked, "Who is this? Another soon to be mage? Or a student of Shangri's getting field experience?"

"No, no this is Nom Carver. He's an orphan from New Keys. Amy and I are taking him with us."

"No magic in him then? Strange you'd take someone like him under your arm. Think he'll make a great warrior then? Training him to fight? Need new armor? That armor is shabby. Feathers? Who would cover up fine shiny metal with silly colorful feathers? Green ones at that! Bah! Give me red and black feathers like the flag of the Tommy Knockers!" At that, Lichtenfrumph pointed to the back wall where there hung the flag of the Tommy Knocker's with its single red gear on a black field.

Nom looked back at the smith and jumped. Lichtenfrumph had come close to Nom when the boy looked away and now reached out and grabbed the boy's sleeve.

"Oh, now I see. Leather. Morsmani this armor is made of hardened leather under woven fabric. No wonder they cover it with feathers. The leather feels tough enough and the fabric will stop most things," the smith grudgingly admitted. "But there's nothing like steel! I can make you a fine set of steel. If you have the money. It's worth more than your weight in gold, boy, but it'll save your life in an instant. My steel has turned many a bronze blade of those foul, foolish scags! It's shattered the stone blades of tribesmen living on the edge of the world! The iron edges of northern swords and spears blunt when smashed against my steel armor! It's a lost art you know. A gift of the Forbears. So, what do you say? A new set of armor? I know Morsmani has the coin, or a trinket or two to trade. A familiar stone perhaps? To enchant a dagger with?" The smith looked up at Morsmani greedily.

"Ah! And young master Duluth! What brings you in today?" Lichtenfrumph asked, turning his attention to Quentin.

He wanted Nom to ponder the prospect of new armor for a minute before Morsmani shot down the proposal.

"Does your ancestor's sword need sharpening again? It's old enough that I'd say it needs a new blade. Keep the handle with its familiar stone and make the blade stronger, longer, and larger. After all, the sword's magic makes it weightless, like Gold's Warhammer of yore! Or do you want a new blade of your own?"

Quentin smiled at the smith and replied, "No, no, Lichtenfrumph, I'm only accompanying Morsmani and Nom about the city today. A sword of my own would be nice. Maybe, someday. I do want to thank you for the silver forks you made us last year, however. They look great and are still working just fine."

The tommy knocker nodded knowingly, saying, "Good, good. I don't usually do silver work, just inlays on weapons and armor. I'm glad the forks are working. Tell your parents to come by some time." Lichtenfrumph leaned forward and whispered conspiratorially to Quentin, "After all, your parents are my richest clients."

Nom was shocked by the smith's lack of humility.

Lichtenfrumph turned his attention back to Nom. He plucked at Nom's shoulders, getting a rough measurement of the boy's width. This close, Nom could clearly see the Tommy Knocker. He was about the same height as Nom, who was short for his age. The smith was bald, with skin so pale that it was almost translucent, and eyes that bugged out and seemed too large for his head. Large bugle shaped ears protruded from the man's head as he stared up at Morsmani questioningly.

"A sword actually is what we need." Morsmani stated, "He's been practicing with one of my short swords, but I need those."

The smith nodded. "A sword, yes. Steel I assume. Do you want it long or short, boy? Long makes a fine weapon of power and finesse. Short would be quicker, both to make and in use."

Nom looked at Morsmani in terror. He had no idea. He'd only ever used the short sword Morsmani had given him and had only recently been getting good at using it.

Morsmani tapped his foot in thought and then answered, "Make it long. Make it kingly. I want this sword to be remembered for as long as men freely walk this world."

"Yes, yes, kingly! You've come to the right place. Kingly is pricey, however. A familiar stone perhaps in payment? A silver folken's stone would be perfect."

"No stones. Would the price be reduced if we provided this?" Asked Morsmani as he pulled out the marlin's spear that Nom had gotten after fighting the great fish.

Lihtenfrumph's eyes lit up at the sight of the bone. He took the spear of bone and said, "Hmm, maybe, maybe. I don't know the quality of the bone. It might not help in the steel."

At this Nom spoke up, "You were very excited when you saw the bone. Do not act like you do not want to use the bone, for whatever you are going to use the bone for. That bone is the sword of a great fish I caught myself and it is as good, if not better, than any other bone out there."

The men turned to look at the boy. Nom suddenly felt as if he should not have said anything and sank a little lower.

The smith sighed and said, "Fine! The boy has good eyes. If they weren't so small, I'd say he'd make a fine Knocker tunneler. The bone will do. It might make the sword cheaper. Might." And with that the smith sauntered over to the furnace area of his forge and began grinding the bone.

As the bone was ground and the metal melted the smith continued talking. Lichtenfrumph liked to talk it seemed. "You're lucky you know. All the other Tommy Knockers have been called back to The Spine. The Lady says there's war brewing and all Tommy Knockers must return to the embrace of the mountains. And so, they have. I'm the last man outside of those mountains who has the knowledge and materials for steel making. Bah! Even amongst my own people I'm one of the last who can do the old art. It's the mining that's the issue. There's not enough material left to risk wasting it teaching the youngsters. Well, there is. But we're using more than we're mining. And we lose Forbear tech every year making it harder and harder to keep up."

The smith checked the metal to see if it was melted yet. It was not. The smith sat back down and continued grinding the bone into meal. "It's not like I don't want to go back to The Spine. I love the tall mountains and deep caverns. But I have to stay to keep up a good relationship with this place. It's the second richest city in Usmer after my hometown, Mariah. So, I stay as ambassador. Also, they tell me something about how Tommy Kockers own the mountains and even a man-made mountain must be ours. Bunch a hoo haa if you ask me. Sure, mountains are ours by right. The Forbears raised them up and then fashioned us Knockers to live in them. This hill, though, no old god made this. No Forbears ever came here in their infinite wisdom and learning. This place was made by mundane humans, and it should stay that way. I know The Lady would love to send an army here to take it, but I say let it lie. At least until this place is as high The Lady's seat in Mariah."

Lichtenfrumph checked the iron metal again, which was now melted. He nodded and said, "All right I'm making the steel now. You have to leave. Proprietary Knocker secrets. Morsmani, we'll discuss payment when you pick up the sword tomorrow evening."

Morsmani nodded, said thank you, and left. Nom followed, also saying thank you to the smith. When they exited the warm smithy, Nom looked up at the Promethean and asked, "Why did he need the marlin bone?"

Morsmani stopped and he slammed his left fist into his right hand exclaiming, "I didn't even ask you if it was okay to use the bone! Amy's right, I'm too airheaded. I'm sorry Nom. Is it okay that the bone is ground up? It's too late to change that, but I really don't want you to be upset at me. Too many people are upset at me as it is. Is it fine?"

Nom was taken aback by this outburst. Adults never apologized to him. Nom was a little embarrassed, so he looked down and toed a circle on the tunnel's floor as he said, "Yes, it is fine. I did not know what to do with the bone anyway. Why did the smith need it?"

Morsmani sighed and answered, "This is a tight kept secret of the Tommy Knockers, but I'll tell you anyway." Quentin and Nom leaned forward. "The trick to turn iron into steel is to put carbon into the molten metal. One of the things that makes bone is carbon. So, an excellent way to make strong steel from iron is to melt the iron and place the bone in the fire used for melting. The bone turns to ash and releases its carbon which goes into the iron, thus turning iron into steel."

"Oh. In that case I am glad you used my marlin bone to make my sword."

"Excellent! Well, we must be off. I have to meet Skalla and the Carrion Feeders, and then we will meet at the Kajscags' stall outside the city. Let's meet there at say, the midpoint between noon and dusk?"

The boys nodded and Quentin asked, "Why are you meeting the kajscags?"

"They will give us passage south, through the Sand Sea to Scagtower." Morsmani replied.

Morsmani headed down the tunnel and exited into the bright sun. Morsmani headed down the mound, leaving Quentin and Nom behind. Nom peered over the road's far edge at the flat lands around Chinchiplas. They were on the north side of the mound and the land sprawled out before them. To the west lay unending, sparkling, rice paddies and to the east grew the coastal swamps. It was a pleasant sight; neat, comfy order blending slowly into green, organic chaos.

"So, Nom, is there somewhere you'd like to go or see?" Quentin asked.

Nom peered around at the stalls and said, "I want to see the top."

Quentin nodded and led the winding way up the mound city. The main road of Chinchiplas spiraled its way up the massive pyramid. Steep streets and staircases branched off the road to markets, neighborhoods, and as they approached the summit, great mansions and palaces.

When they reached the peak of the mound city, Nom quickly ran around the edge. He looked down all four sides and pretended he was a bird flying high in the air. He had been very curious to see what lay directly west of Chinchiplas. The main road went into tunnels on the west side of the pyramid, so Nom had not seen what was over there. He was disappointed. The west side of Chinchiplas's peak was lined with military buildings and the Great Chinchilla's Torch, the massive bonfire that was lit every night. The lands to the west could not be seen.

"Why do they block our sight to the west?" Nom asked Quentin.

"To the west is Kahoke." Quentin began to answer.

"The city where Allison bought her bread?"

"The same. The base of Chinchiplas butts up to Kahoke, which is now the seat of our royal family. Kahoke is their home, and only royalty, their servants, and soldiers can look upon its grandeur."

"Have you ever been there?" Nom asked. He wanted to look west even more now.

"I have, once. My family was invited there to dine after we gifted King Deneth's family with chinchilla fur clothes. My mother and father knew the king when they were young, before he was king."

"Your family is well known! Is it because you are the oldest family in Chinchiplas?"

Quentin laughed and answered, "No, I wish. We are so well liked because we are the richest family in Chinchiplas. We own the largest textile shop in Usmer, which makes the rarest and most expensive fabric in the world. We also own the largest beer brewery in Chinchiplas, and one of the best sake breweries. Also, our inn and tavern do fairly well. The family history is just my mother's pride showing."

Nom nodded. They stood in awkward silence for a minute. Nom couldn't stand it. He began sweating and his ears rang with anxiety. He picked up a stick and brandished it at Quentin.

"You told Lichterfunf that you might want a sword someday. Are you any good at fighting? I just started learning. Do you want to spar?"

Quentin scowled at the younger boy in embarrassment.

"No, I'm not going to play with sticks with you. I'm fifteen, not five. We should be getting to the Kajscag's stalls soon anyway. Let's go."

Quentin turned and left. Nom dropped his stick and quickly followed, red from being shamed.

They wound their way around the mound city, going down, and down, and down. Finally, they came to the inland gate of Chinchiplas. Two stone walls ran out from the north side of the lowest level of the city and in between the walls three stone gates swung open. On the other side of the gates, the land opened up into a flat land covered in rice paddies and dotted with small adobe huts and houses. A square sat a small way down the road from Chinchiplas, where the people who lived away from the mound city could sell their wares. In one corner of the square sat a group of red tents. Quentin led Nom towards these tents. In front, a large stall was set up and a flag flew proudly next to the stall. The flag's insignia was a purple irised eye with three thin maroon triangles hanging from the lower lid on a field of black.

Quentin stopped near the booth and looked around for Morsmani. The Promethean was nowhere in sight. Nom eyed the booth. He figured that the people manning the booth must be the kajscags. They looked slightly different than human, especially the man at the booth.

Three scags manned the stall; an old man, a middle aged woman, and a young girl. The man was of regular height, and muscular. His entire body was covered in short orange hair with blue stripes like a tiger. His hair flowed out from the top of his head in a dark red mane that reached his shoulders. The women did not have body hair. If they had not had tiger stripes on their skin and purple eyes, they could easily pass as humans. They both had intricately braided red hair. All three wore white dresses, although the man only wore the bottom of the dress, leaving his torso bare. Nom later learned that the skirts that kajscag men wear are called kilts. The stall was lined with an assortment of meats, grains, and pottery from the west.

"Don't stare, Nom" A deep voice behind the boy said.

Nom jumped and looked behind him. Morsmani had arrived. The scholar waved for the boys to follow him to the stall.

The kajscag man stood up as Morsmani approached. The two greeted each other like old friends, and Nom stood slightly behind Morsmani, observing the bustling marketplace. Quentin stood to the side, aloof.

Nom heard someone say his name and he looked around at the stall. "This is Nom Carver. He's a traveler sent from New Keys, and is traveling with Amy and I." Morsmani explained to the scags.

The man behind the stall squinted his purple eyes at Nom and his upper lip lifted on one side, revealing a row of teeth with three extra canines. "Do they grow short in the islands, like the Tommy Knockers?"

Nom did not realize that the question was directed at him at first. He just looked back at the man for a while until he noticed everyone was looking at him. He quickly stated, "No, my shortness is just because I am young, I think. They did not have much use for me in New Keys, so they sent me with Morsmani and Lady Amy. It is nice to meet you." Nom then bowed in the customary New Keys fashion with one arm behind the back and the other in front.

The kajscag smiled, revealing all his teeth, which included upper and lower fangs as well as the extra canines. The scag copied

Nom's bow and replied, "It's a pleasure to meet you as well. I am Zarzasrahla, son of Zoli, son of Azranlaq. These are two of my kajscagkin," he pointed to the middle aged woman. "Zoli Zarzan and," now pointing to the girl, who looked about Nom's age. "Zarzasrahla Azra, one of my many daughters." The women bowed in the scag fashion, keeping both arms at their sides. Zarzasrahla continued, looking at Morsmani, "Now then, what can I do for you? I can't imagine you are here to buy meat, since you and Amy don't seem to eat."

"The meat looks delicious, but no I am not here for that. I need to ask you a favor Zoli Zarzasrahla."

The scag nodded, "Favors I may be able to do. What is it?"

"I need passage to Scagtower for Amy, Nom, myself and possibly another person."

"Passage on the sand beasts is for scagkin only."

Morsmani pulled his hand out of one of his cloak pockets but kept a fist around what he had pulled out. "I know this. Amy and I have ridden the sand beasts before, however. We were named as scagfriendkin in the time of you grandfather, Azranlaq. This means we are afforded some rights in scag lands that only scags have, like riding the sand beasts."

Zarzasrahla sighed and stroked his chin. After some thinking he said, "This is true. Scagfriendkin can ride the sand beasts. The other two, Carver and the unknown person, is he the unknown person?" Zarzasrahla noded to Quentin, "cannot ride. This I cannot change. I am sorry Morsmani."

"Fine," Morsmani sighed. "By the way, I heard you have a sore tooth. I hope it isn't bothering you much?"

Zarzasrahla cocked his head to the side. He was a shrewd negotiator and always cautious of human tricks, as most scags are. "Indeed, I have a sore tooth. Many of my wives say I should knock it out, but I fear that would only worsen the pain. Why do you bring this up?"

Morsmani opened his clenched fist and laying in the middle of his red gloved palm was an iridescent tooth. It was what Morsmani had been carving from the sand dollar for so long. After holding the shell tooth out for a few seconds Morsmani said, "I can remove the tooth with little pain and replace it with this one. There will be no more pain after the operation, and you can eat your jerky in peace."

The scag leaned forward when the tooth was revealed, and his eyes went wide. Then he leaned back and glowered at the Promethean. "This isn't free is it?"

"I need passage for my friends and I across the Sand Sea to Scagtower. In exchange I will heal your tooth."

Zarzasrahla stroked his chin in thought. After a little pondering he relented saying, "Fine. You and your companions can ride the sand beasts. They have to help peddle though. And I get my tooth before we leave… And I get a half pound of gold."

Morsmani nodded, "Thank you, old friend. Come by the Green Light Tavern tonight. We'll operate on the tooth then. Bring some of your friends as well. I'm paying for dinner."

After the bargain was made, the scags were all smiles and bade Morsmani and Nom farewell. Quentin, who had stayed out of the conversation followed looking a little worried about having scags invited to his parent's tavern.

*****

That night The Green Light Tavern and Inn was bustling with patrons. Nom's companions were all sitting on the end of one of the long tables discussing what they had accomplished during the day. Amy had replenished the group's supplies, and Skalla had met with the Carrion Feeders in Chinchiplas. His new mission was to help Morsmani and Lady Amy. Nom thought this a strange mission for an assassin but did not question it.

After everyone had made an account of their day Amy pulled Nom aside. She explained that the kajscag clan was coming to the tavern that night and that Nom should know a little about their society before they came. She explained that in scag society, the male of the tribe is the leader of the tribe. He has no title, he simply is the leader, because only one male is born into a tribe. If another male is born it means that the old male is going to die soon. She further explained that because there is only one male, the tribe is entirely female, and everyone in the tribe is either the male's wife, daughter, or mother. The male's mother is named the matron of the tribe and helps lead.

Nom nodded his head in understanding and asked, "Is that true for every scag tribe?"

Amy nodded, "Yes. The Maker never intended for the scags to reproduce but Beatrice Bumble found a way to let them. Which reminds me. Do not say anything bad about Beatrice Bumble or Klart Bumble."

Before Nom could ask why, a hush fell over the tavern. Nom looked around. All of the people in the tavern were glaring at the door where a rectangle of green light slanted into the old building. Standing in the doorway was Zarzasrahla and his tribe.

Annie, the tavern owner, yelled across the tense room, "Come in! Come in! All are welcome! Have a seat!"

Zarzasrahla nodded his head and entered. His tribe followed him. Most of the people in the tavern stood up, scowling.

They filed out of the tavern, muttering about evil beasts and dirty animals being allowed in a city of proper folk. The kajscags took the vacated seats. The tavern was quickly filled again, this time with scags and Morsmani's friends. Nom figured there were at least a hundred scags in the tavern. A man in a cloak broke away from the scags and sat next to Amy, followed by Zarzasrahla and the young Azra.

When everyone was seated, Morsmani stood upon the table and shouted out to the room, "Welcome to the fine old establishment, The Green Light Tavern, great purveyors of fine liquors, soft cloths, and excellent food! You wonderful folk are lucky! For tonight is the last night of crawfish season! That's what I'm eating, and I highly recommend it to any of you. Now let's give a shout for our hosts, Annie and Francis!"

The scags all stood up and bowed towards Annie and Francis and then shouted, "Thank you. May the wind be at your backs and in the eyes of your enemies. May the fires of your hearth warm your feet and light your nights. May the herds of beasts run to your door and allow you to nourish your families with ease."

Annie blushed and stuttered out a soft thank you, clearly embarrassed by the fervor of the scags. Large bowls were brought out and placed in the center of each table. In between the bowls were platters piled high with shellfish. Nom leaned over and asked Amy what was on the plates.

She handed Nom one of the critters saying with a smile, "Crawfish."

Nom held the crawfish in his hands, unsure what to do. A chinchilla watched him with large eyes. At home, his family would eat crab which seemed similar to these creatures, but he would have a wooden hammer to break the shells. Also, only the legs were served. Morsmani grabbed the head of a particularly large crawfish and twisted. The shell cracked loudly and peeled away from the head. Then the purple cloaked Promethean, who had again taken off his helmet, peeled away two rings of shell. Nom copied this quickly and looked back up. He observed

Morsmani grip the tale of the shellfish and pull the meat out of the shell casing entirely. Nom did this and tossed the shell into the large empty bowls in the center of the table. He dipped the meat into a small bowl of sauce that sat near him and ate. The meat was soft, the sauce was brutally spicy, and the tavern was filled with merriment.

On Nom's left, Azra ate the crawfish with reckless abandon. Pieces of shell scattered across the air above her plate as she zealously tore at the animals. Nom watched in apprehension and scooted away from the young kajscag in order to avoid flying shell and meat. Two chinchillas were playing with a large shellpiece that had flown out of Azra's frenzy.

Across the table, the man in the cloak threw back his hood, and rubbed his hands together, glancing around the room. He grabbed a crawfish and tentatively cracked the shell. He winced as the shell cracked loudly in his hands.

After eating the crawfish, he rubbed his forehead and said, "Morsmani, Amy, Zarzasrahla, thank you for inviting me out. I should leave. It's much too loud here. Much too loud. I should go. I wish you all the best."

Morsmani looked up and stated, "Guy, I haven't even introduced you to my new companions. Stay a little longer. Please. This young man is Nom Carver and this ominous figure here is Skalla. Skalla, Nom, this is my good, but anxious friend, Guy Kahoke." Morsmani leaned over across Amy and loudly whispered, so all could hear, to Nom, "If you can believe it he used to be king of this whole city!"

Guy frowned and rubbed his hands more vigorously. "Come now, Morsmani. Please. That was long ago. I'm a potter now. And I much prefer it to politics. No one bothers me, and it's quiet and peaceful. I really do appreciate you having me out here, but I should be going." Guy stood up.

Morsmani waved for Guy to sit down asking, "When was the last time you left your house? This is good for you. You can leave early, but please stay for a little while longer. After all, what do we say?"

Guy sat back down with a sigh, answering, "The sun never shines in closed doors."

"Precisely! Open your door and join the world. I know it's difficult, but stay awhile my old friend. Please."

Guy finally smiled and said, "Okay. For a little while. It's much too loud here. And what a crowd!"

Nom noticed that Zarzasrahla furrowed his brows with every bite of his shellfish and was reminded that the old scag had a sore tooth. Morsmani leaned across the table and whispered something to Zarzasrahla. Zarzaasrahla nodded. Morsmani flicked the scag's cheek and a tooth shot out of Zarzasrahla's mouth with a small spurt of blood. Nom jumped back as the tooth clattered into the no longer empty bowl of cast out crawfish shells. Amy quickly lifted the carved shell tooth, using a tentacle of shadow, into Zarzasrahla's mouth. The dark tentacle retracted and the scag smiled. There was a new iridescent tooth among the white row of teeth.

The scags ate and talked boisterously for a time, and then, when the eating began to decrease, and orders of sake and beer increased, the tavern became contentedly quieter. A group of scags went to the front of the tavern and got out instruments. A bone flute, violin, harp, and tom-tom drums were set out. Azra sighed next to Nom and stood up. She walked with her head down to join the musicians. The tavern had quieted completely.

The violin started with a long, high pitched, painful note. The bow was scraped across the strings, and the violin sounded like it was softly screaming. The sound was not grating; it was sad and eerie. The note ended. Then began again. The flute joined with a slow, soft note of its own, like wind through a keyhole. The violin rang silent, and the flute continued through the silence, until the harp with a few plucks reintroduced the eerie violin. The drums began beating out a methodical rhythm. The sounds increased. The violin got deeper and the flute louder.

Nom was lost in the music that enveloped the dim, smoky dining room. The blue notes of the violin, like a sheet of still water, disturbed in bright ripples by the quick flute. The harp adding warm yellow drops to the ensemble, like drops of sunlight into a forgotten pond. The scene lit up in deep reds and oranges with the steady beating of the drums. The fire of the drums rose, and the tranquility of the pond was nearly lost. And in a moment, when the reds and oranges nearly drowned out the blues and purples of violin, the music hushed. All that remained was the clear blue surface drawn out in long sad notes as the pond lamented. Tears pricked at Nom's eyes. And then the image shattered into a thousand brilliant diamonds of ice and star fire as Azra's voice sang out for the first time. The ensemble came back and swelled louder and louder in hopeful reminiscence. And Azra sang clearly and as beautifully as a peaceful, snow covered mountaintop.

"The world's fallen apart.

There's no one left.

You've all lost heart.

In the cold, dark,
Bereft,
Of all we depart.

But wait, we remark
In the darkest of caves,
There is always a cleft,
Where the sun rains, as shards,
Into the dark.

Do not lose heart,
For the stars heft,

Many tears for our depart.

So fight,
Fight with all your heart.

Fight to widen that cleft.

And open it to direct,
The tears of the stars' hearts,
And make the dark bereft,
Of us."

The final notes of the song rang out and quietly faded into silence. The room stayed, suspended, in wonder. Nom wiped his eyes and Morsmani was visibly crying. Amy stood up and clapped. The spell was broken. The room erupted in applause and cries for more. The musicians bowed. Nom looked at Azra. He had never really noticed her before, but now he did. Her face shone with nervous joy. There seemed to Nom to be a light about her face that lit up her red hair in sparks of fire and shone across her pale face, sprinkled with small freckles, blue tiger stripes and two red triangles pointing down from the bottom of her eyes across her cheeks. Her sparkling purple eyes met Nom's brown eyes and Nom blushed and looked away. As the applause died down the scags left their chairs and filed out of the tavern.

Nom followed Morsmani up to their room. Morsmani hummed and bobbed his head to the beat of Azra's song as they went upstairs. Nom fell asleep to pleasant dreams of exploring coastal waterfalls and collecting colorful shells.

The next morning was much the same as the one before. Nom and Morsmani split off from the rest of the group. First, they went back to Lichtenfrumph's smithy and collected Nom's new sword.

Lichtenfrumph was a little put out. The smith had said to pick up the sword later that evening, and Morsmani was early.

Morsmani apologised and they watched the smith stamp his symbol onto the blade and attach the hilt, before giving Nom his new sword.

The double-edged blade shone of bright silver and stretched further than any sword Nom had ever used. The balance was incredible. Holding the sword made Nom want to practice with Morsmani and Amy. He had been getting very good lately. Amy said he may even be a prodigy sword fighter. The hilt and hand guard were made of the polished marlin bone. There was a faceted obsidian orb protruding from the white bone at the base of the hilt. The stone, Morsmani had explained, was a familiar stone that enchanted the blade so that it would never break or dull.

After the smithy, they went to the lowest level of the city and came to two large, stone slab doors. Outside the doors were two guards. They wore iron armor that left their arms bare. Each had three blue rings tattooed on their right arm, denoting that they were high ranking soldiers of Chinchiplas.

The guards ordered Nom and Morsmani to stop. "Who are you, and what is your business in Kahoke?" the guard on the left of the door queried.

Morsmani answered, "I am the Promethean Morsmani and this is Nom Carver, a representative from the kingdom of New Keys. We wish to speak to the king of Chinchiplas."

"King Deneth is not receiving visitors today. Please come back tomorrow or leave a message with us." The guard replied.

Morsmani sighed and muttered, "Can't be easy can it?" Then, standing straight, Morsmani spoke, "I am Morsmani, The Namer, scholar of the lost Forbear arts and wandering counselor. I must speak to His Kingship, Lord Deneth, about matters of impending war. We will be let in, or would you rather tell Deneth that you refused to let in a Promethean?"

The guards looked at one another and, finally, the guard on the left sighed and relented, saying, "Fine, you may enter. I must ask that you leave your weapons with us, however."

Morsmani nodded and handed over his two short swords, tomahawk, and two long knives. Nom Carver handed over his new marlin bone sword, and tungsten knife. "We need the hammer, sir." Nom looked up and saw that the golden war hammer was still strapped to Morsmani's back.

"I'd prefer to keep this. It's precious to me." Morsmani answered.

"Just let them hold the hammer while we are in there. They will not steal it," Nom stated.

Morsmani looked at the boy and nodded, "Alright. They won't be able to hold it, though. Here you go." Morsmani unstrapped the hammer and held it out with the hammer head towards the ground. The guard grabbed the hammer, and when Morsmani let go, the hammer fell onto the guard's foot. The guard cursed as the heavy metal of the hammer landed. The guard tried to lift the weapon, but it did not budge.

"A little help?" the guard wheezed to his friend. The other guard came over and they both heaved on the hammer. The weapon did not give. Morsmani stepped forward and with one hand, grabbed the hammer handle and effortlessly lifted it off the guard's foot. Without a word, the red armored man leaned the war hammer against the wall and entered the mound of Chinchiplas. Nom scurried after.

The interior of the lowest level of Chinchiplas had one chamber. A large room hollowed out the mound and through the center of the room, rose a thin stone walkway that allowed no more than three men to walk abreast. There were no walls or rails on the walkway and on either side was an eight foot drop ending in stagnant, poisoned swamp water, and large needles of stone. The far end of the walkway could be seen as a small point of light where the walkway left the mound and entered Kahoke City.

Morsmani spoke as they crossed the empty chamber, "We are headed to the walled city of Kahoke."

Nom recognized the name and interrupted Morsmani, "Guy's last name is Kahoke! Is this the city where he lives?"

Morsmani looked at the boy who quailed at the red glass stare of the helmeted Promethean. Morsmani answered slowly, "No. That is Guy's last name. His family made Kahoke at around the same time the Green Light was made. Before Allison was cursed by Shinigorath, Kahoke was the only town in this area and it was governed by the Kahoke family." Nom looked puzzled, so Morsmani explained further by saying, "Guy's ancestors. In Guy's time, however, the throne was taken from Guy and given to Kahoke's and Chinchiplas's new ruler, Deneth Scott. When we are in Kahoke do not mention Guy, or that we saw him last night. Also, don't mention that we saw the scags. Their kind is not much liked in the city."

"Okay. Why do they not like the kajscags?"

"It's an ancient grudge that like many grudges that are held by one group of people against another group of people turned into stereotypes. Stereotypes turn to prejudices, and prejudices turn to racism and hate. Remember, Nom, stereotypes are made for a reason but usually have very little to do with the reality of things. If everyone treated everyone the same and gave no regard or notice of race, the world would much be happier."

Nom nodded and asked, "What was the grudge about?"

"Something that happen long ago. Something that happened before any of this was built." Morsmani waved his hand to indicate the large chamber they were crossing and the surrounding city. "We're coming close. Leave the talking to me."

Nom nodded, and they continued in silence. The room was oppressive. The ceiling felt too close to their heads and the tumbled spikes of stone reached up to them, as if asking the travelers to join them in the waters of Chinchiplas's lowest room.

Finally, they came to the exit of the chamber. The walkway opened out in bright sunlight that bathed a large courtyard. Before Nom Carver and Morsmani was a wide avenue that ran straight to an enormous, red sandstone palace. The avenue, which was wider than Nom Carver's entire childhood village, was flanked by other large sandstone buildings. Every building, including the palace, was shaped as smooth sided pyramids. Behind the buildings to the right of the avenue was a large, ornate garden. Encircling the two lines of smaller pyramids, the behemoth palace, and ornate garden was the fabled walls of Kahoke. The walls were the largest structures made by man until Chinchiplas. The earthen embankments rose one hundred and fifty feet into the air and were wide enough at the flattened top for ten men to stand abreast. No army had ever taken these walls. The avenue was empty, as was the garden and surrounding buildings.

"Where is everyone?" Nom whispered. Everything was so large that Nom felt like a small mite wandering through a termite hive. "This is a very quiet city."

Morsmani laughed. The booming chuckle bounced off the nearby buildings and came back as a deep, menacing echo. Morsmani quickly stopped, worried by his own laugh. He answered, "This is a city for only the royal family and their attendants. There usually aren't many people about."

They arrived at the foot of the palace and began the ascent to the top of the pyramid. 350 steps, and 378 feet higher, they reached the summit of the pyramid of Kahoke. There was the throne of the kings of Kahoke, Chinchiplas, and the surrounding lands. The throne was flanked by two rows of tall sandstone pillars that had been bent and carved into strange shapes by the winds and rain over the centuries. The throne was a simple, white marble slab with no back or armrests. Behind the throne was a large, marble statue of a chinchilla.

Lounging on his side on the marble slab was King Deneth Scott. Nom and Morsmani approached the throne, Nom slightly behind Morsmani. They bowed to the king.

Deneth looked down at the travelers and said derisively, "Morsmani, you return. Why? Is another coup in place? Decided that the Kahokes should still rule this city instead of me? Decided after all these years that I was the wrong choice for ruler in your favorite city? I know you saw Guy the other night. I know you met with the kajscags. Are they the army with which this coup will happen? You've always fought for the rights of those beasts, so why not kill two birds with one stone? Undo the fall of the Kahokes, and give more freedom to your favorite monsters! Am I wrong? Why else would you meet them before coming to see me, your champion? You even have a crow working for you this time. I know his mission is to aid you. I don't know what he will aid you with, however. Will he steal my mail? Spy on me? Or assassinate me? Well?"

Nom could not believe this was the ruler of Chinchiplas. What kind of king accuses people of crimes without any real evidence, and without discussing with them beforehand? King Jin, the ruler of New Keys, was a lazy, selfish man, but he was at least smart and reasonable. This man did not seem to be reasonable. Nom could not decide if the man was smart yet and reminded himself that first impressions were often wrong. He cleared his head and decided to reserve judgement on Deneth's behavior until he knew the man better.

Morsmani stood and answered, "Oh great King Deneth, we come before you to ask your aid. To the south the Terrestrial, the great enemy of the free peoples of the world, is stirring. He has sent his thralls past Isen's Wall and attacked New Keys. We ask that you send your great army with us to the south in order to stop the Terrestrial from coming north."

Deneth grabbed his silver chalice that sat next to him on the marble throne and took a long drink. Then he stated, "No coup then. But you still bring war." Then the king continued in a voice dripping with disdain, "You should rename yourself War Bringer, O great Namer."

Morsmani stood looking up at the king. Deneth took another long drink, which emptied his cup. He threw the chalice at an attendant who quickly tried to catch the cup, and juggling the cup for a few seconds, dropped it. The attendant quickly picked up the chalice and rushed away to refill it.

Deneth laughed and asked, "Who is the boy?"

Morsmani looked at Nom and nodded. Nom stood and stated, "I am Nom Carver, a representative from New Keys." Then gaining courage Nom continued, "My village was destroyed by the Terrestrial's thralls. With your help, no other villages need be destroyed."

Deneth nodded. "Welcome to my city. Tell me, how many villages do you think have been destroyed in New Keys since you left? Or do you think the Terrestrial really stopped after yours?"

Nom gasped. He had not even thought about that. He stuttered, "I-I do not know. I left. How could I know?"

Deneth smiled cruelly at the boy and stated, "Of course you can't know, boy. I'll warn you now, Morsmani is not in the business of saving people. He hurts everything and everyone he touches. When he's not out there destroying things, he's sowing chaos. Leave Morsmani. Go home to your family and protect New Keys. Leave this folley."

Nom opened his mouth, but could come up with nothing to say. Morsmani had saved him from a life of neglect and fear. They were on a mission to save the world. How is that folley?

Morsmani spoke up again, "So your answer is no? We will receive no aid from Chinchiplas? May I ask why, besides that you think we can't win?"

Deneth frowned at Morsmani and spoke, "There is another war going on. A war that is almost at my door. Lord Bairne has conquered all of the north and his army marches south as we speak. Even if I thought you could win against the Terrestrial in a battle in the south, I would not send you soldiers. I need my army here to defend against the closer threat of Lord Bairne."

Morsmani rebutted by saying, "These walls have never fallen from an outside force. You do not need your whole army here. Bairne's army is tired and weakened from a long campaign and many battles. Even a quarter of your great army, the finest fighting force in Usmer, can hold off Bairne's northern rabble. Please, I need your help. I need your soldiers."

"No. My army stays here."

Morsmani sighed and then, his voice getting louder and deeper, he stated, "Fine, give me back the rabbit leg then."

Deneth's eyes widened. "What?" He asked.

"You heard me. Give me my rabbit leg back. You broke our agreement."

"You can't have it. It's mine. You gave it to me. It's mine. I need it."

Morsmani clenched his fists and quietly said, "It was never yours to keep. I will take it by force if I need to."

Deneth stood up on his throne, and trying to look tough, he laughed weakly. "I will call on my palace guards to stop you. I have a hundred of my finest soldiers in this complex. You can't defeat them all!"

The sun darkened and Morsmani seemed to grow in stature. A small flame cloaked the Promethean, and a dark shadow flew out over Morsmani's head like dark wings. In a voice of rolling thunder, the Promethean calmly spoke, "I am no crossroads spirit to make deals with and then break. I am the Namer. I am the lord of shadows. I am Morsmani, created by the Maker, pupil of Klart Bumble, Ally of Gold, friend of the Scag Nation, husband to Amy granddaughter of the Maker. I saw the fall of the Forbears. I fought in the Red Gold Conflict. I have seen the rise and fall of nations greater than any you could conceive of, King Deneth. Your armies would crash against me like sea foam upon the rocks. They are but armies of gnats to me. My hammer, the Golden Key, would sweep your army away like so much chaff in the wind. Now give me what is mine, so I may leave this ant hill, and save your hide from evils you can little imagine."

King Deneth stepped back in fear. He opened his shirt and hanging on a piece of twine around the king's neck was a few small bones tied together with leather where the ligaments had once been. At the end of the bones was attached a thin sheet of green agate about as large as a small sand dollar. Deneth took off the rabbit leg and offered it to the enflamed Morsmani. The fire and shadow around the Promethean subsided, and he took the artifact. Morsmani bowed and left the palace summit. Nom quickly followed suit. He had decided that the King of Chinchiplas was shrewd, if a little paranoid, and that Morsmani was not someone to cross.

They left, collecting their weapons at the gate, and headed to the top of Chinchiplas. At the top of the city, they began practicing their fighting. Nom was trying out his new sword against Morsmani, who was using his tomahawk in his left hand and a short sword in his right. They circled each other. Nom ran through the teachings Morsmani and Amy had given him in his training thus far. A sword is not your weapon, but another part of your armor. The sword is the part of the armor that can end a fight. Morsmani stepped forward and raised his tomahawk. Nom quickly planted his feet and leaned slightly forward, his sword held across his chest. Morsmani shifted right and thrust with his sword at Nom's chest. Nom caught the blade on the edge of his sword, pushing it aside and turning his body so that Morsmani's sword went past him. Each swing, each block, each parry in a fight is one breath away from death for both combatants. One small step can be the difference in winning or losing. Nom rushed forward. His sword scraping Morsmani's sword as the point of the marlin bone weapon rushed towards Morsmani. Morsmani swung down with his tomahawk. The bottom edge of the tomahawk connected with the sword edge and pushed it down and away, causing Nom to stumble. Morsmani quickly stuck out his foot tripping the boy and pointed his sword at Nom's throat.

"I win. What did you do wrong?" Morsmani asked.

"I did not pay attention to your other arm," Nom answered.

"Correct. You watched only your point. You payed attention to only your sword, only your attack. What happens when you go purely on offense?"

"You either kill quickly or die quicker."

"Precisely. I've seen many fights where both fighters only know how to attack. They charge one another like mountain goats and then in one stroke from each, one or both of them dies. Those fights are more luck than anything. When do we go for the kill?"

"When victory is assured."

"Why is this?"

"The good defender need only wait for the attacker to make a mistake. The attacker must force the good defender to make a mistake."

"Good. Now, what is the easiest way to win a fight?"

"To not fight."

"Good. Now again."

Morsmani helped Nom up and they fought again. This time the fight lasted longer. Nom danced back away from Morsmani's blade and harassed his left side, where the shorter tomahawk was. Morsmani won again when he feinted forward, and then, when Nom lifted his sword and leaned forward to defend, Morsmani leaned back, forcing Nom to overextend. Morsmani's sword touched Nom's arm and the fight was over. According to Morsmani any blood drawn in a fight can turn the battle. Pain distracts the fighter. Pain brings in worry and fear. Blood loss weakens the fighter. Even after the battle a small cut can still kill through infection. Therefore, in training, any blow that would result in blood being drawn ends the fight.

Nom sat down to take a break. Morsmani sat next to him and stated that Nom had improved greatly.

Nom nodded and asked, "What is the rabbit's foot?"

Morsmani pulled out the string of bones and looked at it. "It's a charm. It gives its master great luck. More luck than they would normally have. It helped Deneth take the throne of Kahoke."

"Oh. Why did you want it back?"

"I gave it to him with the understanding that it would allow him to become king, and that, when I asked, he would help me. I asked him for nothing, until today."

"So, he broke the deal and you took the rabbit leg back?"

"Yes. I suppose it's for the best. This is a dangerous charm. When the master of the charm loses it the extra luck the person had turns to unluckiness. It is a tool that can help you achieve your dreams, but if you lose it you usually quickly fall down further than you were before."

"So Deneth may lose the throne?"

Morsmani shrugged. "I don't know. He might. I won't hand out this charm again though. Left in the hands of humans it will quickly burn a path of fortune and failure across the world."

Nom nodded. He didn't imagine a little extra unluckiness could hurt someone that badly.

"Now, let's practice your form," Morsmani said as he stood up.

*****

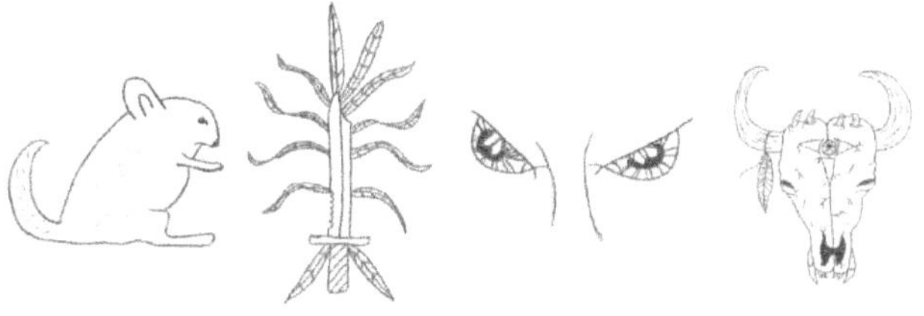

Chapter 5
The Sand Beast

The day was warm. The travelers were waiting at the market outside Chinchiplas's walls for the kajscags. They were leaving the lands of humans again and heading south. Nom had looked at Morsmani's maps and knew that the journey was still long. They would travel through a small strip of forest called Hort's Wall, and then across the great desert called the Sand Sea. After the Sand Sea was a land that was labeled wasteland on one map and marsh on another. That land, whatever it was, was known as Mycostadur. On the border of Mycostadur and the Sand Sea was Scagtower, the capital city of the nomadic scag tribes. They would stay there for a time. Nom supposed Morsmani would try to raise more armies while he was there. After Scagtower, the band would travel south again, across Mycostadur. Finally, they would arrive at the capital of the silver folkens' lands, Urbe. Nom knew nothing about these lands or people. New Keys was far away, and its people kept to themselves. They hated magic and anything non-human, so the different races of Usmer were never brought up except as scary tales told late at night to frighten children. Worship of the Prometheans however was common and encouraged.

The Duluth's had come out to say goodbye. Quentin and Nom stood to the side of the adults and compared swords.

Quentin had brought his grandfather's sword, Nagran's Fang. Nom inspected the two-handed great sword. The sword was weightless and massive. He thought the sword's size would make the weapon unwieldy. Quentin admired Nom's sleek sword.

In the past few days Nom and Quentin had become fast friends. Quentin had taken Nom around the city and the swamps. The older boy had terrified Nom with tales of the five headed serpent, Nagran, who lived nearby. Apparently fighting the serpent was a right of passage for great warriors. While in the swamps, Nom had taught Quentin how to fish with his pole. Quentin had just gotten the hang of accurately tossing the line yesterday.

"Hail, fellow travelers! Today is a good day for a walk through the woods," a loud voice boomed from across the market.

The scags had arrived. Their long red and gold hair blustered in the wind. Three hundred kajscags walked into the market, their purple eyes flicking about the market stalls. At the head of the group was Zoli Zarzasrahla, Zarzasrahla Azra, and a young male kajscag. The young kajscag was Zarzasrahla's son Zoltai. He was sixteen and covered in thick golden fur. He stood out in the tribe not only because he was the only male besides his father, but also because he had no markings. The scags bowed to the travelers who bowed back. The Duluths said their goodbyes. Quentin promised that he would spar with Nom when the boy returned. With a final, wave the travelers departed. As they left, Nom looked back at the Duluths and wondered if he would ever see them again. He wondered if Bairne would really come to conquer Chinchiplas. He missed Quentin's friendship already.

Nom's group was immediately behind the three front scags, Zarzasrahla, Azra, and Zoltai. Azra's red wavy hair bounced with her every step, and Nom could not help but watch it. It was somewhat hypnotic. Every bounce sent a shaft of liquid gold down the strands of fiery hair.

Skalla, who had joined the group again last night, leaned down and said, "Scags are hard women to win, young Nom."

Nom jumped and looked at the assassin. Skalla was wearing his dark blue leather armor again. "I am not trying to win anyone. I was just lost in thought."

Skalla smiled wider and nodded knowingly. Nom frowned, telling himself that adults know nothing, and grumbled under his breath.

The group passed through miles of rice paddies and small adobe towns. The farmers they passed either stared at their procession, or quickly closed their windows and doors. As the sun was setting on their third day of travel, they arrived at the edge of the forest. The forest could be seen for hours before they arrived under its boughs, the trees were so large. The scag party set up camp for the night and slept.

The next morning, they entered the trees. Each tree was at least as thick as four men standing shoulder to shoulder. The tops of the trees could not be seen. The leaves obscured any sight of the treetops and the sky above. The light that came down to the travelers was a dark, filtered green. When the group stopped for a snack between breakfast and lunch, Nom went to a nearby tree and looked at it. A great branch bent down from twelve feet above the ground to where Nom stood. The bough was as thick as Nom's head and was weighed down by the plants growing on it. Nom had thought that the trees grew a lot of leaves and held a lot of moss when he had first entered the forest, but as he looked around, he realized that the trees were actually covered in different plants. There were flowering bushes clinging to the bark of the trees' trunks, and vines curled and hung down from the branches above, while more flowers clung and sprouted from the vines. What bark was left unadorned with plant life was covered in thick layers of moss, which sometimes hung down like beards from the boughs.

Azra sidled up next to Nom and said, "It's said that each tree in Hort's Forest holds more life than all of Chinchiplas.

Look," Azra pointed upwards at a large flower. A lizard crept out from the center of the flower and stood on a petal. It shook; glistening water droplets shot off the lizard's scales. "Those flowerkin are shaped like cups and hold rain water. Lizardkin, birdkin, and insectkin use them as watering holes. Many of the kin in the forest never touch the ground in their whole lives."

Nom touched a leaf near him. The dark green leaf was twice the size of his hand. "That is incredible. My home island has nothing like this. The trees there come close, but they are nowhere near this big."

"Everything's bigger on the continent. Even the people," She added with a sly smile.

Nom's eyes widened, and he looked at the young kajscag girl. "I am still growing!"

Azra laughed and said, "And I'm only joking! You're taller than me anyway. I'm Zarzasrahla Azra by the way. I know my father, Zarzasrahla, introduced us but I wanted to personally introduce myself… Also, I may have forgotten your name. Sorry." Azra looked at the ground and started carving a circle with the point of her right sandal.

Nom smiled, "That is no problem! I am Nom Carver. Why do you have the same first name as your dad?"

Azra cocked her head to the side and replied, "My name's Azra. My father's name comes first to honor him and so everyone knows which tribe I am from. Is Nom not your father's name?"

"No, my father's name was Carlos. Carver is my family name. My family has always been the Carvers."

"Ah, I get it. Your tribe is the Carver tribe, just like I am part of Zarzasrahla's tribe. You humkin just switch the order of the names."

Nom scratched his head and said, "I guess so, yeah."

Azra smiled, nodded, and went back to staring up at the leaves. Nom watched her for a bit, and then, realizing he was staring, he jumped and looked up at the leaves as well.

After a few minutes he asked, "Why is this forest called Hort's Wall? What is it protecting us from?"

Azra looked down at the boy in the feathered armor and replied, "It looks like a wall. It's a thin finger of forest that extends from Hort's massive holdings to the west all the way to the ocean. Walls also separate one area from another. This thin forest separates the humkin lands to the north from the Sand Sea to the south. But most importantly it protects the humkin from the Sand Sea."

"Protects them? How?"

"Have you ever built a sand tower on the beach and seen the waves destroy it?" Azra asked.

Nom nodded.

Azra smiled and continued, "That is how the seas and oceans extend themselves. The waves erode the beaches and rocks on the shores of the lands by breaking them down and dragging them away into the ocean. The Sand Sea is similar, but the opposite. The Sand Sea has great dunes that look and act similar to ocean waves. The wind pushes the sand forward, like the wind pushes ocean waves forward, and when the sand waves hit the edge of the Sand Sea they stop. But, unlike the ocean waves, the sand dunes do not recede back into their sea. The sand piles on itself. So, while the ocean tears down the shores to grow, the Sand Sea builds up its shores to grow. The forest stops this. The sand can't go very far into the trees. Also, the trees stop the sandstorms. Actually, now that I'm thinking about it, I think the sandstorms is the biggest reason for the wall."

"Sandstorms? What are those?" Nom asked.

Azra smiled, revealing her extra pairs of long canines. "You'll see."

"Hey, you two! We're leaving now. Get your packs," Amy called from the edge of the kajscag tribe.

Azra held out her hand and said, "It was nice meeting you, Carver. I hope we can talk again."

Nom grabbed Azra's forearm, which is the custom in New Keys, and responded, "It was very nice to meet you as well. Gracias – um, I mean, thanks for the information. It was really interesting."

Azra smiled again and, bouncing slightly, said, "You're welcome!" She quickly turned and skipped back to the front of the procession. Her hair tumbling up and down across her white dress as she bounced.

The forest was dark and quiet. The path they had followed into the trees in the morning turned into little more than a game trail and eventually disappeared entirely. The humans that lived on the edge of the forest almost never entered for fear of Hort, the forest god. The only people who traveled under the boughs, and between the trunks were the nomadic scag tribes. The night before entering, Zarzasrahla had made a large bonfire at the forest's edge. Each traveler then threw a miniature bronze axe head into the bonfire. When the last of the axe heads melted in the bonfire the two trees bordering the path had bowed towards each other, their branches intertwining to make an arching gate into the forest. The ritual had reminded Nom of the fishing ritual performed in his childhood home. In his village, the fishermen were required to pour a little bit of their finest rum into the water and prick their thumbs before setting out to fish. This showed Backbone, the sea god, that their intentions were good, and to give the sea something in exchange for taking something from the sea.

The ground under Nom slowly changed. The dark mud became lighter and drier. The trees began to thin and there was more underbrush as more light passed between the leaves. As Nom was looking at the ground, Morsmani tapped him on the shoulder. Nom looked up, ahead. The ground stopped. The forest fell away. A large cliff marked the southern edge of the forest. The scags lined the edge of the cliff and looked out. Before them was a vast desert. Large dunes rose and fell. Nom gasped. It was just as Azra had said. The dunes looked like orange waves. Far in the distance was a line of dark clouds that obscured the horizon. Below the nomads, the red cliff face was flat with large, protruding roots. Zarzasrahla led the group to a large root that had erupted from the ground and spilled over the edge of the world long ago. Steps had been carved into the wood. The scags filed one by one down the steps, with the humans, Amy, and the Promethean making up the tail of the procession. The root tapered out a quarter way down the cliff and the steps led to a winding stair carved into the side of the cliff itself.

Nom had always prided himself in his lack of fear of heights. He was the best tree climber back home, and always dared to climb higher than any of his friends. The cliff face however was not a tree and was much higher than he had ever been. The wind caught the feathers of his armor, ruffling them. He breathed deep and continued down. Behind him, Skalla pushed a stone off the side of the steps, and leaning over the edge, watched the stone tumble down the cliff face. He laughed and looked for another stone to toss down. Amy was using her shadow bending to make a rope that was attached to the cliff. She held onto the rope with white knuckles and her constantly billowing brown hair flung itself straight back and up. At seemingly random places on the stairs were recesses with carved totem poles. The totem poles depicted scags.

After an hour and a half, the group reached the end of the stairs. Waiting for them was a delegation of beescags. Nom could not help but stare. While kajscags look human except for their purple eyes, extra canine teeth, tiger markings, and the males being covered entirely in fur, the beescags looked nothing like humans. They looked like giant rainbow scarab beetles that ranged from nine to twelve feet long. They stood on their back four legs and used their front two legs as arms. The front beescag reach up to his head as the group approached and pulled back on his single horn. The exoskeleton on the scag's head peeled upward like a mask and revealed an overlarge, dark, rainbow speckled human face. The scag's eyes were large black marbles and took up half of its gaunt face. The beescag smiled, revealing many sharp, black teeth.

"Welcome to the edge of civilization," The scag said.

The kajscags all bowed and then Zarzasrahla stated, "Hello, Korki. We're heading home."

Korki nodded and two large iridescent wings flung out from his back and rubbed together to make a buzzing sound. "I know. It's almost time for scagmoot. We heard that Morsmani and his beautiful wife were coming with you, so we prepared The Beatrice sand beast for you. Scagfriendkin are rare, and godkin even more so. Who are these others?"

At the question Skalla stepped forward and said, "I am Skalla of the north. I am a humble servant of Ruhk and companion of Morsmani."

Korki nodded. "A carrion feeder. The beescag tribes are not afraid to go to war with Ruhk. Don't hurt my people, and make no mistake, you're only allowed to travel with us because of Morsmani and Amy. And who is the childken?"

Nom stepped up next to Skalla and bowed. "It is a pleasure to meet you, Korki of the beescags. I am Nom Carver, a representative from the New Keys Kingdom."

Korki rubbed his wings together again and said, "The pleasure is mine, I'm sure. Now, let's get out of the sun. We depart tomorrow morning."

Korki and his people turned around and went into a cave in the base of the cliff. The massive cave sloped slightly upwards and eventually turned into a large open room. The room was lit by candles placed on stones around the chamber. In the center of the room were four large wooden machines, the sand beasts. Each beast had upwards of forty legs and had spiraling sails above the beasts' curved backs. The sand beasts were designed to look like beetles and used ancient, repurposed Forbear parts to run.

As they entered, Korki waved to the largest sand beast and said, "We will be traveling in the pride of the eastern Beescagkin, The Beatrice. It is our largest beast and its carapace is made of the finest hardened leather to help protect her and her passengers from the great sandstorms of The Sand Sea. It is also the best transport we can offer to the great Namer and his irredeemably beautiful queen, Amy."

Zarzasrahla rolled his eyes at Korki's flattery and said, "They're just people, Korki."

Korki rubbed his wings together and scratched the top of his head as he replied, "But such powerful people. A Promethean, and the Titaness of Shadow. Now pack your things into The Beatrice and get some sleep. Tomorrow we leave for Scagtower!"

*****

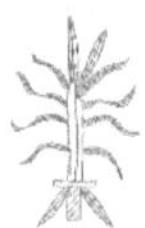

The next morning the large sand beast, Beatrice, was pulled by the Beescag tribe out of the cave. Ropes were attached to the front of the machine and the scags pulled. The slope of the cave and the design of the machine made the pulling of the beast an easy and quick affair. Once out of the cave, the spiraling sails were lifted and the first pedaling crew began pedaling the sand beast forward. Nom wandered about the inside of the machine. The entire beast was a dome that consisted of three levels. The lowest level was devoted to the pedaling crews and the mechanic's rooms, the second level was the living quarters, and the third level was the bridge, armory, and dining hall. There was a platform on top of the beast for observation and to access the sails, and a balcony that circled the third level of the beast. From the ground to the floor of the first level was fifteen feet and the beast stood a total of sixty feet tall, including the fifteen-foot-tall sails. The Beatrice was 150 feet long and 100 feet wide at its widest point. Nom was exploring the lowest level and entered the front mechanic's room.

The beescag working the room looked up when Nom entered and said, "Hello."

Nom replied, "Hola. I am Nom Carver. Is it okay if I look around in here? This machine is incredible. I had no idea there were things like this."

The beescag had no expression on her face. Her carapace helmet was down, so Nom had no idea what the scag was thinking. The scag's teeth clicked together and she said, "Okay, you can look around. If something looks sharp or dangerous, it most definitely is, so don't touch it."

Nom smiled and bowed saying, "Thank you!"

The room was above the first row of feet. There was a total of fifteen rows of feet. The feet were placed next to each other in five-foot intervals along each row. So, the longest row, in the middle of the sand beast, had 20 feet, and it was the eighth row of feet from the front. This row had only three feet. At each of the feet, there was a slot in the floor of the room for the top of the leg to enter. In the slot Nom could see the central axle that all the legs on this row were attached to. Each leg had a piece that rotated around the axle, which translated into the foot stepping forward far below them. On each of the pieces that rotated about the axle were three chains. Two of the chains ran parallel to each other towards the pedaling rooms. Scags and passengers pedaled, which caused the rotation of the leg and the forward movement of the sand beast. There were two sets of pedals for each leg. The third chain ran upwards. Nom knew that that chain would go to gears that would rotate when the wind caught, and spun, the spiral sails on top of the beast, which would then cause the beast to move forward. The spiraling, corkscrew sails allowed for the machine to move forward no matter the direction of the wind.

Nom noticed some of the chains were made of a white material and the others were made of metal. He asked, while pointing at the white chains, "Why are these chains different?"

The Beescag looked at the chains and replied, "Those are bone chains. We can't make the old metal chains anymore, so when the metal ones break, we make chains out of animal bone."

"Why can you not make the metal ones anymore?"

"Well, we never could. Most of the machinery in these sand beasts are old Forbear stuff we repurposed. Take the gears for instance, no one can make those. If a gear breaks it's done. We have to hope we can find an unused gear from some Forbear scrap. The chains are like that, too. We used to be able to get the Tommy Knockers to make us new chains when the old ones wore out, but they haven't done that for us since my grandpa was leading people across The Sand Sea. Steel making is a Knocker secret that they keep heavily guarded."

Nom frowned and said, "That is silly. Would it not be better if everyone could make steel?"

The scag clicked her teeth and replied, "It probably would, but then every nation could have steel armor and steel weapons. The Tommy Knockers would no longer have the advantage of better weapons in war. Also, I'm pretty sure they've lost the knowledge on how to make steel. Last I heard, there's a few families that know how to make steel, and they keep that knowledge from the rest of them. So even for the Tommy Knockers there's a shortage of steel."

Nom pulled out his marlin bone sword and stated, "I have a steel sword made by a Tommy Knocker."

The scag peered at the sword. "Steel and bone. Just like the inner mechanics of a sand beast. Keep that sword safe. It may be one of the last steel weapons ever made. It might be one of the last steel anythings ever made. The Forbears' technology gets further and further away with every year. Does that seem right to you?"

Nom put his sword away. "I do not know. The Forbears were ancient gods before the world as we know it was made. I think it is reasonable we cannot make what they made."

"True. I guess we're lucky we can even make some of their lesser materials."

Nom stayed for a while watching the parts of the machine move and rotate. He wondered why, so long after Shinigorath burned the world, people were still moving further away from the Forbears? How could people be losing knowledge instead of regaining knowledge? He finally decided that as long as people do not work together, knowledge will not be shared, and the world will be thrown further into darkness.

Nom Carver left the machine room. He wandered through the pedaling rooms where the beescags sat and pedaled four pedals at a time. In a few hours, the shifts would change and the kajscags, and Morsmani's companions would be the ones pedaling.

Upstairs were the living quarters. There were rows and rows of hammocks hung three high like bunk beds. The kajscags and beescags on the night shift for pedaling were sleeping. Nom tip toed through the living quarters and up the stairs to the dining hall.

The dining hall was a large, open, half-domed, wooden room. There were rows of low wooden benches where diners would place food while the diner himself would sit on soft cushions on the wooden floor. There was a door in the wall nearest the front of the sand beast. Through that door was the armory and the bridge, where Korki and Zarsasrahla commanded The Beatrice. The other wall, which curved around the entire dining hall, was made of sliding, wooden panels. This allowed the dining hall to be open to the air in fair weather. Most of the panels were open when Nom entered. In the center of the hall was a large metal plate above a wood pile. Nom did not know what the purpose of the plate was but figured he would see its purpose at dinner.

He wandered over to the wall that separated the dining hall from the armory and looked at a painting hanging there. It was the only painting on the sand beast, and it was a large painting. There were three panels. The first panel on the left depicted a red-haired woman dancing with a blond-haired man. Below them was a young child playing with rocks. The central panel showed the three people again, but now the woman was wreathed in flame, and instead of a dress had golden scales on her body. The man stood behind, and above the woman, and had beams of white light bursting from behind him. The child was still below them, but was no longer playing. He appeared to be writhing in pain and his skin was now covered in blue fur. Horns twisted out of his head. The last panel showed a large battle in the background. Above the battle, flying in the air, was the man and the child. The child now was a grown man. The blond man appeared to have ripped the blue haired man's head off of his body, and was holding the head in one hand, with the body in the other. Below them was the red-haired woman. She was lying on the ground mortally wounded. She was lifting her hand to a chocobscag woman. Bright white light was coming out of the red-haired woman's finger as she touched the chocobscag, who was kneeling next to her crying. Nom stared at the painting for a while and figured this must be a depiction of the old legend, The Tragedy of the Bumbles, the story Morsmani had told on the shipwright's ship.

"That's Korki's favorite possession, Beatrice's Tragedy Triptych. Do you know what it's about?" Someone behind Nom asked. Nom jumped and turned around. Azra was sitting on a cushion behind Nom, watching him.

Nom nodded and said, "It is the story of Klart, Beatrice, and John Bumble. It shows them as a happy family. Then, I assume the middle picture is them being transformed by the Maker. The last panel is the battle where John kills Beatrice, and Klart kills John. Why is there a person with wings on the bottom, though?"

Azra smiled. "You're correct! The chocobscag, that's what the person with wings is, have you never seen a chocobscag? On the bottom is the first Incarnate, Sola. As Beatrice died she knew that the scagkin would be hated for siding with Red in the Red Gold Conflict, and she wanted to help her son's people. She understood why the scagkin had joined Red instead of the Golden Council and did not want to see them be harmed after the war. So, as she died, Beatrice gave her spirit to the scag Sola. Since then, Beatrice's spirit is reincarnated in different scag women. These women are known as Incarnates and are the leaders of all of the scag tribes."

Nom had never heard of this before and he asked, "Who is the current Incarnate? Are they technically a dragon, since Beatrice was a dragon?"

Azra laughed and said, while patting the cushion next to her for Nom to sit on, "No they aren't a dragon. They have the soul of a dragon, and can control fire, and can appear as a dragon, and have the strength of a dragon, but they are not a dragon. They are a scag. They can commune with Beatrice and all of the previous Incarnates for knowledge, however."

Nom sat down next to Azra, and felt uncomfortably close to her, even though he was a foot away on a different cushion. This feeling had never happened to him before, and he did not like it. He said, "Oh, so who is the current Incarnate?"

Azra shrugged. "No one knows. The last Incarnate died fourteen years ago, and Beatrice never reveals herself until the current Incarnate is sixteen. It will be a kajscag though." Azra stated proudly.

"How do you know that?"

"The reincarnation cycles through the different tribes. The last Incarnate was a chocobscag, and the kajscagkin are next!"

Nom thought this over and then asked, "How old are you?"

Azra whipped her head around at Nom. Her purple eyes were narrowed into angry slits and she bared her teeth, showing her large canines. Her red and blue markings were no longer interesting designs on her skin, but menacing, alien, war paint. She answered in a high-pitched growl, "You're not supposed to ask a girl that, Carver."

Nom paled and quickly said, "Sorry. I did not know." He looked down at the ground and wondered why he was not allowed to ask that. It did not seem like a rude question. Why would someone want to keep their age a secret? Was she embarrassed by her age? No, that wouldn't make any sense. He shrugged internally and stored the question away for later deliberation.

Azra smiled, and bouncing a little on her cushion, said, "It's okay! I was just messing with you. You really shouldn't ask someone that, though. It's rude. I'm fourteen. What about you? How old are you, Carver?"

Nom sighed and queried, "Why can you ask me how old I am?"

Azra frowned and replied, "Because I told you how old I am…"

Nom scratched his chin and said, "Oh, okay. I am thirteen. I only asked you, because if you are fourteen, which you are, you could be the next Incarnate. Right? Beatrice's spirit will immediately travel to the next Incarnate when the old one dies, right?"

Azra's face lit up. She leaned forward towards Nom and exclaimed, "I never thought of that! You might be right. I could be the next Incarnate! Oh, my goodness, that's incredible!"

Nom smiled and continued, "You even look similar to Beatrice. Or, well, at least you look similar to the Beatrice in the painting."

Azra turned to the painting and looked sideways, suspiciously, at Nom. "Maybe," she replied. Then suddenly the kajscag girl jumped up and said, "Come with me. I want to show you something." Azra rushed away to the balcony that circled the dining hall. Nom quickly followed her.

Out on the balcony Azra was talking, not realizing that Nom had fallen behind. "You asked me what a sandstorm was, and I said, 'you'll see,' or something like that. Well, here it is. This is the Sand Sea Storm. A never ending storm that rages in the middle of the Sand Sea."

Nom stood next to Azra and looked out. In the distance was a brown cloud that sat on the ground. The edges of the cloud billowed and spiraled upwards like brown and gold buttresses and towers. The great dunes, flowing in peaks six hundred feet tall, and diving in sharp valleys, disappeared into the writhing storm. The sight of the storm calmed Nom. It reminded him of his small hut, his last home. The storm looked like The Sundering, just brown instead of grey, and shorter. He remembered long days swinging on his swing while he waited for Esmira to bring him his weekly allowance. It was a bittersweet memory. Those were lonely days, but he could at least count on each day being similar back then. Now, every day was different. Every day was filled with new adventures, new people, new places, and new discoveries. Nom had not decided which life he preferred yet. He looked at Azra. Her fiery hair billowed across her face, and the red triangles below her eyes, and blue lines across her face, shone against her pearlescent skin. *'At least I am not so lonely anymore,'* Nom thought.

*****

That night at dinner, the passengers on the Beatrice filed into the dining hall. They each grabbed a cushion and a large clay bowl. They sat down at the low benches and looked to the large metal plate in the middle of the hall. The chef entered. She was a smaller beescag whose carapace was mostly speckled with golden flakes. Her exoskeleton helmet was pulled up and her large black eyes observed the room. When everyone was seated she lit the pile of wood below the metal plate on fire and raised her hands.

The scags around the room raised their bowls into the air and chanted, "We thank you for this food, our kin. Though we must kill to eat, we do so with regret, and hope for your forgiveness and understanding. When we pass from this life may we return the favor."

After the chant, the scags all stood and made a long line around the outside of the dining hall. The curved, outer wall was lined with tables. On the tables were bowls and platters filled with vegetables, uncooked meats, oils, sauces, and noodles. The scags filled their clay bowls and handed them to the cook. The cook was joined by three helpers. The helpers and cook threw the contents of each person's bowl onto the metal plate above the flames. The food sizzled on the hot metal and cooked quickly. Nom was near the back of the line, and was one of the last to sit down. He sat next to Morsmani with an empty seat on his other side. The empty seat was quickly filled by Azra.

Nom took a bite of food and gasped. "This is delicious!" he exclaimed.

Morsmani nodded. He had taken off his mask's mouthpiece so that his beard and mouth were exposed. "It is," he replied. "I love the scag barbecue. You get to choose what you want to eat, and it's cooked fresh for you. Do you want some tea? It's excellent."

Nom frowned at the pot Morsmani offered him. The boy asked, "It is not like the caff is it? That stuff was no good."

Morsmani smiled and laughed. "No, no. This is not nearly as bitter. It's good."

Nom shrugged and Morsmani filled both his own cup and Nom's cup with the dark liquid. The Promethean took a sip and sighed, "That is the strawberriest of spoons."

Next to Nom, Azra laughed and leaning forward asked, "What does that mean?"

Morsmani looked at her and asked, "What does what mean?"

Nom answered, "You said 'that is the strawberriest of spoons.'"

Morsmani frowned and said, "Ignore that. It's nonsense. Word salad it is."

Nom took a sip of his own tea. The tea was warm and clear. There was a light, bitter taste. The tea, while not Nom's favorite, was refreshing and pleasant. Nom turned to Azra and asked, "What was that chant before dinner about?"

Azra quickly finished sucking up a mouthful of noodles before she replied. Her bowl was mostly noodles with a small spattering of buffkin meat. There were no vegetables. Nom thought that if his mother was here, she would have made sure Nom had vegetables. He looked at his bowl. There were noodles, bell pepper slices, mushrooms, and pork in his meal.

"That wasn't a chant. It was a prayer. Everything is connected you know? So, when we kill something to eat we kill a relation. Everything is kin, and when something dies its soul travels to another body, and has a new life. So, before eating we apologize for ending our kin's life, and ask its forgiveness."

"Oh!" Nom exclaimed. "Is that why you call everything kin?"

Azra thought about that for a second, then replied, "Maybe? Kin is used at the end of a word for an animal or plant. It means more than one. Ken means one. For example, you,

Carver, are a humken, one. You and that assassin are humkin, more than one."

"Oh, that makes sense." Nom replied.

A kajscag next to Azra leaned forward saying, "I doubt he understands. He's a humken. Humkin are cruel and mean. They are the lowest of creatures. We should never have let them on the sand beast."

The kajscag that spoke was Zarzasrahla's son, Zoltai. Nom had thought the kajscag had no markings on his yellow fur but now saw that Zoltai had two thin red lines that traveled from his tears ducts down to his chin.

"Why do you not like humans?" Nom queried around another bite of food.

Zoltai growled and replied, "Because humkin are monsters. You enslave and hunt scagkin. You don't let us into your cities, and give us less money for our goods than what we deserve. You humkin chop down forests and burn fields to build your overlarge houses. You have no respect for anything."

Nom frowned but did not say anything. He had no counter points to Zoltai's allegations. Azra and Zoltai talked for the rest of the meal, while Nom quickly finished his dinner in silence and left.

*****

Chapter 6
Deneth's Fading Favor

Back in Chinchiplas, in a back room of the Green Light Brewery sat an odd group of conspirators. The Duluth family sat on one side of a rectangular table. Quentin sat between his mother Annie and his father Francis. Across from them sat Guy Kahoke. Also in attendance were a magpie and a vulture from the Carrion Feeders. At the head of the table floated Shangri, a Promethean from the north. Behind Shangri stood three of Shangri's students who had traveled south with their mentor.

Francis stood up and addressed the room. "Thank you all for coming. First, I think it would be best if we all introduced ourselves and explained how we came to be here. I am Francis Duluth, proprietor of the Green Light and your host. I was told by Morsmani that you would all be coming here tonight. That's all I know. I don't know why you are here, or what we will be discussing. This is my wife Annie, and our son Quentin."

The people at the table all nodded, and the vulture stood up. He wore a dark red robe and his shaved head was painted white with a red skull on his face. He stated, "I am Quin, the vulture's beak of Chinchiplas." He saw the blank faces of the Duluth family and explained further, "I am the leader of the Carrion Feeder branch in Chinchiplas. My orders come directly from Ruhk, and I control all assassins in Chinchiplas and the surrounding lands. This is Hul, the magpie's claw." Hul was a small woman dressed in black and white robes and a silver beaked mask. She nodded as Quin continued, "Although she is a lower level magpie, she is very discrete, and very intelligent. I am personally training her to become a vulture like myself. She will deal with the money and logistics of this political assassination. We came here on orders from Ruhk. We do not know much about this contract except that it is the largest since the last coup in which Guy here lost the throne."

Guy shriveled into his seat as the vulture gestured towards him. He took a deep breath and stood up, rubbing his hands together nervously. "Hel-hello everyone," Guy began. "I'm Guy Kahoke. I'm a potter, and I was kidnapped and brought here by Shangri's students." The small man quickly sat down.

Shangri smiled and flipped himself upright. His bare porcelain-like feet floated a few inches above the brewery's dirt floor. Shangri wore a faded orange robe that allowed all four of his pale arms freedom to move. His head was bald, and if he stood, he would stand seven feet tall. He was covered in jewelry. Each piece contained at least one polished familiar stone. His solid purple, pupilless eyes surveyed the room. Some people speculated that Shangri's eyes were actually his familiar stones, the stones that contained a magical being's soul and power, and not his eyes at all. Shangri smiled and said, "I am Shangri, Collector and Keeper of Souls. I have traveled south from my temple with three of my strongest artificers to fight this world's greatest foe, the Terrestrial. I was contacted by Klart Bumble on the way down, however, and instructed to come here first. It seems I am the only one here who knows our mission." Shangri paused to peer around the table. He then continued in his calm, colorless, serene voice, "We must dethrone Deneth, and muster an army for Morsmani."

The table was silent in thought. Finally, Annie spoke out. "Another coup? Was the last one not enough? Why must we do this again?"

The Carrion Feeders stayed quiet. They were simply there to be given a contract and money. They did not care about the political landscape of the world.

Shangri answered her questions, "Yes, another coup. The last coup was to set up Chinchiplas for the coming of the Terrestrial…"

"Wait!" yelled out Guy. He had stood up suddenly but now seemed nervous at everyone looking at him. He sat down and continued, "I thought the last coup was because my older brother wasn't fit to rule, and I didn't want the throne after him. Deneth was the most ambitious and chosen to rule. Is that not true?"

Shangri nodded, "That is true. However, those are small disputes of mortals. We Prometheans do not get involved in your affairs for such trivial matters. Morsmani and Amy helped the last coup in order to gain a treaty with Deneth and his descendants. A deal that he knew the Kahokes would never agree to, but a man desperate for power would, when the deal seemed the only way to gain desired power."

"And this deal was?" Francis queried.

"To deliver an army under Morsmani's control when asked. A one-time deal. The idea was that Chinchiplas is the furthest southern human city. Therefore, an army from Chinchiplas would be the first line of defense and the quickest to march south against our enemy."

"So Morsmani knew the Terrestrial was mustering for invasion?" asked Annie.

"He always has been. Ever since he came to this world he has been trying to conquer it. He has been stalled by the machinations of various Prometheans and the Silver Folken, but now he moves. Either he is running out of resources in the south, or he is now strong enough to attack us, or we have weakened so far as to be vulnerable. Most likely all three options are true. In any case he attacks, and Morsmani needs an army."

Annie then stated, "And Deneth did not provide one."

Shangri smiled sadly and shook his head. "The deal was broken. It is left to us to fix it, if you are willing."

Now Quentin spoke, though he was nervous being in a room of his elders. "Why did Deneth not provide the army? He can't be foolish enough to anger a Promethean, can he?"

Guy Kahoke answered, "It's because of Prince Bairne. Bairne is leading an army from the north as we speak. He has conquered every city to the north of us from the eastern seas to the Smoky Mountains. Chinchiplas will be attacked soon." The table stared at Guy. Guy flushed and defended himself, saying, "I was once a political power. I pay attention to these things. It's simply a habit."

"Impressive, and insightful, Guy," complimented Shangri. "Mr. Kahoke is correct."

Again, Quentin spoke up, "Is King Deneth not correct then? If a conquering army marches towards us, should we not defend ourselves? If we send our army south, won't we lose Chinchiplas to Bairne?"

Shangri sighed and replied, "You are correct. This is why I leave the decision to you. This is not my city. Its fate is not mine, but yours. Just know there is a war coming. It will be a war on two fronts, and never have I seen a war won by the middle nation when attacked on both sides. I would suggest putting all your strength in fighting the Terrestrial in the south. Fighting next to the Silver Folken, Prometheans, like myself, and hopefully the great scag tribes. The Terrestrial is the larger threat. If he breaks through the Silver Folken, he will take everything. Bairne is simply a man, not a god. He will be easier to deal with later. But I am biased and have no holding in Chinchiplas."

The Duluths and Guy sat in silence for a while thinking. The Carrion Feeders put their heads together, discussing the logistics and price of a contract to kill a king.

After a few minutes, Shangri spoke again, "I forgot to mention, the coup is unavoidable. The King will die no matter what you do."

The table looked startled and then suspicious. "Why?" asked Guy.

"As some of you know, Deneth was given an artifact to help him gain the throne. The artifact was made by Shinigorath but was in the possession of Morsmani."

Annie gasped, "The rabbit foot. Did Deneth lose it?"

"He did."

"But it only increased its master's luck. Deneth's luck should be back to normal, yes?"

Shangri smiled, "No. Shinigorath, the god of death, madness, and chaos was firstly a trickster. As you know, Lady Annie, Shinigorath's artifacts always have more than one purpose. Many that seem hurtful at first actually help their users in the end. The Duluth family can attest to that, since their fortunes began with the chinchilla staff. But many that seem beneficial at first, end up hurting their users, often driving the users insane or killing them. The rabbit leg is one of these objects. Deneth's luck has run out, and when a king is unlucky, his kingdom is even more so. If Deneth stays in power Chinchiplas will suffer and fall from within. There are already the mustering rumors of locusts to the west. Hort and The Tormented claim they have seen more grasshoppers than usual, and in more dense clumps than in recent years. Would it not be bad luck for a king if the winds caused his city to be assailed by locusts? What of droughts? The winds that carry clouds shift, not through man's or Promethean's will, but by the magic of nature. This city and her holdings will suffer with Deneth on the throne, that cannot be changed."

Quentin blanched at the speech and quietly accused, "Are you threatening us Shangri?"

Shangri observed the young man, "No, no, I am not threatening. I have not the power to summon locusts or rain. Only three beings could have such power, and they are all occupied. I simply speculate what could be. Again, the decision is yours. We will meet again tomorrow, same time, same place. Hopefully, a decision will be made by then. Time is short, and if we wait too long, the decision will be forced upon us."

Shangri floated out of the room with his three pupils following him. The Duluths, and Guy stood, and after apologizing to the vulture of the Carrion Feeders for not making a contract yet, left. Quentin would lay in bed all night thinking about wars, disasters, and political assassinations. He had never thought that he would be involved in such things. He had imagined his future spent owning his family's brewery, inn, tavern, and textile business. He had imagined he would simply be the richest man in Chinchiplas and nothing more, like his father.

As he drifted off, he thought of Nom and how the boy was traveling south with Morsmani. Nom had not mentioned that he was going to war. Quentin wondered if Nom was nervous or scared.

*****

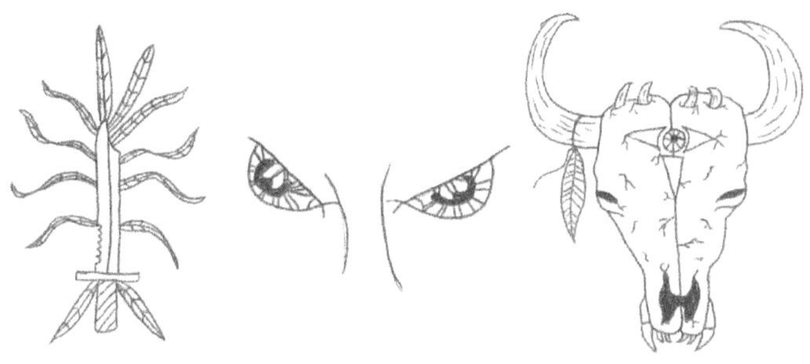

Chapter 7
Nom's First Kill

The sand beast, Beatrice, had entered the everlasting sandstorm of The Sand Sea two days ago. The sliding doors of the dining hall were closed tight, and the sand blasted the outside of the machine. Nom had awakened in the night after dreaming again of the cannibalistic matriarch. In the dream, they had not escaped, and the island people had cut up Nom and his friends and placed them on the scags' barbecue, and said a prayer thanking the waves for bringing such a feast. He was still shaking from the nightmare as he entered the dark dining hall. The wind whipped and whistled around the outside of the beast. The doors rattled continuously. One sliding door was left ajar, and a small pile of sand slowly grew where the door opened. Nom moved towards the opening nervously, the memory of his dream fresh in his mind, giving him a sense of anxiety. Outside the door was pitch black. Nom grasped the edge of the door and slid it open, so he could slip out. On the other side of the door was Amy.

Amy smiled, "Hello, Nom! Come out, come out. I made a cocoon to see the storm through."

Nom stepped out of the door and closed it carefully behind him. Amy, using her shadows, had made a small, spherical, black room that enclosed both her and Nom. The far side of the cocoon's shadow was less dense, allowing those inside to view the storm without being battered by the winds and sands. Nom looked out. The sand dunes, now larger than ever, rose and fell away in the distance. A great orange ocean, its waves cresting nine hundred feet above their valleys. Sand blew from the tops of the dunes like golden mist, and the backs of the dunes were great vertical cliffs.

"Couldn't sleep?" Amy asked.

Nom shook his head. "Nightmare."

Amy nodded, saying, "Ah yeah, I get those too sometimes. Just remember they're all in your head."

Nom thought about that and then asked, "Why are you up?"

"There's no rest for the dead and damned, Nom." Amy answered.

Nom had no idea how to respond to that, so he stayed silent and instead peered into the storm. There was something relaxing about viewing a storm when you cannot hear or feel its effects. It felt to Nom as if he and Amy were in a dream, and the storm was a distant memory a thousand miles away. He could watch the destructiveness in peace and quiet. Nom appreciated the beauty lying beneath the terror. Far away shapes began to appear on top of the dunes. They were small dots moving along the ridges of the dunes. The shapes disappeared into a valley.

"Did you see that?" asked Nom.

Amy squinted as she asked, "See what?"

"There were shapes moving out there. There they are again! On the dune's ridge."

Nom pointed, and this time Amy saw them. They were closer and looked like roly poly bugs. They were approaching the sand beast at speed.

"Ohmkin!" Amy whispered, then yelled, "Get inside! Grab your sword and knife. Prepare for battle! I must alert the scags. Hurry!"

Amy's shadows pulled open the door and shoved Nom inside. A hundred inky, black tubes with fluted ends extended out in front of Amy's face. They grew and snaked to every compartment of the sand beast.

Amy shouted into the near ends of the tubes, "Ohmkin! Ohmkin! Wake up, prepare for battle! Ohmkin! Ohmkin! Grab your weapons, and head to the top of The Beatrice! Ohmkin! Ohmkin! Retract the legs! Prepare for Battle!" The message was shouted through the tubes, traveling into every room, and every corner of the sand beast.

The sleeping scags below awoke in fervor and alarm. They quickly put on their armor and grabbed their weapons. The pedaling scags all stopped and opened up the floorboards, which allowed the legs of the sand beast to bend into the belly of the beast. The Beatrice was slowly lowered until it rested upon the sand. The back legs were still extended so that the beast was level. The scags rushed into the dining hall and out of the sliding doors. Nom pushed against the tide towards the ladder down to the sleeping halls. He reached his bunk. His marlin bone sword, tungsten knife, and helmet were quickly snatched up. The rest of Nom's armor was already on him. The woven armor was quite comfortable, so Nom almost never took it off. Nom quickly scrambled back up the ladder. The dining room was almost empty now. The elderly scags and children were lifting large, wooden beams into holders on the sliding doors. The beams would reinforce the doors, making it harder for an enemy to break in. Nom moved to the only open door left.

Skalla stopped Nom from leaving by blocking the door.

"Let me through," Nom demanded.

Skalla, who was in his blue, leather armor, and wearing his raven cowl, shook his head. "No," he shouted over the winds and commotion. "You are too young to fight. You will stay here with the children and elderly."

"I know how to fight! Morsmani taught me! He says I'm one of the best he's ever taught!"

A deep, gravelly voice then spoke into both Skalla and Nom's minds. 'You have the most potential to be a great warrior that I've seen in many years, Nom. I would hate to see that potential lost to this fight. Stay safe and live to see another battle. One which you will surely win.'

Nom looked around but did not see Morsmani. Nom made a mental note that apparently Morsmani could speak to people in their minds. Nom nodded to Skalla and moved back into the dining hall. The last of the warriors left the interior of the sand beast, and the last door was boarded up.

The wind howled, rattling the doors. The scags in the sand beast sat in silence, waiting. Then, the ohmkin came. Through the wind Nom could hear the clash of swords, the screams of the warriors, and loud booming. The battle raged outside the sand beast for thirty long minutes. Ohmkin crawled over the top of the beast, their large footsteps clunking across the ceiling of the dining hall. Below Nom and the non-fighters, bows could be heard twanging as the scags below protected the underbelly of The Beatrice. Nom could only imagine what monsters the ohmkin were, and what was making the booming noises. He gripped his sword tightly in his right hand and his knife in his left.

With a great gust of wind and flurry of sand, two of the doors into the dining hall tore asunder. An ohmkin pushed halfway into the hall. The beast's large body would not allow it further into the room. The scags all screamed and ran to the opposite end of the dining hall. Nom stood frozen, staring at the ohmkin. The giant pillbug had six blood red eyes, and three long horns protruding from its forehead. The giant insect's short legs scrabbled at the wooden floor, attempting to gain purchase. The feathers on Nom's armor prickled and stood straight out, making Nom look twice as large as he was. He looked at the cowering scags behind him. Azra stood in front of them holding up two knives. She glowered at the insect, her purple eyes slits, and her teeth bared. Her red hair stood up around her in a great, ginger globe. Then her hair fell in a cascade of red, illuminated by a bright blue-white flash. With a deafening bang, lightning arced through the dining hall, connecting with an elderly beescag. The beescag fell limp. Nom jumped back, looking for the lightning's source.

Morsmani spoke again into Nom's head saying, "The ohmkin. They control lightning. The sand in the air creates large static charges that the ohmkin can discharge through their three horns."

Images appeared in Nom's head of swords and axes breaking upon ohmkins' exoskeleton. Then images of swords and spears sliding behind the plates of the ohmkins' exoskeleton, and black blood leaving the insects. Nom understood and jumped towards the beast. The ohmkin scrabbled at the floor, and swung its head towards Nom. The monster's horns knocked Nom against the wall, and his breath was torn out of him. Another burst of lightning lit the room. A jagged line of white fire crossed Nom's vision. The lightning burst was so bright everything else fell to black, except where the lightning connected with a girl in white robes. Her red hair thrown up and her pale face wide with shock. Nom, still unable to breathe, pushed off from the wall. He ran behind the ohmkin's head and quickly thrust his marlin bone sword under the exoskeleton plate of the ohmkin's head. His sword plunged into the neck of the giant insect. Black blood sprayed across the walls and floor. The ohmkin shuddered and fell dead.

Nom looked across to the scags. He saw the old beescag, clearly dead, and Azra, lying on the floor. Nom dropped his weapons and rushed over to Azra. He knelt over her. The robes on her right shoulder were blackened and singed, and the skin under them was burst open, bleeding, and burnt.

Azra smiled weakly, and asked, "How did you know how to beat that thing, Carver?"

Nom shrugged and replied, worriedly, "Do not mind that. Are you okay? I do not know how to fix…" Nom trailed off looking at the seared flesh on Azra's shoulder.

Azra looked over as well. "It looks like barbecued buffkin meat, haha." Her laughter died out, and she fainted.

Nom was pushed aside by an old kajscag healer. Nom scooted away and watched the healer apply a poultice to Azra's shoulder. The battle outside slowly died down, and the ohmkin left. The Beatrice and her cargo had survived the onslaught.

*****

The storm had lessened slightly the next morning. A weak, orange sun peaked through the clouds and flying sand at the scags as they prepared their dead. Thirty scags and ten ohmkin had died in the battle. The ohmkin were being taken apart for meat and materials. The hard exoskeleton would make good armor and building materials. The scags were being laid out in a circle in a relatively flat valley near the sand beast. Thirty stone pillars had been brought out that morning. Beescags and kajscag were busy carving designs onto the pillars. Nom watched the scags erect the first pillar at the feet of a dead beescag. The pillar had a beetle head on the bottom, then stars spiraled up the pillar to the top, which was carved into an ohmkin.

Azra left the Beatrice. Nom watched her walk out towards the dune he sat upon. Her arm was in a sling and a large bandage covered her shoulder. She climbed the dune and plopped down next to Nom.

"How is your arm?" Nom asked.

Azra squinted into the wind, replying, "Not great. The healer says it will heal though. Do you want to see it?"

Before Nom could answer no, Azra had taken off her sling and peeled back the bandage. The injury did not look as bad that morning. The area that had been burned and bleeding the previous night was now a jagged scab. Red lines ran out from the scab like leafless branches of a creeping vine down her arm.

Azra put the bandage back on her shoulder. "See? It's not that bad. I won't even have any scars. I got the sling because my arm was tingly and hard to move this morning, but it's fine now." Azra paused, then asked wide eyed, "Do you want to see my foot?"

Nom stuttered, "Why would…"

Azra had taken off her left sandal and removed another bandage stuck to the sole of her foot. There was a blackened hole on the ball of her left foot. Nom gasped and held back a gag.

"Gross huh? The healerkin didn't catch this injury last night. Morsmani told them to check for an exit wound on my feet. Apparently lightning travels all the way through us when we get hit, and leaves through our feet," Azra excitedly explained. She enjoyed learning new things and sharing what she knew with others. She then added quietly, "I'll have a gross scar there though."

Nom looked away from the injured foot. He sat in silence for a while, unsure how to respond. Finally, he said, "Well, the scar will be on the bottom of your foot. No one will see it most likely. Will those red lines fade?"

Azra beamed at Nom. "You're right! No one will see it. That's good. Really good. I'd hate to have an ugly scar. The red lines will fade. Why, do you think they're ugly too?"

"No, I think they look cool. Like an ornate, red tattoo. They match the red triangles on your face."

Azra studied the red lines and replied, "They match my markings? I guess so. They do look interesting."

Nom watched as another pillar was erected. This one was at the feet of a kajscag. The bottom of the pillar was a large cat's head. Then, two crossed tomahawks, a buffkin head, four smaller cat heads, a short, plump man, and finally, on the top, an ohmkin.

Azra looked at Nom and asked, "So, what are you doing up here?"

Nom shrugged and said, "Watching them carve those pillars. What are they for?"

"Those aren't pillars. They're totems. They mark where a scag died, and chronicle their life. When a scag finally reaches enlightenment, they can see all their past lives, but they have to go on a journey. They have to travel to all of the places where they died. That way they tie together the broken string of their whole existence, and can see the circle that is life. The totems help the journey.”

“Oh,” Nom stated. He didn’t really understand the scag religion. Nom said, “In New Keys when someone dies they are placed on a reed boat, sailed out to sea, and the boat is set on fire. It is supposed to show Backbone, the god of the ocean, how the dead served the ocean and was at the ocean’s mercy their whole life. The fire and burning is to pay respect to Shinigorath, the god of death, madness, and chaos, who burned the whole world save Usmer.”

“Why is burning a person paying respect to a god? He sounds like a terrible god.” Azra stated.

Nom picked up a handful of sand and said, “Well, Shinigorath is an evil god. We do not worship him in New Keys. He is the enemy of all living things. We have to pay respect to him when someone dies, because he is the god of death. That person’s soul is now in Shinigorath’s domain.”

“No his soul isn’t. It’s been reborn in a new body.”

Nom shrugged. His father had told him from a very young age that religion often divided people, and it was best not to bring it up unwarranted or argue with someone about it.

Nom asked, “What will they do with the bodies? Will they bury them?”

Azra shook her head, “No, we leave the deadkin for the birdkin and the beastkin.”

Nom looked shocked. Azra quickly explained, “We eat the birdkin, and beastkin, so we are just returning the favor. After all we, scagkin and humkin, are just smarter beastkin of the land. Also, if only bones remain of the dead, the soulless dead can’t rise and kill us.”

“Does that happen? The dead rising?”

Azra shrugged and laughed, “There are stories about it happening.”

Nom nodded. A piece of sand flew into his eye. His eye immediately watered up. Nom quickly rubbed his eyes, hoping

Azra didn't notice and think he was crying. Azra did notice, and she wondered if Nom had teared up from seeing the dead from the battle. She thought that was sweet of him. Azra looked down at her feet and began pushing them in and out of the dune's sand.

After some time Azra quietly said, "Carver, my dad and brother say I can't talk to you anymore. They say scagkin don't mix well with humkin."

Nom looked up his eyes red from sand and rubbing. "What about Amy and Morsmani? You can talk to them!" he said, hurt.

"They're scagfriendkin. They've been named friendkin to the kajscags, so all scags know it is safe to be around them."

Nom glared at Azra. His eyes were watering again, this time with anger and hurt. He liked talking to Azra and was mad that someone would not allow it just because he's a human. "So what? Humans are dangerous to scags? As far as I can tell scags and humans are basically the same. The Maker took some humans and turned them into scags. We are not so different! I do not understand."

Azra sighed and looked at her feet. She said, "You come from islands where scagkin never journey, so you don't know how we are treated. On the mainland scagkin are hated and hurt by humkin. They view us as beastkin and demons. In the west, on the other side of the Spine Mountains, the humkin and dragonkin hunt us for sport. The Tommy Knockerkin buy us as slaves. Here, in the east, we are not allowed in humkin cities, and often cannot trade with the humkin. Do you know why we have so little money, but so many small trinkets?"

Nom shook his head.

"Many humkin think that scagkin don't deserve money. Money is for civilized races, not beastkin. So, they trade small trinkets for our meats and pottery. This stops scagkin from buying land, or anything really."

Nom sat in silence staring at Azra. He said, "I am sorry. I did not know any of that. That is horrible. I would never treat anyone like that."

Azra smiled and replied, "I believe you. My father and brother don't trust you. You are a humken."

"Is there anything I can do to convince them otherwise?"

Azra smiled wryly. "It'll be difficult to convince them that you're not humken, even with that armor making you look like a chocobscag."

"No, no, no. Convince them that I am trustworthy!" Nom quickly corrected.

Azra touched Nom's hand, saying, "I was just joking, Carver. There's nothing I can do. I'm sorry. I liked talking to you. You're different from the scag boykin I play with at Scagtower."

Nom nodded, trying to hold back tears. Azra stood up, wincing on her foot, and left. Nom's hand burned comfortingly where Azra had touched it.

*****

Chapter 8

Locusts

Chinchiplas was in trouble. King Deneth had tripped on his way down the stairs of the Great Pyramid of Kahoke. He was bedridden with a broken leg and a large concussion. A few days later his wife became sick, and the healers of Kahoke could not determine what the sickness was. She lay in bed all day and night, moaning and sweating.

Word had begun to spread around Chinchiplas about an evil demon in the south. Rumors were spread about the doom of the world, and the necessity to prepare for armies of evil to march on Chinchiplas. These rumors were all started at the Green Light Inn and Tavern, but they had spread so fast and so far, that no one remembered where they had first heard the rumors.

While these whispers were spreading, and fear was growing, a strange monument appeared at the docks of Chinchiplas. The monument was a ring of eleven, twelve-foot-tall obelisks made of granite. In the center of the ring was a thirty-foot-tall obsidian monolith. The monument's construction had started when six men had appeared in Chinchiplas dragging the obsidian pillar. They had raised the obelisk at the dock and began chanting about being one. More people showed up to the monument and joined the vigil. These newcomers were locals of Chinchiplas. They had abandoned their jobs and homes to come worship at the new monument. Some of the people worshipping left a few days later and returned dragging large slabs of granite. The chanters set about carving the smaller obelisks, still chanting about being one. The worshippers never left. They ate, slept, and chanted at the monument. Their jobs were left empty, their homes abandoned, and their families wanting.

The bedridden royalty, rumors of the apocalypse, and a strange new religion had the people of Chinchiplas worried. They were concerned as news of the queen's health deteriorated. They were in fear as rumors about the Terrestrial's power and might grew ever more outlandish. They were angry and shocked as more and more chinchiplasians left their lives to worship at the new monument, The Monument of Order.

Then, as Chinchiplas was beginning to become truly restless, the locusts came. They came in a great cloud sweeping over the land. They left the trees and plants stripped to bark in their wake. Food stores were ravaged, clothes eaten through, plants killed long before harvest. The lands of Chinchiplas suffered. The farmers, merchants, and craftsmen had no food, and many families slowly starved.

Then, the locusts came to the city of Chinchiplas. The great mound was surrounded by the flying insects. The sun could not be seen during the day. The wind from the locusts' wings beat upon the air, making Chinchiplas sound like the inside of a dragon brood.

The swarm lasted for a week in Chinchiplas. No one left their homes, except for the city criers, Men of Order, and a few rumor mongers hired by the Duluths' and Shangri. The criers sent word about how the royal family was no better, and how there was no food anywhere. The Men of Order chanted at their monument, and went door to door, saying how the swarm of locusts survives strongly together, while the individual grasshopper dies. The rumor mongers claimed the locusts came at the behest of the Terrestrial to make the lands weak before invasion.

On the final day of the locust swarm the only child of King Deneth lay crying in his crib. His cries could not be heard above the storm of insects outside the shuttered windows of the palace. His sick mother could not come to him. The maids and wet nurses did not come to work for fear of the locusts. No one was there to help the heir of Chinchiplas.

The child cried. A woman entered the room. She was dressed in dark blue robes that covered her entire body. A dark hood was thrown over head. A beaked mask covered her face. She crossed the room and flung open the large window. A few locusts flew into the baby's room. The woman sprinkled rice and sugar on the window sill. More locusts came in and followed the rice further into the room. The child's chamber was now filled with the insects. They crawled over the floor and walls and flew all over. They began eating the bed sheets and curtains. The woman went to the crib. Locusts do not eat meat. The child was safe. The woman pulled out a crystal jar filled with fire ants. She sprinkled sugar on the baby and shook the jar of ants, emptying its contents onto Deneth's baby boy. The ants, enraged by the shaking, immediately began biting the child. The child cried out in pain, and feebly tried to brush the ants off. This only made the ants angrier. The woman went back to the window and broke the latch that held the shutters closed. That way it would appear that the shutters broke open from the beating of the insects.

After a few minutes, the baby's crying quieted. The woman looked at the child. It was swollen from the fire ant bites, and its breathing was slowing. After a few more minutes the child was dead. The woman sprinkled sugar in a line across the bed. The fire ants followed the sweet food, and the woman scooped up the insects. The assassin, her clothes now in tatters from the locusts, left the room.

The locusts left the next day. During the week of the storm, Deneth's broken leg had become infected. His wife, the queen, had become even sicker. When she learned of her son's passing due to the locust swarm, she became depressed and refused to see anyone, even her doctors.

She said, when the healers came, "Shinigorath's wrath has descended upon our city. Who am I to fight the god of death?"

She too passed not long after. Deneth's infection grew. No doctors had dared brave the swarm to come visit the king and check on him. Because of this, it was too late to amputate the king's leg. King Deneth died of infection a few days after his wife. There was no king in Chinchiplas.

*****

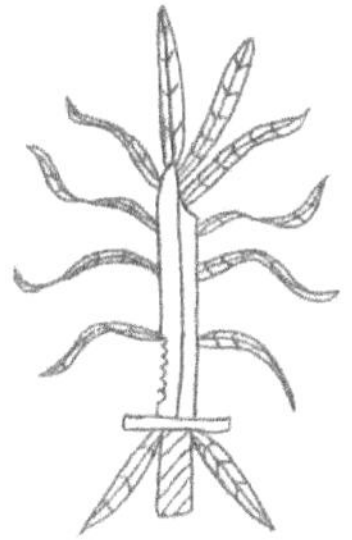 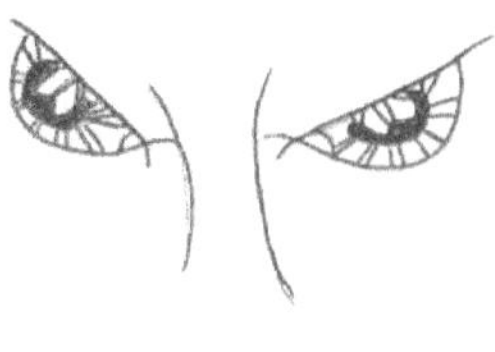

Chapter 9
Tales of Drought and Starvation

The Beatrice was on the move again. The dead had been honored, the sand beast fixed, and wounds healed. Up and down the dunes the scags and Nom travelled, getting ever closer to the scags' capital, Scagtower. Nom and his companions, Morsmani, Amy, and Skalla, sat in the dining hall of the sand beast; their shift of pedaling recently ended.

"So, how did you like the battle, Nom?" asked Skalla. "You killed an ohmkin. No simple feat. How does it feel?"

Nom thought about that for a while. He replied, "I am not sure. The ohmkin was just an insect, and it was stuck in the door. It was no different than killing a fish really. They are both just animals. The battle was a little scary." Nom admitted tentatively.

Amy laughed good naturedly. "Battles are always scary. If you aren't scared going into battle, you're either an idiot, or suicidal, or my husband."

Nom nodded, feeling better about himself. From the stair flew a small, green and gold beetle. It must have flown in through the leg holes on the first floor of the sand beast. The insect landed on the ground in front of Morsmani's cushion. Its back broke open into four leaflets, and a piece of paper tied to a small metal plate rose out of the beetle. Nom was quite shocked until he realized the beetle was not alive. It was made out of glass and metal. The beetle was completely mechanical, and its head was an emerald familiar stone. Morsmani grabbed the piece of paper and read its contents.

"What does it say? And who is it from?" asked Nom. He was extremely curious about the beetle. He had never seen anything like it.

Morsmani finished reading the message, and then said, choosing his words carefully, "The message is from a colleague of mine, Shangri. He's a Promethean who studies enchantments and runs a school up north. He's currently in Chinchiplas. He says that a locust swarm just hit the city and that the swarm is now heading south towards us."

"Will the city be okay?" asked Nom.

Amy replied, "Chinchiplas will survive. They won't have much food this year and it will be hard on them, but they will survive. Don't worry, the Duluths will be fine."

Nom nodded, thinking about the Duluths. He wondered how they would be able to keep the tavern and brewery open if there was no food. He also wondered how they could stop Prince Bairne if his army came that far south. Bairne would conquer Chinchiplas easily if its citizens were already starving.

Nom was broken out of his train of thought by Skalla. "Speaking of people's friends, how are you and Azra doing, Nom?" Skalla asked.

Nom shrugged.

"Did you two break up?" Skalla goaded.

Nom flushed and replied, "No! We were not...we were just friends. She is not allowed to talk to me anymore."

Skalla ignored the last part of what Nom said and started on a story of his own. "I once had a scag girl you know. She was a buffscag; large, muscly, blue haired, with fangs and two horns the size of my forearms. I had been sent to kill a Tommy Knocker in The Spine Mountains, which I did. In order to complete the job, though, I needed help from the Tommy Knocker's buffscag house slave. So, we escaped together. But, on our way down from the mountains, a blizzard blew in. We were trapped in this little sheltered valley near the Scagway for a week. It was just the two of us, alone, in the snow and ice. And, well, you know how things are. One night she came into my tent…"

"Maybe this isn't the best time for that story, Skalla," Amy cut off the assassin. "What happened between you and Azra, Nom?"

Nom clutched his knees to his chest and explained, "Zarzasrahla and Zoltai told Azra she cannot talk to me anymore. I am a human and cannot be trusted. It is not fair! I did nothing wrong."

Morsmani tapped the nose of his helmet and said, "They talk to Amy. And they talk to me."

"You are scagfriendkin. You can be trusted. Also, neither of you are human. Do they talk to you Skalla?"

Skalla shook his head. "No, they don't. Most people avoid me once they find out what my profession is, so I didn't really notice. Sounds to me like you need to become a scagfriendkin."

Nom nodded saying, "It is pronounced scagfriendken, not scagfriendkin. Kin is plural. Ken is singular. I wonder how I can become a scagfriendken? How did you do it, Morsmani and Amy?"

Amy and Morsmani looked at one another. "You tell the story," Amy said to Morsmani.

Morsmani began. "Fine, it was a long time ago. In the time of Zarzasrahla's grandfather Azranlaq. This story happens at Scagtower. The scag capital, Scagtower, is a large tower in the middle of a desert oasis. It was built by the Forbears long ago. The tower stands over a large lake called Tear Lake. It used to be called Beatrice's Tears Lake but was shortened to Tear Lake over the years. This lake is fed by an underground waterway that was also constructed by the Forbears. Many years after the fall of the titans this water way clogged, and Tear Lake began to dry up. It lasted a few generations, but by the time Azranlaq's generation was getting old, the lake was almost gone. The oasis of Scagtower was shrinking and could no longer hold the growing scag population. So, the scags began the discussion of moving away. They were going to lose their ancestral home. They were going to lose one of the few places where they were safe. That's when Amy and I showed up. We overheard the worried scags, and set about solving the problem.

"Do you know what the Golden Key is? It's my hammer, but it wasn't always a hammer. It was once a key. It was a tool fashioned by the Forbears to control the water in their cities. It could open and close the Forbear waterways, cisterns, and aqueducts. I had just recently come into possession of the Golden Key. It was gifted to me by my good friend Gold, the god of war, in his will.

"Amy and I searched through the Forbears' water ways. These waterways are large tunnels, larger than most peoples' houses, made of stone that stretch for miles. They are dark, wet, and filled with all manner of beasts and monsters. We discovered that these large tunnels were fed by smaller tunnels. Tunnels that one had to crawl through. And these smaller tunnels were fed by even smaller tunnels. We traced all of these tunnels back to a large lake in the hills miles away from Scagtower. The lake, like the tunnels, and the tower, was made by the Forbears. They had made this lake to catch water for their now lost cities. This lake was overflowing. Its drainage was blocked. Amy used her shadows to find and unclog the waterways that were too small for us to crawl into, and I used my hammer to open up closed water ways that were otherwise clear of debris. They had simply been closed by someone long, long ago. Water flowed back into Tear Lake, and the scags were saved. Azranlaq and the kajscag tribes labeled us scagfriendkin and gave us each a tomahawk in commemoration. Amy lost hers long ago, but I still have mine."

Nom nodded. "So, you saved the scags' capital. I cannot compete with that. There is no way I become scagfriendken."

Skalla patted Nom on the back and said, "Don't worry little buddy. I bet you'll find a way. And if you don't, I'll show you the beautiful redheaded girls of the north."

Scags began filing into the dining hall. It was dinner time. The great barbecue was lit and scags said their prayer and began eating. Nom looked across the room at Azra. She was talking to Zoltai, the heir to Zarzasrahla's tribe. She laughed at something Zoltai said and looked across the room. She made eye contact with Nom. Her face went blank. She quickly looked down at her bowl. Zoltai glared at Nom, his sharp teeth bared slightly into a snarl. Nom looked down at his own barbecue. The Beatrice continued to ride the great dunes of The Sand Sea through the night.

*****

Chapter 10

Matters of State

Quentin Duluth sat at the meeting hall's large, round, cherry wood table. The leaders of Chinchiplas had been called together, and as heir to the Duluth estate, Quentin was allowed to come. Around the table sat: the Duluths, Guy Kahoke, General Francis, Lichtenfrumph, Master of Coin, the Dock Master, Healing Master, Master of Cloth, Forge Master, Governor Altec, Sake Master, Shangri, and a representative from each of the fifteen levels of the city.

General Francis stood up and addressed the group, "I called you all here to discuss the recent problems our lands have faced and ways to mitigate future problems. First, the king is dead. His heir is dead. His wife is dead. I am the acting leader of Chinchiplas until the Quetzal's Calling can commence to choose a new king."

The general let that sink in. His white brows furrowed as he looked around the table.

Governor Altec spoke up, "I don't care about the new king. My people are starving. They have no food, and no money to get food. They have no food to sell, which means that they will have no money for food next year. Master of Coin, can you spare some money or seek out foreign aid? Surely someone will send us food if we pay them?"

Before the Master of Coin could answer, the General stated, "We can discuss that issue later."

"But…" Altec began

He was cut off by General Francis. "I will make committees at the end of this meeting to solve the other issues. Our lack of leadership is the pressing problem. Prince Bairne bears down upon us from the north. He has taken every city save Chinchiplas and Shangri's Temple. He marches south to our borders. We need a king to defend our city."

Shangri now spoke, "What of the Terrestrial to the south? Is he not of concern?"

The general scowled at the pale Promethean. "Those are baseless rumors. I will believe that an ancient demon is coming towards us when I hear of the death of the Silver Folken and see scags running from their homes. I know Bairne is coming. That is who I will prepare to fight. Lord Shangri, you were invited to this meeting to give advice, and as a courtesy. You are known as one of the wisest Prometheans, but I begin to wonder whether that wisdom lies only in spiritual guidance and does not extend to wisdom in governance."

The general stared angrily at Shangri. Shangri held his tongue and smile passively as he floated a few inches off his chair.

"Now," continued General Francis. "I want candidates for kingship. Do any of you here want to nominate someone to be king?"

The table erupted in shouting. Most of the people at the table were either nominating themselves or berating others for nominating themselves. The Duluths, Shangri, and Lichtenfrumph watched this with curious detachment. Guy Kahoke slumped down in his chair and pulled his hood over his head. He could not stand the noise.

The general shouted for quiet. No one listened. The general shouted again, but to no avail. The leaders of Chinchiplas were too emotionally invested in their yelling. A loud shrill screaming sounded, which drowned out all of the shouting. The people in the room clapped their hands over their ears and wilted into their seats.

Shangri closed the locket he was holding. The banshee scream ended. Shangri looked at General Francis and said, "The table is yours."

"Thank you," Francis admonished. "Now we will go around the table, one by one, and name candidates. We will start with the Duluths."

The Duluths posited that they had no candidates and were simply at the meeting to be in the know and part of the committees. The name saying continued around the table. Everyone nominated themselves and no one else, until the last four people, General Francis, Shangri, Lichtenfrumph, and Guy Kahoke. The general was not allowed to name himself, so instead he named the head of the archers as his nominee. Shangri offered no nominee. Lichtenfrumph named Guy Kahoke.

Guy jumped in his seat and quickly stated, "I don't want to be king! Why would you nominate me? I've been king. I failed horribly! Horribly! You just want to weaken Chinchiplas for the Tommy Knockers, don't you, Lichtenfrumph?"

Lichtenfrumph smiled and said, "What? Me? No, never. I like this city. Although it could do with some more Tommy Knocker charm."

General Francis cut off Lichtenfrumph. "Stop messing around Lichtenfrumph. Guy, do you have a nominee?"

Guy nodded. "Yes, yes, um, ah, well, I know you all will probably dislike this nomination, but well, I think he'd make a good ruler. He's young, smart, honorable, and has good counseling. Quentin Duluth is my nomination."

Quentin's ears rang. He wasn't sure if he had heard Guy correctly. He could not be king. What about the family business? The table grumbled as everyone muttered their thoughts about the nominations. When the scribe had recorded all of the nominees, General Francis called together the small council meetings to deal with the various catastrophes around

Chinchiplas. Quentin, not being part of any of these groups, and having too much on his mind, left the meeting chambers. Shangri followed.

Quentin went outside. He leaned against the railing of the balcony outside the meeting hall. The meeting hall was a room on the topmost level of Chinchiplas. The balcony looked over the compound of Kahoke City, and the rice paddies beyond. The sun sank slowly in a blaze of orange beyond the endless rows of rice. Shangri floated next to Quentin.

Quentin looked down at Kahoke. The large pyramids glowed blood red in the dying sun and appeared like small ant hills from the top of the mound city. Quentin wondered what it would be like to live there, to rule there. He wasn't sure he would like it. He wasn't sure if he could do it. Plus, who would take over the family business when his parents left?

"Are you wondering what it would be like to be king?" Shangri asked.

Quentin nodded, not wanting to be broken out of his reverie.

Shangri pulled his legs up so that they crossed like the northerners' pretzels. He stated, "Ruling is difficult. You must make decisions that will hurt people. Most people will hate you, and many will try to kill you. Most rulers I've met ended up being mad, dead, or lonely. But I've seen a few rulers who rose to the status of gods. Their names were sung through the streets. They were loved by all and died happily and content. Do you want to rule Chinchiplas, Quentin?"

Quentin answered, "I don't know. I doubt I'd make a good ruler. I'm not even the best server at my parents' tavern. Plus, what would happen to my parents' businesses?"

Shangri nodded. "Kings do not serve. But to have a king who served, and who knows he was a bad server, is a more valuable asset than a king born from a bed of gold. I do not know what will become of your family business. Your parents are yet young. I daresay your devotion and concern to the business you think you will one day own is a sign that you will treat the city you may yet rule with compassion and attentiveness."

"I don't know if I want to rule though."

"Good. Most of the good rulers ruled not because they wanted power, but because it was their duty," Shangri replied.

Quentin thought about that for a while. He decided that maybe, maybe, he could rule well. He would rule like Klart Bumble, with a soft hand, never given to anger, and listen to all advice given. He would try his best to follow the wisest path and admit his mistakes when he made them. Then his mind froze. He would immediately have to decide to go to war, or to stay and wait for war, when he came to power.

Quentin looked sideways at the comfortably floating god next to him. He asked Shangri, "Are you trying to see if I will march my army south to fight the Terrestrial?"

Shangri's roughhewn, purple, garnet eyes sparkled. He smiled and said, "The decision is yours. I try not to meddle, just advise." Shangri reached in his robes and pulled out a large ruby. The vitreous stone reflected light from a thousand different faces. "Do you know what this is, Quentin Duluth?"

"A ruby. I've never seen one so large."

"Half right. This is a ruby. It is so large because it came from a dragon. Many years ago, long before your great grandfather had his great sword forged, I traveled with a group of Tommy Knockers into the cold desert on the other side of the Spine Mountains. They were hunting wild dragon for sport. Many of their houses view dragon hunting as a way to show that the young men of their house are true men, and great warriors. I went along, because I wanted to see their hunting techniques. Dragons, even the wild ones who have no intelligence, are fearsome beasts. They do not fall easily and live forever. Indeed, many view the first generation of dragons as Prometheans. I personally do. I do not like the killing and hunting of things, but it was a fun journey, nonetheless. The Knockers brought down a large, golden scaled dragon. They took its head and hands to mount, and its meat to eat. I stayed behind, for my prize was still in the dragon.

"I prayed to the dragon's soul for a fortnight. The dragon was three hundred years old, and powerfully magical. It did not yield its soul to me easily. Eventually I gained the magnificent animal's trust and was rewarded with this." Shangri held up the ruby, which lit on fire in his hand. The Promethean had put on a leather glove with pearls running around the bottom edge. The fire did not harm the glove or The Collector of Souls. "This is the dragon's familiar stone. Large as her years, and wild as her anger. Now tell me, do you know why it is shaped the way it is?"

Quentin shook his head. He was enraptured by the flames, and the myriad rainbows cast off by the faces on the stone.

Shangri nodded, "The faces tell of the major events of a life. When a magical being is born their familiar stone is a perfect sphere, untainted and pure. With every great event, every large decision, every trauma and joy, the stone is chipped. Eventually the small chips cause the stone to shear and a face is made on the stone."

Shangri peered at Quentin and stated, "Just in the conversation tonight I saw in you a caring son, a hardworking man, and a nervous child. Which one of these is truly you? Are any of them? Every person has many facets, like a cut diamond. You only show the world a few of the facets, a few of these faces. Even if you spend your entire life with someone, you only ever see a few of their faces. Only they ever know the true radiance of their own souls." The ruby lit up into a million rainbows as light from the fire and the sunset refracted off every face, every facet, of the stone. "No one knows anyone but themselves. That is why I study familiar stones and use them to enchant artifacts. Not for their powerful magic, but because I can come closer to knowing these people, knowing their souls, by looking at their stones. The decision to march to war, or wait for war, is a decision that in itself would cut a new face on your stone, Quentin, if you had one. Whatever decision you make, or don't make, will change who you are. The people around may not notice the change, but you will. Therefore, I will not try to sway you one way or the other. It is your decision."

*****

The next morning, the conspirators were again meeting in the Green Light Brewery's back room. Money between the Duluth parents and the magpie Hul was exchanged before Quentin came into the room. The vulture, Quin, was attending the meeting as well. Quentin entered the room and surveyed the conspirators. There was Shangri, his three students, Quentin's parents, Guy Kahoke, Hul, and Quin. The same group who conspired to end a king's rule. Quentin sat down, and the meeting began.

Annie opened the meeting, saying,, "King Deneth is dead and his heir is gone. It seems the rabbit leg did its job well, and I am very glad it is no longer in Chinchiplas. Now, Quentin has been nominated for the throne." Annie paused, and the room clapped. Francis patted Quentin's back. Quentin blushed, and beamed.

Annie continued, "This means we now have to work hard to get Quentin votes at the Quetzal's Calling. As you all know, each level of Chinchiplas gets one vote at the Calling, the military gets three votes, Kahoke gets two votes, and the surrounding lands get two votes. That's 22 votes total, and we need a majority vote to get Quentin the throne."

Quentin interrupted his mother by saying, "I'm sorry, but what is the Pretzel Calling?"

Annie answered, "Right, you weren't born yet when Guy lost the throne. The Quetzal's Calling is a celebration where the votes for the new king are tallied, and the new king is crowned. I suppose you want me to explain how the voting works?"

Quentin nodded.

"Okay. The week before the Calling all of the people of Chinchiplas go to their respective voting booth and cast their vote for the new king. The nominees are posted at the booths, but the people can vote for whoever they want. On the day of the

Quetzal's Calling, the votes are tallied at each booth and whoever gets majority at each booth gets that booth's vote. You need a majority booth vote to be crowned."

Quentin nodded. "So, we only need twelve booth votes to win? If we get the military, Kahoke, and the surrounding lands on our side that would count for seven votes. Then we only need five of the fifteen levels on our side. Which levels should we target?"

Francis, Quentin's father, smiled and said, "Slow down a little. Remember, this is a fight between more than just you and one other person. There were 25 nominees at the meeting yesterday. Now Governor Altec, the Sake master, and most of the level representatives have pulled their names out of the competition this morning."

Shangri asked, "How do you know this?"

Quin, the vulture's beak, stated, "I told him. He payed me last night to collect information. My ravens were busy all night and this morning gathering news on these affairs. They will continue to do so, even if the Carrion Feeders do not get money for our efforts. Information at a time like this can easily be turned to gold."

Shangri nodded, and gestured at Francis to continue.

Francis began again, "There are now only five nominees: Quentin, Guy, Master of Cloth, the archer whose name I forget, and Master of Coin. We just have to have more booth votes than any of the other nominees."

Quentin turned to Guy and asked, "Why have you not rescinded from the competition?"

Guy touched the tip of his nose with his right pointer finger, and explained, "Well, I figured, I'm not going to win, and if there's more nominees, less people will want to join the competition. Cause there's already so much competition. And, I mean, I can try and pull votes away from the other nominees. You work on the booths you want and then I'll work on the booths you aren't working on. That way I get a few votes, and all the other nominees get less, because of me. You won't need as many votes to have a majority that way. I'm no threat. I already lost the throne once. I gave it away. I told Morsmani, I told him, I do not want to rule. I can't do this. I can't lead meetings, and make speeches, and go to war. I am on your side, Quentin."

Quentin cut off Guy, saying, "Okay, okay. I think that's a fine plan. So, when do we begin campaigning?"

Annie smiled, and stated, "Now."

*****

Chapter 11
A Vision of Order

Nom Carver slept soundly, a thing he had recently not been able to do. His dreams were plagued by nightmares, anxiousness, and, strangely, conversations with Azra. Tonight, however, he slept well.

His nonsensical dreams became a vision. He saw a world split into a thousand pieces, floating in the sky. A bright white sun shone upon the broken world, and Nom felt homesick. He saw his home. The small huts with palms on the roofs. The mangroves growing at the edges of the village. The clear water lapping the soft sand.

An image of Morsmani swum into Nom's vision. With the image came a feeling of resentment. This Promethean, this unknown god, had taken Nom away from his home. He had taken Nom on an adventure full of terrors and brushes with death. The nightmares were from the travel's tribulations. Who was responsible for the way the adventure had gone?

Morsmani', Nom's voice spoke in Nom's head.

Nom shook his head, "No. that is wrong. He did not cause the problems. He was as much a victim of them as me."

Then a different voice spoke, a voice of calm. It said, "This world is broken. This world is fractured. It's chaotic.

Cannibals on islands, assassins as friends, giant bugs killing giant bugs, children abandoned and forgotten. Lost children."

Nom saw himself on his swing outside his hut. His silhouette lay bare and bleak against the looming greyness of The Sundering. He remembered those days of hunger and loneliness. No one in town would talk to him. He was the monster who survived the burning of a village. Maybe he destroyed the village? Maybe he's a demon? He went weeks without human interaction. Esmira would leave a basket of money once a week outside his door. She would not knock. She dropped the basket and left. Nom was alone, Nom was sad, and his feeling were reflected in his silhouette by The Sundering.

Then Nom was given visions that were not his, but in line with his thinking. He saw the broken world of floating islands. He saw friends and happiness. Then suddenly a cage came down, and Nom floated through the stars for an eternity. He floated forever, until one day he came crashing onto a new world, Nom's world. Nom saw his world in a whole new light. He saw the grasses flash past his face as he ran as a mouse through the fields. He saw the jungles of his home islands below him as he flew as the quetzal. He saw the towering buildings of the Forbears, lit by their artificial suns. He saw the mechanical dragons of the ancient titans, and the rumbling behemoths that the Forbears rode.

Then in a flash the buildings lit on fire. The behemoths were tossed like chaff into the air, the mechanical dragons spiraled to the earth. The sky turned from blue to orange, and the earth burned. The plants and animals disintegrated. Once again Nom was alone.

He stood in a desert of heat blasted trees, looking at a wall of golden light. He was alone and sad. He knew on the other side were people and animals. He could not go there. He was not allowed. For hundreds of years he watched the wall. For hundreds of years he waited. He waited for the cruel jailors to relent, to free him. They did not. They have not.

"Help free me, Nom. Join me and others like you. Join us, and never be alone again. See the world through a thousand eyes. Find more friends than you could even count. We will be your family, more understanding, more supportive than any you have ever had. Join me, and we can go home."

Nom jerked awake to a final vision of his island village floating in a sky filled with a bright white sun. He shook his head and thought, *That was the strangest dream I've ever had.*

*****

Azra was awake as well. Her pedaling shift had just ended, and she wandered the dining room chewing on buffkin jerky. Lady Amy crossed the dining hall and left through one of the sliding doors. Sand swept into the room and dusted the floorboards. Amy quickly slid shut the door.

Amy's behavior peaked Azra's interest. Azra walked to the door and slid it open. Amy was climbing the ladder at the back of the sand beast to reach the top of the machine. Azra followed.

Azra found Amy standing on the edge of the roof of the sand beast, looking east. Azra approached the shadow bender, her white skirt flying about her in the strong winds of The Sand Sea.

"What are you doing out here Lady Amy?" Azra shouted into the wind.

Amy jumped and looked around for the voice. The gusty wind made hearing difficult. When Amy finally saw the slight figure of the kajscag girl beside her, she smiled. A cage of shadow fell around the two of them, with a small, eastward window. Azra jumped back and ran into the wall.

Amy quickly said, "Don't worry, don't worry. This is my room. We don't have to shout anymore."

Azra picked herself up and nodded. "What are you doing out here, Lady Amy?" she repeated.

Amy, her dark, silken hair still fluttering about her head though there was no more wind, stated, "I'm looking for the wreck of the Bumble Bee."

Azra's eyes widened. The Bumble Bee was the greatest sand beast ever built. Its purpose was war, not transportation like The Beatrice. The entire sand beast had been made of metal and was twice as large as The Beatrice. The Bumble Bee had gone to war in the early days of the world. It had defeated many of the scags' great foes, but on one of the sand beast's journeys home to Scag Tower, the beast had fallen. It was rumored that the

Promethean of The Sand Sea, Gerud, had become envious of the way the scags could travel across his lands so easily. So, Gerud had broken The Bumble Bee and killed all of the scags on board. It was the worst sand beast accident in history, and The Bumble Bee's loss marked a decline in scag power and influence.

"Can you really see it from here?" Azra excitedly asked.

Amy nodded and pointed. Out in the distance, a great domed shape rose out of the side of a dune. A weak moon peaked between the blowing sands and was dully reflected back at the two women.

Azra gasped, "That's incredible! I wish I could go and explore it. Where's Morsmani? I'm sure he would like to see this."

Amy peered out at the sand, and replied, "He's out doing something right now. He would have loved to see this though."

Azra wondered what Morsmani could be doing. *'He couldn't have left the sand beast,'* she thought. *'No one does that. It's too dangerous.'*

Then quietly Azra stated, "Nom would have liked to see this too. He likes old stories, and I could have told him all about The Bumble Bee."

Amy looked at the young kajscag and nodded sadly.

Azra asked, "Does he hate me?"

"Who?" Amy asked.

"Carver. Does he hate me for not talking to him, for ignoring him?"

"No." Amy shook her head. "He's more upset at your father. He thinks it's unfair that the two of you can't talk. After all, you were the only person his age he talked to on this journey. He doesn't blame you. He knows you are just following your father's orders."

"So, he's angry at my father then?"

Amy shrugged. "Maybe. Nom doesn't seem to get upset easily. He's hurt, because he thinks it is unfair that he gets blamed for things other people did, but he isn't angry, I don't think. He's lonely though. He lost the only friend close to his age he had made since his village was destroyed."

Azra thought for a while. Finally, she stated, "I wish I was like you."

"Why do you say that?"

"Because you don't have to listen to anyone. You can do whatever you want. And you're really pretty."

Amy laughed. "When you're older you can do as you please as well. Just be patient. Also, I'm no prettier than you."

Azra replied petulantly, "I don't want to wait! By the time I'm an adult, Nom will have forgotten me. And you're a lot prettier than me! You don't have ugly freckles."

Amy smiled and ruffled Azra's hair.

Azra glowered as Amy said, "A face without freckles is like a night without stars. But remember, the night's beauty is determined by the stargazer not by the night. Nom will never forget you."

Azra looked at the ground. She asked, "Can I go now? I want to go back inside."

The shadows disappeared around the women and Azra quickly walked back to the ladder. Her hair whipped about her face, as if her wavy red hair was really fire. At the bottom of the ladder she was overcome by emotion. She leaned against the wall and screamed. Her voice was taken by the wind and disappeared. Hot tears were swept off her face in the gusts.

*****

Across the dunes The Bumble Bee lay. The husk of the ancient sand beast was filled with sand but was not empty for the first time in hundreds of years. Five northern men sat around a fire in the old machine's armory. It was the only room where they could get away from the storm and build a fire. They had cast off their furs and leather armor in the heat and sat in only their cotton shirts and pants.

"Gods, I hate this job," one of the men said.

"Would you rather be trying to storm the walls of Shangri's Temple?" another asked.

"Ha, no. That's a suicide mission. Those artificers are crafty and mean. I wouldn't want to fight one in open battle, let alone fight however many are in that school. And they have the walls! Bah. That's a job I'm not envious of."

Another of the men spoke up. "Still, this job is terrible. Who wants to dig up an old wreck like this? It doesn't even work. Its sails are gone, most of the siding is cracked, or fallen off, and the gears are all gone. How the hell does Bairne the Unkempt expect us to fix this old metal bin?"

The men snickered at Bairne's old nickname. The last man who called Bairne the Unkempt to his face was still tied to a rock, upside down, with his head below the high tide line. He had drowned during the first tide change, but his body was still there as a reminder.

The leader of the group, his yellow braided hair and beard sparking gold in the firelight, stated, "We have replacement gears graciously given to us by the Knockers, and this beast does not need sails. It runs on the same potion that runs the Shipwrights' ships. We dig up the machine, replace the gears, and give this old monster her medicine. Then, we take this pile of junk back to Chinchiplas to pick up Bairne and his army of northern screamers. Or help take Chinchiplas if Bairne's too slow to do that in time."

The men nodded and grumbled. They heard the same speech every day. The leader, Aegil, figured this mission was his break. After this mission was successful, he would be given a bigger command. So, he talked about how to complete the mission every day with the firey zeal of ambition in his eyes. Everyone else was tired of digging dry sand and eating hard tack.

The first man spoke again, "I'm tired of this. I hate sand. It's everywhere. In my clothes, in my shoes, in my hair, in my bloody ears and eyes. I'm starting to wonder when I'll just turn to sand out here. I say we take the gears and potion and leave. We head over The Spine Mountains. We sell the gears and potion in the dragon cities out west. We would be richer than anyone. And Bairne wouldn't follow us that far."

"And how do we cross the mountains, idiot? The Tommy Knockers, those damned dwarrows, are taking the Scagway soon. When they do that there ain't no free way over the mountains. We'd be lucky to get off as slaves to those Knocker troglodytes. We finish the mission," Aegil stated simply.

The man who kept complaining grunted in agreement and pulled out his axe to sharpen it. After running the axe edge over the whetstone twice, he swung the axe at the man next to him. The man looked at the axe buried in his side. Blood ran down the axe edge and his shirt turned red. He slumped over, expressionless. The three other men shouted in shock. The axe wielder stood up and bellowed. The three men scrambled up as well. The group's leader came at the axe man with his golden gilded sword. The axe swung high at Aegil's head. Aegil ducked and plunged his sword into the traitor's guts. Aegil turned and saw his last two companions. One was on top of the other. The one on top was stabbing the other man repeatedly muttering, "Why won't you stay down? Why won't you stay down? Why won't you stay down?"

Aegil approached the man and yelled, "What are you doing?"

The last man alive besides Aegil looked up and said quietly, afraid, "He, he, he wouldn't stay down. He can't stay down. Will you stay down?"

The man lunged at Aegil. Aegil swung his sword, which buried itself halfway into the man's neck. Aegil sat down and looked at his crew. He could not believe what had happened. Then he saw a figure enter the room. Aegil jumped up and faced the figure. The newcomer was hidden in shadow. It had two horns that curved upward and a great war hammer.

"Who are you? What do you want?" Aegil challenged.

Fire wreathed the silhouette. Red glass eyes flashed on the figure's masked face.

The figure stated in the voice of an avalanche, "I am death, and I want the same."

The hammer came up, then down. Aegil lifted his sword to block the blow. The sword shattered just like Aegil's body.

*****

Nom woke up in his swaying hammock. The scags around him were snoring and snuffling in their sleep. Nom got up, put on his woven armor, brushed the feathers down, and went upstairs to the dining hall. Azra and Zarzsrahla were the only other people in the dining hall. Nom grabbed a biscuit and jerky from the cold barbecue and sat on the other side of the room from the kajscags. Zarzasrahla's fur was unkempt and sticking up in tufts along his arms and torso. Nom watched the old scag eat. Azra stared at Nom. Nom glanced at Azra, who gave a quick shake of her head, and looked back down at her breakfast. Nom took the shake to mean 'do not stare,' and looked elsewhere. Zarzasrahla finished his food and left for the bridge. Nom stuffed the rest of his biscuit in his mouth and quickly followed. Azra gasped and gestured at Nom to not go into the armory. Nom glared at her and slipped into the armory after Zarzasrahla. The armory was a wide hallway with weapons and armor on the walls and in a long rack running along the middle of the room. On the far side was the door to the bridge. Nom crossed to the bridge.

When Nom entered the bridge, Zarzasrahla turned around. There was no one else in the command center, Korki had gone to sleep a few minutes ago.

"Only chiefs and matrons are allowed on the bridge humken. Leave," Zarzasrahla demanded.

Nom shook his head. "I will leave, but not yet. Why will you not allow Azra to talk to me?"

"You are a humken. Humkin hunt, kill, and enslave scagkin. Would you let your favored child talk to a grizzly bear?"

Nom glared and replied, "I am no bear. I am a human. I am as smart as any of you, and I do not want to hurt anyone. Azra was my friend. My only friend. I want that friendship back."

"You have Skalla, Morsmani, and Amy to talk to. Or are they not your friendkin?"

"They are adults. They are like family, not friends." Nom paused. Zarzasrahla looked at the boy with no sympathy. Nom continued, "Why am I being punished for things I never did? I never saw any scags until I came to Chinchiplas. I do not hate you people. I do not wish to hurt you people. I do not understand why other humans treat you so poorly. Why am I being punished for others' crimes?"

Zarzasrahla stated, "You are humken. Azra will be my son's first wife, and the matron of his son's tribe. She, above all my children, must be protected, for she is the best of my daughters. Humken are dangerous, and I do not want her to talk to them."

"She will have to talk to them when she is older."

"True, but she will be older. She will be stronger and wiser. She will be more able to protect herself. I do not think you will hurt her, but I do not want her to be influenced too heavily by you. If she thinks humkin are friendkin, then she will put her guard down and get hurt."

Nom thought about this. That did not make any sense to him. Everyone was different. So how could an entire race of people be boiled down to a few simple truths?

Nom then stated, "You say when she is wiser. My father told me intelligence comes with age, wisdom with experience. Would Azra not benefit from the experience of interacting with a friendly human? She would learn how humans think and be wiser to their ways, right?"

Zarzasrahla replied, "She will get that experience when she's older."

"She will get that experience when she is older, and her head is filled with prejudices and fears. Then she will be just like you and Zoltai! Scared of a little boy, and unable to see anyone for who they are! How can an adult act like this?"

Zarzasrahla charged Nom, grabbing him by the throat, and slamming him into the wall.

The scag yelled, "You dare to insult me and my son? No one would question me if I killed some humken who trespassed onto the bridge, so get out before I decide to hurt you, you insolent little child."

The retractable claws on Zarzasrahla's hands came out, and the kajscag bared his fangs. Nom ducked under the arm that held him against the wall and quickly left the room. Out in the armory Nom was met by Azra.

"Are you okay?" Azra asked.

Nom rubbed his neck. Zarzasrahla's claws had pricked Nom's skin and he was bleeding a little. Nom asked Azra, "Did you listen to the whole thing?"

Azra nodded.

Nom blushed a deep red. Azra pulled out a piece of cloth and said, "You're bleeding. Let me clean that."

Azra brought the cloth close to Nom's neck to wipe away the blood. Nom, embarrassed and surprised, brushed Azra's arm away and stormed out of the armory. Azra was left looking confused, hurt, and worried.

*****

Chapter 12

Call of the Quetzal

The day was bright and warm. Quentin was sweating underneath his chinchilla fur shirt in the sweltering heat. His parents had insisted he wear the shirt while campaigning. They said it represented the family values of persevering in the face of the gods. The shirt reminded the people of Chinchiplas how Allison Duluth had turned a curse placed upon her into a profitable business for her and her descendants. Quentin felt like most people who saw the shirt would simply be reminded who had all the money in the city. A shirt like the one Quentin was wearing was worth more than the entirety of the second level of Chinchiplas.

He wore the shirt though, because today was an important day. Today Quentin was meeting with Governor Altec, the man in charge of the lands surrounding Chinchiplas, and the military leaders. If Quentin convinced both Altec and the military to vote for him, he would have five votes. Over the last few days Quentin had been meeting with the other leaders of Chinchiplas and Kahoke. Kahoke was firmly behind Guy. They remembered when Kahoke was ruled by Kahokes and wanted a return to those days. That was fine. Guy wouldn't win and any votes he took would mean less votes needed for Quentin's victory. The Master of Coin would put his votes towards Quentin. He figured having a business leader as king would help fill the coffers of Chinchiplas. The Sake Master and Cloth Master were also backing Quentin's claim to the throne. The King of Chinchiplas was not allowed to own or invest in any businesses. If Quentin, the only child of the Duluth family, was king, the biggest rival to their own businesses would be gone. If Quentin could garner votes from Governor Altec and the military today, he would be all but guaranteed the throne.

"So, tell me Quentin what brings you out here to the farmlands?" Governor Altec asked as he walked beside the boy.

"I wanted to help the farmers and people who live around Chinchiplas. I know that your people lost almost everything when the locusts came, and I want to help as much as I can." Quentin answered.

They had met in the marketplace and headed out into the farmlands. The market had been empty, and tired. The only customers of the few stalls still open had been dust devils and flies. A few stray, emaciated, chinchillas played in the square when they had met. It was a sad sight. No one had anything to sell, and no one had anything to buy with. The farmlands were in similar condition. The wheat fields were simply lines of barren stalks, the grain eaten away. The rice paddies lay as muddy pools, the water poisoned by dead bugs. Some farmers were seen wading into the paddies, looking for more crawfish, and planting more crawfish eggs. The crawfish season had ended just before the swarm, however, so most of the crawfish found were not good eating, and the newly laid eggs would not hatch. It was an exercise in futility, but it kept some farmers active. The other farmers simply sat outside their adobe houses, staring at their ruined fields. The hot air was filled with the chirping of cicadas.

Governor Altec asked, "How will you help my people? They have no food, money, or goods. Most barely get by each year, and this year is, well, the worst I've ever seen."

Quentin sighed, "I know. I know it's hard for your people. My family has large stores of rice for our sake, and grains for our beer. If your people come to The Green Light Tavern, my family will give them a pot of their choice of either rice or grain. One pot per person. Three pots for families."

"That's very generous. You get people to come into your tavern, which I'm sure is as empty as my marketplace, and you get votes for king. Very smart. Now, will my people have to bring their own pots, and if so, what size is allowed?"

Quentin shook his head, "Guy Kahoke will provide the pots."

Altec raised his eyebrows. "Guy will? His pots are very expensive. If they are usual Guy quality, then the pots are worth more than your food. Aren't you worried about Guy getting the votes? He is running against you still, yes? One of the final three candidates?"

Quentin gave what he hoped was a winning smile, and answered, "He is running against me. This isn't to get votes, Governor. This is to help Chinchiplas. Without the farmers there is no rice for sake. Sake is our main export. The farmers here," Quentin pointed to the farms they were walking past, "are the true foundation of Chinchilpas. Chinchiplas was built around my family's brewery, but my family's brewery was built from the rice and barley of these farmers. Chinchiplas needs the farmers more than the farmers need Chinchiplas. I just want to help."

Governor Altec nodded and smiled. "I believe you. Although you did not stay for the council meetings. I will tell my people of your offer and urge them to come within the next week. After all, the Quetzal's Calling is at the end of this week, and much will change."

Quentin and Altec continued walking and talking. They discussed that year's crawfish harvest, the return of Morsmani, and other smaller matters. They parted ways just before noon, a new friendship just beginning to bud. Quentin headed back into the mound city and climbed the spiraling road to the top of the mound.

Along the way, Quentin passed each level's voting booth. At each booth were three people yelling rhetoric for their respective candidate into the crowd. The Duluth's representatives spoke of an ancient family who had built Chinchiplas from the ground up, a family who brought business and money into the city, a family that all the people of Chinchiplas could rely upon in these trying times. Guy's representatives spoke of tradition. They spoke of old royal blood, of how after the first line of kings, chaos and death had fallen on Chinchiplas. They said if the old royalty of Kahoke was reinstated, Chinchiplas would return to the days of prosperity. The archer's representatives, Quentin did not remember the archer's name, spoke of war. They spoke of an invading army to the north, a looming evil to the south, a creeping darkness in Chinchiplas itself. They asked how a businessman, or a politician, could stop these threats? They claimed only a military leader could save Chinchiplas. Quentin had to admit that the military representatives were the most convincing. Fear has a way of moving the masses.

Quentin arrived at the military training grounds some time after noon. General Francis and the archer were waiting. They ushered Quentin into the general's office and closed the door. The office was next to the large meeting hall they had met at to name candidates for kingship. There was a bedspread in the corner and a pitcher of water. On the far wall was the general's iron armor and sword. The three men sat on the clay floor among the dried threshes and began to talk.

Francis began, "The two of you have not met before. Quentin this is Morrin, Morrin this is Quentin. Now, Quentin, you asked for this meeting. What do you wish to discuss?"

Quentin nodded to Morrin, who nodded in return. "I wanted to ask Morrin to pull out of the race for kingship."

"No," Morrin stated simply. His voice was raspy and dry.

Quentin smiled. "Fair enough. I also wanted to ask your advice on the coming wars. One of us will win, and if it so happens that I win, I want to make the right choice military wise. Should the army go south to Morsmani, or should we keep the army here to protect against Bairne?"

The soldiers looked at each other, and Morrin answered by asking, "Do you know how many times the army of Chinchiplas has marched out and gone to war?"

Quentin shook his head.

"Zero times. Chinchiplas's army has never left its own lands. Our army is equipped for defending the walls of Kahoke and the mound city. And our army has been successful at just that for hundreds of years. We have never been conquered. Never. We will not be conquered any time soon, as long as we have an army here. Let Morsmani lead his army of beast folk south. If the god of order defeats the Silver Folken, scags, Morsmani, Lady Amy, Shangri, Myco, Gerud, and Hort, and arrives at our city, we will be ready. I find it unlikely that the Terrestrial will make it here. Bairne on the other hand, will arrive here. He still holds Shangri's temple under siege, but we have reports that a large portion of his army has been sent south. We are the only place left to conquer. We can hold off Bairne, if we have our army here. We need our soldiers here."

Quentin nodded. He had come to a similar conclusion, but it was good to hear someone else say it. Quentin stated, "That is what I have been thinking, but for different reasons. Shangri told me that it is nearly impossible to win a two-front war. He supposed that the best course of action was to attack quickly to the south, and then when Bairne comes we will only be fighting a war on one front. But I've been thinking that if the army leaves, and Bairne comes before the army returns, we lose. We would have abandoned the city. That we cannot do. So, I agree with you. We should keep our army here and defend against whatever threats may come." Quentin paused, and then asked, "If, however, the new king asked you to go south, would you?"

General Francis nodded. He stated, "The soldier obeys the king's command."

✳✳✳✳✳

It was the day of The Quetzal's Calling. Quentin, Morrin, and their entourages arrived at the market outside the city walls as the sun peaked above the horizon of swaying swamp trees. General Francis arrived and stood before the voting booth. He waited.

When the sun was half over the horizon he stated, "We have to start now. Where is Guy Kahoke? Is he coming?"

Quentin Duluth shrugged, and Morrin shook his head to show that he did not know.

"Fine," General Francis said. "We will begin. If Guy does not show by the time we reveal the farmland's vote, he concedes." Francis paused to gather his thoughts, and began, "We are here for The Quetzal's Calling. The old king is dead and left no heirs. So, it is left to the people of Chinchiplas, Kahoke, and the surrounding lands to choose a new king. A king of man who, like the great Quetzal the king of birds, will rule from on high. A king who will see the world and lands he controls laid out before him, and protect them from far reaching enemies, and tribulations at home. There is a total of twenty-two votes. The person with the majority vote wins."

From the crowd, Lichtenfrumph spoke up, "What will happen to Guy's votes if he doesn't show up? Will those votes go to the second place?"

The general shook his head. "His votes will be counted. If Guy wins, we will hold a meeting to discuss what course of action to take. I warn you, however, I'm not sure on the leniency he will get."

Lichtenfrumph opened his mouth, but was cut off by Annie Duluth who said, "Quiet Lichtenfrumph! You are just stalling so that your candidate can show up. He is late, and we need to get going. Please continue, general."

General Francis nodded. He walked to the booth and opened the voting box. Votes had been placed into the box through a slit in the top. Each vote was a clay token with an enscribed symbol for the candidate chosen; an arrow for Morrin, a pot for Guy, and a chinchilla for Quentin. The tokens were placed in stacks for each candidate. Morrin's stack began rising quickly then faltered and stopped as Quentin and Guy's stacks rose higher and higher. Finally, the stacks showed that Quentin won the vote by two tokens. The watching crowd clapped and Governor Altec presented Quentin with a wooden statue of a crawfish. The candidates, their entourages, and some of the crowd moved into the city to the lowest level, the dock level.

As the crowd wound its way around the great mound to reach the docks, Quentin thought. He knew this level would be an easy win for him. Green Light Inn and Tavern, Green Light Brewery, and Green Light Textiles were all on this level. Most of the people who came to the infamous lowest level of Chinchiplas did so to visit the Duluth's establishments. The residents of this level were the poorest, but they respected the Duluth's for staying on their level through all these years. This level was Quentin's without any questions. They arrived at the docks. The wind wafted dirty air from the neighboring swamps. The cisterns added their own ripe smell to the air as sewage dumped into the water not far from where the group stopped. What bit of air was not tainted by the sewage or swamp scum was filled with the smell of dead fish. Quentin was used to the smell. He did not mind. Most of the crowd, however, covered their noses in disgust.

The voting booth had been placed next to the new Monument of Order. All that remained of the booth was ash and charcoal. The booth's keeper rushed over to General Francis and explained what had happened. Quentin overheard most of what was said. It seems the followers of the new religion had burned down the booth last night. They had yelled about not needing a king when all were one. For if there is only one, then there is none to follow and none to lead. The booth keeper was badly bruised and burnt. The followers of Order had been locked in the Kahoke prison that morning. General Francis explained what happened and stated that the dock booth could not be used. The crowd moved to the next level.

As the sun reached the highest point in the sky the crowd had finally reached the top of the mound city, the military level. Quentin had six votes, Guy had six votes, and Morrin had four votes. The tokens were being stacked. This level had many people living on it and it would take a while to count the tokens. Quentin wandered over to the eastern edge of the level and looked out over the swamps which stretched to the horizon. He saw movement in the waters near the docks below and peered down. The military's ships were all set up in the docks. Men could be seen like ants carrying supplies onto the ships and arming themselves. Quentin wondered what the navy could be doing. Maybe the zorscags were becoming unruly again, and the Chinchiplas army was preparing a raiding party, or maybe they were simply drilling. Quentin shrugged and went back to the voting booth. The tokens were finished stacking. Morrin won to no one's surprise, and he was gifted a silver tipped, golden arrow. The crowd moved down the mound to reach Kahoke, the final voting booth. General Francis and Morrin whispered behind Quentin as they went. Quentin could not help but eavesdrop on his opponent.

"Why was the top level so quiet? Did you give the men the day off?" whispered Morrin.

General Francis whispered back, "I did not give them the day off. I will see what happened after the feast tonight. Maybe the men decided to ignore orders and not work today since the military leaders are all absent for The Calling."

Quentin wondered how strong of a hold General Francis had on the army. He would have to watch that if he won the throne. Quentin also wondered at the absence of Shangri. Two of Shangri's artificers were in the crowd, but the Promethean was nowhere to be seen.

They arrived at Kahoke. The final booth was at the top of the Great Pyramid in front of the throne. All of the people of Kahoke, and many of the people of Chinchiplas, had come out to see the final results of the voting. No one was allowed onto the pyramid except for the candidates, and General Francis. Quentin, Morrin, and General Francis left the large throng in the wide avenue below and mounted the many steps to the pyramid's top. Once at the summit, the two candidates watched in silence as the general began stacking the tokens. Two votes would be won here. If Morrin or Quentin won the votes, they would win. If Guy won the votes, he would tie with Quentin at six votes, and Morrin would win with seven votes. The stacks were even throughout the voting. Quentin sweated under his chinchilla fur shirt. The loose sand from the sandstone of the pyramid was picked up by the wind from the west and blew about the candidates' heads. Finally, the stacking finished. Quentin peered at the stacks, his breath held. He had won. He had beat Guy by one vote. Quentin was king.

General Francis strode to the top of the stairs. He shouted, "The vote is finished! The vote is finished! The vote is finished! The person called forth to be a king of man is…" General Francis paused to let the tension build, and the crowd to quiet. Then he yelled, "Quentin Duluth!"

There was a roar like an oncoming hurricane from the crowd. The people below shouted, and danced, and sang.

A great feast was held that night in the great hall of the Great Pyramid. Three buffkin were roasted whole over fires. The great horned beasts of the western plains were enough to feed an entire level for a week. That night they were eaten in but a few hours. Fish from the swamps and seas were served with fruit and vegetables. Rice, piled high in mountains of grain, was devoured ravenously by the people of Chinchiplas. Gifts were exchanged amongst the great people. Sake and beer flowed like the winding waterways of the bordering swamplands. That evening the people of Chinchiplas forgot about their food shortage. They forgot about the approaching armies. They forgot about the new religion. That evening the people of Chinchiplas celebrated a new king, who would lead and protect them.

Quentin watched a soldier enter the great hall and speak to General Francis and Morrin. The soldiers got up and quickly left. Quentin scanned the feast. Most of the revelers were stumbling and singing under the giant gilded statues of the spirit animals; chinchillas, quetzals, buffkin, crocodiles, and snakes. Guy and Shangri had never appeared at the feast, and now Quentin could not spot the artificers. Quentin stood up and crossed the feast to Lichtenfrumph.

"Where are the northern artificers?" Quentin asked the Tommy Knocker smith.

Lichtenfrumph looked at the new king. The smith's eyes were glazed, and his pallid cheeks red from drink.

"I don't know," he yelled. His words sloshed around his mouth. Then Lichtenfrumph said, as if remembering suddenly, "Wait, no, they're at the docksh… er, I mean they're at home. Yesh they're at home… shleeping. They're definitely not wish the fighting peoples…"

Quentin stared at the drunk smith and stated, "You're an untrustworthy fellow."

Quentin turned and quickly left the feast for the docks. On the way, he stopped at The Green Light Tavern and grabbed his great grandfather's sword, Nagran's Fang. With the sword hung across his back, Quentin continued to the docks. He hoped the sword would be unnecessary, but Quentin suspected treachery from the wise Promethean.

The docks were lit by the small horned moon. The military ships Quentin had seen earlier were almost completely loaded and ready for a long journey. Men and women worked quietly to load the remaining stocks onto the ships. Presiding over the preparations were Shangri and Guy. Quentin came onto the stone docks and strode towards the man and god. He unslung Nagran's Fang. The sword's blade, as long as a spear, and as wide as an oar head, rose far above Quentin's head. The sword weighed almost nothing, such was the enchantment placed upon it by the familiar stone gained from the third daughter of The Quetzal, and the sword's bite was imbued with the poison of a thousand snakes, such was the power given it by the familiar stone gained from a head of Nagran, the five headed snake.

Quentin shouted, breaking the silent toil of the soldiers, "Guy, Shangri, what is this? What are you doing?"

Guy and Shangri turned to Quentin. Guy shrank back and rubbed his hands together. Shangri answered, "We are loading these ships for a voyage south."

"For what purpose are you using these ships?" Quentin asked.

Shangri smiled, and stated simply, "War."

Quentin, his anger rising, commanded, "I forbid it. I am King of Chinchiplas, and I command you to stop. I will decide what the army will do tomorrow. All you men go home. Rest, and tomorrow resume your training and work as usual."

The soldiers stopped and looked at their new king. Then a man, the head of the Chinchiplasian navy shouted, "Get to work, you lazy slobs! We have a god to kill!" The soldiers quickly scuttled back to work.

Quentin, now truly upset, yelled, "Why? Why now? Why would you do this?"

The naval leader had come up the dock, and he answered, "Because the god of order needs to be stopped. You, Morrin, and General Francis," He spit at the ground after naming the general. "You all wanted to keep the army here. Shangri's little bugs overheard your meeting. You keep the army here and fight what enemies will come. Good, fine, we hold back Bairne. But how can we hold off the Terrestrial? Do you think he'll send his armies at our walls? Look around, boy. You see the ashes of the voting booth. You heard their chanting in the night. You've seen the empty homes and abandoned children, left behind when their parents heeded the call of Order. The Terrestrial's already here.

We can't stop him, not unless we start killing our own. Which you already have by sending out our food for your campaign and your feast. This city is lost. It can't hold up in a siege with no food, and our greater enemy already has a hold here stronger than yours."

Quentin shook with fury. He lifted his sword and swung down at the treacherous man. Shangri put out his hand, and with his pointer finger, stopped the blade's motion.

Shangri stated, "I missed this old blade. Made from the soul of a close friend and a bitter enemy. It will not hurt me, for I made it. Quentin, I know you disagree with us, and this is not the way things should have been done. I'm sorry, really, I am. But this is how things are. If it's any consolation I think you are the best man to leave in charge of the city."

All of the fight left Quentin. The new king sunk to his knees and watched as his army piled onto the shallow bottomed ships and left. Quentin wondered how long his reign could last now. He wished he could just go back to serving customers at his parent's tavern.

*****

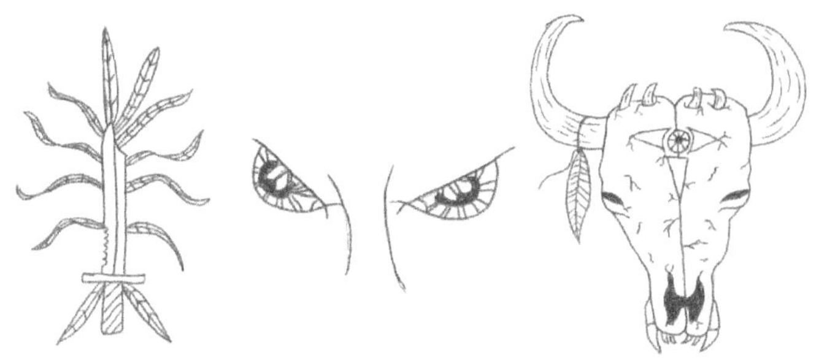

Chapter 13
Scagtower Upon Tear Lake

The sand dunes lessened in height, from towering mountains to short hillocks. The black clouds turned to burnished gold, dark orange, and finally wisps of white. The billowing sands slowed from hurricanes of polishing missiles to flurries of soft intent. Then one day the sands stopped blowing, the sky was clear, and the dune the sand beast climbed was not made of sand, but compact sandstone. When the sand beast reached the zenith of the sandstone hill, it stopped. The passengers filed out of the machine. Nom, standing next to Skalla and Korki, looked out upon a sight illuminated by unobstructed sunlight. The scene was made all the brighter due to his eyes no longer being used to the sun, having lived in twilight since entering the Sand Sea.

Before Nom was a large, shallow bowl, the sides made by the sandstone hill. In the center was Tear Lake, shaped like a rain drop. On three sides of the lake, great white columns sloped upward towards the center. The columns met one hundred feet above the waters, and turned upwards, spiraling around one another in a triple helix. Between the spiraling columns, floors and rooms could be seen, and in a few places, glass yet remained. One of the columns had crumbled long ago about half way to the top of the tower. The remaining two columns continued up to the flat top, two thousand feet above the lake. Thus rose Scagtower, capital city of the scag tribes, erected long before the world was young. Made when the titanic Forbears ruled the earth.

Nom peered at Tear Lake and asked, "Can I swim in the lake?"

Korki, his carapace helmet up, buzzed his wings and nodded. Nom smiled, but before he could rush down to the water, he was stopped by Morsmani.

Morsmani stated, "Not yet, Nom. Introductions and welcomings first, play later. Otherwise some people, upset. They'll be upset. Wait just a little bit. Okay?"

Nom nodded. Zarzasrahla's kajscag tribe, Korki's beescag tribe, and their guests walked down the hill towards the nearest column. They reached the base of the column. Nom was astounded. He had been amazed at the size of Chinchiplas, a mountain made by man, but Chinchiplas paled in comparison with Scagtower. The column was as wide as King Jin's castle, the largest building in New Keys. This was a building built by the Forbears. Only ancient titans could make such a thing. Then Nom remembered his vision. He saw again the Forbears' buildings being blown away like sandcastles. Nom realized that that vision was of when Shinigorath burned the world. Nom peered straight up at the top of the tower, which now was hidden behind a cloud, the only cloud in the sky. He wondered how many buildings like this there had been when the world was ruled by the Forbears. He wondered how many of the buildings in his vision had been as large as this one. He shivered thinking about how one god could destroy a building like Scagtower in an instant, and then in the same instant, destroy countless more across the entire world.

The returning scags and visitors were met at the base of the column by the leaders of the scag nation, all of the men and matrons of the tribes currently at Scagtower. The scags all intermingled and talked amongst themselves. Nom watched the scags. There were other kajscags, three with ink black fur, and two with black spots on yellow fur. A few other beescags from other tribes. Their carapaces shiny blues, greens, and golds. Strangest of all though were the graceful Chocobscags and beastly Buffscags. The Chocobscags were all skinny people. They looked completely human except for the feathered wings sprouting from their backs. They wore white togas, which allowed their wings freedom to move. The buffscags, like the kajscags, were covered in fur, except that even the females were completely covered by thick hair. The buffscags towered over everyone, even the beescags. Their fur was uniform in color. One group had dark blue fur, another maroon, and another white. Great horns grew out of the buffscags' heads, and long fangs protruded from behind their lips. The buffscags' eyes were overlarge, black, and without any whites. Nom quickly looked away from the buffscags and watched Azra meet with an old kajscag matron, her hair yellow, striped with black.

After the greetings and small talk was finished, the crowd moved to climb up the tower. Crude stairs had been carved into the column; the original entrance having fallen into the lake long ago. The group mounted the column, each step a shallow indent barely large enough for a single foot. The column was steep and tall. Nom was behind Azra, who bounded up the column in her usual perky manner. Behind Nom was Amy who crawled up the column in fear. At the top of the column was a small, metal door, stronger than the gates of Kahoke. Through the door they went, into Scagtower.

The group was met with a cacophony of sound. The center of the tower was hollow and open all the way to the top. A staircase wound around the open space, spiraling to the tower's top. The balconies of the floors above were filled with the scags of the tribes already at the tower. They shouted and sang in welcome. Drums were beat upon, flutes were played, and string instruments were plucked and fiddled. Nom was amazed at how many scags there were, and how even with so many scags the tower still seemed empty.

The newcomers took to the stairs. They walked four abreast, passing floor after floor. Each level was emptier and emptier. When they reached the point where one part of the tower had collapsed, there were no more scags. The tower was empty beyond here. The chocobscags and beescags took wing and flew the rest of the way. The remainder of the group continued on foot. Rope bridges with wooden slats had been built across where the tower had collapsed. Lady Amy clutched the rope railings and closed her eyes whenever these bridges were crossed. Azra leaned over each railing to see how far up they were and laugh at the world below. Nom felt uneasy whenever she did this and wished she would stop. The floors near the top of the tower were worn down. There were holes in the walls, ceilings, and floors. Very little glass remained in the windows, and the wind rushed through the building. When they reached the top seven floors however the tower was alive again. These were the floors that the flying scags, the beescags and chocobscags, lived in. The group was greeted by music and welcome as they ascended the last few stairs and rope bridges to the flat top of the tower.

Nom's childhood village could fit upon the tower top twice, even with a large part of the tower missing. There were a few buildings, constructed from the fallen pieces of Scagtower, erected on top of the tower. These were the meeting places for the tribes' leaders. The group wound their way between gardens full of food that the scags had planted on the tower top, to the smallest structure. It was a small hut made by leaning three large pieces of the Scagtower's grey stone together in a pyramid shape and covering the front of the hut with a buffkin drape. As the group approached, the brown furred drape was pulled aside and a frightening figure stepped out. The man who stepped out of the hut was golden in color, like he was covered in sand from the Sand Sea. He stood a head taller than anyone else there. His four arms hung down past his knees to his mid thighs, and ended in long, thin fingers. Most frightening however was the man's face. He had no eyes. Above his mouth a semi circular, flat shelf of yellow bone protruded upward covering the rest of his face and ending a few inches above his head.

The frightening man threw his upper arms wide and reached out his lower arms to shake Morsmani's hand. He exclaimed in a high-pitched voice that rent the air, "Namer! Amy! Scagfriendkin, and the tribes of Zarzasrahla and Korki! Welcome back to Scagtower. I have been eagerly awaiting your return. How was the journey?"

As Morsmani answered the strange being, and told tales of ohmkin and incoming locusts, the Promethean sensed Nom's fear of the man. So, to quell Nom's trepidation, Morsmani sent the boy visions of the man's past.

*****

Nom saw a tribe of beings like the man. They were all women except for an old man, and a young boy. They were a scag tribe who lived in The Sand Sea and were called the Gerudscags. Morsmani showed Nom flashes of war and enslavement of the Gerudscags, and Nom understood that this tribe he was seeing was the last of the Gerudscag tribes. The tribe lived in the desert, surviving off of ohmkin meat, oases, and yucca plants. They survived by having a great war beast. Nom heard Azra's voice call it the Bumble Bee in his head, and a darkness fell over Morsmani's visions for a second. He saw the Bumble Bee crawling over the great sand dunes in the never ending sandstorm. A dark cloud rose on one side of the war beast. The cloud moved to cover the Bumble Bee. Nom sensed evil and anger in the cloud.

Nom was shown inside the Bumble Bee. The young boy was playing with small warriors made of woven yucca in the dining hall. The metal sliding doors rattle and shook. A few black specks of sand entered the hall and hung in the air. They reminded Nom of the ashes that floated lazily down from the burning houses of his home village. He felt sad and scared. More dark sand entered. Now the sand that had entered gained energy and beat at the doors of the dining hall. The metal quickly lost its burnished look of many years. The metal became shiny, polished by the scouring sands, then the doors became dull grey as the sand blasted the metal. The boy listened to the black sand, mesmerized, his four hands lazily holding his toys. Nom wanted to yell at the boy to run.

The latch on the door snapped, made thin and brittle by pounding sand. The door slid open with great force, and black sand poured into the hall. The last gerudscag warriors ran into the dining hall. Their spears held ready for attack. The women's spears found no enemy to pierce. There was only swirling sand. The women were sand blasted just as the door had been. They turned red under the abrasion instead of dull grey, and eventually fell. The young boy had crawled under a pile of cushions. He could not see, the gerudscags are blind, but he heard the chaos, and screamed out in fear. Nom felt sick. Finally, all of the scags in the dining hall were dead, their sand scoured bones all that remained. From below, the sand swept up the old man. He had been handing out masks to protect his people's faces in the pedaling room below. There were no more people to give masks to now. The dark sands swept him up to the dining hall and pinned his two legs and four arms behind him, so that he knelt with his head held high and chest pushed upwards. His mouth opened. Sand poured into his open mouth and nostrils, choking him, until he died.

The boy lay under the cushions for some time. Eventually he crawled out. His four hands feeling the sand covered floor. They alit upon the bones of a scag. The boy cried out and retreated to the cushions. He ventured forth again after he calmed himself. This time he found his father, the old man. He sat and wailed into the wind. His whole world had gone into the blustering, blasting sands.

Eventually, the boy became hungry and thirsty. The Bumble Bee was no longer usable, so the boy set out on foot. He stumbled for days over the dunes to the nearest oasis.

Here the visions became faster and jumped over large spans of time. Nom saw the boy grow older in his travels. He visited old totems of his past lives. He ran among the great buffkin herds upon the central plains. He met with dragons and saw the great northern ice shelf. The boy grew old and died.

Then, a gerudscag was born to a western buffscag mother. The buffscag killed the boy, thinking the child was a demon, for the gerudscags were no more. Then, the boy was again born. This time to a chocobscag. The chocobscag was the Incarnate of her time and recognized the boy as the wise and unfortunate man she had met in a past life. She raised the boy. Nom saw the cycle of death and rebirth over and over again. Morsmani interjected a name into the visions, Tuar.

*****

Nom came back to the present. He heard Tuar ask, "Who are the humkin you have brought here, Namer?"

Skalla and Nom stepped forward. Skalla introduced himself first by saying, "I am Skalla of the north. A raven's beak of the Carrion Feeders tasked with helping Morsmani and Amy."

Tuar nodded stating, "A smart assassin. You take after the crow well. And you child?"

Nom, the feathers on his armor blowing in the wind, answered, "I am Nom Carver, a representative from New Keys. It is nice to meet you Tuar of the Gerudscags."

Tuar smiled, showing two rows of sharp teeth. Tuar reached out and touched Nom's face with his four hands. "A humkin boy, cloaked in feathers, like a chocobscag. Crowned by the tail of a quetzal. Last disciple of the Namer. There is greatness in you, Nom Carver, last of child of New Keys. Will there be justice and mercy? Or will your pacifism give way to hate and domination?"

Before Nom could ask what Tuar meant by all of that, he was led away. The leaders of the group went to a nearby meeting house to discuss the news of far lands. Nom and Skalla were led back down to the base of Scagtower.

*****

Skalla and Nom stayed in the guest tower for the next week. The building was a thin white tower on the south side of Scagtower. The tower had four triangles protruding from its base to hold it upright. The outside and inside were made of the same strange material that King Jin's castle was made of. It was white, reflective and smooth. On the outside of the guest tower were giant, ancient runes. Neither Nom nor Skalla could read them. During the week in the guest tower Skalla taught Nom a dice game, and Nom taught Skalla dominoes. They exchanged tales of their home. Nom told fantastical tales of sea creatures and sailing. Skalla shared mythical stories of snow monsters and warriors.

A week after coming to Scagtower, Morsmani visited the humans. He asked how they were, and Skalla and Nom replied that they were fine. Nom asked what the runes on the tower meant.

Morsmani answered, "Those are runes from the Forbears. The runes say ISEN."

Nom's eyes widened at the name. "Isen. Is this tower named after the Star of Isen?"

Morsmani shook his head. "No, Isen is named after this tower. This is the spear upon which Isen fell to the earth. She was named after the runes on the spear."

Skalla interjected, "This tower can move?"

Morsmani's helmeted head nodded. "The Forbears sent towers like this into the heavens, to explore amongst the stars."

"And Isen came from the stars?" Nom asked.

"Indeed," answered Morsmani. "Isen, the Terrestrial, and the fire and ice tyrors fell from the heavens. And with them came the God Spring. Now, this is not why I'm here. There is a feast planned in a couple days. You are both invited. It will be two days after the swarm leaves."

Skalla asked, slightly concerned, "What swarm? A swarm of what?"

Morsmani replied, "Locusts. A swarm of locusts is coming. Close all the openings of this tower when they come. Don't go outside."

Nom and Skalla nodded. Morsmani stood up and headed for the ladder down the tower. As he reached the top of the ladder he turned back and said, "I almost forgot! Nom, you can swim in the lake. No fishing. Skalla, I suppose you can swim as well. I didn't ask about you, but I mean, if Nom can..."

The Promethean disappeared down the ladder.

*****

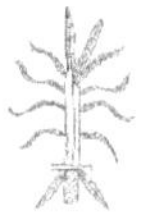

The locusts came to Scagtower. Their wings beat the air for three days. The scags had locked away all of their food and shut tight their doors. The locusts, finding no food save the unripe crop of the scag's gardens, left. The people of Scagtower came outside after the swarm's leaving with large pots and baskets.

Nom came outside and stared at the landscape. The ground was littered with dead locusts. The bugs crunched under his feet. A yellow feathered chocobscag handed Nom a woven basket and told him to collect the bugs. Nom did so. His basket quickly filled. Once he could carry no more bugs he headed for Scagtower to find out what was being done with the insects. As he got closer to the tower he heard music. The scags were dancing and playing songs in celebration. Children were running about giggling as they made a game of collecting bugs. Nom saw a line going up the entrance pillar and got in it. Behind him Azra and Zoltai joined the line.

Nom turned around, saw Azra, turned beet red, and faced forward again. Then he turned around again, opened his mouth, saw Zoltai behind Azra, and quickly faced forward again. Zoltai glared at Nom. Azra pretended she did not see Nom. When Nom was halfway up the pillar to the metal door, he decided he did not care what Zoltai thought.

Nom turned around, glanced at Zoltai, who glared right back, and asked Azra, "What are we doing with these?" Gesturing at the locusts.

Azra now turned bright red. Her face was a deeper red than her wavy hair. She looked around and fidgeted. Nom continued staring at her, waiting for a reply. Azra said, "They're —
".

She was cut off by her brother, Zoltai, who said, "We're taking them to the cooks. For the feast. Don't talk to Azra, humken."

Azra stared at the ground. Nom glared at the kajscag boy, who glared back. The line moved forward, forcing Nom to turn around. In the large open area at the center of Scagtower many fires had been lit. Scag cooks were roasting locusts over the flames. Large mountains of dead insects covered most of the floor. Nom threw his locusts onto one pile and shuffled back out to collect more. The festivity of the day was lost on him as he seethed internally at Zoltai.

*****

Nom arrived at the feast with Amy. Amy had collected Nom before climbing the tall staircase to the top of Scagtower. She had said that she was getting Nom to make sure he made it to the top safely, but Nom suspected she may have just wanted to climb the stairs with someone. Nom had a strong suspicion that Lady Amy might be scared of heights.

The top of Scagtower was brightly lit in the twilight of the dying day. Candles had been placed along tables and in lanterns hanging on ropes. Amongst the candles and tables all of the scags at Scagtower mingled. This was the homecoming feast. The scags had a feast every year at around this time to celebrate the tribes that came back home, and to herald the beginning of the yearly scagmoot, the meeting of scag leaders to discuss laws and events. Nom closely tailed Amy as she wound her way to join Morsmani at the high table. Here sat all of the scag men and the honoured guests of the scags. Nom knew he could not sit there. He began scanning the feast for Skalla to find out where he was allowed to sit.

Amy tapped his shoulder. Nom looked at her and she said, "Don't go anywhere just yet. Stay here until after the announcements."

Amy sat down next to Morsmani and Nom stood awkwardly behind them. He felt like everyone was watching him. He scratched nervously at the feathers on his sleeve.

Morsmani spoke into Nom's head, "Calm down. We always assume everyone notices all we do. The truth, however, is that almost no one notices any of us. Most people only pay attention to others in passing. No one is watching you, Nom."

Nom nodded and took a deep breath. As he did so, Tuar stood up and hit a small gong he was holding. The scags all became quiet and found their seats. When all were seated Tuar, began the announcements.

"Thank you all for coming to this year's homecoming feast. We are unfortunately missing many of the western tribes. There is fighting against the tyrannical Tommy Knockers along the Scagway. Many could not make it here this year. We hope they will come home next year." Tuar paused. The crowd had begun whispering, but quickly quieted down.

Tuar continued, "While our brethren are fighting in the west, we have been blessed this year with a bounty of locusts! We are serving a few dishes made with the benevolent bugs tonight. And when each tribe leaves Scagtower, they will leave with forty pounds of locusts!" Tuar again paused. This time he did not pause for whispers but shouts of joy as the scags thanked him. Nom could not imagine the locusts tasting very good. He decided he should probably try some at the feast.

Tuar raised his hands, and the crowd quieted again. "Before we thank the gods for bountiful harvests, and their sacrifices to us, we must welcome a newcomer to our midst. This boy, who is nearly a man, has traveled across the ocean, through jungles and swamps, and across the treacherous Sand Sea, to fight a dark being far stronger than any of us here. Along the way he has made many friends and helped many scags. On the Sand Sea the sand beast Beatrice was attacked by ohmkin." At this many scags gasped and turned to look at Korki, who smiled and waved a reassuring hand. "One ohmken broke into the sand beast and killed a brave scag woman. All the warriors were occupied outside the sand beast. There was no one to protect the children and the elderly inside. The ohmken could do as he pleased." Tuar paused for dramatic effect. "Then, out of the shadows a young humken boy appeared. He was clad in feathered armor and held a sharp sword with a black jeweled hilt. He attacked the ohmken and killed the beast! Saving all of the scagkin inside. This humken's name is Nom Carver. Nom! Step forward!"

Nom nervously made his way around the table to stand next to Tuar. Tuar pulled out a silver necklace with a large ring made of woven yucca leaves. Suspended by strings in the center of the ring by strings was a black and white stone. A single hawk feather hung from the ring's bottom. Tuar put the dream catcher on Nom and stated, "Nom Carver is now and forever named scagfriendken! He can come and go here as he pleases and will be treated by us as if he was a scag himself. May your days be long and without ailment."

The crowd clapped and shouted. A chant of Nom's name started. Nom blushed in embarrassment. Morsmani beckoned Nom to sit next to him. On Nom's other side was Zarzasrahla.

The old scag leaned over and said, "I want to apologize, Carver. I treated you badly. You have to understand that's just our rule, to be wary of humkin."

Nom nodded, unsure of what to say or feel about the apology. This was the second time an adult had apologized to him. It felt strange, adults were supposed to know what they were doing and follow their convictions, not apologize to children.

The food was served. There were three full roast pigs, platters piled high with buffkin meat, giant wheels of cheese, dishes of fried locusts, fruits and vegetable platters, and mushrooms from Mycostadur. Nom grabbed some pig meat, fruit, a piece of soft white cheese that had herbs in it, mushrooms, and a few locusts. He wrinkled his nose in minor disgust as he picked up the bugs. He went back to the table and began eating. Next to him, Morsmani had taken off the mouthpiece of his helmet. The Promethean was busy devouring some locusts.

"Are they good?" Nom asked.

Morsmani smiled, showing a mouth of broken, missing teeth. He said, "They are excellent! Avoid the ones with little breading. Insects don't have much flavor or texture on their own. And just don't think. Don't think about what you're eating. And do not look at them, because they look like bugs." Morsmani shivered and put down a locust he was halfway done eating.

Nom nodded and grabbed a locust. The insects were fried and covered in a chili powder. They smelled of garlic. Nom took a bite. The locust was crunchy, and spicy. Nom gasped and began sweating from the spiciness. His mouth hurt, and his eyes watered, but he liked the insects. The heat of the food reminded him of Green Light Tavern's red rice dish. Nom wondered how Quentin was doing. He chowed down on the food on his plate and went for seconds on the locusts.

As Nom was eating his second plate, performers came onto the floor in front of the high table. It was customary for each scag race to perform something at the homecoming feast. The beescag performers played a fast-paced song on their drums as beescag dancers spiraled and pirouetted through the air on their insect wings. The six buffscag men at the feast, each a chieftain of their own tribe, performed two songs of throat singing, the traditional buffkin style. Next, the chocobscags performed an elaborate dance to their famous woodwind instruments. The final performance of the feast was from the kajscags. This is the performance Nom was most interested in. He felt a certain affinity for the kajscags; both because they were the most human like besides the chocobscags, and because they were the first scags he had known. The kajscags set up their string instruments in front of the high table. Azra stepped out from behind a yellow haired kajscag's cello and walked up to the high table.

She smiled at Nom and then asked Morsmani, "Ready?"

Morsmani took off his helmet. He replied, "I suppose."

The Promethean joined the kajscags in front of the high table. Azra and Morsmani stood side by side. The kajscags began to play their instruments. Azra began to sing in her clear voice. Morsmani quickly followed, the gravel of his voice becoming soft sand.

Upon temples of cloud,
I look down,
Upon the world of azure,
and allure.

The old people toil,

Building higher and higher,
The stars they wished to reach,
In their towers of babel.

From the great turmoil,
Above from the stars,
A great jealous screech,
The God Spring did tumble.

Upon temples of cloud,
I look down,
Upon the world of azure,
and allure.

The old people took,
The God Spring to home,
The stars had come,
Now finally to ground.

Great creatures they shook,
Into new shapes and new bones,
Monsters so fearsome,
The new gods thus crowned.

Upon temples of cloud,
I look down,
Upon the world of azure,
and allure,

Great vines crept up,
Inside my wrinkled head,
Spider webs of dark,
Insufferable intent.

The fires lit up,

The world all red,
For the God Spring did hark,
The end of the old people's interment.

Upon temples of cloud,
I look down,
Upon the world of maroon,
Ended too soon,

The old people now gone,
Their world left,
Broken and ruined,
Empty now

We are whats left,
Broken and weak,
We must fix what is left,
For the Forbears we shall follow.

Upon temples of cloud,
I look down,
Upon the world of maroon,
Ended too soon.

      The strings slowly stopped as the singing ended. Morsmani and the scags bowed and returned to their seats. Azra turned her head back as she walked away and smiled at Nom. The candles seemed much brighter to Nom all of a sudden.

      After the performances, dessert was served. There were fruit pies, cakes, and fried dough covered in sugar and cinnamon. Nom grabbed two pieces of pie, apple and rhubarb. Skalla was next to Nom as Nom put the pieces on his plate.

      The assassin leaned over and said, "Apple and rhubarb? You should get something exotic. Like this banana pie."

Nom glanced at the dully yellow cream pie and stated, "I had a banana tree outside my house growing up. Bananas are common. Rhubarb I have never heard of."

The pies were delicious. The rhubarb turned out to be extremely tart and paired well with the copious amounts of brown sugar used in the pie. The diners all leaned back after finishing with sighs of content. Many of the scags loosened their waistbands to allow room for all of the food they had eaten.

Now that the food was gone, the fighting competitions began. The great warriors of the different scag tribes would come forth and challenge other scags to duels. The rules were first blood. If blood was drawn the fight ended and the bleeding party lost. If either fighter left the fighting circle they also lost. Nom watched the fights with interest. The kajscags were fast and more agile than any person he had ever seen. The beescags threw their opponents around the fighting ring like stormy waves tossing a small canoe. The chocobscags jumped high in the air and attacked from above. No one challenged any buffscags, and no buffscags stepped forward to fight.

As the challenges wound down, Zoltai stepped forward to challenge someone to a duel. The scags all whispered amongst themselves as he stepped into the ring. Men hardly ever dueled at feasts. The political strain that could be caused by a tribe leader dueling was too risky.

Zoltai looked directly at Nom and loudly proclaimed, "Let us see firsthand the fighting prowess of Nom Carver, our new scagfriendken. I wish to witness the strength that singlehandedly brought down an ohmken! What say you, Carver?"

Nom glanced at Morsmani. Morsmani, his mouth guard still off of his helmet, smiled and nodded. Nom gulped and replied, "I will fight."

"Your weapon?" The young kajscag asked.

"My sword and knife."

"I will use my tomahawk and buckler shield then."

A chocobscag flew to the guest tower to retrieve Nom's weapons. When the chocobscag returned, Nom stepped into the ring where Zoltai was already armed. The scag's tomahawk was iron with an oak handle. The weapon was intricately engraved with gold runes and turquoise stones. The buckler shield was fully covered in gold leaf and had a spike in the center. The night wind rustled the feathers on Nom's armor.

They began. Nom circled right, looking for an opening to the scag. The buckler shield was tiny. It offered Zoltai little protection but did not weigh down the kajscag. Zoltai lunged forward with a downward strike of the tomahawk. Nom dodged and stabbed forward with his tungsten knife, which scraped the side of the buckler. The fighters broke apart. Nom had the advantage at longer range with his sword. He knew at close range his knife was useful, but the scag's claws might be more useful. Zoltai lunged again, this time with a sideways swing. Nom jumped back keeping the distance. This continued for three more attacks, until the scag overextended on a downward strike. Nom dodged slightly to the side, dropped his sword, and grabbed the tomahawk. With a quick pull of the tomahawk and Zoltai's arm the scag tumbled over the boy and onto the stone floor. Zoltai barely touched the stone before he was back up. Nom cursed the agility of the kajscag as he blocked another downward strike of the tomahawk with his knife. Zoltai dropped his shield and swiped at Nom, his claws fully out. Nom sucked in his stomach, barley avoiding the slash. Nom danced away. Zoltai followed with quick swipes of claw and tomahawk. Nom barely dodged each blow, until finally, at the edge of the fighting ring, Nom blocked the claws with his knife. Zoltai's claws clanked dully against the flat of the knife, and the scag grimaced in pain. Nom quickly twisted the blade so that the claws scraped up the knife towards Nom, carried forward from the momentum of Zoltai's attack. Before the claws reached the boy, however, the knife edge struck the scag's palm, drawing blood. Nom had won.

Tuar jumped up and exclaimed, "Nom wins! It seems his strength did not win the fight, but his precision with his blade did. Good fighting, both of you."

Nom bowed to Zoltai, who glared back, his lips curled up, revealing his extra canines. As Nom returned to the high table, Morsmani shot out of his chair with a grimace. There was a commotion behind Nom. Turning around Nom saw Zoltai frozen in the motion of throwing his tomahawk at Nom. Nom glanced in shock at Morsmani.

Morsmani's voice left him in a thunderous rage. "You will not attack my charge, kajscag! Nom is under my protection and the protection of your people. Are you so ashamed of being defeated by a human boy? Accept your defeat with head bowed and shoulders high! Keep your shame to yourself and use it to better yourself. Do not use it for rash action! Action which has now brought shame to all the scags here!"

Morsmani sat back down. Zoltai quivered in the fighting ring. With a wave of his hand Morsmani released the scag, who promptly fell onto the ground. Zoltai screamed, writhing, yelling, "Get out of my head! You demon! You demon! Why is there so much rage? So much anger and fear! Get out! Get out!"

The feasters stood up and began packing away the food. Zoltai was left muttering and crying in the ring as people began leaving. Zarzasrahla came to his son and comforted him with a stern face.

*****

Chapter 14
The Brick Kilns of Chinchiplas

The day was hot and humid. Moisture rose from the dark waters of the swamp and permeated the air of Chinchiplas. Quentin stood in front of what remained of the Chinchiplasian army. Guy Kahoke had taken three quarters of the army with the navy when he fled south. Quentin looked back. The army stood, sweating under their brass scale armor, their rectangular shields held high, their spears held ready. General Francis, in the center of the front line, nodded at Quentin. Quentin jerked his head. The army moved forward. They quietly rounded the corner and came out upon the docks. The clinking of metal and stamping of feet was all that belied the coming of the host before it rushed into the open. The army circled the Monument of Order.

When the monument was surrounded, King Quentin Duluth stepped forward to address the people worshipping. Since the navy left, the throngs of followers of Order had grown exponentially. Most of the stores and farms were empty. Businesses had shut down. The docks were empty, with no one to help unload incoming ships. Children were abandoned. Quentin had decided that something needed to be done about this new religion. If Order's followers could not work, could not support Chinchiplas, the religion had to go. And now the army surrounded Order's place of worship.

Quentin addressed the worshippers. "Followers of Order! Go back to your homes! Go back to your businesses and farms! Go back to your families! Renounce your new religion! Chinhciplas is slowly crumbling without your care. Your families are abandoned and starving while you stand here and listen to this obelisk. Leave this place! We will let you go in peace."

The throng of worshippers turned to Quentin. There were six score zealots in the Monument, men, children, and women. They answered as one, "Chinchiplas is already ruined. I wait here for the city to fall and become king of the rubble. The city will be rebuilt in my image. The image of Order. The image of the Terrestrial. No corruption, no competing businesses, no stratification of wealth. But above all, no political squabbles that leave children dead, families destroyed, and the poor starving. We will become me. And for that end I cannot leave this Monument. Send your army forward. We are but a small portion of I, and more will come, more will join. So, come, young king, declare war upon my legion."

Quentin sighed. He had been worried about this. He waved his hand, signaling the army to move forward. The army swept around the king, and into the tall standing stones. The worshippers did not move. They watched as the soldiers pushed past them towards the large obsidian pillar in the center of the monument. The first soldiers at the obelisk knelt down and took out hammers and chisels and began chipping away at the black stone. Those soldiers fell first. The worshippers pulled weapons out from their robes, and quickly attacked the soldiers in their midst. Blood ran over the stones of the dock. The inside of the stone circle became a dusty red. Blood dripped from the standing stones and ran into the swamp waters.

When the fighting ended, the army of Chinchiplas stood victoriously over the bodies of the followers of Order. There were no cheers for the victory. These were the bodies of their friends, neighbors, and family. In somber silence, the soldiers took out again their chisels and hammers and knelt at the Obelisk of Order and the standing stones. As the first chisel bit into the obelisk's black skin a voice reverberated through the air.

"Let us show you what we are building."

Quentin saw Chinchiplas. The city was full and alive with bustling people. There were no shops selling things. People grabbed what they needed from the stalls. The people worked in silent content. There were no beggars. The children were fit and healthy, and they followed their parents, helping with the work. Quentin looked out at the green rice paddies to the west. He could see farther than ever before. The city rose to three times its current height. The top of the mountain city opened above Quentin like a yellow lotus. A great obelisk, as tall as five levels of the city, rose out of the opening summit with a roar like a thousand crocodiles. The obelisk, spewing fire, rose into the sky and disappeared into the clouds. The people of the city below continued to work efficiently and contentedly.

Quentin thought to himself, *'The city is too quiet. Where is the laughter of children playing? Where is the haggling of the merchants and shoppers? Where is the singing of the brick layers? Where are the funny chinchillas playing their games? This city feels content, but neither sad nor overly happy. I want a city full of joy. I want a city of music and laughter, not this city of emotionless happiness.'*

A voice sounded in Quentin's head, "You want a city of joy? A city which sings of dreams? Dreams lead to ambitions, ambitions lead to struggles, struggles lead to conflict, and conflict leads to pain and suffering."

Quentin asked, "But does not the person feel joy when they overcome those conflicts and achieves their ambitions? Should not the people have the chance to fight for their dreams?"

"Do you feel joy when you awake in the king's bed every morning, Quentin Duluth? Do you feel joy now that you achieved your ambition of ruling? The joy you felt lasted a fleeting moment as one dream came to fruition and another superseded it. Ambition does not sleep; ambition is an unending hunger that gives momentary morsels of joy to the few who achieve their ambitions and leaves the rest of people in discontent and melancholy. Our world would have nothing but the dreams and ambitions of One, of the collection of souls that is I. We all would struggle together, towards one singular goal, and feel joy together as One. Is this not better?"

"Who is the One?"

"Everyone is One, there is no The One. We are One. We all have the same dreams."

Quentin watched a child drag a large brick along the ground to the brick layers. A slight smile played on the child's lips. Quentin thought, *If there is one thing that is true about humans, it is that we do not usually agree. How then can everyone be following the same dreams and goals? They all could not have agreed. The point of a king is to lend a direction for the people to go in, but it is foolish to assume the people want to go in that direction. Yet here, all the people willingly go in one direction. Someone must be telling them where to go, what to dream for. Is it the god of order controlling them all?'*

"No," the voice answered. "There is no god of order. I am a collection of all those who join us. We move forward together as One."

"No, you lie. These people who join you lose their individuality to you. They lose their free will. They are simply appendages for you to use like the fingers on my hand, or the toes on my feet."

Quentin opened his eyes. He was laying on the ground. Morrin, the archer, was shaking him, telling Quentin to wake up. Quentin stood up and looked at the Monument of Order. The soldiers in the monument had dropped their chisels and hammers. Many seemed to be asleep, muttering in their dreams. Some writhed on the ground, holding their heads. A few soldiers knelt, heads bowed, unmoving. Quentin moved among the standing stones which encircled the obsidian obelisk. The blood of the battle, choked with dust, was already drying in the heat of the sun.

Quentin knelt in front of a kneeling soldier. The soldier was muttering about being one with the world. Quentin knew he was lost to Order. Quentin went to a sleeping soldier. He shook the soldier awake. The soldier stared in fright at Quentin, but as he realized where he was, the fear left his eyes.

"I saw Usmer from far above, sir. It was below my feet like a marble in ink, green and blue. What does it mean, your majesty?"

Quentin shook his head, "I don't know. It may be the ravings of the Terrestrial, or the dreams of the collective whole. In any case, we need to help these people. Wake the others. Get everyone out of this damned stone circle. Leave the praying ones, they are lost. Drag out the ones writhing on the ground if you have to. I want as few people to turn to Order as possible. Hurry."

The soldier nodded and went to work. Soon every soldier who had not turned was outside the monument. The people in pain slowly awoke. They claimed a shadow had grabbed their minds and filled them with fear and rage. General Francis, one of the ones who had been writhing in pain, sat cross legged and stared at the dust, turned red by rivulets of blood.

Quentin sat next to his general and asked, "Their weapons, where did they get them? Those weapons were not in the style of Chinchiplas's brass spears and swords. Those weapons are iron longswords, and knives."

"Steel," croaked Francis. "Those are steel weapons. Fine steel." Francis pulled out a knife he had taken from one of the worshippers. The knife shone silver in the sun. "This is greater craftmanship than Lichtenfrumph. They made these, but I do not know how they learned such skill. Not even the greatest Tommy Knocker craftsmen could match this. This knife looks like an artifact from the Forbears."

Quentin asked, "Where are they making the weapons?"

Francis shook his head, "They would need large smithies to make this many weapons."

"Maybe the weapons were shipped in?"

"No," Francis stood up. "There has been little trade since we lost our rice. No merchant wants to come to a city that has nothing to sell. I have seen every ship that has come in since you came to power. There were no weapons. These swords and knives were made here, but in whose smithy?"

Quentin shook his head.

Morrin stepped forward and bowed his head. "I'm sorry for eavesdropping, sirs. I think I may know where the weapons were made."

Quentin quickly turned to his old political opponent and asked, "Where?"

Morrin smiled and stated, "The brick kilns. The brick layers have slowed down recently, and there are enough fires and materials at the brick kilns to set up a very large smithy."

Quentin nodded. "That makes sense. Round up the men. We're going to the brick kilns."

*****

As the soldiers neared the brick kilns, Lichtenfrumph, the Tommy Knocker smith, rushed up to Quentin Duluth.

"Quentin! What's with the soldiers? Running a drill for when Bairne comes?" Quentin opened his mouth, but before he could answer, Lichtenfrumph continued. "Anyway, I have an issue. My iron has been stolen. All of it! And there was a lot of it. It's all gone and, seeing as you're king now I figured I should let you know. That way you can start an investigation. I own the most profitable smithy in town, and from one businessman to another, shutting down until I get my next shipment of iron from The Spine Mountains would… well, not be good. I'm not sure when the iron was stolen. I haven't had much business, so I haven't gone into my storage room in, oh I dunno, three days, maybe five? Anyway, the thief could be a long way off by now. They might be out of your lands."

Quentin looked at the short Tommy Knocker, who was holding a red umbrella to ward off the sun. He had never seen Lichtenfrumph outside in the day before. The smith's almost translucent skin burned easily. Quentin was still upset at Lichtenfrumph for what happened on the day of the Quetzal's Calling.

Quentin answered, "You must be very worried, coming outside in the sun like this. Don't Knockers catch fire in the sun?"

The smith turned a bright red. "No, we don't catch fire. We just don't like the sun is all. Look, I need my iron back. I'm one of the only shops still running in this city. Will you help me?"

Quentin nodded, "Yes, I'll help you. I think I actually know where the iron is."

"Really? Well let's go there now! Or, after your drill of course, your majesty."

Quentin nodded. He smiled at 'your majesty' and waved for Lichtenfrumph to follow him. They continued to the brick kilns. The brick kilns were just inside the landward gate to the city. The kilns burned inside a large walled complex. There was only one entrance and exit into the muddy square of the brick builders. The soldiers rushed in after Quentin and blocked the entrance. The spearmen made a line, their large rectangular shields making a wall of bronze. Behind the spearmen, out of sight of the people inside the square, the archers nocked their arrows. The kilns, all one hundred of them, burned bright in the noon day sun. They added their fires to the heat of the tropical day. The mud on the ground felt cool to the touch. The people making bricks turned to the newcomers. The Brick Master stepped forward.

"Ah, King Quentin, welcome! Are you here to inspect the brick making? In the past, the King always set an appointment. But never mind that. The brick making goes well. We are a little behind quota but, I suspect, you knew that. It is hard for the citizens to come and make their mandatory bricks when there is no food and the army flees. May I ask, why did you come with so many soldiers?"

Lichtenfrumph leaned over to Quentin and asked, "Why *did* you bring the soldiers here?"

Quentin ignored the smith. "I have heard rumors that these kilns are not making bricks. Is this true Brick Master?"

"Of course not!" The Brick Master answered, shocked. "I don't know how to make anything other than bricks. Plus, these are brick kilns, not pot kilns, or whatever you think we are making here."

Quentin smiled, "I am not worried about clay pots. I am worried about iron, about steel."

"What would we make with steel?" The Brick Master asked innocently.

Just then a shower of sparks flew out of the top of one of the kilns. A man behind the Brick Master glanced nervously at the kiln. Quentin saw the glance and stepped towards the kiln.

"May I see inside please?" Quentin asked, gesturing at the kiln.

"Sir…" General Francis began.

"I'll be fine. Morrin, cover me," Quentin commanded.

The Brick Master opened the kiln and stood back. Quentin did not lean in closer to see inside. He heard a twang, swoosh, and thud. Behind Quentin, the Brick Master gasped in a pool of his own blood, holding a steel knife. Quentin ran back to the soldiers and faced the brick makers. All of the people in the square held swords or knives.

As one, they spoke to the man who had glanced at the kiln. "You gave me away, new blood. Now, you leave the collective whole."

The man blinked rapidly, and then gasped as if coming out of water after a deep dive. "No! No! Wait, please! Let me leave! I'll go with the soldiers. I'll—"

He was cut off by a sword hitting his throat.

"Stop!" Quentin commanded. "Lay down your illegal weapons, and surrender."

"We have steel. You have bronze. We will win." The crowd mocked.

Quentin smiled and answered, "You have knives. We have arrows."

Quentin dove to the ground, dragging Lichtenfrumph with him. The spearmen stepped to the side, and the archers moved forward. The air hummed with feathered shafts, the ground again soaked red.

Lichtenfrumph got slowly up and wandered over to a fallen sword. He picked up the weapon and stated, "Steel. Fine steel. Better than I could make. Gods I hate saying that! Quentin, what is this? Were they rebels?"

Quentin shook his head sadly and answered, "Not rebels. They were a conqueror. I think we only stubbed its toe."

"Who's toe?"

"The god of order, the Terrestrial."

*****

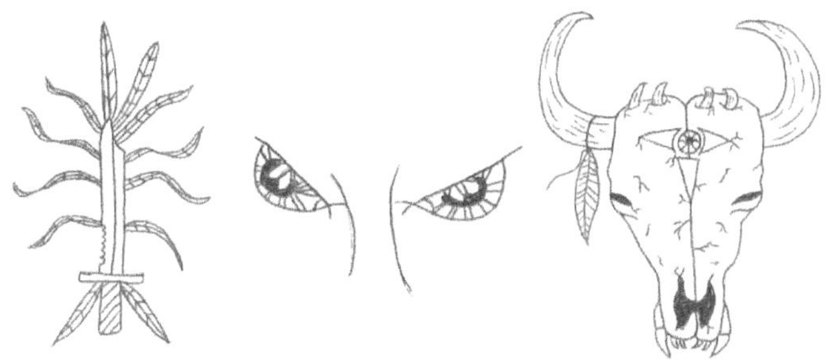

Chapter 15

Scagmoot

The water was brilliant blue and cool in the noon day sun. Nom paddled around the edge of Tear Lake on his back. He had missed swimming. In his village he had swum almost every day. There were the winding rivers and marshes next to his village where he could swim between the roots of the mangroves and among the small fish of the rivers. Then there was the ocean. The salty waves used to lift him up and mellowly sway him. The schools of bright fish surrounded and flitted about him in his youth. Tear Lake had very few fish, no waves, and little plant life. The lake was, from Nom's perspective, a shallow, sandy pit filled with water. Nom, however, was not bored. The lake was relaxing. He did not have to worry about crabs pinching him, undercurrents, large waves, snapping turtles, crocodiles, or any other worrisome thing from home. This lake was calm and serene.

"Hello Carver!" a bright voice yelled from the shore.

Nom turned over in the water and saw that Azra was waving to him. He swam to the shore, coming up next to the kajscag girl. Azra was bent over opening a box. She pulled out a small string instrument and bow to play it with.

"You can call me Nom you know," Nom joked.

"Okay. Hello Mister Nom."

Nom furrowed his brows. "No Nom is my first name. So, it would be Mister Carver, not Mister Nom."

Azra plucked a string on her instrument and began tightening the keys at the top. She replied with a smile, "Fine then. So, Mister Carver Nom, where've you been?"

"It is Mister Nom Carver. You got it backwards. And you know where I've been."

"Okay, okay. Let me try again." Azra took a deep breath, and with a glint in her eye said, "Hey Mister Carver, where've you been?"

"You know! I've been here."

"Oh. So, what are you up to?" Azra asked while tightening the keys on her instrument.

Nom shrugged. He could not wrap his head around this conversation. He began to feel warm. Warmer than he should have felt in the noon heat.

'Why was talking to Azra so difficult sometimes?' he thought.

He answered her question by saying, "Swimming. Do you want to join? The water is really nice!"

Azra shivered and glanced at the lake. "No," she replied. "I hate swimming. Sorry."

Nom suddenly felt sad. He said, "Oh. I love swimming. Why do you not like swimming? Do you not know how?"

Azra flushed as she quickly stated, "I know how to swim! It's just, well, I'm not very good at it. I don't float. I sink right to the bottom."

"Really? Are you floating properly?"

"Yes! I think it's a kajscag thing. I've never met a kajscag who likes swimming or was good at it."

Nom thought about that. "Hmm I guess that could be. What are you doing here then?"

Azra struck a pose with her instrument on her shoulder and pointed the bow at Nom. "I'm here to practice!" She exclaimed. "I just got this fixed and wanted to play it. I like playing by the lake. It's really relaxing. You don't mind if I play while you swim, do you?"

Nom took a step back. The tip of the bow had almost hit him. He shook his head while saying, "You can play! Music will probably make the swim more relaxing. There is nothing more relaxing than a nice swim." Nom enticed.

Azra scowled, her purple eyes narrowing. "I doubt it's very relaxing under the water." Azra brightened and continued, "And anyway I can't play my viol in the water."

Azra sat down on a piece of grey stone that had fallen off Scagtower in years past. Her feet were planted in the sand and her back was straight as she began playing. She started slowly with soft brushes of the bow across the strings. The viol made a wonderful sound. Nom sat down on the warm sand to watch and listen. Azra picked up the pace of her playing. The bow moved faster, back and forth, and her fingers moved along the neck of the viol. The song was not very intricate but was beautiful in its simplicity. A high-pitched shriek came out of the viol. Nom jumped. Azra put down the viol, her face matching her hair in hue.

Azra stated glumly, "I'm not very good at this either. Why aren't you swimming if you like it so much?"

Nom's eyes widened as he stuttered a response, "I – I wanted to hear you play. I thought you were great! I enjoyed it."

"Really?" Azra asked excitedly. "It was a really simple piece. They usually teach it to little kids when they start playing," She added sadly.

"I could not play that piece. And I thought it was beautiful."

"Oh, well thanks," Azra replied, averting her gaze. She had blushed again.

Nom nodded. Then he asked, "So, um, is it okay for us to be talking now? Since I am a scagfriendken?"

Azra looked back at Nom. Her face was its usual pale color. There seemed to be more freckles sprinkling her nose than usual. Nom figured she must be spending more time in the sun.

Azra answered, "Yeah! We can be friends again!"

Nom nodded. Dark clouds rolled away in his head, and happy sunshine fell upon his mind.

"If you want to be friends with me…" Azra added nervously.

"Of course I want to be friends with you, Azra!" Nom exclaimed, then asked, "Do you want to be my friend?"

Azra nodded emphatically.

"Good," Nom stated.

"So, you don't hate me?" Azra asked.

"No. Why would I hate you?"

"Because… Because I wasn't talking to you. I was being mean. I was ignoring you!"

Nom stared at Azra. First Zarzasrahla apologizes, and now Azra apologizes.

'If they both felt bad about ostracizing me, why did they do it in the first place?' Nom thought.

"You were ignoring me because your father told you to. I would not expect you to go against your father. I do not blame you," Nom explained.

Azra looked down. A lock of red hair fell off her shoulder, blocking the lower half of her face from Nom.

"So, you hate my father then?" She asked.

Nom shook his head. "No," he answered. "He apologized to me last night. I do not hate anyone."

Azra's eyes went wide. "He apologized to you?"

Nom nodded.

"Good. I'm glad." Azra ascertained. "You must hate something, though, right? Don't you hate the Terrestrial? Aren't you traveling with Morsmani and Amy to get revenge for your parents?"

"I dislike the Terrestrial. I don't really hate him though. He is a god who I do not understand. I have a hard time hating someone for something they did when I do not know why they did it. All I want to do is see the person who took my village and try to stop him from doing something similar to others."

Azra turned fully to Nom. She narrowed her eyebrows and stared at the boy. She asked, "How do you plan on stopping the Terrestrial?"

Nom shrugged. "I have no idea. I am not even sure why I was brought on this journey. The only fighting skills I have were taught to me by Morsmani and Amy. I have no magical powers. I am not very strong, I mean, I am even short for my age. I do not know what use I am to Morsmani. I guess I will tag along and see."

Azra reached out and grabbed Nom's cheeks. Her hands were warm, comforting, and filled Nom with a strange wanting.

Azra stated, "You defeated my brother in combat. He's the best fighter in my tribe besides my father. You are a great fighter. You saved me from the Ohmkin. I still have the scar on my foot. You may not be a god like Morsmani and Amy, but I'm sure you'll do great things. Don't doubt yourself, Nom. Never do that. Never."

Nom reached up and put his hands on Azra's hands. Her skin was soft under his touch, but the palms of her hands were rough from her rugged nomadic lifestyle. He felt tears welling in his eyes. No one had comforted him like this since he lost his family. *'Don't cry. Don't cry,'* he thought.

Azra moved her hands away from Nom and stood up. "I forgot!" She exclaimed, "Morsmani sent me to find you. That's why I came to talk to you. I was planning on playing my instrument when Morsmani told me to find you. Did you know he can talk into your mind?"

Nom answered, "Yeah. He has done that to me a couple of times. What does he want?"

Azra cocked her head to the side, thinking. Finally, she answered, "He said to tell you, 'They've been asking … wondering why you aren't at the scagmoot?'"

"That sounds like Morsmani. What and where is the scagmoot?"

"It's a yearly meeting with all of the scag tribes that came to Scagtower that year. It's for the tribal leaders and special guests. I guess you are a guest this year, Mr. Scagfriendken. It's outside Tuar's hut."

Nom scrambled to his feet, threw on his shirt and sandals, hurriedly thanked Azra, and sped off to the tower entrance.

*****

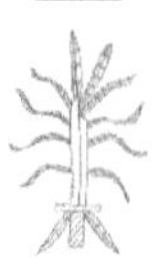

The scagmoot was held in front of Tuar's hut on the top of Scagtower. The only people allowed were the men of the scag tribes, the tribe matrons, and guests invited by Tuar. Nom's invitation had been implied, and no one had told Nom. The scags sat cross legged in a large circle. Nom sidled into the circle and sat down between Morsmani and Amy. A kajscag man with black fur covering his entire body was discussing how the buffkin herds in the west had changed their migration patterns to avoid being hunted by the wild dragons. He worried that this change may be difficult on his tribe and requested extra provisions this year. A vote was made, and his request was granted.

After the vote, Tuar tapped his small gong to announce that they were moving to another topic. He introduced Morsmani to the scags by saying, "And now the scagfriendken, Morsmani, has an announcement and movement to propose to the scagmoot. Please stand, Morsmani. State your case."

Morsmani stood. His purple cloak billowed in the wind and the red scale armor glinted in the noonday sun. The Promethean took off his helmet. This was the third time Nom had seen Morsmani without the helmet. Morsmani's wild red hair stuck out in every direction like an uncontrollable fire. His yellow eyes with the strange curved pupils gleamed out from his scarred face.

"The Terrestrial moves in the south," Morsmani began. "Long ago the Golden Council and Silver Folken locked the Terrestrial in the south on the other side of Isen's Wall. Now the Terrestrial moves north. He has designs to escape his lands and come here."

A buffscag matron stood and asked, "If he comes to our lands what will he do? Will he not just be another Promethean wandering the world, exerting his power in his domain, like the other Prometheans? I see no issue with having another god here. You Prometheans generally mind your own business."

Morsmani smiled at the buffscag. "Long Foot, you are correct. The Prometheans in Usmer generally mind their own business, but many have control of areas you would never enter, right? Myco controls Mycostadur, Hort controls most of the forests, Gerud controls The Sand Sea, Backbone patrols the oceans, The Tormented has his tower, and many other Prometheans claim smaller lands, many of which mortals are not allowed to enter. Would you not be upset if a new Promethean came and claimed lands your tribe uses and barred you from entering them? Or allowed you to enter them and then took advantage of you, like Gerud did to the Gerudscags, the last of which sits with us now." Morsmani nodded toward Tuar. The blind gerudscag did not notice the nod.

Morsmani continued, "The Terrestrial does not want a small domain north of Isen's Wall. Neither will he be a wandering god like Amy and I, and he especially will not be a patron god of a people like Beatrice is to you scags. He will be all there is. He wants his domain to be the world. He will not wander, for he will see and control everything from his throne. He will not be a patron, for there will be no people or things other than him. He wants everything and, if he escapes the south, he will have everything."

Now a chocobscag stood. His red and green feathers ruffled as he asked, "How can he escape from the south? And if he can, why now?"

"Why now, I don't know. We put him down there because there were very little resources for him after Shinigorath burned the world. Either the Terrestrial has gathered enough resources to finally go to war with us, or he has almost run out and is desperate and thinks that if he does not win now he never will. I hope the second option is the truth. For your first question, he can escape. Not physically yet, but his influence has escaped. He has sent emissaries from his lands. They went around Isen's wall, through The Sundering, and back into our lands. A difficult journey. I have only known two men and one Promethean to make such a journey and live. Of course, the Promethean, Gold, god of war, died on the other side due the continued burning of the world. These extensions of the god of order came into Usmer and began making Monuments of Order; large obelisks from which the Terrestrial can exert influence and take over the minds of the people and animals here. I have seen these monuments in many cities already. They dot the wilderness as well, and I'm sure some of you have seen these monuments in your wanderings."

Some of the scags from the nomadic tribes nodded in agreement.

Morsmani continued, "He will continue to gain followers in this way until he has an army that can assault the silver folken from this side of Isen's Wall; the less defensible side. The wall will fall, as will all here when Isen's Wall no longer stops the Terrestrial. Already he has control of many people in the north and has begun his war. Nom Carver here lost his village to the Terrestrial. Some emissaries from the South came to his village and burned it to the ground, killing everyone, save Nom. The war has begun, and I want the scags' help. Will you march south with me and fight the god of order at Isen's Wall? Will you help protect this land from being ruled by a single entity? An evil alien being? Will you protect this land so that your children can run freely over the grasses of the plains and sands of the deserts?"

Morsmani sat down. There was silence as the scags thought.

After a time Tuar announced, "The floor is now open for debate. We will discuss this matter today and vote tomorrow."

A beescag stood. "We do not take part in the wars between gods. Do not forget, fellow scags, that last time we joined in the fight between gods, we lost. We chose the side of Red and he died. Now, because of that blunder, we are hated, hunted, and enslaved like beasts. We should not make such a mistake again."

A chocobscag stood and rebutted, "But this could be our opportunity to redeem ourselves. If we win, then maybe we will be treated as equals."

A kajscag now stood and stated, "I care not for redemption or more damnation. What of the other wars in the land? What of Bairne in the north and the Tommy Knockers in the mountains? Our lands are getting smaller as the humans and the blasted dwarrows move against us. The Scagway is under attack as we speak. I don't think I need to tell you all what will happen if we lose that pass."

Nom nudged Morsmani. Morsmani spoke into Nom's mind, "Of course you don't know what will happen. The Scagway is the only pass over the Spine Mountains that the scags are allowed to take. Right now, the Tommy Knockers, also called the dwarrows, which is a derogatory name, are fighting the scag tribes for control of the Scagway. If they lose access to it the western and eastern scag tribes will be split, and all of the nomadic tribes will lose some of the lands they wander in."

Another kajscag stood and said, "How can we hope to win a war against a god without Beatrice? The Incarnate will not be revealed for a few more years. Until then we should not march to war. We should remain and protect our lands until our patron goddess returns to us."

A buffscag stood. His hair was blue, and he towered over all the other standing scags. One of his horns was broken. His voice boomed out loud and clear stating, "The buffscag are not afraid! We will fight! I care not if war comes to us or we go to war. We will fight! I, Shatter Horn, have never lost a battle! I will follow this wandering god to war. I will break the southern god's face with my fangs! I will rend his body in two with my claws! Then I will return and break Bairne's back and tear down the mountains around the cowardly dwarrows. This I will do while you other scags cower in your holes and run away across the plains. The buffscags are not scared! The buffscags will show a god mortality! Who needs a patron goddess when we have claws, horns, and fangs?"

The other buffscags all cheered in their deep voices and began chanting their war songs. Tuar clashed his gong for order. The chanting subsided and the gerudscag stated, "We will vote tomorrow. Please, Shatter Horn, think over your vote tonight."

Shatter Horn responded, "I do not need to think! A god and goddess come here and offer to let us fight an enemy stronger than any I have faced. I relish the opportunity!"

"You do not think. That is clear," stated the beescag who had warned against joining in the wars of gods. "This is not an enemy you can beat in a fist fight. I think we should stay here. Defend our lands against the enemies who are at least our equals.

Enemies you can break with your fists, Shatter Horn, not gods who control armies on the far reaches of the world."

All of the scags then began arguing amongst themselves. Tuar rapped on his gong, but the gong could not be heard above the tumult. Finally, Morsmani scowled and projected his voice into everyone's mind. "Silence! Like children you squabble. Quiet. Listen to Tuar."

The scags stopped talking immediately. They looked warily at Morsmani. Tuar rapped his gong again, signaling the end of the topic.

"We will vote tomorrow on whether or not the scag tribes will march to war with Morsmani. Now, Korki, you have a proposal to discuss?"

As Korki stood, Amy and Morsmani left the circle. Amy grabbed Nom and took him with her.

The three of them went out of the tower and stopped at the side of the lake and sat down.

Nom asked, "So will you get an army this time?"

Amy shook her head. "Most of the scags are against it. I think only the buffscags will come with us, and of them only the eastern tribes."

Morsmani sighed. "If only Beatrice were here. If the Incarnate went to war with us, the scags would follow."

Across the lake Azra was still playing her viol. The soft sounds of the strings wafted across the water. Every now and then came a screech from the instrument and a curse from the girl. Amy glanced worriedly at Morsmani. Morsmani, his helmet back on his head nodded.

Staring at Azra he said, "I know, I know, Amy. It's dangerous, but a choice we don't have. Nom, meet us later tonight. We will be on the thirtieth floor, in a room without windows."

*****

The room was barren and small. A fire in the center of the room gave light to the group of people circling the flames. As Nom entered, the group looked up. There was Morsmani, Amy, and Azra. Nom sat down.

"Good. Everyone's here now." Morsmani stated. "Now as you know, or may know, I don't know, Amy and I are here to raise an army. We must fight the Terrestrial. Unfortunately, the scags will vote against war. I can't blame them. They have enough problems here without helping me with mine. But we need their help. That is why I have brought you all together."

Nom looked around. Morsmani acted like he was addressing a large crowd but there was only the four of them in the room, and surely Amy already knew what was going on.

"Azra," Morsmani continued. "We need your help. Normally the decision to go to war lies on the door of the Incarnate. The Incarnate will not awaken for another two years. You can change that, Azra."

"How?" Azra asked.

Amy replied, "You are the next Incarnate. Inside you lies dormant the soul of Beatrice Bumble, mother of dragons, protector of scags, queen of the gods, wife of Klart Bumble, goddess of fire."

"Yep, yep, yeah," Morsmani affirmed.

Azra looked from Amy to Morsmani. After a few seconds of silence, she asked, "Wait, what? Really?"

Amy and Morsmani nodded in affirmation. Azra looked at Nom, who shrugged. He was as shocked as Azra was.

Azra tentatively said, "Okay, sure…How does that help us though? I can't claim to be the Incarnate, if I am actually the Incarnate, until I show Beatrice's power."

"We'll awaken Beatrice early. If that's okay with you?" Morsmani explained.

Azra nodded. "That's fine by me." She paused and shook her head. "Wait, I still don't understand. I mean… how am I the Incarnate? How do you know?"

"Because I am the Namer, and I name you Incarnate! Now Amy, do it."

Amy stood. Black tendrils of solid shadows jumped from her towards Azra. The shadows rushed into the girl's mouth and nostrils, and wrapped themselves around her neck, cutting off all air. Azra gagged. Tears of pain formed in her eyes. Nom looked on in terror. He yelled at them to stop. He could barely hear his voice over the buzzing panic in his mind. He didn't know what to do. Azra's face paled. Morsmani watched, slumped against the wall, as if tired. Amy was crying. Nom didn't understand.

He grabbed the tungsten knife from his belt and threw it. The blade buried itself into Amy's chest. Her grip on Azra did not loosen as steaming, black blood flowed from under her tunic. Nom fell to his knees, crying and screaming. The fire was too bright, the room too dark, and the buzzing in his head too loud.

Azra's eyes fell shut. She slumped in Amy's grasp. Nom felt nothing in his shock. A single red hair floated over to Nom and alighted in his open palm. A farewell from his last friend.

Then, Azra's eyes opened. Her eyes were not their usual purple, but bright white, shining through the gloom. Her markings glowed like flowing lava, and her hair radiated like fire, dancing about her head. Azra reached up her hand and touched the shadows around her neck. The shadows crumbled away in flame like old parchment, moving faster and faster backwards, toward Amy. Amy shrunk away from the fire but was quickly enveloped by them. She exploded into a thousand wisps of smoke; a few embers left on the floor.

"Hello, old trickster. What do you name yourself these days, Namer?" Azra asked. Her voice was amplified by the voices of all the previous Incarnates. A cacophony of voices all speaking together. They were powerful and ominous.

"Hello Bumble Bee. Call me Morsmani." Morsmani answered.

"Your names for yourself never made much sense. While your names for others are mocking. Don't call me Bumble Bee, I will burn you like I did Amy."

Morsmani nodded quickly.

"Why have you wakened me, Namer?"

Morsmani sighed, then said shyly, "I need your help."

"Against the Terrestrial?"

"Yes, yes. So, you know? That will save a lot of time." Morsmani said hopefully.

"I know. I have been watching from Azra's eyes. Bairne is a passing problem, which you have already begun to fix. The Tommy Knockers will destroy the west until the west is lit on fire anew, and all there dies. Soon, you will set that in motion as well, Namer. Is this your new apprentice?" Beatrice was peering at Nom with her luminescent eyes. Nom swallowed.

"Well, we haven't discussed it formally, but I think so. He's a good kid. He tried to kill Amy back there to save you," Morsmani answered.

"He seems gentler than Ruhk. I like him better. Don't make him a monster, Namer. Klart has plans for him. And Azra has dreams for him."

Morsmani nodded and asked, "So will you help us? The Terrestrial is the most powerful being after your husband. We need all the help we can get."

Beatrice, her fiery hair billowing out, answered, "You would have me give my people over to you to lead to war and death. Every battlefield you have graced ended with only you left standing. You will lead my people to death. Why would I let you do that?"

"Because we're old friends?" Morsmani hoped.

Beatrice glared at Morsmani. Her hair flickered and sparked. Morsmani quailed under her gaze.

Finally, Beatrice spoke, "You are a fiend. A mad dog. But you are right. The Terrestrial is our greatest threat. You may lead my people south. I will help. Azra shall become the Incarnate and protect my people." Beatrice paused, then added quietly, "And you are my friend. I'm sorry this world is so hard on you."

Azra's eyes faded back to purple. Her markings and freckles returned to their normal color. She fell limp to the floor. Nom quickly crawled over to her. He held his hand above her mouth. He sighed in relief when he felt her soft breath on the back of his hand.

*****

Nom arrived at the scagmoot early instead of late the next day. He was nervous. He wasn't sure why he was nervous. He was worried he would make a fool of himself, or Azra would make a fool of herself. He saw Morsmani standing, staring at the sky. Nom hunched his shoulders and wandered over to the purple cloaked man.

Nom stood next to Morsmani. Morsmani continued to look at the sky. Many of the scags around Morsmani were also peering upwards. Eventually curiosity got the best of Nom and he asked Morsmani what he was looking at.

"The sky. Nothing," replied Morsmani. "This is a fun game I play sometimes. I stare into the heavens, at nothing. Then people start to wonder what I'm looking at, but instead of asking me they look upwards too. To see what I see. But there's nothing to see. Pretty soon, when enough people are looking up, and everyone's forgotten who the first person looking up was…Oh wait, here it is."

"I think I see it. Look there! Do you see it?" asked one black feathered chocobscag to an iridescent red beescag. The beescag squinted and shook his head slightly.

Morsmani continued, Nom could tell the Promethean was smiling underneath his mask by the mirth in his voice. "Eventually people will pretend to see something. I think it's so they don't feel left out."

"So, they lie?" Nom asked.

Morsmani shook his helmeted head. "Not really. If anything, they lie to themselves. They trick themselves into believing they see something that isn't there. No fault to them. I just like this game, cause I think it's funny to trick a crowd of people into staring into the sky for no reason," Morsmani finished with a little chortle.

"Are you a god or a demon?" Nom asked.

Morsmani jumped. He looked at the boy. Angry tears played at the edges of Nom's eyes.

"I don't know," Morsmani answered. "That isn't for me to decide. That's for you and everyone else to decide. When I was young, there was a saying, 'Only God can judge me.' Most people took that to mean that people couldn't judge them, and they used the saying to get away with being terrible people. I don't think that's what it meant though. It meant that a higher power is the judge of you; not you, not your neighbor, not your best friend, but something else. Now, that religion died long, long ago. The higher power now, in my opinion, is society. It is the people of the world. The judgement of the masses is what tells you if you are good or bad. Now, you're thinking, 'Shouldn't you know if you are good or bad?' And you should have an inkling, yes. But you shouldn't judge yourself too much. The people who judge themselves and shut out the opinions of others oft times end up in the pits of hubris and arrogance, or in the lonely plains of anxiety and depression. What you should do is try to be the best you can be and listen when others tell you what they think of you. Then, adjust accordingly. It also doesn't hurt, when you're feeling down, to ask people you trust what they think of you. They'll probably tell you what you want to hear, but they might not. That's also a good way to see who you can trust the most. The people who want to help you will tell you the truth. The people who want to help themselves will tell you what you want to hear. So, I don't know if I'm a god or a demon. Most days I feel like a lost child. Do you think I'm a demon?"

"I do not know," Nom answered. "You took me away from New Keys, where everyone hated me, and I was sad. I am a lot happier now. You and Amy have also saved me many times. You seem like a good person. But, a lot of people do not seem to like you, and what you did last night was terrible. Were you going to kill Azra if Beatrice did not wake?"

"She was in no danger. We had to make it seem real. The Incarnate has a reflex that, when they are about to die, Beatrice takes over their body and attempts to destroy whatever it is that is killing them. That's why Amy was the one who put Azra in that state. Amy is not killed easily."

Nom brightened despite his anger at Morsmani. "Amy is fine?" the boy asked.

Morsmani nodded. "She's over there."

Nom looked over and saw Amy, her dark hair playing about her face in an unseen, unfelt wind, talking to Korki. "Is she hurt from my knife?"

"No, she's fine. She's stronger, better, than any of us," Morsmani reassured.

Tuar stepped out of his hut. The scag leaders made a circle abound the gerudscag. They began the second day of the scagmoot. First, they discussed irrigation problems in the western chocobscag's pueblos. Then, they discussed the dragons hunting scags along the plains. They switched from topic to topic, and Nom grew bored. He yawned. His anxiety was all but gone for the moment. The hot sun beat down upon the circle. Nom was sweating under his feathered armor. The long quetzal feathers fluttered in the wind. Finally, Tuar introduced the topic of war again.

"Now, the final discussion of the day, war. We are beset on all sides by our enemies. The Terrestrial in the south, Bairne to the north, and the dread dwarrows, the Tommy Knockers, in the center. Who do we fight?" Tuar turned his eyeless face towards the sun, waiting.

Korki stood, "You are our leader, Tuar, in place of the Incarnate. What is your council?"

Tuar smiled in recognition of Korki, and answered, "I have always voted against violence. I will now as well. With the Incarnate we are a strong nation of many peoples. Without her we are a loose band of scattered tribes. I vote we defend this tower until the Incarnate awakes."

Many of the scags nodded in agreement. The buffscags scowled.

Shatter Horn stood, "You are weak! Scared of a little blood! The buffscag will fight. We will fight in the northern cities. We will fight in the dwarrows' caves. We will fight the very gods in the south! And the buffscags will show the world that the gods are but mortal after all!"

The buffscags in the circle yelled and chanted. They stamped the ground and beat their chests. Nom was glad they were on his side. They would make terrifying enemies.

Tuar opened his hands and stated, "Now, we vote. Polished stones are for war, rough for peace. Place your stone into the bag when it reaches you… Azra?"

Tuar turned around. Azra entered the circle from behind Tuar's hut where she had been hiding during the scagmoot.

Zarzasrahla stood and shouted, "Azra! What are you doing? You are not allowed here. Leave. Now!"

Shatter Horn guffawed. "Zarzasrahla, you have grown soft in your old age. First, your son dishonors us at the homecoming feast, then your favorite daughter sneaks into the scagmoot. Have you lost control of your children?"

"Mind yourself buffscag," Zarzarahla answered. "Azra, what are you doing here?"

Azra had looked at the ground in fear when her father had first yelled at her. She now raised her eyes. Her red hair blazed in the sun and the wind atop the tower. Her eyes shone a bright white, her marking lit up. She floated up into the air as her hair became fire.

"I came to vote," she stated in the voice of all the previous Incarnates. Their voices augmenting her own in tidal wave power. "I am the Incarnate, Beatrice reincarnated. I was shown the last war against Order. The god of death and the god of order ripped the world asunder until all that remained was Usmer, barely holding on. The other gods abandoned the god of death, Shinigorath. They said he was mad, evil, and untrustworthy. Only Klart listened to him. Only Klart helped him fight the unseen enemy. Now, Morsmani has taken up the fight in place of Shinigorath, and again, no one has listened. Chinchiplas refused to help, and now you vote against him. I will not abandon Morsmani. I will not abandon Usmer to the wiles of the Terrestrial. I march south with Morsmani and Amy."

The scags stared in silent wonder. Then a chocobscag shouted, "What trickery is this? Beatrice was not to awaken for two more years! What have you done Morsmani?"

The circle looked expectantly at Morsmani, who now stood. "I awakened Beatrice early. I need the help of the Incarnate. Azra may be young, she may not be as wise yet as she should be when she becomes the Incarnate. She is strong, though.

And, she is right. You said yesterday that the scags do not join in the wars of the gods. That is wise. Our wars are brutal, and often long. But, the gods do not join in the wars of mortals. Our servants may intervene. Shangri may send artificers out as councilors. Ruhk may send out his assassins. But the Prometheans themselves never join. And, we never ask you mortals to join. We are now. This fight is not a grudge match between two gods, but a fight for the survival of Usmer. Would you ignore the council of The Incarnate? Your messenger to the gods, the reincarnation of Beatrice Bumble, Queen of the gods, Mother of Dragons, Protector of Scags, goddess of fire?"

Azra landed back on the tower top. Her hair fell down upon her shoulders, and her eyes and marking returned to their normal colors.

Shatter Horn yelled, "To war! Who are we to ignore the request of the gods? To war!"

The other buffscags join in the chant. Then Korki and Zarzasrahla joined. Zarzasrahla hugged Azra proudly as the rest of the scags started shouting along with the chant. Morsmani had his army.

*****

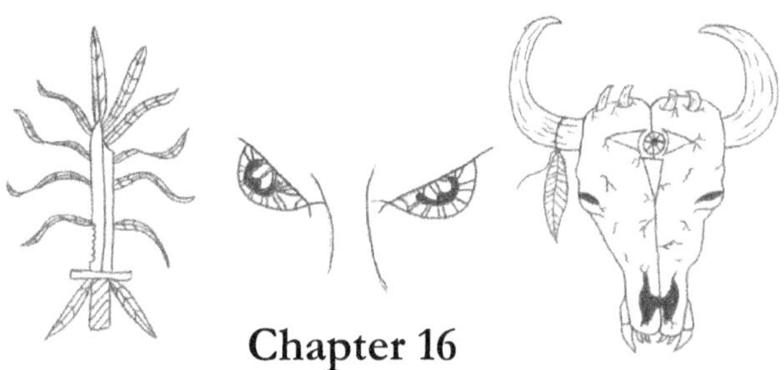

Chapter 16
Mycostadur

Nom, Skalla, Amy, and Azra crept to the hill crest. Nestled amongst the fungus which dominated Mycostadur they looked down upon the Monument of Order below them. Nom, Skalla, Amy, Morsmani, and Azra had left Scagtower four days ago. The scag army would follow once they had prepared. Nom wondered why Azra had decided to go ahead of the army with Morsmani, but he had not asked her for fear of offending the scag girl, and because he was quite happy that she had come.

Mycostadur was the strangest land Nom had seen in his travels thus far. The land was marshy and wet. Mushrooms as tall as the trees in Hort's Wall grew sparsely across the land. Their shade provided the perfect environment for fungus to grow and algae to cover the pools of water. Often clouds covered the sky and fog hung heavy between the tall fungi. There were no plants in Mycostadur. All of the vegetation was fungal, mostly tall, thin pale stalks that stood upright like the ends of oars sticking out of water. At night, luminescent mushrooms lit up the ground in an eery glow. Nom found the squelchy land, strange multicolored vegetation, and the quiet of Myostadur unsettling.

Skalla, on the other hand, seemed to love it. He was very excited when they first enter Mycostadur. He rushed around collecting samples for his potions and poisons explaining that many ingredients could only be found here.

On the fourth day, Morsmani stayed at the camp. He had received a beetle from Shangri and wanted to send a reply. The group went ahead to scout and scavenge. Some distance from camp they discovered a Monument of Order. The monument was large; five rings of rough standing stones circled a monstrous obsidian obelisk. In the distance, framing the monument, was Fungal Fortress, home of Myco, the Promethean who oversaw this domain. The scene was ugly; the grey standing stones reflected in the puddles of grey-green standing water, the sprawling, overgrown mass of the fortress in the distance, and in the center the strangely alien obelisk. Nom shuddered.

From among the standing stones wandered out a man and two strange creatures. The humanoid creatures had four arms each, a ring of horns about their heads with open flames burning at the horn tips. Their skin looked like dark grey porous stone. Red light escaped through cracks in their tough hide. Wherever they stepped the waterlogged ground sizzled and released vapor.

"What are they?" whispered Azra.

"Fire tyrors," answered Amy.

Nom drew in his breath in fear. Fire tyrors, evil demons of fire, appeared in the most frightening and darkest tales told in New Keys. The legends state that the fire tyrors were spirits of stars who descended upon Usmer to seek vengeance upon the Forbears for creating their own light, and for extinguishing from the sight of man the stars in the night.

"What do we do? I've never seen a tyror. Ruhk and the elder Carrion Feeders have always said that if we saw a tyror to run and pray, and that almost certainly the gods would forsake you. Do we go around?" Asked Skalla.

Amy grimaced. "No," she whispered. "We have to destroy that monument. Look at the ground around it. The ground is dead. Myco has died where the monument stands. We must destroy the monument. I will cover our approach, and then we attack. You can hide in the shadows, right, assassin?"

Skalla answered, "Yeah, but there aren't any…"

He stopped talking as the air darkened around them. A dark mist rose up around the group. Nom knew it was only shadow created by Amy, but the illusion of a dark fog was well made. Soon they lost sight of the man. The fire tyrors could be seen as glowing blobs in the shadows. The group moved down the hill. The mushrooms dampened the noise of their footfalls as they approached. Nom pulled out his knife and sword. Azra held up both her knives. Amy crouched behind her spear. Skalla brandished his obsidian knife and held a kunai knife in the throwing position. They stopped just short of the glowing monsters.

The monsters were talking in a strange tongue which involved mostly clicking and growling. Skalla threw his kunai knife at a tyror. The shadows disappeared in an instant as the group charged. One tyror was clutching his upper right bicep, where Skalla's kunai knife had landed. With a wave the other tyror caused the puddles between the groups to boil. The attackers stopped so as not to burn themselves in the scalding waters.

"Hello Amy, Azra, Nom, Skalla," stated the man with the tyrors. His voice was strangely raspy and high pitched, sounding like he didn't speak often. "Good attack. Now you should leave. Or you could join us. Be a part of me, of us."

"We will never join you!" yelled Nom.

"Pity," the man replied. "I knew I couldn't get Amy, granddaughter of the Maker, or Azra, keeper of Beatrice, but you two, Skalla, Nom, I could use very effectively. Kill the men, capture the women."

One tyror scowled and asked in his wispy voice, "Why not kill?"

The man, apparently annoyed at being asked questions, yelled, "Because they will just come back! I do not want to chase across the whole of the world for them. Now, go! Fight!"

The tyrors' arms became large clubs of black stones dripping lava. They stepped into the boiling water toward the travelers. Amy threw her spear. The black shaft went through the man and lodged itself in the dead mushrooms behind him. Amy created a new spear and stabbed at one of the approaching tyrors. Nom joined Amy in fending off one tyror while Azra and Skalla fought off the other. Amy retreated slightly and made a net of shadows which she spun over her head and threw at the tyror she and Nom were fighting. Nom jumped out of the way as the tyror shot fire at the net. The net disintegrated into a million wisps of shadow.

The other tyror slowly advanced on Azra and Skalla. His weapons of fire were longer than Skalla's and Azra's and they were having difficulty fighting the monster.

Amy and Nom charged together at their foe who parried both of their weapons with his upper arms. His lower arms swung inward, each striking an opponent. Nom's ribs broke, Amy's spine twisted like a wet branch. Amy crumpled to the ground. Nom stumbled away.

Azra, distracted by Nom's shout of pain, was seized by the other tyror, and tossed into the boiling water. She screamed and flailed her way to dry ground. Skalla yelled in anger and charged the tyror, who brushed aside the obsidian blade and kicked Skalla in the chest.

Nom stumbled and fell. The tyror he had been fighting was occupied by keeping Amy on the ground. Amy cursed at the tyror as she writhed beneath him. She laughed as ten black spikes erupted out of the marshy ground and pierced the tyror. The tyror could not move. He was stuck.

The other tyror stepped over Skalla and rained blows down on the man. Skalla blocked the hits with his forearm, which quickly lost its rigidity and swung loose like a wet mat of grass; broken and now unusable. Azra, her eyes glowing, her hair wild, sent a tongue of flame at the monster. The rope of flame wrapped around the tyror's four arms. Skalla, taking the opportunity, cut off his sleeve, revealing his buffkin tattoo. He rubbed blood from his wounds over the tattoo and slapped the ground. A buffkin appeared in the midst of the fight. The buffkin's brown fur stood on end, smoke steamed out of his nostrils, his horns glimmered, his large hooves stamped the ground. The large beast of the far plains eyed the tyror with hate.

Skalla shouted, "Get on the buffkin, Nom! Go for help! Go to the fortress, it's closest!"

Nom stood frozen. Amy had passed out before delivering the final blow to her enemy, who writhed on his spikes. Azra struggled against the strength of the other tyror. As Nom watched, the tyror held by Azra pulled his bonds until his hands came together. Azra's flames disappeared and a pile of molten rocks formed up around her. The rocks cooled, encasing the scag. The tyror turned to Nom with hatred and glee in his eyes. The buffkin rushed towards Nom, hooked a short horn into Nom's armor, and lifted the boy onto his back. They rode away.

The tyror shrugged and walked over to his companion. He began breaking the spikes. As he did he talked in his wispy voice, like steam escaping a volcanic cleft.

"Goddess of fire…I think not. You are a weak being who uses fire like a child with a match. We are true gods of fire! Come from the heavens. I would kill you if my master would let me."

"We should kill them," the other tyror interjected. He was busy pulling the spikes out of himself. "He's not here. He will not know. We say they forced us to kill them."

"No, we follow orders, or we die."

The injured tyror nodded. His wounds were dripping with what looked like lava. As his friend turned around, the injured tyror stabbed forward with a spike. The spike went through the loyal tyror's head. A great sound rent the air like a bonfire being lit in an instant. Red light left the dying tyror and rushed around the killer. When the light disappeared, the remaining tyror was fully healed and appeared taller than before. The tyror sighed. He went and stood over Amy. Lifting his arms and head, a great geyser of fire engulfed the tyror and shadow bender. Azra shouted from her stone tomb. Skalla had passed out, blood pooling from his ruined arm. Azra attempted to call upon the powers of Beatrice, but nothing happened. She was badly burned from the boiling water and the molten stone. Everything hurt. She tried again. Nothing. She cursed herself and tried a third time. Still nothing.

"Morsmani! Your buddies need you. Morsmani!" A bright voice thrilled across Mycostadur.

*****

The buffkin carried Nom away from the fight. Nom wanted to jump off the animal and run back to protect his people, but he was scared. He was frozen. His head felt light on his shoulders, and his eyes seemed to peer through dark tunnels set far back in his skull. Everything felt unreal. He observed his fear objectively. His desire to return was like the anxious whisperings of a different person. He could not move or feel. The world was too bright, too loud. The world was empty.

The buffkin thundered towards the Fungal Fortress. The beast's speed was great, and the fortress loomed closer. As they approached the broad, shapeless building made of petrified fungus the buffkin stopped.

"Hello!" A bright voice around Nom greeted.

Nom looked around. There was no one near him.

"Oh, right! I haven't talked to anyone in a long time. Just a moment."

Next to the buffkin, on the side where Nom's head hung, a shape of a skinny woman appeared. The figure was made of what looked like a pink powder which floated and twirled in the air.

"There! Now you can see me. Well, you can see me everywhere haha. I'm Myco! Nice to meet you. Why are you thundering on that buffalo towards my fortress?"

'She is made of spores. That is what those pink things are,' Nom thought and then he answered. "My friends are in trouble. I was sent to get help. They are fighting near the Monument of Order. Can you help them please?"

"Nope! If I could do something about that monument it wouldn't be there right now, would it? Every time I get close my shrooms and spores simply die. If you could tell your friends to die a ways away from the monument that would be wonderful, though! They'd make great food for my shrooms."

The figure of the lady disappeared. Nom cursed.

"Wait! Don't go!" Nom shouted into the air before despair fully overcame him.

The figure returned. "I didn't leave, silly. The fungus here is me. What do you need?"

"Can you call Morsmani? He is at our camp. He can destroy the monument."

The figure fluttered quickly in excitement.

Myco asked, "He can? He must be strong indeed. Let me find him." The pink spores assembled into a shape of a woman thinking for a few seconds.

Then, from every mushroom, fungus stalk, mold, and various other fungi, came a shout in Myco's voice. "Morsmani! Your buddies need you. Morsmani!"

*****

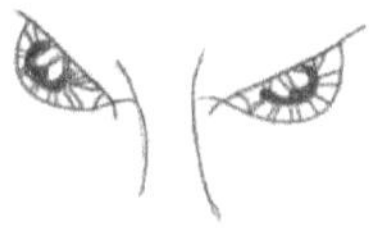

The shout reverberated through the air for a time. The tyror had stopped his column of fire when the shout began. It looked around, worried. Azra watched in apprehension. Then on the top of the ridge appeared a figure in red armor, his purple cloak flapped behind him as he rushed down towards the tyror.

The tyror hurled fire balls at Morsmani. Shadowy figures jumped in front of the fireballs and disintegrated. The tyror turned to retreat as Morsmani approached, but it was not fast enough. Morsmani swung his hammer, the Golden Key, at the tyror. The demon flew back through the air and slammed into a standing stone. The stone cracked and fell, crushing the tyror. Red light spilled from under the stone and disappeared into the sky. Morsmani continued into the midst of the standing stones. Azra watched as the obsidian obelisk fell, followed by the rest of the stones. Morsmani ground each stone into dust with his hammer.

After the monument was destroyed, Morsmani came to Azra and began chipping away at the volcanic stones surrounding her. With a rush the stone fell away in front and she fell to the ground. She could not stand. She could not move. Everywhere the molten rocks had touched was burnt to a crisp. Morsmani covered her disfigured body with his purple cloak. He gestured apologetically, paused, then rushed to Amy. Amy was gasping on the ground. She was in a similar state to Azra. Morsmani stamped his feet, wrung his hands, and walked in a circle. He continued doing this with a few glances at Azra and nods and shakes of his head until Nom returned.

Nom rode up on the back of the brown buffkin. The boy leapt off the animal and winced in pain as his broken ribs felt his landing.

"You did it! You beat the tyrors. Is everyone okay?" Nom Carver asked.

Morsmani shook his head, tapped his helmet where his nose would be, and replied, "No, no, no… Broken, burnt, and broken. I'm sorry, Nom. They, they… it's not good. I should've been here. I should've been here. I should've been here."

Nom tried patting the Promethean reassuringly, but Morsmani moved away from him, still repeating "I should've been here."

Nom went over to Skalla, who was just coming to. Nom gave Skalla some water. After checking that Skalla was okay, Nom moved to Azra. He cried out when he saw her. She was covered by the purple cloak. One arm hung out from beneath the garment. The arm was no longer pearly white, but was black and red.

"Azra?" Nom asked quietly as he knelt next to her.

Azra replied in a strained voice, jokingly mocking Nom, "Carver?"

Nom missed the mocking tone and became even more worried. "How are you feeling?" he asked.

"I'm not," Azra replied. "I can't feel anything."

Nom nodded and tried handing her his water skin. "Your arm is badly burned."

Azra laughed and then grimaced. She could not grab the water skin. She could not move her arm.

Azra said, "Everything's burnt like a buffkin steak. Except my face. Cause that's what I need, a stupid face and nothing else."

"Your face is not stupid. I like your face," Nom immediately stopped and turned bright red.

Azra beamed and laughed weakly, "Well, thank you. Too bad I can't fight the Terrestrial with my face."

At this point, a strange creature sidled up next to Nom and stated, "I've heard of looks that can kill, but your face is just too pretty for that."

Azra screamed. Morsmani rushed over, his hammer held ready.

The creature immediately fell back, shouting, "Sorry, sorry! I didn't mean to scare you."

The creature was about three feet tall and looked like a human. Instead of hair there was a large toadstool on its head. The thing's shirt was made of what looked like moss, and the creature had a large mushroom cap around its waist which looked strikingly like a skirt.

Nom recognized the bright voice and jumped inbetween Morsmani and the newcomer.

"Stop!" Nom shouted. "This is Myco, the Promethean of this land. She helped us. She called you."

Morsmani lowered his hammer. Myco wandered over to the ruined monument. She jumped about on the broken stones for some time while Nom saw to Azra, and Morsmani tended to Amy.

"You're pretty strong, Morsmani. What are you?" Myco asked from atop a broken standing stone.

"A Promethean, like you."

"Hmm, I don't remember a Promethean named Morsmani. Did you change your name? I recognize your hammer. That was Gold's hammer. Why do you have his hammer? Are you two friends?"

Morsmani grunted. He took off his helmet and turned. "I'm also called Namer. Gold gifted me his hammer when he died."

There was silence. Myco perched on top of a shattered stone. She stared at Morsmani.

"Gold's… Gold's dead? Well I guess death would catch up to the god of war eventually, eh Namer. You'd guess that too, wouldn't you? Because I know who you are. You're Gold's best friend, god of –

"He was my best friend!" Morsmani interrupted. "I don't want to talk about it. Now, can you help us with our companions?"

Myco nodded. Without prompting, fungi rose out of the ground and formed rickshaws around Amy, Azra, and Skalla. Morsmani, Nom, and the buffkin each pulled one rickshaw back to their camp. On the way there, Amy woke up and quietly pleaded with Morsmani for something. Nom did not know what was plead, but he could tell by Morsmani's silence and agitation that he loathed whatever it was Amy wanted.

Their meal that night was somber. Amy slept. Nom fed Azra. Skalla was finally up and able to move about. His arm was in a cast made of hard, dried fungus. Myco was bursting with energy but had enough sense not to say anything.

As they finished eating, Azra muttered loudly, "How can we defeat an army of those things if we can barely defeat two of them?"

*****

Chapter 17

Defenders of Chinchiplas

The morning was overcast. Fog from a low hanging cloud enshrouded the top of Chinchiplas. The remaining fit people of Chinchiplas were gathered on the peak of the mound city. In front of the crowd on a raised wooden stage stood Quentin, his parents, Morrin, and General Francis.

Quentin spoke to the crowd, "A terror from the north bears down upon us. Bairne marches his army south to conquer fair Chinchiplas. We have been through much, these past few months. Our king and his family died. Locusts ate our crops. A new religion has taken men and women away from the fields and their work. Through all this you people standing before me have survived. You have come out stronger than before!" Quentin paused. He had thought the crowd would cheer at this point, but he was met with steely gazes instead. He continued, "You have made it thus far, and I would ask one more thing of you. Will you help defend our home from the northern invaders? You will each be provided with your choice of weapons and armor. Your help in defending the city will be rewarded with food for you and your families, money for your services, and spots higher up in the city. Chinchiplas has never been taken, and it will not be taken now!"

Again, there was no cheer. The crowd stared up at their king with tired looks.

A man in the back shouted, "Where's the army? Shouldn't they defend us?"

Quentin ground his teeth. The people knew well enough where the army was, they just wanted to hear Quentin say it.

Quentin answered, "Some of the army went south to help Morsmani fight the Terrestrial. Do not worry! With our remaining forces and you all augmenting our ranks, we will have enough manpower to easily throw back Bairne's army."

Another voice spoke up from the crowd, "Bairne has taken Shangri's Temple. If the artificers can't stop Bairne, how can we?"

Before Quentin could answer another voice yelled out, "This city's already dead. We are what's left of it. The fields lay fallow, the shops are empty, the docks are closed. King Quentin, I leave this mound of dirt to you! I will not lay down my life for a city that is already dead. I am leaving, and any who wish to join me can!"

The crowd murmured and shuffled about. The people began to disperse. Quentin shouted, but the noise of the crowd was too loud. No one heard him. When the leave taking was over, there remained only a third of the original crowd. Quentin despaired. This was not enough to defend the city. He kept his face stern, not showing his worry or fear. He turned to Morrin and instructed the archer to give all of the people who left armament and some food for their journey. Then, Quentin went into the crowd to thank the people for staying.

After the crowd had left, Quentin's mother, Annie, came up to Quentin. She put a reassuring hand on his shoulder and told him, "Long ago Chinchiplas was just your ancestor Allison. Shinigorath tried to destroy Chinchiplas then, and failed. As long as there is one true son or daughter of Chinchiplas to defend us, there is hope."

*****

A week later Bairne's army came. At first, there was a trickle of small groups of men. They snuck into the lands surrounding Chinchiplas at night. They set about raiding the farmlands. Quentin watched the fields burn at night. He dared not send men out to fight the northmen. The villagers still outside the city were killed and enslaved.

A few days later, Bairne's army arrived in full. They made camp around the mound. Governor Altec's body was strung up on display outside Bairne's great tent. The fires of the northmens' camps stretched to the horizon in all direction. General Francis assured Quentin that many of the fires were unattended. Bairne lit extra fires in order to make his army appear larger.

Two days went by before a messenger from Bairne rode to Chinchiplas's gates. Quentin opened the gates and met the man with Morrin and General Francis. The man approached on horseback. He was resplendent in jewelry and wore an arrogant smile.

The messenger rode up before Quentin and stated, "I am Dullson, messenger of Bairne the Beautifully Bearded."

"I am Quentin Duluth, King of Chinchiplas. What do you want?" Quentin replied.

"My King desires much, but from you he only wishes your knees upon the ground. He wishes you to keep ruling Chinchiplas as you have, but in return you will swear fealty to him."

"I already have Chinchiplas. Why would I give something to your king to keep what I already have? If you had a rice ball that you could eat, would you give me a glass of sake in order to eat the rice ball, or would you simply eat the rice ball?"

The messenger smiled. "You are smart. A great king, I see! But the offer is not to give what you already have, but to allow you to keep what you have. Chinchiplas will be ours within a week."

"And what of my people? Will they be allowed to keep what is theirs?"

"That depends on the person. For example," The messenger reached into a saddle bag behind him. Next to Quentin, Morrin placed an arrow on his bowstring. With a flourish the messenger lifted the contents of the bag over his head. Hanging from the ringed fingers of the messenger dangled a few heads on a chain. Quentin recognized the heads as being some of the people who had left Chinchiplas. "For example, these men were running away. There is no need for such men in Bairne's empire. However, men like you three, strong, powerful, smart, will thrive in our empire. We would gladly have you."

"Not too long ago I was offered to join something larger than my city. I refused then, and I refuse now." Quentin answered. "Go back to your king, Son of Dull, and prostrate yourself in front of his unkempt beard. Tell him Chinchiplas will not fall to his tyranny."

The messenger scowled as Quentin turned and returned to the city.

*****

That night General Francis joined Quentin at the top of the Great Pyramid of Kahoke. They looked at the fires dotting the landscape, like stars in the night.

"Do you regret it?" Francis asked.

"What?" Quentin asked in return.

"Your decision to stay. Do you regret not going south?"

"No. Even though the decision did not matter in the end, I would still make the same choice. Chinchiplas is home. I would not abandon it. Do you wish you had left?"

Francis shook his head. "That's not for me to decide. I follow the king, and the king stayed."

Quentin nodded. "Do you think we can win?"

"No. We have enough food for a month. I have shifts of people on the walls. Most of them are too young or too old to have left, so they stay and fight a battle that they are too young or too old to fight. My hope is that we can hold back Bairne until our navy returns."

"Do you think it will? Do you think the navy will return?"

"If it does not, then Bairne is the least of our worries."

"When could we expect them to come back?"

"They most likely will arrive at the Silver Folken lands any day now. So, assuming they fight the Terrestrial for a day and immediately return, we could expect them in a few weeks."

"So, we're doomed?"

"We won't know the end until a spear pierces our hearts. Until then, we fight."

*****

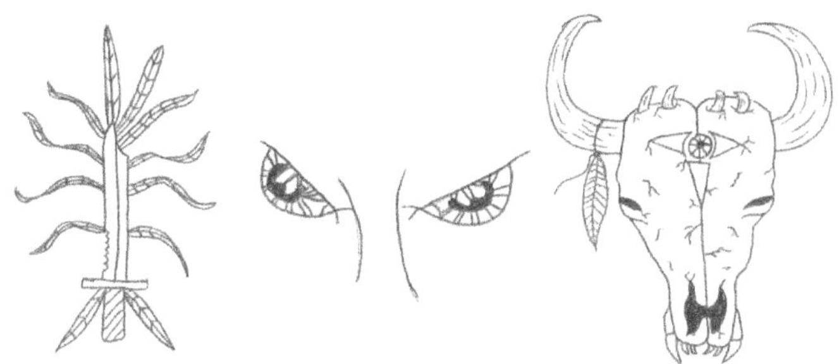

Chapter 18
Isen's Hidden Light

The twilit sun glanced over the low hills. The travelers set up camp for the night. Nom had unpacked his things and went to Azra. Azra sat upon a soft chair of shadow fashioned by Amy, on the back of the buffkin. Nom patted the beast's cheek and led it up the hill. At the top of the hill, he stopped and looked out at the capital of the Silver Folk, Urbe. The city was comprised of great glass towers rising into the sky. The tallest of the towers was half the height of Scagtower. The city sat within the golden light of Isen's Wall, which rose higher than the clouds. Nom was reminded of The Sundering back in New Keys, both walls had been made by the Silver Folk. One wall made of Isen's light, the other steam from the ocean floor. One to hold back the Terrestrial, and one to stop Shinigorath's wrath from burning Usmer. Just outside the wall, to the north of the city, sprawled another city, Ghet. Morsmani had explained that the non-silver folk who lived and visited Urbe lived in Ghet. Only Silver Folk and distinguished guests were allowed to enter Urbe proper. Ghet was comprised of a vast network of wooden and adobe buildings, none of which were more than two stories tall. Smoke rose from the narrow dirt streets.

"I wonder how many people live there?" Nom asked. He had never seen a city as big and sprawling as Ghet.

Azra shrugged, then asked, "Why hasn't Morsmani sent me back to my father?"

"Why would he do that?" Nom asked in return.

"Look at me. I can't fight like this. I can't move anything below my neck."

Nom sighed. Azra had become rather depressed after the fight in Mycostadur. She had brightened a little when they had arrived outside Urbe. But the happiness was fleeting. Azra had sunk back into sadness as she glared at the massive, glowing mushrooms they passed on their way south.

Nom answered, "Maybe he wanted to help you with your training? There might be a healer that can help you in Urbe."

"I doubt it. My training now is just discovering my past lives. I wish I was Amy. She healed in a night, and her injuries were just as bad as mine!"

"Did you ask her how she healed so quickly?"

Azra nodded. "She said Morsmani helped her. Then, when I asked if Morsmani could do the same for me, Amy said that there was a terrible price to pay for that type of healing. I'd pay it."

"They probably have a reason to refuse you. We have to trust Amy and Morsmani. They are the leaders of this group."

"Maybe they think that if they heal me, I won't be any help anyway. After all, I couldn't call on Beatrice's power when it mattered most in the fight against the tyrors. Why would I be able to call on her in a real battle?"

Nom glared at Azra as he stated, "That was your first battle. Most people do not survive their first battle. The first battle I saw I was frozen with fear. Everyone I knew died. Everything I had known went up in flame. The next battle, I was not so scared, but only Skalla, Amy, Morsmani, and I survived, and I was no help in the fight. It took me until my third battle to do anything to help, and all I did was stab an enemy that was trapped in a doorway. You survived your first battle. That is an achievement."

Azra smiled weakly at Nom. "Thanks, but with these injuries I won't be fighting in any more battles."

That night Nom had trouble sleeping. He lay awake, staring up at the cloud covered night sky through his dreamcatcher, which he hung above his head each night. This was the first night with nightmares since the homecoming feast. In the blackness he heard Morsmani and Myco talking.

Morsmani asked Myco, "Are you leaving tomorrow?"

Myco's cheerful voice answered, "No."

"Really? Why?"

"I'm lonely, Namer, and traveling with your friends made me realize how much I miss people. I cut out all human contact so many years ago, I forgot how nice it was. So, I'm staying. Also, the Terrestrial hurt my mushrooms. I won't let that stand."

"You'll join us?" Morsmani asked.

"I will."

"Thanks."

There was a long pause in the conversation. Nom began to drift into sleep. He saw fire tyrors hurling balls of flame at ancient forbear buildings.

Morsmani spoke again, "I'm sorry, Myco."

Myco sounded apprehensive as she queried, "For what?"

"I bullied you when you were a child. Even that name I gave you is a mockery. I'm sorry, truly. Will you forgive me?"

Myco did not answer for some time. Then she stated, "No, I won't. That pain is so old and so far buried into who I am. It's a part of me; one of the spores that makes me, well, me. I can't forgive you, but I won't fight you. When I realized who you were I wanted to fight you, to kill you, but I saw these people you were with. I saw how they looked up to you, and I couldn't bring myself to fight you. You seem to have grown a lot, but I still see the mean teenager who called me Stink Cap, and hid tippler's bane in my bed. I still remember how you burned all of my mushrooms."

There was more silence.

"I understand, I understand, I know," Morsmani said. "You don't have to forgive me, and I don't blame you for not… That's your right. Forgiveness is yours to give and mine to ask, not demand." Then quieter he said, "After all I find it hard to forgive myself for what I've done."

*****

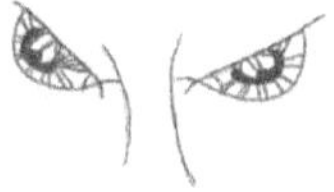

The next morning, while Nom was eating breakfast, Skalla and Morsmani entered camp. Behind the men wandered a bound and gagged silver folken. The prisoner was tall, bald, and his skin was completely silver. He shone of a light all his own. His eyes, which pleaded to the camp, had no pupils. They were simply silver spotlights. Morsmani sat down next to Amy. Skalla pushed the silver folken into a sitting position and stood protectively behind him.

"Why is he tied up?" asked Nom.

Morsmani ignored Nom. The Promethean took off his helmet. His cuttlefish eyes seemed sad. He looked at Amy and stated, "If I could trade the whole world for just five more minutes with you, I would."

Amy replied, "But I won't let you, because you are much too important for the world, and me."

Morsmani jerkily nodded his head, nervously tapped the tip of his nose with his pointer finger and turned to the silver folken. When the silver folken saw Morsmani's face, he recoiled. He gasped and muttered, trying to yell around his gag. Skalla bent down and sat the prisoner upright again. The prisoner twisted and flailed in apparent terror as Morsmani leaned forward and touched the man's forehead with the palm of his hand. The silver folken and Morsmani both spasmed. They both dry heaved. The silver folken lay back. His face was empty, serene, and unperturbed. His silver light dimmed. Morsmani stood. His hair quickly receded as his pale skin quickly paled further and began to shine. His scars receded into smoothness.

"What did you just do?" asked Nom, slightly worried.

Morsmani turned to Nom. The golden eyes with horseshoe shaped pupils were replaced by silver globes. Morsmani looked identical to the captured silver folken. Morsmani answered in a voice that sounded like the yowling of a cat in the night, "I stole…" Morsmani cleared his throat. "I stole," Morsmani continued in a slightly higher pitched voice than normal, "His skin. I need it, need it… to get into Urbe."

"Why?" Azra asked. Morsmani looked puzzled, so Azra elaborated, "Why can't you get into Urbe normally? Wouldn't they let a Promethean in?"

Morsmani smiled and chuckled. "Oh no! I can't get into Urbe. Actually, I am an enemy of the silver folken. We had our differences in the past. I think they might try to kill me on sight. Which means I can't exactly ask them kindly for the Great Star of Isen."

"So how are we going to get the Great Star of Isen?" Nom asked.

"Steal it." Morsmani replied. He saw the children's horrified faces and quickly added, "I'll give it back. It's just to kick start the action, otherwise nothing will happen until it's too late. So, without any further dithering and dothering, let's go to town. Nom, I need your help. You girls and Skalla, go have fun in Ghett!"

Amy opted to stay and help the captured silver folken, who was now staring into the distance asking where he was, and who he was. The rest of the group headed out. Myco turned herself into a small toadstool which Azra held in her lap. Skalla, his arm still in a cast, limped behind the group.

*****

Ghett was a large, dusty city. The arid region just south of Mycostadur barely saw any rain fall, so the streets of the city were choked with swirling dust and dirty peddlers. The city was overall poor. The small buildings and shacks lay haphazardly around each other, crowding the alleyways like drunks crowding a warm fire. The group split up. Nom and Morsmani wound their way towards the large wall of golden light.

Nom asked, "Will that silver folken be okay?"

Morsmani said, "Maybe. Hopefully. Amy's the best person to help him. It was an unfortunate thing I had to do."

Nom nodded and looked at the merchants on the side of the road. They sat on rugs with their wares spread out in front of them. One merchant, who was selling roasted mushrooms on sticks smiled a toothless grin at Nom. Nom shivered.

Eventually they arrived at Isengate. Isengate was a free-standing stone archway set into the edge of Isen's light. It was the entrance to Urbe. A silver folken guard stopped Morsmani and Nom.

The guard asked, "Draconi, who is the child?"

Morsmani, who looked liked Draconi, looked at Nom and answered, "The child is a follower of Order. I found him in Mycostadur. I want to bring him before the council for questioning."

The guard sighed, "That, I think, is not wise."

Morsmani said, "Kalli wants to investigate Order's growing restlessness. The boy will be cut away from Order's control inside Isen's Wall. It will be safe."

"Fine. If Kalli wants this, let it be on her head. Isen, let them in."

The light in the archway shone brightly, then disappeared. Behind the arch was a long hallway that stretched to Urbe. The arched ceiling and walls of the hall were made of the golden light of Isen's Wall.

"Do not touch the light, Nom," Morsmani said into Nom's mind. "The light strips away any magic it touches. Your sword and scag pendant would be ruined."

At the end of the long hallway was another arch. This one was made of copper slowly greening with age. Urbe was magnificent. The capital of the Silver Folk sat in a bubble inside Isen's Wall. The city was bathed in golden light. The buildings were all green glass spears sticking proudly into the sky. Nom held his breath at the sight. Then he noticed the quietness of the city. There were no animals or plants. No buzzing of insects or quiet conversations could be heard. In fact, there were no people in sight. The city seemed empty.

Morsmani led Nom to the tallest tower in the center of the city. The city looked larger from the outside. Nom counted the buildings in the city and found there were only twenty. The central building was slim. They entered, still seeing no one. The trespassers went into a small room with metal sides. A door slid shut behind them. Nom jumped and turned around, there was no way out of the room.

Morsmani waved his hand. The floor shook. Nom fell down in terror as he felt himself get heavier for a second. The feeling of heaviness passed, and Nom stood. Morsmani stared ahead. Nom was about to ask what they were waiting for, when the door slid open again. Nom gasped. The hallway had changed. Instead of the entrance to the building, he looked out at a landing far above the ground. Somehow the room had teleported upwards. They exited the small room and went towards a door at the end of the landing. Nom looked down at the ground. They were at the top of the tower. There was only one floor above them.

At the door at the end of the landing they were stopped again by a guard, the first person they had seen inside Urbe.

The guard asked, "What are you doing here?"

Morsmani said, "I am taking this boy to Isen."

"Why?"

"The boy is controlled by Order. Kalli wants him questioned, but first he has to be purged of Order."

The guard stared at Nom. Then, he said, "So he has to see The Great Star?"

"Obviously," replied Morsmani.

"This is very irregular."

"Of course it is. How many thralls of Order do we host here? Let us through, please."

The guard tapped his silver spear on the ground a few times in thought, but finally relented and let them through.

Inside the door was a wide staircase of onyx leading to a raised dais under a great green glass pyramid, the top of the tower. On the dais was a single white jewel, which shone so brightly that the midday sun darkened to twilight in comparison. Nom squinted as they approached the jewel. When they reached the dais, Morsmani reached for the fallen star. Before he could touch the jewel, however, a cylinder of golden light surrounded the trespassers. Morsmani cursed. A group of three silver folken entered the room.

The one in front, a bald lady of serene silver light, stated, "Welcome, Shinigorath, to Urbe."

*****

Chapter 19
First Defense

The drums thundered; the bells rang. Quentin shot out of bed, his head racing. Quickly, he put on his armor and ran outside. He had been sleeping in the army barracks on the summit of Chinchiplas ever since the northern army arrived. The king rushed to the edge of the summit and looked down upon the rice paddies. Fog hung over the fields in the crisp, early morning. The city's bells rang in warning terror. The enemy's drums thundered like hell's steeds; their bagpipes squealed like carrion crows. Bairne's forces marched towards the city walls.

Arrows and stones began to shower the approaching army. Bairne's men floundered and sloshed across the rice paddies, their iron armor causing them to sink in the waterlogged ground. The yelling began. The defenders screamed orders and hurled abuse, as well as projectiles, at the attackers. The attackers let out their battle cries and screamed in their death throes.

At the summit, ziplines had been set up that led to different defensible locations throughout the city. This way the upper garrison could quickly and easily be deployed as reinforcements anywhere in the city. Quentin grabbed a line and flew down to the city walls. He arrived at the same time as the first attackers. Ladders swung up onto the outside of the earthen walls. Grappling hooks spun over the wall's sides. The hooks found nothing to grab onto and simply fell back to the attackers. The walls of Chinchiplas were the tallest in the world, but, like the city they protected, were earthen mounds. As such, the walls were not vertical but were still too steep to climb in armor. The ladders, however, made climbing the walls a simple task. Quentin grabbed the nearest pot of boiling tar and tossed the black sludge down the nearest ladder. The climbers screamed in pain as they were hit by the tar. They tumbled down the wall. Quentin threw a torch down after them. A line of fire now burned where the ladder had once been.

Along the wall more fires were lit upon the steep slope. The wall was ablaze. The attackers had to navigate through a few fire free pathways up the wall. Their success was limited. Defenders began falling from being hit by arrows. A great siege tower made it through the marshy farmland. All others had floundered in the wet ground. A ramp extended from the tower to the top of the wall. Northmen poured from the tower. Their faces painted blue, their hair and beards plaited, their iron glinting. The bronze weapons of the people of Chinchiplas bent upon the attackers' iron armor. The invaders were taking the wall.

Quentin rushed to the fight. His sword, Nagran's Fang, cleaved through the enemy. The sword's weight, though hidden to its wielder, allowed the blade to break through nearly anything. The attackers fell, retreated, and were finally routed by Quentin's fury. Quentin ran up the ramp to the tower and with a swing of his sword, he broke the beams that held up the tower's topmost floor. The tower collapsed around him, and Quentin fell.

He landed in the mud beneath the tower. Dazedly he looked around. The flames from the wall flickered in their pale reflections upon the rice paddies' red waters. Bodies sunk into the mud all around Quentin. One man nearby cried as he tried to close his stomach with his hands. What little ground was not covered in bodies or fire, was red with rivers of blood. The air stank of coppery blood and burning flesh. Quentin felt sick. The enemy drums gave three loud beats as the bagpipes gave a low, long tune. The invading army retreated, leaving behind their comrades and siege towers stuck in the mud.

Quentin crawled to a ladder left by the attackers and climbed to the top of the wall. There he was greeted by the shouts of the victorious defenders. The people of Chinchiplas were tired, beaten, and injured, but their faces were happy. They had thrown back the northern army. They had won the day.

Quentin raised his hands. His army quieted. Quentin yelled out, "We have thrown them back this time! Good work! Tonight, we celebrate, while they lick their wounds. But remember, they will return. They will attack again, and we must be ready! Like we were today!"

The crowd cheered and stamped for their victorious leader. Quentin looked down and saw the Sake Master lying on the ground. His head was opened by an arrow. Pale insides spilled from the hole on his temple. Quentin vomited.

*****

<u>272</u>

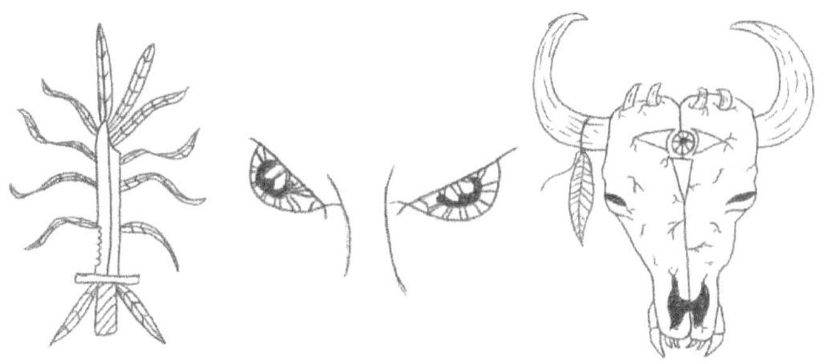

Chapter 20
Machinations from a God

The day of Morsmani's, Shinigorath's, trial was at hand. Nom had the cell next to the Promethean. They had been imprisoned for three days, and interrogated. Nom had not said anything to the man he once knew as Morsmani in that time.

Nom broke the silence, and asked, "Are you really Shinigorath?"

"Yes," answered Morsmani.

"The god of death, madness, and chaos?"

The three people in Morsmani's cell looked up and each said, "Yes."

Nom looked at the three people through Isen's golden light, which made up the walls of Shinigorath's cell. There was Morsmani. His armor had been taken away. His thin, scarred frame looked weak and frail inside his large purple cloak. Pacing the cell was a man who looked nearly identical to Morsmani, but his hair waved wildly like it was in a gale, and he had no scars. Sometimes Nom had seen this second man erupt in angry flames. In the corner of the cell, crouched the third man. This man was also identical to Morsmani, but had more scars, and was covered in a dark shadow.

The crouching man muttered to himself, "He talks to us. He talks to us, but he hates us. I don't blame him. I am terrible, terrible, terrible people."

The pacing man kicked the crouching man.

Morsmani sighed and said, "Nom, can we talk?"

The boy nodded.

"Good," Morsmani stated. "The scared guy," Morsmani pointed at the crouching man, "Is Gorath, god of madness. The other one," now pointing at the pacing man, "Is Shini, god of death. These are my demons. After I burned the world, I split them from myself with Amy's help. Usually they are trapped, somewhat, in my familiar stones in my helmet. Gorath in the Crown of Madness, Shini in the Mask of Death. They're out right now because Isen's light is blocking me from my stones."

"Who are you then?" asked Nom.

"Morsmani, Namer, god of chaos."

"So, you admit to destroying the world?" asked the boy.

Morsmani nodded. Gorath moaned and rocked back and forth. He started picking at his fingers, small flakes of skin falling away from his cuticles.

"We didn't destroy the world!" said Shini. "You're still here. Usmer's still here. We only destroyed a civilization we didn't understand and didn't fit into. Then we built this world. We fit here. You fit here. It's better. It's worth it. I had fun, damnit!"

Morsmani stood up and faced Shini. "I did not burn the world because I didn't fit in. I did it to stop the Terrestrial. You may have enjoyed it, you sick bastard, but I hated it."

"Hated it, hated it, hated it," muttered Gorath as he rocked in his corner.

"Shut up!" yelled Shini, who then kicked Gorath. Gorath's shadow darkened and covered himself.

Gorath sang softly from inside his black shadow, "Inside my shadow, dark, dark, dark. It's cold and quiet without Shini's angry spark, spark, spark."

Shini lit on fire as he yelled, "I will tear you to pieces, coward! I will rip you apart and feed you to Zorscags. Who needs you? You're scared all the time. You can't talk straight. Worthless worm!"

"Quiet, both of you!" Morsmani admonished.

Shini glared but became quiet. Gorath's shadow lessened, and he reappeared. His fingers bled where he had been picking them.

"Why does he do that?" asked Nom, pointing at Gorath's fingers.

"You can ask him yourself," said Morsmani.

"Why do you do that?" Nom asked Gorath.

Gorath touched his nose with his pointer finger and said, "Dermatillomania."

No one said anything after that. The silence dragged on. Shini paced, Gorath swayed, Morsmani stared contemplatively into the distance.

Finally, Nom asked, "Are we the bad guys?"

"You aren't, Nom," said Morsmani. "I was for a long time. This mission we are on, however, is a good mission. A righteous mission."

"A mission to war! Always good, always good, always good. War, it never changes, and I always miss it," said Shini.

"War's scary. So loud, so violent. Stressful," said Gorath.

Shini replied, "You like war. You get a bunch of weirdos like yourself from it. It's great! People die. The ones who don't die go insane. And it's all caused by the chaos of battle! Which you appreciate Morsmani, no?"

"War is terrible," said Morsmani. "I do not want to sow chaos. I have in the past. Many times. For the last few hundred years, I have tried to get rid of chaos, unsuccessfully."

"Bah, you failed old man," said Shini. "You failed, and now you're starting another war. Kinda ironic, eh?"

Morsmani glared at his tormentor. "It's not ironic, it's unavoidable. I'm glad you're excited about our mission, Shini, but do not lose your head."

Shini lit on fire again. "I was part of your head! Your head! That was me up there. The three of us made a whole Shinigorath. You split us apart! I hate you! Hate you! Treat me like a child. Look at Gorath! Look at what he's become. Don't you feel ashamed?"

"No," stated Morsmani. "Having the two of you in my head ruined my childhood. Caused me to bully people like Myco, kill the families of my own bullies, kill the Maker's family, and destroy 99 percent of the world's population, while simultaneously making most of the world uninhabitable for a thousand years. Since splitting away from you, I have been able to control my panic attacks better, and I do not wantonly kill."

"You're repressing me!" shouted Shini.

"Sorry, I suppose," replied Morsmani.

*****

The central square of Ghett was full. The crowd of people and scags jostled and pushed to get a view of the men standing in a cylinder of golden light on the raised stone platform. Morsmani scowled and twitched, Shini paced angrily, and Gorath hung his head despondently behind them. Behind Morsmani, along a long wooden table sat the leaders of the Silver Folken, the Silver Council. Nom, still in his feathered armor, was chained next the cylinder of light. His head was buzzing, and the bright sun bounced blindingly from the ground to his eyes. He had never felt so low and embarrassed. The crowd darkened in the middle and parted, allowing a group of strange people through. Amy, Azra, and Skalla stood before the raised platform. Azra was sitting on a floating chair made of shadow. A small morel mushroom sat upon her lap. Azra stared at Nom. Nom's eyes filled with embarrassed tears and he quickly looked away.

The woman who had captured Nom and Morsmani, Kalli, stood and addressed the crowd. "We are gathered here today for the trial of these two men. They were caught in the act of stealing the Great Star of Isen in Urbe."

The crowd murmured to themselves.

"Yes, yes," Kalli calmed the crowd. "If they had succeeded, we would have been defenseless. For this crime the punishment is usually death."

The crowd cheered. Nom had seen similar spectacles in the New Keys Capital. Never a trial, just a reading of crimes, pronouncement of the judgement, and then an execution. Nom had quickly realized that the people who went to these events cared very little about the crimes, and less about the judgement, as long as that judgement was death. All they actually cared about was the execution. Watching the crowd, Nom recognized the same type of people. His stomach plummeted, and he despaired.

Kalli raised her hands. Silver light flitted over the crowd, which quieted. "However," she stated. "The boy, Nom Carver, did not know of the crime he was committing. For his young age, and ignorance, should we let him free?"

The crowd sneered and booed. They were not here for acquittals and apologies. They were here for the safe sights of public death and gore. The Silver Council members raised their hands with fingers pointing up. One finger up meant innocent, two meant guilty. Of the thirty one members, only five had two fingers up. Kalli nodded. She waved her hands and Nom's chains fell away. He was free. He stood staring, not sure what to do. Morsmani jerked his head towards the crowd, and Nom quickly jumped from the stage and stood next to Amy and Azra.

"Now, this man, who attempted to take the most powerful object in all the world, says he did so to save us all from the terror to our south!" Kalli said. "We will now let him speak and explain to us why he thinks taking away our protection will, in fact, protect us."

The crowd jeered. They jostled forward, pushing Nom.

Morsmani lifted his head and said, "I am Shinigorath."

The crowd immediately silenced. A few people asked each other if they had heard correctly. Morsmani's voice rumbled over the crowd again, "I am Shinigorath, god of death, madness, and chaos. I am the Namer. I am a member of the Golden Council, fighter of Red, friend of Gold, pupil of Klart Bumble, killer of the Maker, burner of the world, trickster, thief, husband, teacher, murderer, and fiend."

The crowd was still silent. Shini and Gorath now stood tall behind Morsmani.

Morsmani continued, "Before this world was made, when the Forbears ruled the Earth, the Terrestrial came down from his throne in the heavens. He came down and began conquering. No one saw this. No one knew this save me. I fought him alone the only way I knew how. By making thralls. That was my specialty. I took over the minds of the masses, just as the Terrestrial did the same. Our thralls fought the world over. His ordered, and disciplined. Mine, angry, uncontrolled, violent. I was losing and had no help, had no hope. In desperation I set out to end the Terrestrial in one fell swoop. I burned the world. I killed billions in a blinding blink of an eye, and I failed. All I did was stall him. I had killed his thralls, his army. After Red was defeated, Klart instructed Isen's Wall be built in order to keep the Terrestrial at bay."

Kalli interrupted by asking, "And you want to tear down this wall now? Why?"

The crowd perked up. Most of them had never seen a god before. Most of them smelled the scent of execution in the air. Most of them figured the death of a god, especially one as powerful as Shinigorath, would be a sight to behold. They licked their lips in anticipation.

Shinigorath nodded his scarred head. "I did. He moves, the Terrestrial, in the south, and the east. New Keys has been attacked by his thralls. Monuments of Order have been erected all throughout the lands north. He aims to circumvent Isen's Wall. Desperate, he is. But so are we. We have not the strength to fight him once he gets a foothold here. We must stop him before then. We must stop him at Urbe. If Isen's light disappears, the Terrestrial will snap at the bait and move against Urbe. With a great enough force, we can destroy his army and force the god of order to come out himself. Then, when he does, I will destroy him using Isen herself upon my hand."

Kalli walked up to the edge of the light and spoke quietly so that the crowd could not hear what was said. Nom strained forward and heard Kalli ask, "This great force you speak of, is it the combined forces of the scag tribes and Chinchiplas? Is that why we have these armies marching uninvited towards our lands?"

Morsmani nodded. Kalli scowled and stepped back. Turning to the crowd she yelled, "What say you, people of Ghett? Should Shinigorath be executed for the crimes of murder, torture, genocide, thievery, and terrorism?"

The crowd went wild. This was the moment they had been waiting for. They stamped their feet and gnashed their teeth. They went wild to show how much they hated the gods of death, madness, and chaos. They yelled to the heavens in exultant pleas to see the death of a god. They begged to witness the incarnation of death becoming mortal and snuffed out upon the square. Kalli turned to the Silver Council. Before the stoic silver folken could raise their luminous hands, however, a cloud appeared on the stage. Out of the cloud swept an old man. He looked familiar to

Nom. The crowd hushed, waiting to hear what this ancient interruption was about. Kalli quickly bowed before the man.

The old man walked over to Shinigorath and said, "I'm dreadfully sorry old friend. I had an inkling this may happen. Do not despair, not all is lost, we are still upon the best path to win."

Shini smiled and asked, "How can we be if you had to step in? Are things so desperate even the King of the gods must step down from his throne and join the fight?"

The crowd gasped. Not only did they get to see Shinigorath, The Enemy of All Living Things, but also Klart Bumble, the God King. The crowd bowed. They no longer thought of public sanctioned killings. They simply hoped that these gods would not smite them for their insolence.

Klart laughed. His voice, an unassuming tenor, rolled out over the crowd. "Get up, get up, good people of Ghett and Urbe. Fear not. I have not directly harmed anyone in a very long time, and I'm not about to start today. I am upset at you Kalli, though. You drag a man out in the streets to be tried by the mob for crimes that occurred when this mobs' great, great, great grandfathers' great, great, great grandfathers weren't even a twinkle in their great, great, great grandfathers' eyes."

Klart paused to let this sink in. All this statement really did was muddy up the crowd's already excited heads.

"Don't tell me you did not notice the growing strength of the Terrestrial. The Silver Folken have always known the movements of all the great things of this world. This trial is a farce to exact vengeance and judgement upon your ancient enemy. These wounds incurred so long ago have festered and blinded you all. Do you not think that maybe in a few hundred years Shinigorath has changed? Are you the same silver skinned girl who helped erect the Sundering Wall? I do not think you are. So, then, why would Shinigorath be the same. You do not know this man you are trying. His ancient crimes should be punished, yes. But, perhaps, his punishment may be less taxing now."

Kalli was silent.

Klart Bumble turned to the crowd. "Nom Carver," he addressed. "You once asked Shinigorath if he was a god or a demon. Now I offer you the chance to determine this answer objectively. Talk to the people who have known Shinigorath. Hear what they have to say about this Promethean, the good and the bad. You will be his judge."

The crowd, including Nom's friends, edged away from Nom. He stood alone in the crowd, the feathers of his armor rustling. Nom turned around. He looked at his companions, at Morsmani, the closest thing to a father he had had since his village was destroyed, and he walked away. He left the crowd. Once he was out of sight of the crowd, he took off his helmet and threw it on the ground. The helmet rolled into the garbage filled gutter on the side of the dirt road. Nom ran. He ran back to their camp outside of Ghett. When he got there, he began to pack his things. He was going to leave. He was going to leave and never see any of them again.

When his bags were packed and strapped on his back, he left camp. He walked into the marshy land of Mycostadur. As he walked, he began to see things in the swampy waters. First, they were murky images in the corners of his tear filled eyes, then they came into focus. He stopped at one puddle and saw in the murky waters the marlin he had caught so long ago on the shipwright ship. His sword hung at his side, a comforting weight. He remembered training with Morsmani and Amy. The exhilaration of learning a new technique. The pride of mastering it. The happiness in Morsmani's voice. He heard Morsmani saying, "He's my new apprentice." Nom hardened his heart. Morsmani, no, Shinigorath, had only been training Nom to be a killer. After all, why would a demon need an apprentice?

Nom walked on. He ignored the images on the ponds, so spores rose out of the fungi around him and assumed shapes. The first was the shape of the black and white dreamcatcher he had received as the token of becoming scagfriendken. Azra's smile rose in his mind. A twinge of guilt hit him. He shook his head.

"Do you hate me?" Azra's voice asked.

Nom whirled around. There was no one there. The spores behind him formed into a shape similar to Azra's. They asked again, "Do you hate me, Nom?"

Nom shook his head. The guilt of leaving was now filling his every thought. Every fiber in his body screamed at Nom to tear them out for the guilt was too painful. Hot tears stung Nom's eyes as he collapsed. His head pounded. He rocked back and forth in between the ponds of Mycostadur, his tears feeding the giant mushrooms looming overhead.

Later in the evening, Nom returned to camp. Amy, Skalla, and Myco had made camp and cooked food. Azra was propped up on a springy mushroom couch. Klart Bumble was drawing stick figures in the dirt. When Nom entered camp, Azra looked up. She had been crying. Her eyes were red, and the red marks on her cheek shone with tears. The guilt rose in Nom again and a twinge of anxiety came with it.

Nom cleared his throat and said, "I did not know where to go."

The rest of the camp looked up. Amy and Skalla beamed, Klart look relieved. Myco, now the strange mushroom creature again, shrugged, then could not contain herself and danced a little jig.

Klart stood and said, "Good. The boy returns, even if it is only because he has no where else to go." He winked knowingly at Nom and continued, "So, as my first sign of appreciation to all of you for helping in this matter with the Terrestrial I want to thank Azra. Without you convincing the scags to join us we would be in very dire straights indeed. And look what it has gotten you. This won't do, you know. Here."

Klart flicked his hand at Azra. Azra was filled with golden light and lifted into the air. She hung there, serene, and angelic. Then, in a breath stopping moment, the light disappeared and she fell. Nom rushed forward to try and catch her. He was too late. She hit the ground on her hands and knees.

Nom skidded to her side and yelled at Klart, "How could you do that? She's paralyzed!"

"Nom," Azra whispered.

Nom looked down. Azra was looking up at him, a sheepish grin on her face. "My hands are cut. I can feel them. I caught myself." She stood up and yelled at the world, "I caught myself! I caught myself! I can walk!"

The girl grabbed Nom and hugged him. She lit on fire, and ascending, floated above the ground. The fire warmed Nom but did not hurt him. His mixed emotions of guilt, anxiety, hurt, anger, and now relief and happiness overwhelmed him, and he sobbed in her arms. Azra cried tears of joy onto his shoulder and whispered in his ear, "I'm glad you came back."

They slowly descended onto the ground again. Klart had tears of his own in his eyes. He turned to leave. Nom let go of Azra and rushed after Klart.

"King Bumble wait." Nom implored.

Klart stopped and turned to the boy. "I am no king. That is a title I do not wish, and certainly do not claim. I am an advisor, and a meddler, but I rule nothing. Now is not the time for you to talk to me. Talk amongst the people you know. Ask them why, as you think, they lied to you about Shinigorath. Ask them about him, then ask others you don't know about him. After you get your answers, come to me and we will talk, Oh King of Kings."

Before Nom could say anything, Klart had disappeared. Azra tapped Nom on the shoulder. Nom turned around and was presented with his helmet.

"I saw it on the ground and figured you would want it back," she explained.

Nom nodded. "Thanks," he said. "Can we talk later? I want to talk to Amy, but afterwards can we talk?"

Azra nodded.

When Nom came up behind Amy, who was sitting in front of the fire, Amy asked, "Do you want to talk Nom?"

Nom said, "Yes", and sat down next to Amy.

"Why did you lie to me?" the boy asked angrily.

"I didn't lie," Amy replied.

"You told me his name was Morsmani. His name is Shinigorath. Why did you not tell me who he was?"

Amy sighed. "My husband's name is Morsmani. He changed his name from Shinigorath a long time ago. A name is just what people call you. We didn't tell you who Morsmani was, Nom, because we thought it would upset you."

Nom, his anger still rising, did not fully listen to Amy. He asked, "How can you marry someone who destroyed the whole world? Someone who murders people?"

"Don't be angry, Nom. I understand why you are angry, but please try to calm yourself. Tell me, Nom, what titles have you heard me be called by?"

Nom was about to retort by asking who cares, but then he stopped. There must be a point to the question.

The boy slowly answered while thinking about the question. "You have been called Lady Amy, a scholar, Master Shadow Bender, um, goddess of shadow… that is all I can think of."

Amy nodded and said, "Here are a few more; Titaness of Shadow, Phoenix Goddess, and this last one you may have heard me called in Mycostadur, Granddaughter of the Maker."

Nom glared at Amy, who continued to stare into the fire. Nom could not figure out why Amy had asked him to list her titles. Is it a show of strength, to remind him who she was? No, that could not be it. Amy reached down to the fire to adjust a log. Nom watched her hand grab the log and noticed that the fire could be seen through Amy's arm.

"What is wrong with your arm, Amy?" Nom asked. "I can see through it."

Amy brought her hand to her face and looked at it.

"You can," she agreed. "I'm fading. My power comes from Morsmani, and since he is locked away behind Isen's light, I am cut off from his power. So, I am fading. Nom, do you know the story of my grandfather, the Maker?"

Nom nodded. "I do," he said. "Why –

"Give me a quick synopsis of the Maker's story, Nom," Amy interjected.

Nom paused and said, "The Maker was a powerful Forbear, who granted the power of the gods to the humans. He turned humans into the scags, silver folken, dragons, and Prometheans. He locked his creations away in his palace dungeons, so that the other Forebears would not know of his creations. Klart Bumble broke out of the Maker's palace and then freed everyone trapped inside and then released the God Spring. The Maker and his servants had to run and hide from the other Forbears, who wanted to kill them for giving humans great powers. They were also chased by some of their own creations as well. Shinigorath was one such. Shinigorath caught the Maker, his servants, and family in the Spine Mountains. A great fight ensued, and in the end, Shinigorath killed the Maker, his family, and his servants." Nom paused in telling the story. Then, puzzled he asked, "That can not be right, can it? You are the Maker's granddaughter. Did Shinigorath not kill your whole family? How could you marry your family's murderer?"

Amy said, "Shinigorath saved my brother Jason. Jason became Shinigorath's first apprentice, and was renamed Ruhk, leader of the Carrion Feeders. I died in those mountains. One of Shinigorath's thralls smashed my head in. I hated him for a long time. Do you know why Shinigorath gave up on using thralls like the Terrestrial does?"

Nom replied by asking, "If you died, how are you here?"

"I'm a shade. A summoned warrior. Do you know how summoning works?"

Nom shook his head. "I know Skalla can summon buffkin."

"He can. He made a contract with the buffalo spirit, Tatanka. That is what his buffkin tattoo symbolizes. If he places some of his blood on the tattoo and places his palm on a surface, he can summon a buffkin. Morsmani can do the same with shades."

"What are shades, and who does he have a contract with?"

"There is no contract. Shinigorath is the person people wishing to summon shades go to for those contracts. Shades are the spirits of dead warriors. They only appear in this world through being summoned, and the summoner can only summon warriors they themselves have killed. So, I am summoned by Shinigorath, since he killed me. Now, Nom, do you know why Shinigorath does not use thralls?"

Nom shook his head.

"Shinigorath, like the Terrestrial, can make thralls. He can take over the minds of others and control them. Shinigorath can become a hive mind like the Terrestrial. That is why he has been fighting the Terrestrial when others have not. He is, or at least it was assumed that, Shinigorath was the best equipped to fight the

Terrestrial. He was one the few who could sense where the Terrestrial's thralls were. In their first war Shinigorath and the Terrestrial raced each other to make the most thralls. Shinigorath lost. His thralls were monsters. They could not be controlled. They raged and killed unchecked. The Terrestrial's thralls, as you've seen, are extensions of the god of order. Like fingers, they have no will of their own, and simply follow every whim of the Terrestrial. Shinigorath's thralls on the other hand were beasts of rage. Their minds were gone and all that was left was Shini's anger. Shinigorath could not control his thralls."

Nom jumped into the story by stating, "He still killed your family though, even if he could not control the thrall that killed you."

Amy replied, "True. In the mountains he was the ultimate cause of my family's death. The only person he killed himself, however, was my grandfather, who was a terrible man. Shinigorath did not want anyone else to die. He tried to save me from the thrall but failed. I hated him for a long time. He summoned me to help him fight. Summoned shades have little control over what they can do. Most have to do exactly what their summoner tells them to. Some can twist their summoner's wishes and find loopholes to allow them to do things differently. I can refuse. When he summoned me the first time, I tried to kill him. Shinigorath was intrigued and summoned me again. I tried to kill him again. This continued, as Shinigorath attempted to understand why I did not listen to him like the other shades."

"Did he know who you were?" Nom asked.

"He did. He tried to apologize every time he summoned me. Eventually, he managed to have a conversation with me and explain himself. He apologized for killing me, and that he never wanted me to die. He showed me how he has no control over his thralls. I believed him. I still hated him, but I believed him. After that point, when I was summoned, I simply stood and refused to help him. I ignored his orders. I saw his fights. I saw his madness control him. He had episodes where he was just as deranged as any of his thralls, and much more dangerous. He had other episodes where he was so scared he could not move. He would hide in a corner for hours, afraid of nothing, afraid of everything. Then he burned the world."

"Why?" Nom asked.

"Hmm?"

"Why did he destroy the Forebear's world?"

"The Forbear's world, the world I grew up in, was filled to the brim with billions of people. At the end, more than half of those people were thralls of the Terrestrial's. No nation, no Promethean, no Forbear, could hope to fight such an army. The Terrestrial had won. All that was left in those days was to wait for the Terrestrial to slowly close his iron fist around the world while the Red Gold Conflict continued, unaware of the tightening noose. So, to destroy the army, which comprised of most of the world, and hopefully kill the god of order, Shinigorath burned the whole world. His goal was to kill everything, even himself. He had not considered that the silver folken would raise The Sundering Wall to defend Usmer from the burning. He is incredibly grateful to them for that. Shinigorath's best hope for the burning was that a few people would survive and rebuild the world from the ashes. Shinigorath's burning hit one of its goals. Order's army was decimated. This brought Shinigorath little joy.

"I was summoned in the aftermath of the Burning. Shinigorath did not mean to summon me. I stated before that in order to summon something, you need your own blood placed upon the summoning mark. On that day, the god of death's tears ran along his summoning tattoos, and I was summoned from beyond. I saw the destruction, and I saw Shinigorath amongst it. He was sad and broken. I have never seen someone in such despair. He had won, but he hated himself for it. I helped him return to Usmer. I helped him break Shini and Gorath away from himself, so that his episodes would be less common, less extreme."

"Does he still have episodes? Does he still go into murderous rages?"

"Not very often, and the rages are no longer for no reason. Now something needs to upset Morsmani before he gives into his rage. Before, his rages came unexpectedly, and without purpose. He is a good man, Nom, who suffers from his own demons, and from what he was forced to do."

Nom thought about all that he had heard.

"You want me to pardon Shinigorath?" he asked.

Amy nodded her head. Her hair fluttered about her head more than usual. Nom wondered if the unseen wind which always blew Amy's hair was a wind from beyond the grave. He shuddered.

Nom said, "Thank you for telling me all this."

Nom wandered away from the fire. Skalla and Myco were huddled together a few feet away. Fluorescent mushrooms gave Skalla's face a green underglow. Myco was a pink spore cloud in the shapely form of a sensuous woman. They were discussing poisonous mushrooms.

"This is one of my favorites," Myco was explaining to Skalla. "It kills slowly, but silently. It grows in small, wet crevices, like in the tight spaces between walls, or cracks between stones. You breathe in the spores." Skalla quickly covered his mouth with his hands. "Then, over the next few weeks little, itty bitty mushrooms, they're really cute little guys, grow in your esophagus. Eventually you suffocate. Silent, deadly, untreatable, and best of all for your profession, undetectable, unless the body is cut open postmortem."

Skalla lowered his hands when he realized that the mushroom was not going to release any spores here. He rummaged in his pack and pulled out a few small, pale mushrooms.

He said, "These are my favorite. I mix these in their food. Then, when they eat them, they start to see the spirits that circle us all the time. Usually they become very frightened, act crazy, and either attack people, or lock themselves away. What usually happens is they get killed for attacking people, and if they don't then they see things for the rest of their lives, and are locked away forever, which in essence means I completed my task."

Myco nodded, "Effective, but kind of a gamble, no? Won't the client be upset when they find out that instead of killing the target you made the target go insane?"

Skalla shrugged, "Sometimes, but I'm hired for difficult cases. I can always fall back to the excuse that killing them would be too difficult, or impossible to do discretely."

Skalla saw Nom passing by at this point and called over to the boy, "Nom! Azra's asleep. She told me to told, er, I mean, tell you, that she was going to bed. Do you want to talk?"

Nom sat down and said, "Okay."

Myco seemed miffed for a second at the new company. Nom noticed this and thought it was strange that the people loving Promethean did not want more company.

Skalla replied, "Okay then. You probably want to know what I think about today's events?"

Nom nodded.

"Well," Skalla continued. "First, I want to ask you if you think I'm evil?"

Nom opened his mouth to declare that of course he did not think Skalla was evil, but then closed his mouth again before saying anything. Skalla was, after all, an assassin. He was a high level assassin who had joined them after assassinating some Lord Goram for Bairne.

Skalla stated, "I'm an assassin, Nom. I kill people for money. But I don't think you think of me as being an evil person, right?"

Nom nodded.

"That's because you're too close to me. Remember, Nom, even the worst of people have friends, and no one thinks of themselves as being bad. Everyone is a hero in their own eyes. If you are going to judge Shinigorath fairly, you have to step back and see him as someone who you do not know. You cannot look at this case through familiar eyes."

Nom thought about this for a while. Then asked, "Are you a bad person?"

"Maybe. I think about it sometimes. I go back and forth with thinking I'm evil, and good. My excuse is that I'm only doing a job, and it's the only job I know how to do, and I do it well. I'm sure Amy and Shinigorath gave you their excuses for what they have done."

"Could you not change professions?" Nom asked.

Skalla shook his head, "I don't think so. I joined the Carrion Feeders when I was a little older than you. My father died. I come from Hatten, far to the north. Bairne had just taken the city. His warriors had burned and looted as they conquered. The lack of shelter and amount of dead left on the streets after the fighting caused a sickness to spread through the city. My father was eaten by the plague, leaving my mother to care for my young sister and I. She could not find any jobs, and one day she left to look for a job and never returned. My sister and I waited for a few days. The food ran out. It ran out for everyone. Bairne's screamers feasted in their newly won towers while the Hattenians starved; our food stores having been burned down in the war. My sister and I were desperate, but we were two orphans who could not work, and could not get food. So, in desperation I stole a loaf of bread from a baker. I was caught. Instead of beating me and sending me on my way the baker turned me over to the guards. I was locked in jail for two weeks. When I got out, I went home and found my sister's body. She had starved. In my anger I went back to the bakery and killed the baker who I had tried to rob. That night I was visited by Ruhk, the titan who leads the Carrion Feeders, he offered me an escape from the city and a new family. I accepted gladly. I've been an assassin ever since. It's all I've ever known. Now, tell me, am I evil?"

Nom replied after thinking, "I do not think you are evil. You are kind and friendly to me, and it sounds like you did what you had to do to survive."

Skalla scowled. "You aren't thinking about this objectively, Nom! Forget how I treat my friends. Of course I'm kind to you. If I wasn't kind to my friends, I wouldn't be here. The facts are that my family died in war, like so many others, and so I resorted to stealing and murder to survive. That is not good. The only reason you think I should not be arrested and executed is because you only know me as a friend. If you are to judge Morsmani fairly you have to think of his crimes objectively. Forget that Morsmani is your teacher."

"Do you think Shinigorath should be executed?" Nom asked.

"My moral compass points straight to hell. Do not ask me to judge another man's crimes."

Nom put the question to Myco, who responded by saying, "I'm apathetic to this whole thing. The Shinigorath I knew was a mean, confused, teenager with anger issues and mood swings. Now he seems like a capable adult, if a little strange. All I know is that people change, and it seems that he may not be the same person he was a few hundred years ago when he committed the crimes he is on trial for."

"He is also on trial for trying to steal the Great Star of Isen." Skalla interjected.

"The Great Star of Isen is the last piece of Isen's soul that we have. It's a sentient thing. You mortals seem to think that if something is not humanoid it has no rights of its own. The Great Star of Isen is not an object that can be owned or stolen. The silver folken do not own Isen. Isen chooses to live with them. If anything, Shinigorath attempted a kidnapping. But no one asked Isen if she was fine with going with Shinigorath or not. It may have been mutual. Isen may want a change of scenery, or she may want the same thing as Shinigorath. No one has asked her though, because everyone thinks The Great Star of Isen is just some magical stone, not a person, just like none of you will talk to me unless I assume a human like form."

Nom asked, "So maybe Isen is being held hostage on top of that tower?"

"Maybe. A damsel in distress at the top of the monster's tower, and Shinigorath is the brave hero attempting to rescue her. Or she's the princess with the tower room, and Shinigorath is the roguish kidnapper trying to steal her away."

Nom thought about this and finally got up and left. Skalla and Myco continued their conversation about the potent effects of various fungi.

*****

Azra leaned over Nom in the foggy morning. She tickled his nose with one of the long quetzal feathers on his discarded helmet. Nom's nose twitched, he rolled over. Azra sighed and went around to his nose again. She scratched with the feather. Twitch, roll. Azra moved again to Nom's nose and began tickling. Nom's nose twitched, and his mouth opened wide. He sneezed, sitting straight up. His head hit his dreamcatcher, which he hung above himself every night. Nom blearily brushed his dreamcatcher to the side, as he looked for the reason he was awake.

"Carver Nom! I challenge you to a duel!" Azra cried into the marshy air pointing at Nom with the long feather like a sword.

Nom sat wide eyed, staring at the girl in shock.

After a few seconds of staring, Azra added, "Well, not an actual duel. Just sparring. I want to spar, and you're the best person to spar with. I'm really excited! Look at what I can do!"

Azra performed a cartwheel in front of the bemused Nom. Nom, while not upset about being woken up by Azra, was still trying to collect his whereabouts.

"What time is it, Azra?" Nom asked.

"It's time for walking!" Azra replied, full of gusto.

"It is too early. Can we spar in a little bit? No one else is up yet."

"Amy's up."

"Yeah, and the ocean is wet. Amy does not sleep."

Nom lay back down. Azra frowned and sat next to the boy.

"Please, Nom? I could hardly sleep last night. I want to run around! I can walk again. I'm too excited. I can't sleep anymore."

Nom grunted.

Azra, with a sly grin said, "I've been thinking about you all night. I've been wanting to do stuff with you all night, now that I can walk. I've felt like I've been a burden on the group, especially you, since you've been helping me the most. So, I wanted to play with you today. Come on, let's spar before everyone else gets up."

Nom flushed a bright red but remained on his side facing away from Azra. He waited for his heart to stop pounding, which had begun with Azra saying she had been thinking about him. He sighed. He could not fall asleep now that he was so excited. He rolled back over.

"Fine," he said. "What time is it?"

Azra jumped up. "It's sparring time, silly!"

They went to the other side of the hill next to the camp. The fog covered the land, nothing could be seen of Mycostadur, Ghett, or Isen's Wall. The world was a grey cloud with a black hill sloping up next to them. Azra held her two long knives, and Nom brandished his sword and knife. They clashed. Azra had lost none of her speed or skill in her hiatus from fighting. After a few blows they separated, panting.

"Why are you so fast?" Nom asked.

"Because I'm a kajscag. 'Faster than a kajscag' is a saying for a reason."

To prove how fast she was, she rushed back at Nom. Her face dappled with morning dew. Nom barely got his sword up in time. Their blades locked and Azra pushed forward. Nom pushed back. Their faces were inches from one another. Nom looked at Azra's purple eyes.

"I'm sorry, Nom." Azra said. "About Morsmani. You really liked him, didn't you?"

The fight left Nom and Azra fell forward. The two of them fell in a heap on the ground, and quickly disentangled themselves.

"Yeah," stated Nom.

Azra waited, but Nom didn't seem to want to elaborate. Azra jumped up, exhilarated by her agility. She offered her hand to Nom, who took it, and they quickly went back to sparring.

After a few minutes, Nom said in the middle of a bout, "He was the closest thing to a father I had since my village. I knew he was strange and weird, but Morsmani and Amy were the first people to not treat me like a monster. They were nice to me. They seemed to care about me."

Azra lessened her attack as she replied, "I think they do care about you. Why else would they bring you along? And I know how it feels to find out your father's not the greatest person."

Nom stopped. "That is the thing. I know not why they brought me here. They barely knew me when they offered me the chance to come. I went with them because I was lonely and hated where I was, but I have no idea what use I am to them."

"Not everyone needs to have a use for you. Some people just like your company. Maybe Morsmani wanted a new apprentice, and you fit the bill."

"A small boy from a fishing village, with no magical abilities, or fighting skill?"

"A cute boy who was lonely, lost, and afraid, and has the potential to do anything," Azra retorted.

Nom smiled. "Thanks," he said as he went on the offensive. He swept aside Azra's blades and his knife went up to her throat. She froze. Nom tapped the tip of her nose with his sword saying, "Touch."

They sat down, exhausted. Azra leaned on Nom.

Nom asked, "What do you mean you know what it is like to find out your father is not that great?"

Azra jerked and looked away. "When my father banned me from seeing you," she began. "I was so confused and angry. How could my father be so stupid? You were no threat to us. Sure, most humkin are mean and cruel to scagkin, but you were nice. How could he not see that? It wasn't until later I realized that he did see that. He forbade me from seeing you out of principle of what you are, not who you are. When I realized that, I no longer saw my father as a god, but as just another person. It hurts, that realization. I think you had a similar realization about Morsmani yesterday?"

Nom looked at the mud between his shoes. She was right. Morsmani had always gotten them out of every situation. He always knew what to do, and how to do it. He could be trusted. Then, when they had been captured, Nom had seen who Morsmani really was. He had seen Morsmani defeated, saw his demons and faults, and had been told of his crimes. Nom's hero had become a villain. Had always been a villain.

"Did you forgive Zarzasrahla?" Nom asked.

Azra nodded. "Everyone makes mistakes, and he apologized to you."

"How can I forgive Shinigorath?" Nom asked.

"Forgive him for what? He's always been nice to you. Has he ever done anything bad to you? If you didn't know his past, would you think he's anything other than good? He doesn't want your forgiveness, he wants the world to forgive him, and for all we know that's what he's been seeking since he burned the world."

Nom replied but the words never got anywhere. The world was silent. There was no noise in the misty morning. Azra tugged on Nom's armor. Nom looked at where Azra was pointing. On the top of the hill was a shadowy, hunched shape. The figure sparkled alabaster. Its hands hung by its side, its fingers pointing into sharp claws. The figure was hairless. The teenagers got onto their feet and crept up the hill. When they neared the white beast, another figure appeared. A woman with dark, flowing hair came up to the monster and hugged it. The mists cleared in a gust of unheard wind, and Amy was revealed to be letting go of the monster. The monster sensed Nom and Azra and turned uncannily quickly to them. The beast seemed to be made of stone. Its eyes were green marbles set into two gouges on its flat face. The vertical slits for nostrils opened and closed rhythmically above the thing's mouth, which was a jagged line. The fingers of the beast were pointed shafts of white marble. The beast moved forward. Nom stepped in front of Azra, holding up his sword. Azra stepped up next to Nom, her knives bathed in flame.

Amy put a hand on the monster and said, the silence disappearing, "Pet, these are my friends, Nom Carver and Azra Zarzasrahla. They mean you no harm, you just frightened them. Right?" Amy asked, looking at the children.

Azra and Nom nodded. Azra added, "Of course. I've never seen—"

With a rushing sound like storm waves washing away from ocean cliffs all of the world's noise disappeared. The monster moved forward again. Its movements were uncanny. It seemed to move very far without moving its body. Sweat beaded

Nom's forehead. He was glad he was also covered in mist so that Azra would not see that he was frightened.

The monster screamed. The whole universe filled with an unending screech of pain, fear, and hate. How the clouds did not run away, and the ground did not shatter, Nom did not know. Then the world darkened, and Amy walked in front of the beast.

She yelled, louder than the beast's ongoing, never ending scream, "Stop! She spoke quietly enough and knew not that you hate noise. Now be quiet, like you'd like them to be quiet, and let me introduce everyone." She turned to Nom and Azra and said, "Nom, Azra, this is Pet. Shinigorath's Pet. Pet, Nom, Azra. Now, since that's done, I am heading into town to see the arriving armies. Your father's here, Azra."

Azra and Nom followed Amy into Ghett. Pet stayed behind, preferring the quiet of the empty camp to the city. In the square where Nom and Shinigorath had been tried, there were now tents being set up for the recently arrived army leaders. The armies themselves were setting up camp outside the city. Azra spotted her father's teepee and left Nom and Amy to visit. Amy went to a tent with Chinchiplas's sygil, a purple chinchilla on a yellow field. Nom followed Amy.

Inside the tent was cool and serene. The light filtered through the tent's sides in muted yellow hues. Guy sat at a table next to a strange bald man in orange robes. Nom wondered where King Deneth was.

"Hello, Guy, Shangri," Amy said. Nom made a mental note that the strange man was named Shangri. He also noticed that Shangri was floating cross legged above his chair.

The men nodded to Amy.

Nom asked, "Where is King Deneth?"

There was a pregnant pause, then Guy answered, "King Deneth died, Nom. He got sick."

Nom nodded then asked, "Is it because Shinigorath took away the rabbit's foot?"

This time the pause was longer. Finally, Shangri stated, "Yes, it was. How do you know the mad god, child?"

"I am his apprentice."

Shangri smiled and asked, "Do you follow death or madness? Do you wish to learn how to heal insanity and stop death, or to cause madness and death? Morsmani has the power for all that you know."

Nom took in a deep breath and did not answer. He had no answer.

"You are a Promethean," Nom stated.

Shangri nodded. "I am The Collector and Keeper of Souls, Shangri, Supreme Artificer. You are?"

"I am Nom Carver of New Keys."

"My condolences, Nom, New Keys is in terrible shape. Now, Amy, where is your husband? Or are we supposed to make battle plans without him? I don't mind. He was never one for plans anyway."

Amy said, "Morsmani is in jail. The silver folken keep grudges for a very long time. And, yes, I'd like to discuss the coming battle."

Nom wanted to know what Shangri meant when he said that New Keys was in bad shape, but he did not dare interrupt the adults. He stood quietly next to Amy and listened. Chinchiplas had brought their entire navy, which unfortunately were not trained very well for fighting on land. They had also brought a sizeable portion of their army. Their soldiers were equipped with bronze weapons and armor. Amy stated that the Terrestrial's fine steel weapons would slice through their armor like cleavers through lard. The scag armies numbered four times as many as the Chinchiplas warriors. It seemed that in the end, all of the eastern tribes had been convinced to join in the fight. The western tribes had attempted to return home but were currently fighting the Tommy Knockers along the Scagway. Their weapons were as diverse as they were; the kajscags brought knives and tomahawks, the chocobscags, spears and bows, the beescags, hammers and maces, and the buffscags brought their claws and horns. The scags also brought a war beast to use as a mobile base in the battle.

Amy told of their travels south and mentioned that the Incarnate was ready for battle. "She is young and does not know her own strength yet, but she will be valuable on the battlefield.

Also, Myco has joined the fight. The Terrestrial stung her in her own domain, and she seeks vengeance."

Shangri inhaled sharply in surprise and Guy smiled widely.

"Myco?" Guy asked. "One of the nature gods? Surely we can't lose with her on our side!"

Nom finally spoke up. He said, "The Terrestrial beat her in her own lands. He had a monument there with two fire tyrors. Morsmani had to destroy the monument. Myco could not."

This sobered Guy. Then Guy asked, "Speaking of Morsmani, will he join the fight? What do the silver folken plan to do with him?"

Amy looked at Nom and smiled. "Tell them," she implored.

Nom took a deep breath. He did not know how to explain the situation. It was ludicrous. He was barely more than a child and was in charge of judging a god. The god who was reportedly the third most powerful being in the world.

Nom looked at the wall in between Shangri and Guy and stated, "I am in charge of trying and passing judgement on Shinigorath. Klart Bumble volunteered me."

Shangri laughed. "Here I was thinking that maybe you wanted to be one of my apprentices after this war, but it seems Klart already claimed you. He has plans for you, like he does with every important person." Then he became more serious and said, "That is quite the task. Do you need help? How are you conducting the trial?"

Nom looked at the Collector of Soul's eyes. They were rough purple orbs. For a second, they reminded him of Azra's purple eyes. Her eyes were bright and lively, Shangri's were dead and frozen. As Nom stared at them, he realized that they might not be eyes at all.

"I am interrogating people who knew Shinigorath. Which, actually, I should talk to the two of you about. I do not know you Shangri, but you seem to know a lot about Shinigorath. And Guy, you did not seem surprised to know Shinigorath was here. You knew Morsmani was Shinigorath, did you not?"

Guy rubbed his hands together nervously and replied, "You're good. I'm a worshipper of Shinigorath. I have been for a while now."

Nom nodded. Amy patted Nom on the back, whispered good luck in his ear, and left the tent. Nom stared at the men across the table. Guy averted his gaze nervously. Shangri peered at Nom in interest.

"What do you hope to achieve being Shinigorath's apprentice, Nom?" Shangri asked.

Nom shrugged.

"I do not know," Nom answered. "I never really thought about it. I mean, until a few days ago I thought Shinigorath was Morsmani, a traveling Promethean scholar. I figured I would learn all about the world and its people. Now, I have no idea."

Shangri nodded. "From my experience there are two paths for Shinigorath's teachings; to hurt and to heal. Ruhk used the powers he gained from Shinigorath to hurt, to kill, to become rich and powerful. Amy used the powers she gained from Shinigorath to heal. She gives council to people who suffer."

Nom thought about this. He could not remember a time when Amy had ever been mean to anyone. He remembered the silver folken that Morsmani and Skalla had captured before going into Urbe. The man had suffered after his skin was taken. Nom had seen him a few days later, and he was fine then. *'Amy's the best person to help him,'* Nom remembered Morsmani telling him that morning.

"I would like to help people. But I have always heard that Shinigorath is an evil demon who only hurts and kills." Nom explained.

Guy now looked at Nom and said, "That's not true. He's helped me. I was horribly unfit to be king. I'm a nervous fellow, I think you can appreciate that. I could not be king. Shinigorath came to Chinchiplas at the beginning of my rule and tried to help me. Him and Amy counseled me on how to deal with anxiety and panic attacks. It helped, but in the end, I was unfit to rule, and they placed Deneth on the throne. They always visit and make sure I'm okay."

Shangri spoke up before Nom could say anything. "Nom, how has your sleep been?"

Nom paused, taken aback by the abrupt change in topic. "Fine," he said simply.

"You used to sleep fitfully though, right? I recognize the stone on your pendant, your dreamcatcher, there. Amy used to have that. It was taken from a spirit bear who died as it hibernated in the winter. Shinigorath gave it to Amy so she could sleep at night. Now, I assume, he gave it to you, so you could sleep at night. Keep that dreamcatcher safe, there's only one of its kind."

Nom nodded rubbing the stone on his dreamcatcher.

"What do you think I should do? Do you think I should judge Shinigorath guilty or innocent?"

Guy looked away. He tapped his feet and rubbed his hand, and Nom knew no answer was forthcoming from him.

Shangri smiled thoughtfully and replied slowly, "Klart has a plan. He's a powerful seer, and an incredible tactician. You'll probably do nearly exactly what Klart wants you to do. However, Shinigorath did burn the world. He has murdered and killed in anger and in cold blood. He has sown madness through the ages. He is guilty. You can choose his punishment or pardon him. That's up to you, Nom, that's your task. I will give no advice here. I will warn you, though, against asking that question of others. Before asking what someone else thinks should be done, you first should consider why you are asking them that. Are you hoping they will give you an answer better than one you could come up with yourself, and thus free yourself of this burden? Are you hoping they will affirm what you already think, and thereby prove to yourself you are correct? Or are you hoping they will steer you down a path you know you must go down but do not think you have the strength to go by yourself? Or are you perhaps interested in hearing their opinion, and going to consider their advice without bias? That last one is the most impressive and most difficult to do. Most people have not the wisdom for that kind of thinking. You must also consider the conflict of interest of having you as the judge. Shinigorath's enemies will hate you all the more if you spare him, but Shinigorath's friends may think you weak and traitorous if you judge him harshly."

Nom stared at Shangri. That advice did not help. Now the trial seemed even more terrifying. He had even less of an idea of what to do. Nom left the tent, his head buzzing and his heart skipping in small panic at the titanic task ahead of him.

*****

Chapter 21
Bairne

Quentin shot out of bed. The bells and drums were ringing, as they had every morning for the past days. Quentin could not remember how many days. Maybe the bells had harkened every morning for years. Quentin was tired. He stumbled out of his room at Chinchiplas's summit. The bells seemed more insistent today, more panicked. Quentin shook his head. He looked down at the fighting. The attacking army massed themselves against the earthen walls of Chinhciplas like ants. He grabbed a zipline to get down to the battle. He was not thinking. There was no time for thinking. Even if there was, he was too tired, too hungry, too hurt. He was simply doing what he had done for as long as he could remember.

He looked down again before riding the zipline. The ants were swarming the wall. They piled over the wall. Quentin saw the defenders in their bright steel armor that they had taken from the Terrestrial's men, flee into the city. The drums beat out the retreat signal. Quentin stared down for a little while, mesmerized by the fast-moving people below.

"Sir!" a soldier behind Quentin exclaimed.

Quentin turned around. His head still swam with visions of insect hordes swarming over one another. He frowned at the soldier and tried to rub the sleep from his eyes.

"You must go to Kahoke, your majesty. The army is retreating there now. Take this zipline."

The soldier led Quentin to the zipline to Kahoke's palace. Quentin grabbed the zipline and stepped off Chinchiplas's summit. He flew to the top of the palace. The cool morning air swept away much of his tiredness as it rushed by him. The panic began to set in. Bairne's army had broken through his defenses. Quentin landed, and he rushed over to his throne on the top of the pyramid. Behind him the rope of the zipline was cut and fluttered down upon the wind. Far below him two figures ran through the empty royal city. Two fleas fleeing on a great red ribbon between large anthills. Quentin knew who they were. It was Francis and Morrin coming to protect the king.

Quentin sat on his throne. The marble bench was uncomfortable. The coldness of the stone chilled him. He stared across the small royal city at the gates of Kahoke. At first, he could not believe Chinchiplas had been taken, but the more he sat waiting, the more he accepted his city was lost. For the past few days, or weeks, or years, Quentin had lost count, he had watched his people slowly die. Every day more people died, and every day there were less provisions. The shifts became longer as there were less people to man the stations. Sleep became a precious commodity as soldiers and civilians were given double and sometime triple shifts. In recent days, sickness and lethargy had begun to take hold. Half rations of old rice while fighting every day did not lead to strong soldiers; it led to hollow, wasting men.

Morrin and General Francis ascended the steps to the summit of the pyramid. At the peak, they spoke to Quentin about the fall of Chinchiplas and how he must stay here. The army was defending the outer gates and the chamber into Kahoke. Bairne would never make it here.

Quentin barely listened. He stared at the mound city of Chinchiplas. The rising sun behind the mountain turned Chinchiplas into a black silhouette. The city was silent, already dead. The only sound was the distant fighting of the armies. The noise was quiet as it came from the other side of Chinchiplas, outside the gate into Kahoke. To Quentin it sounded like the buzzing of flies upon a fresh corpse. Chinchiplas was already lost. Even if his armies could hold Kahoke against Bairne there was not enough food for them. They would starve, and Bairne would enter the royal city walking over fallen soldiers, killed not from sword and arrow but from starvation and plague.

Far away a shuddering filled the air. The outer gate to Kahoke had fallen. Quentin knew the northern soldiers would now be rushing into the lowest chamber of Chinchiplas. There they would meet the few remaining defenders in groups of three upon the causeway over the poisoned water. He imagined the fight would be more a meatgrinder than a battle.

Quentin wished that time would stop. That he could sit here forever, the last king on his marble throne. Below him the gate shuddered inward. The defenders of Chinchiplas ran down the causeway pursued by the fierce northerners. Quentin saw flash before his eyes, the deaths of his friends, colleagues; his citizens. Each had fallen over many days. Quentin had not even shed tears for the last few. He had no more tears, and even if he did, death had become normalized. He was numb to suffering and pain. His retreating army was swept underfoot. They were slow and tired from their lack of sleep and food. Bairne's army was well rested and fed. There was no competition.

The attacking army came to the base of the pyramid. Morrin stepped to the top stair of the palace and pulled back his bow. Morrin looked at Quentin. Quentin shook his head.

Quentin said, "We've lost. I don't want to lose you too, either of you. We'll surrender and then escape. We'll find Morsmani, Nom, and Guy and come back with our navy. If we fight now, we die."

Morrin retorted, "If we surrender, we're cowards. I'm not afraid to die."

Francis said, "Lower your bow, Morrin. Better to live to fight another day than die a needless death."

Morrin lowered his bow. The army marched up the steps led by a man wearing a bear skin. The bear paws rested on his hands and the bear's head hung behind his neck. On his head was a crown made of twisting goat horns connected by a gold band. He reached the summit, the blue tattoos outlining his skeleton shone darkly in the morning, as the large, skinny, conqueror towered over the three final defenders of Chinchiplas.

He smiled, stretching the large scar on his cheek, and said, "So this is the great southern city of Chinchiplas. Fabled for its unassailable walls. I'm a little disappointed, I must say. I expected more. There were no citizens to chase and murder. No children to make cry as their houses burn. There wasn't even any good looting. This city was a bore. I wanted massacres and hell fire. I wanted blood to run from the city's summit in waterfalls. But, I suppose that's what happens when your citizens desert you before battle. Did you like their heads? I figured you might want them back. I have the bodies somewhere too, if you want those. The crows picked at them pretty nicely though, so no telling who's who. Maybe Scagtower will provide more entertainment."

Quentin had heard enough. His anger rose above his depressed apathy and he grabbed his sword, Nagran's Fang. Bairne's soldiers tensed behind Bairne. Bairne gestured and the soldiers lowered their weapons. Quentin jumped from his throne and ran at Bairne. The conqueror threw something at Quentin's feet. Quentin slowed to avoid what was thrown at him. There were his parents' heads. Quentin stopped and fell to his knees. He felt empty, unreal.

"They fought my soldiers when we went to their tavern. They did not fight well," said Bairne.

Quentin looked up at his great enemy and stated in a hollow voice, "I surrender. The city is yours. My lands are yours."

Bairne laughed. "The city and lands were mine when I set foot here. What is your name, boy king?"

"I am Quentin Duluth, King of Chinchiplas, Kahoke, and the surrounding lands. I presume you are Prince Bairne?"

Bairne nodded, "Maybe my armies have moved too quickly for news of my new titles to reach you before me. I was prince when I united the northern tribes. I was king when I conquered a few cities. Now, I am Emperor Bairne, Lord of Eastern Usmer, and ruler of the first empire this world has ever seen. Oh, and for what it's worth, you aren't king of Kahoke, Chinchiplas, or any lands. You just ceded them to me, boy."

Bairne looked at the scowling faces of General Francis and Morrin. "Kill the extras," Bairne instructed.

Arrows flew from the invading army and struck Morrin and Francis.

Quentin yelled, "No!" and leapt to his feet, his shock replaced with anger. Bairne slapped the boy. The slap was not hard. It was a disdainful stroke which took all the fight out of Quentin.

The emperor said, "Do not tell me how to handle my fallen enemies. I will do as I please with them, as I will with you, boy."

*****

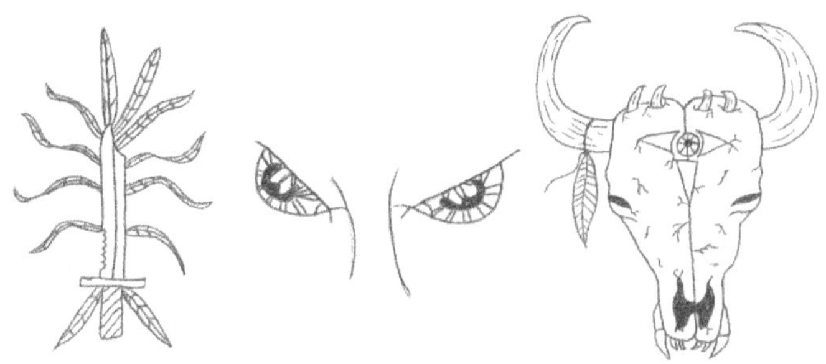

Chapter 22
Death's Final Judgement

Ghett was boisterous. The coming of the armies had sparked the interest of the people of Ghett as well as trade in the city. The streets, which were usually dusty, and empty, save for a few disheartened souls, were loud with the noise of merchants selling their wares and the soldiers laughing as they enjoyed themselves. The people of Ghett were on the edge of the world and were only ever visited by scags and the lowliest of merchants. With the isolation of Ghett and the lack of trade, it was difficult for the locals to leave. The new visitors were a welcome sight even if they harkened the threat of impending war. Nom and Azra wandered the streets in the early morning. The teenagers had been invited to the war meeting in Urbe and had decided to see the city before going.

They entered the main square. The square was busy with the last drunk soldiers leaving the taverns for bed and the first merchants setting up their stalls. In the corner of the square sat the stocks and gallows, and in one stock, sat a man covered in blue fur. Shatter Horn glared up at the noisy square from his wooden trap. Azra and Nom approached the buffscag and said hello.

"Hello to you too," replied Shatter Horn.

"What happened?" asked Azra.

Shatter Horn grumbled and replied, "Some humken called me and my ladies a bunch of blue bellied varmin last night."

"Why are you in the stocks then?" Nom asked in reply.

"Well, I told the humken that buffscag women are more graceful than the antelope galloping across the far plain. They are more awe inspiring than the golden eagles of the high mountains, more majestic than the buffkin herds galloping across the golden fields of grain. The humkins laughed at me and spat at my companions."

Nom and Azra waited for more of the story. When it seemed clear that Shatter Horn was only going to sit and stew Azra asked, "And then what happened?"

"I ripped out the offending humken's throat. Figured he wouldn't need it anymore." Shatter Horn said.

Azra stated, "You certainly aren't yellow bellied, but you have to admit your fur makes your belly blue."

The buffkin glared at Azra. "I am descended from the ilk of the proud buffkin. We buffscag are as far from vermin as lightning bugs from the sun. But I wouldn't expect a kitty cat like you to understand."

Azra narrowed her purple eyes and bared her teeth. "I am the Incarnate, watch yourself, Shatter Horn, lest I break your second horn."

"You are an untrained girl who can't yet talk to the ancestors. But you show the fire in your belly. I think we will be friends, young spirit dragon," Shatter Horn replied

Nom was appalled. "Are they putting you on trial for murder?" he asked.

Shatter Horn laughed. "No. I'm important for the war effort. Plus, this city won't miss one more drunkard. How's your trial going, young scagfriendken?"

"It is moving forward. I think I have a judgement. We, I mean Azra and I, are going to the war meeting. I assume you were invited?" Nom said.

Shatter Horn nodded. His one good horn clicking against the wood panels holding his head and hands. Azra's index finger erupted into blue flame. She moved the finger close to the leather strap which held the stock shut around Shatter Horn. Nom touched her shoulder and shook his head. He looked around the square for a guard. He spotted one talking to a potter as the potter set up his bright stall. Nom rushed over to the guard. His hand burned happily at the memory of Azra's warm skin. Azra was wearing a formal kajscag dress for the meeting. The dress was a blinding white sheet that fell to her knees. The top of the dress left her shoulders and arms bare. Loops of fabric went from the top edge of the dress to her elbows and jumped again to her wrists like falling cascades of bright mist from cool waterfalls. Skalla had whispered to Nom in the morning how the dress's arms looked like decaying, white, bat wings. Nom had scowled and silently disagreed. The dress had captivated Nom with its elegant beauty, although Nom suspected that his interest in the dress had more to do with who was wearing the clothing rather than with the clothing design itself.

Nom approached the guard and explained the situation. The guard looked from the boy in the strange armor covered in bird feathers to the locked up beast. Eventually the guard agreed and let Shatter Horn go with a warning to not cause any more trouble. The three of them headed toward Isengate.

*****

Nom, Azra, and Shatter Horn entered the council chamber of Urbe. The room had been difficult to find. Their guide through Urbe had walked fast and the visitors had quickly discovered that while the outside of the towers of Urbe were entirely glass, once you went out of range of those windows there was no lighting. Silver folken glow with a fluorescent silver light of their own. They do not need candles to find their way through the dark. Because of this, their buildings do not have torches or windows on the inside. Their guide rushed them to the council chamber, obviously miffed at letting foreigners into Urbe, especially scags. Nom, Azra, and Shatter Horn entered the room panting for breath.

Klart Bumble announced the newcomers to the room by saying, "Shatter Horn, leader of one of the eastern buffscag tribes. Nom Carver, representative of New Keys, and apprentice of Shinigorath. Azra of the tribe of Zarzasrahla, Incarnate, Protector of buffscags, chocobscags, kajscags, and beescags. Welcome."

As the newcomers sat down at the large round table Amy burst through the door.

"Sorry, am I late? I got lost in the shadows. There were no torches," She explained breathlessly.

Klart announced Amy. "Amy Milliken, Phoenix Titan of Shadows, Wife of Shinigorath, Granddaughter of the Maker, Penultimate Forbear. You are just in time."

Nom looked around the room as he sat at a large chair from which his feet could not reach the floor. Around the table sat the leaders of the scag tribes; Zarzasrahla, Korki, Shatter Horn, Azra, and others whom Nom had not met. Next to Zarzasrahla sat Guy Kahoke, the leader of Chinchiplas's navy, Amy, Shangri, Shangri's three artificers, Klart, the Silver Council members, and in the largest chair sat Kalli.

Kalli began the meeting. "Now, since everyone is here, tell us the plan for this war you've constructed for us Klart."

Klart smiled and replied, "Well, it isn't really a war, and I did not construct it. It was going to happen; I'm just nipping it in the bud. Because if it flowers, we lose. So, what Shinigorath and I have come up with, with the wonderful help of Lady Amy, of course," Klart nodded towards Amy, who smiled slightly, looked away and tapped the table, embarrassed. "is a battle of attrition. Obviously, the Terrestrial has the numbers, but we have the flexibility and better soldiers. So, we will meet his army outside the walls –"

"You mean on the walls? Why would we fight outside the walls?" Kalli interrupted.

"We have to draw Order here. He won't attack us if we hide behind walls. He will simply walk around the walls, which he is currently doing, and crush us. It only takes one person to fall to Order in a village for that village to fall, and he is very persuasive. He has no reason to fight a battle against encamped enemies."

"But he will attack us if we leave the walls? Won't he just ignore us if he can win without fighting?" Nom asked.

The table turned to the boy. Nom flushed and looked down at his feet.

"Who is this child, Klart? You bring a demon and two children to fight the god of order. You have always been strange, but I fear you may have lost your mind," Kalli said.

Amy stood up in anger. "Nom and Azra are fine soldiers and are here representing their people. Nom will not be in the battle, but it is Morsmani and I's wish for him to be here. He is much smarter than you would think."

Nom felt pride warm his chest as embarrassment warmed his dark cheeks to a dull red blush.

Klart answered Nom, "The Terrestrial would most likely ignore us, however on the south side of this city is a deep chasm with an ancient bridge across it. On the other side of the chasm sits Order's Monolith, the seat of the Terrestrial's power, the castle upon which he arrived to Usmer in, a shard of the God Spring. We will cross the bridge. To the Terrestrial we will appear to be making for his home, he will not allow that. He will meet us in force, both to protect himself, and to exact vengeance. We will force his hand to fight, and he will seize the opportunity as a chance to destroy us and make his plans happen that much sooner. We will make our stand on the bridge where his numbers mean little.”

Kalli snorted, “So your plan is to pretend to invade his lands and then hold his armies at the bridge? His army is massive, and powerful. Also, he does not care if his people die. His soldiers falling in battle is like having your hair shorn. He does not care.”

“True,” Klart admitted. “That is why it will be a battle of attrition. The only way to defeat the Terrestrial is to kill him. As long as he is alive, his numbers will continue to grow, his armies will continue to come. We must draw him out and kill him. If we destroy his armies in front of his home, he will meet us personally in battle, for his home is the key to his dreams. We hold his armies at the bridge. Once his army is in shambles, the Terrestrial will show his face. When that happens, we strip him of his power with The Fallen Star of Isen and kill him.”

One of the Silver Council members whispered, “So Shinigorath wasn’t lying. He really did intend to use Isen.”

Kalli glared at the council member and asked, “Who will wield Isen’s power? None here can, save the humans, and they lack the resolve.”

Klart held up his hands. “You would be surprised at the strength some the humans here have. Remember, Kalli, you were once human, but you were never weak. No, the original plan was that Shinigorath would wield The Fallen Star and kill his ancient enemy. He volunteered.”

“Won’t that kill him?” Asked Zarzasrahla.

Klart shrugged, “Isen might. But if Isen’s power kills Shinigorath, then it will surely kill the Terrestrial. And if it does not kill either, they will at least have a more even fight. So, that is my plan, just the upper level of it. If there are no objections I would like to get to the nitty gritty details of the battle.”

There were no objections. For the next few hours the leaders discussed how best to use their soldiers. Nom listened with great interest at first, but his mind began wandering. He looked over at Azra, who was listening with great care. Her eyes flashed back and forth as she tried to stay on top of the conversation. Nom caught himself staring at her purple eyes and the fall of her wavy red hair on her bare shoulders. He turned his attention back to the battle plans. His eyes soon wandered back to Azra.

Eventually the discussions ended, and the leaders of the assorted tribes and armies began to leave. Nom asked Kalli and Klart to stay so that he could ask them a few questions. Klart gladly remained. Kalli made a show of annoyance but agreed to stay behind.

Once the large room was empty Nom asked Kalli, "Kalli, you are the lawmaker in Ghett as well as Urbe, right?"

Kalli nodded, "I am. Why?"

"Shatter Horn killed a man last night and was placed in the stocks for a night. Why is he not on trial for murder?"

Kalli looked down her nose at Nom to show the boy that she thought it was silly for a child to ask her questions of how she ran her nation. She answered, "Shatter Horn is an honored guest, who we need for this war, and he is a buffscag."

Nom tilted his head. "What does being a buffscag have to do with anything?" He asked.

Kalli answered, "Buffscag are violent beasts. It does not surprise me that a buffscag male would kill someone who insults him. It is in their nature." When Nom continued to scowl, trying to think this over, Kalli added, "I would be pleasantly surprised if less than six of my citizens were killed by buffscags by the time the scags leave."

"So, you let him go because he is needed for the war, and it is in his nature to kill?" Nom asked.

Kalli nodded.

Nom said, "Yet you want to execute Shinigorath, who is much more important to the war effort and for whom it is also in his nature to kill. Buffscag may be violent, but Shinigorath is the god of death, and madness. His entire identity is that he kills and can not control his killing. Do you not see the hypocrisy?"

Kalli scowled, "It is not hypocrisy. Shatter Horn leads a tribe of powerful fighters, and he killed one person. Shinigorath leads you, a child who cannot fight, a dead woman, and an assassin. Shinigorath did not kill just one man. He murdered entire families, whole cities, the entire world. Billions have died at his hands."

Nom nodded, "I agree that he must be punished for burning the world."

Kalli said, "Good. You might not actually be that dumb."

Nom turned to Klart and asked, "Can we win the battle without Shinigorath?"

Klart smiled, "I've seen much of the future. We can win without him, but it is always a close thing, and leaves the world in dire straights for the coming conflicts. With Shinigorath our chances, while still slim, are better. Kalli, Shinigorath may not lead any troops, but he has time and time again singlehandedly defeated nations and armies. He defeated the Forbears at the height of their strength almost entirely on his own. He is worth three armies of ten thousand men, maybe more. Also, who else will wield Isen? Will you?"

Kalli snorted. "Who's to say that he won't run the moment we free him? And *will* he fight for us? He's also known as a trickster, and the silver folken and Shinigorath are ancient enemies. I fear he wants to destroy my people or take a shot at finishing off the last piece of the world, the only piece that survived his burning."

Nom piped up and said, "Those are fair concerns, and I do not know your history with Shinigorath, but I know he will not run, and he does not want to destroy anyone besides the Terrestrial. He has been preparing for this war since the world burned, and in that time, he has helped the people of Usmer survive. He created Chinchiplas by giving them his staff. He used the Golden Key to save Scagtower from drought. He helped Guy Kahoke and Deneth achieve their dreams. He cares about this world."

Kalli said, "Fine. You are the judge. Dismiss my concerns, even though I have lived fifty of your lives."

Nom replied, "Age does not give wisdom, experience does. You may be immortal, but underneath you are human just like the rest of us and have the same flaws as everyone else."

Kalli glared at Nom, who simply looked back at her expressionless. Finally, she stormed out of the room.

When the door slammed shut Klart laughed and said, "For someone who has so little experience you seem very wise, but not very prudent. Morsmani taught you well. Have you made your decision?"

Nom nodded, "I think I have. I want to see Morsmani one more time before the trial, but I think my decision is made. Do you want to know it?"

Klart shook his head. "No. Your decision is your own. I will not cloud your judgement with my thoughts. That is why you want to tell me, no? To see if I agree?" Nom blushed and looked down embarrassed. Klart continued, "Keep the decision to yourself. Knowledge like this, when told to others, spreads like wildfire. It is contained as easily as water in cupped hands. I believe you will make a good decision."

*****

In Urbe's prison Morsmani sat cross legged in his golden walled cell. Shini paced the cell, and Gorath sat next to Morsmani leaning forward nervously. Nom approached the cell and sat down on the other side of Isen's light. The prisoners were having a strange conversation.

Shini said, "That boy ain't right. He killed those people, all five of those families."

Gorath rebutted, "But he wasn't in his right mind, judge. He was angry, and confused, and the boys of those families attacked him."

"Those boys attacked him well before this boy sought revenge! That is no excuse," Shini said.

Morsmani looked over at Nom and nodded at the boy.

Nom asked, "What are you guys doing?"

Morsmani explained, "We're reenacting our first trial."

"What happened in your first trial?" Nom asked.

Gorath replied, "We lost."

Shini stated, "We died."

Morsmani said, "We were found guilty of killing five families, around 25 people, and sentenced to death. The Maker spirited us out of prison and gave us the powers of the gods after that."

Nom asked, "Why are you reenacting your first trial?"

Gorath explained, "We're preparing for this next trial. We're," Gorath glanced at Shini, "Morsmani and I are scared to death about this upcoming trial. So, we are preparing by reliving this old trial. I mean, we could either sit in terrifying, terrified, silence and think about this trial and that trial, and worry and fret about what will become of us at your hands, or we could just act out what we are already thinking about. Otherwise we'd fall into despair and panic and there'd be no way, no way, no way, for us to, I mean, there'd be no outlet for that despair. So, we avoid it by doing… by doing this."

Nom nodded. He did not really understand why they were doing what they were doing, but he agreed anyways.

"Did you kill those families?" Nom asked.

Shini shouted, "Rejection! We aren't on trial for those murders, we don't have to answer your questions about them."

Morsmani replied, "We did. The sentence was just."

Nom nodded again. He looked at Morsmani. This man, whom Nom had thought invincible, sat now in a prison cell awaiting a trial that may end in his death. Morsmani looked like a tired vagabond, not a powerful god. With sudden clarity Nom saw Morsmani not as the strange, powerful man that had taken him from New Keys, or the Promethean whom Nom had begun to see as a father figure and protector, but as an old and broken man. Nom saw Morsmani as the flawed person that he truly was. If the gap in age was smaller, if Nom was older, Nom would see Morsmani as an equal, and Nom felt pity.

"Do you have a sentence for us?" Morsmani asked.

"I do." Nom said. "But I wanted to see you first. I want you to know I do not hate you. And even if the sentence is a bad one, I still respect you. I guess, really, I wanted to thank you. You took me on an incredible journey, and I have met so many people and seen so many new things. You taught me so much. I am glad you brought me here, and I am sad that it has to end this way."

Morsmani smiled and said, "Thank you, Nom. Whatever your sentence is I will take it. Whatever your sentence is, it will be just. Do not be sad for me. In truth a small part of me is happy that I am finally being judged. I have tried to fix my crimes. I have tried to negate my sins by helping others, but no matter what I did I never felt like I was doing enough. I felt like I was hiding from justice, from penance, by hiding my name and face from all but my closest friends. Now, the world will judge me, and I will know if I am a god or a demon. Whatever your judgement is, Nom, I will gladly accept it, and maybe then my conscience can be at peace."

Nom stood up. He could not reply to Morsmani even if he knew what to say. He was choking on emotions. Nom quickly walked away, and when he was out of sight of Morsmani, Nom began to cry large tears of sadness and pity and anger. When he finished crying in the dark hallways of Urbe, Nom left. The trial was tomorrow at noon in Ghett's square. Nom did not feel prepared but had no idea of what to do to prepare.

*****

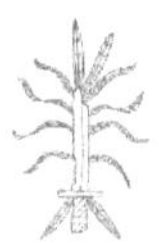

Ghett's main square was filled. The citizens and soldiers stood shoulder to shoulder from the base of the raised platform to the buildings that lined the square. Children sat on their parent's shoulders. Some people had climbed the buildings and sat on the roofs to watch the trial of Shinigorath. The Silver Council and Klart sat on chairs at the back of the raised platform. Nom stood in front of them. Morsmani was led out by a group of ten fully armed silver folken. A section of Isen's light stretched from the wall, arching over the city, and surrounded Morsmani, Shini, and Gorath like an amoeba's pseudopod.

The crowd cheered and jeered as Morsmani was led out. This time they were certain they would get to witness the death of a god. The crowd's blood lust filled the square with a tense energy and anger. Nom stepped forward.

"I have been tasked with judging and sentencing Shinigorath, the god of death, madness, and chaos. For the past few days I have interrogated the people that know Shinigorath best, both his friends and enemies. The crimes Shinigorath has committed are many and heinous. He will be punished for them, however, Shinigorath is necessary for our fight against the Terrestrial. Shinigorath has confessed to all his crimes and has promised to help us in our fight. For his help and cooperation against in the coming war, and the acts of kindness Shinigorath has performed since he burned the world, he will not be executed."

The crowd grumbled. Some people shouted up at Nom, demanding to know what punishment will be handed out. Nom waited for the crowd to quiet.

Once the crowd quieted, Nom continued, "Shinigorath will be banished from Usmer after the Terrestrial is defeated. He will live to the south of Isen's Wall until such time as the people north of the wall deem to forgive Shinigorath's crimes, if such a time comes to pass."

The onlookers stood silent. Then, they erupted into angry shouting. They had come for a show, and instead got to hear some politician give excuses. The crowd yelled at the Silver Council. Some threw food up at the raised platform. Nom was hit on the head by a toadstool. The scags in the crowd bellowed and began fighting the citizens of Ghett. Throwing food at a scagfriendken was akin to throwing food at a scag, and the scag tribes would not have that. A massive brawl was forming in the square. The silver folken guards lifted their hands. The dirt ground turned to thick mud. The people sank into the mud up to their knees. The silver folken lowered their hands and the mud turned back into hard, dry, dirt. The brawlers were stuck. Some still tried to fight each other. They threw punches at those nearest to them while trying to twist out of the dirt trap. Eventually all the fighting stopped. The silver folken went down to the square and released the people one by one.

*****

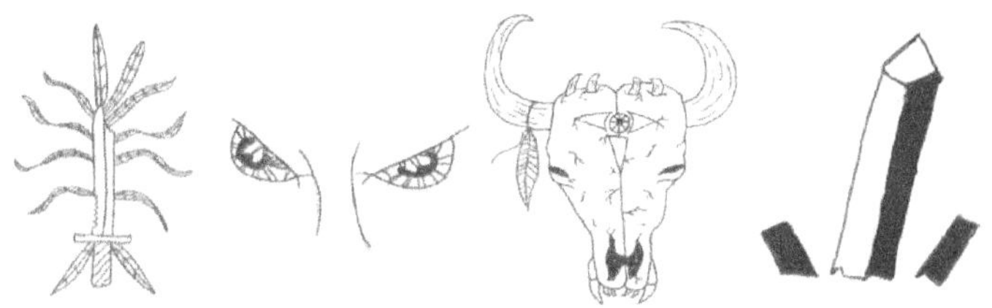

Chapter 23
Chaos and Order

It was the morning of the battle against the Terrestrial. Nom stood in the predawn dimness outside Urbe's southern gates. Isen's Wall had been taken down at midnight and all that remained where Isen's light had stood yesterday was a tall stone wall. Carved onto the southern face of the wall were great statues and images of warriors, representations of the people who protected the north from the terrors of the south. Nom stood beside Azra. Azra was dressed for battle. Adorned on her head was the Dragon Helm, the helmet that the Incarnates had worn into battle from time immemorial. The rest of her armor was the typical scag armor; leather vest to protect her chest and back, a knee length leather skirt with bronze plates to protect her legs and allow for movement. More bronze plates covered her arms, shins, and chest. Her hair spilled out from under her helmet making it appear as if the Dragon Helm was already on fire.

The scag tribes filed out of the city one by one. Each male tribal leader greeted Azra and continued to the battlefield in front of the bridge, which lay a hundred feet to the south. Nom noticed most of the scags' armor, which was made of hard leather and bronze like Azra's, was also adorned with bones. In a break from greeting tribal leaders, Nom leaned over to Azra and asked why there were bones on the armor.

Azra explained in between greetings, "The bones are for extra protection. Bones are hard and light, so we put them on our armor for extra protection. May the wind fly under you feathers, Anu," Azra said to a passing Chocobscag.

The chocobscag replied, "May your flame never waver, Incarnate."

Azra continued as the rest of chocobscagkin passed, "Also the bones are rather scary and show how great of a warrior you are. You can only get bones for your armor from fallen enemies, and you are only allowed one bone per fallen foe."

"Why only one?" Nom asked.

"Korki! Nice to see you. May your heart be as strong as your carapace." Azra greeted Korki as he passed.

Korki had his exoskeleton helmet lowered. He replied by rubbing his wings together to make a loud buzzing noise. "Azra, Beatrice bless you, good luck," the beescag said.

The beescags passed. Each of them rubbed their wings together as they passed, making the air hum. Azra could not answer Nom until the scag tribe passed. The next tribe was Zarzasrahla's.

"Father!" Azra exclaimed. Under her helmet she turned bright red. "Um, I mean, Zarzasrahla, may your claws be ever sharp, and may your feet never leave the wide plains."

Zarzasrahla laughed and hugged Azra. Nom could see Azra's eyes widen in surprise behind her helmet, then soften into contented happiness.

When she was released, Azra admonished, "I am the Incarnate, and we are preparing for battle! You can't hug me, father. It makes me look weak."

Zarzasrahla laughed again and replied, "This pomp and circumstance is silly. Its only purpose is to show that you are in power, and a good Incarnate does not need all this to show how powerful she is. Everyone already knows, Azra, so relax."

Azra nodded.

Zarzasrahla asked, "Is your armor tightened down? Did you sharpen your knives? Did you pray to the ancestors for protection?"

Azra sighed, "Yes. I did all of those things. Don't worry, and stop making a fuss, it's embarrassing. I'm not a child anymore." She glanced at the kajscags behind Zarzasrahla. They were all smiling and giggling. Azra clenched her fists in embarrassment.

Zarzasrahla smiled. "You may lead the scag tribes, but you are still young, and you will always be my daughter." Zarzasrahla left to the battlefield.

When Zarzasrahla turned away Azra quickly tightened down the straps on her gauntlets and answered Nom's question. "We are only allowed one bone per person, or beast, because any more and the bones will actually hurt you."

Nom looked confused, so Azra explained further, "The fallen warrior is obligated to protect you when you wear one of their bones as a token of defeating them in battle, however any more than one bone, and it upsets the dead and they haunt you until your death. The western tribes believe that taking more than one bone breaks the body apart too much and the soul cannot be reincarnated, which is why the soul of the deceased haunt you. Personally, I think the people who take more than one bone are simply cursed for being greedy. The dead's soul already left the body for its next life."

The last tribe came up to Azra. This was a northern buffscag tribe, who lived in remote woods far to the north. Their fur was shiny white, and thick.

Azra greeted the tribe leader by saying, "Moon Tooth, may your enemies be valiant, and may they lie at your feet."

Moon Tooth, who had a longer than normal fang curl down below his lower lip like a scythe, answered, "Incarnate, may your dragon fire burn the scags' enemies. May your fighting prowess be proven in the coming battles."

Nom watched the buffscags pass. He realized that the buffscags did not wear leather or bronze armor. The only armor they wore was bones tied together with twine. The youngest buffscags wore nothing, having never defeated an enemy, and therefore having no bones for armor. Luckily the buffscags' thick fur covered everything.

When the last scag passed, Azra turned to Nom. "I have to go, Nom," she said.

Nom asked as Azra turned away to leave, "Incarnate, are you scared?"

Azra looked at Nom over her shoulder and replied, her voice breaking with emotion, "Terrified."

Nom rushed over to Azra and hugged her from behind. Azra stiffened, and then relaxed. She turned around, breaking the hug, and took off her helmet.

"Be careful, okay? And good luck," Nom said.

Azra nodded. "Nom," she began, then faltered. Nom waited, standing in front of her. The feathers of his armor touched her leather armor when they stood straight in the breeze. Azra looked up at Nom. Her face was flushed, and her purple eyes sparked with emotion. Nom, looking in her eyes, saw fear there and something else. Azra leaned upwards, and in an instant that Nom could remember even unto his deathbed, her lips pressed against his. Azra stepped back and put her golden helmet on again. Nom stood there, his head a rush of thoughtless euphoria.

Azra laughed, her eyes glowed white behind the helmet and Beatrice and Azra spoke to Nom, "Nom, scagfriendken, may your wanderings be warmed by the hearths of your friends. May your journey end at the threshold of your home."

The girl turned and left for battle. The boy remained behind, forbidden from joining the fight. Nom watched her go. The horizon was turning a deep red in preparation for the sun's rising. The red light glinted off the small bit of bronze on Azra's armor, making her appear enshrouded in divine flame.

Nom went into the city to join Klart Bumble. Klart had told Nom that he was saving a spot on the walls for Nom to watch the battle with him. On the top of the walls, Nom found Klart talking with Amy and Morsmani. Nom realized, as he approached, that Klart looked so familiar to him because he was the old man who gave him his armor at the Shripwright's Dock. His memory had been sparked when he saw Morsmani and Klart talking on the wall, similar to how they had talked on the ship. As Nom approached, the Prometheans stopped talking and turned to Nom.

Morsmani, now dressed in his usual red scale armor with his helmet on his head, greeted Nom and said, "You can stay on the wall, but don't get in the way of the soldiers up here. If Order breaks through our army and comes to the wall, defend it. Hopefully that won't happen."

Nom nodded, then said, "Morsmani, I'm sorry for –"

"The silver folken are assembling." Morsmani interrupted. "We have to go, Amy. Klart, watch the boy. Nom, stay safe."

Amy hugged Nom and then walked off the wall with some hesitation. Shadowy stairs descended under her as she walked down to the ground.

Morsmani stepped up onto the wall's parapet and said to himself, "Shini, where does death lay claim, and linger?"

Wings of flame erupted behind Morsmani as Shini replied, "The battlefield."

Morsmani said, "Gorath, where does madness breed best?"

Black shadow enshrouded Morsmani in a cloud as Gorath replied, "The battlefield."

Morsmani hefted his hammer, the Golden Key, above his head and asked, "Where is chaos king?" Then, he jumped from the wall. Amy caught him in a net of shadow and lowered him to the ground.

Nom peered over the wall. At the entrance of the bridge, stood the ancient war beast the scags had brought with them. The machine was covered in steel plating. In a few sections where the steel had been damaged, the scags had placed bronze plates. Unlike The Beatrice that Nom had ridden across the Sand Sea this beast's outer walls were vertical. When the legs of the beast were retracted the machine sat flat on the ground and rose thirty feet, making it an unassailable tower. Around the war beast stood the wingless scags and humans. The chocobscags, beescags, and Azra stood on the edge of the cliff, prepared to fight in the air. Behind the scags and humans stood the silver folken. Nom had no idea how well the silver people fought. The leaders of the various factions were ordering their soldiers into position and explaining the battle plans.

Nom watched for a time. The early morning air was filled with energy. It felt the same to Nom as the air before the hurricanes back home. In his childhood, he would rush outside to see the black clouds roll towards his village over the darkened waves. There was never any wind or noise. All the things of the world had hidden themselves from the anger of the coming storm. His mother would yell from their house to come inside. Nom would ignore her for a few moments as he stood in the silent sense of doom which overcame the world before great storms. The still, heavy air carried upon it the warnings and fear of impending death, and the inky blackness under the clouds whispered of the wrath hidden in its depths. That is how this morning felt, except instead of dark clouds on the horizon there was a strange slanting tower on the other side of the chasm, and instead of fear and anger there was fear and excitement.

Nom looked across the chasm at Order's Monolith. The tower, which appeared to be made of a single piece of obsidian, jutted out of the ground at a steep angle. If Nom did not know better, he would say that the tower looked like it had been thrown there like a javelin by some giant. The tower, even at its strange angle, rose higher than Scagtower. It loomed over the southern field, casting a dark shadow. Nom did not like the look of the south. To the south of the chasm was a dry field with small, brown bushes. Ancient buildings made by the Forbears dotted the field in the distance. They were squat, square, grey buildings that were slowly decaying. As Nom watched, he saw figures wandering north towards the bridge.

As the armies of Order began amassing, Nom turned to Klart and asked, "Why do you not end the fighting? You could simply go to Order's Monolith and kill the Terrestrial, right? Why not do that instead of watching all these soldiers die?"

Klart sighed, "I've been asked that many times, and have as many answers. Last time I fought I killed my only son. That is not the reason why though. I could win this battle with a snap of my fingers. If all of the Prometheans joined together and fought me, they would all die before I even began breaking a sweat. It would be easy to order the world the way I want it to be through force. However, that is no way to make the world. Do you know why I am considered to be the king of the gods?"

"Because you are the strongest, and because you lead the Prometheans," Nom replied.

Klart shook his head. "I am the strongest, but that is not why I am called king. I am not the wisest, or smartest, or most popular. Those titles belong to others. No, I am trusted. I see the future, Nom. The future stretches out from this moment in a million twisting paths. Each path branching into a million more. I discern which paths are the most likely to occur, and which is the best to take. Then, I move the necessary pieces to make that path even more likely to occur. So far, my schemes and plans have turned out for the better, so the Prometheans trust my judgement and follow my advice when I give it. The mortals fear my power, so I have others deliver my advice to them. It would be easier if I simply forced the world into the shape I want it, but I have seen those futures. They are not bright futures. They are futures of a world darkened by slavery and fear. A world I rule with iron."

Nom thought about this, then said, "But if you only use force sparingly, like for this battle, then those futures might not happen."

Klart shrugged, "You may be right. The future is variable and ruled by probability. There is a level of randomness to what happens. But I will not risk it. In all of the futures it starts with what you suggested. I step into a situation and win through force. Then, at some point in the future another situation arises similar to the first. Again, I step in, this time there is less debate, less doubt, in my mind whether I should or not, and I win even more easily than before. Each time after that I hesitate less and less before intervening, and I intervene in more and more trivial problems. Problems I could solve through guidance and advice I instead solve through a show of force. Eventually I lose myself and rule everything as an immortal, tyrannical, god king. That is not a future that I, or any good person, want. So, I avoid the situation entirely by not fighting, only watching."

The figures on the far side of the chasm had grown in number. They stood watching the armies amass. In their midst, like torches, stood fire tyrors, the generals of Order's armies.

"Why do they not attack? Why are they just watching?" Nom asked.

"Because the Terrestrial does not know what we are going to do. Morsmani has hidden our minds from him. Oh, look, the armies are ready. Please excuse me for a moment, Mister Carver, I have to address the troops."

*****

Chapter 24

Passing of the Staff

"I'm giving you away," Quentin said to Shinigorath's staff.

Quentin had awoken on the last day of the Age of Chaos to knocking on his door. He had been called to see Bairne while he was under house arrest. Quentin looked around his family's old estate. The tavern was empty now. Motes of dust floated around the large room. The invaders had left Green Light Tavern and Inn unharmed except for the famous light outside. That, they had smashed when three men had tried to take the green lantern at the same time. Anything of value had also been taken. Luckily the looters had left Shinigorath's staff. When the tavern was ransacked, the staff had transformed back to its original twisted shape. The looters must have seen the staff and left it thinking that taking such an evil looking totem would bring bad luck.

"I'm giving you away," Quentin said again. "But only for a little while. I'm giving you to a man who destroyed the family you belonged to, a man who I don't think will understand the lesson you teach. For Bairne, you will be only a curse upon him, and if he learns your lessons and tames you then he is a better man than I thought."

"I will still hate him." Quentin whispered into the empty air.

Taking the staff, Quentin left the tavern. His guards led him through the city to the docks. The city was quiet. The few people that wandered the streets were soldiers, the soldiers' women, and women who would become a soldier's woman for a bit of time and a bit of money. The houses built of wood had been burned. The heads of the defenders of Chinchiplas adorned the streets on spikes. Quentin had been forced to watch the ritual sacrifice of the surviving defenders. The northern priest, dressed in a skirt of animal bones with great elk antlers on his head, had cut out the hearts of the prisoners. The hearts had all still been beating. Blood covered the priest's tattoos of the gods he communed with as he raised the hearts one by one and proclaimed them as offerings to the gods and spirits. First to the spirit of the goat, then the bear, boar, and whale. Then hearts were offered to Ruhk, Shinigorath, Gold, Hort, Myco, and many others. Quentin wondered if the gods knew about the sacrifices. He wondered if the spirits and gods actually appreciated the offering or were indifferent to the suffering of mortals. The bodies were tumbled down the Palace steps.

They had arrived at the docks. The Monument of Order still stood. Bairne had forbidden his men from walking near the monument. Quentin wanted to tie the northern king to the obsidian monolith and watch Bairne go mad. The docks were busier than the city. Ships were coming and going, delivering and taking supplies. The navy supplied Bairne's armies with necessary items like food, armor, and reinforcements. Bairne stood at the edge of the dock, looking into the dark, twisted swamp, munching a chicken leg.

The guards approached Bairne and, slamming their spears on the ground, announced, "Quentin Duluth, last king of Chinchiplas."

Bairne turned around. He was still wearing his bear skin coat and goat crown even in the sweltering southern heat. He was not wearing a shirt under the bear skin. His torso was covered in blue tattoos that traced the bones that stuck out of his emaciated form. He looked down at Quentin, took a bite of his drumstick, and smiled.

"Quentin, King of Nothing, how is the house? In order I assume? How do you like what I've done to the city? I haven't had much time to fix it up unfortunately. Hell, I might not fix it. I might leave it as is. A reminder of what happens to those who challenge me. A warning that even the strongest city will fall before my empire. I might ransom it to the Tommy Knockers. Those dwarrows have had their sights on Chinchiplas for a long time. But I digress. Quentin, my boy, what lives in the swamp?"

Quentin was taken by surprise by the question. Why would Bairne care about the things in the swamp? What did he want to know? Quentin wondered if he should tell Bairne that the spirits of the crocodile and snake lived in the swamp, that Nagran still roamed the deep waterways, or that the humans who died in the swamp never truly rested but wandered at night.

"Many things live in the swamp. Not even the wisest of men know all the secrets hidden there," Quentin finally answered.

Bairne waved his drumstick. "I know that, boy. It's the same everywhere. No one knows anything. We're all just guessing. That's what happens when you kill the people who did know everything."

"Who were they?" Quentin interrupted.

Bairne's eyes narrowed. He did not like being interrupted. "The Forbears," he said. "They knew everything, that's why they could fly without wings, and they could curse the ground to lie fallow and poisonous for a thousand years. Next time you interrupt me your heart will be offered to Backbone so you can learn some manners, and your skull will be my new chamber pot. Actually, no, if your head was my chamber pot, then nothing would change about it. Your head would still be full of shit." Bairne paused to let his sentiment sink in. The guards sniggered quietly behind Quentin. Then he continued, "My soldiers have reported strange sightings in the swamp. They say the swamp seems angry and quiet. Are there creatures in the swamp that give your people trouble?"

Quentin frowned. "The zorscags sometimes raid our lands. They might be preparing for another raid since my people are gone."

Bairne spit on the ground. "Scags!" he exclaimed. "Disgusting beasts. It will be a grand day when I take Scagtower from them. Thank you for the answer. I don't think we have much to worry from some swamp scags. Well, in that case I'll head back to Kahoke."

Quentin and his guards walked, followed by Bairne, to the city side of the docks when Quentin remembered the staff.

"Um, excuse me, Emperor Bairne, I have a gift for you. To show my allegiance to your empire. I see now how powerful you are and how it was futile to fight you," Quentin explained.

Bairne stopped. Quentin and his guards took a few more steps before they stopped. Bairne's back was facing the water.

"What is this gift?" Bairne asked.

Quentin replied, "It is Shinigorath's staff, sir. This is my family's oldest heirloom and the secret to our wealth. It summons chinchillas."

Bairne's eyes lit up. "Oh!" he exclaimed. "That's how you do it. I've been looking for chinchillas everywhere since I arrived and saw none." Bairne took the twisted staff from Quentin and peered at it. "A bit ugly, no? Oh, there's one!"

A muddy, unkempt chinchilla had appeared at Bairne's feet. Bairne leaned down to peer at the rodent. His nose wrinkled at the animal's smell, but he did not seem to mind too much.

Quentin smiled. *'Eventually,'* he thought, *'Bairne would be tired of the smell and probably, hopefully, overrun by chinchillas.'* The emperor would call Quentin to help with the rodent problem and Quentin would feign ignorance of the issue. Bairne would order Quentin to deal with the chinchillas. Quentin would then have to stay near the emperor, which would allow him a position to either become a court member, or more likely, assassinate Bairne. Even if none of that transpired, Bairne would at least be cursed.

Quentin looked out at the swamp, happy in his scheming. He saw dark skinned, feathered figures crawling up the sides of the docks. Small reed canoes shot out of the trees and capsized a northern longboat. The figures on the docks killed two of Bairne's men. One of the men screamed as he fell. Bairne turned around and stepped forward, his axe in hand, his chicken leg discarded on the ground.

"Those aren't zorscags, boy!" he yelled at Quentin. "Those are chocobscags!"

"No, your majesty, they have feathers on their clothes. They're humans," a guard said.

Quentin looked at the newcomers on the docks. Bairne's men were rushing forward and engaging the intruders. More feathered men were swarming out of the swamp. Quentin recognized the feathered armor. It was the same armor Nom wore, and the newcomers had dark skin like Nom.

Quentin yelled, "They are soldiers from the New Keys Kingdom!"

Bairne grunted. "I care not where they hail from. If they come to my lands with violence in their hearts, they will soon learn of my charity."

The New Keys soldiers fought silently against the northerners. Many fell on both sides. Bairne yelled some commands and his men fell back, making a shield wall. The New Keys soldiers stood still, looking dazedly at the northern soldiers. Behind them, out of the swamp's muck, crawled women and children. The children held knives, and the women held bows.

The people of New Keys said in unison, "Look, Quentin Duluth, I have arrows now too."

As the arrows were placed on bowstrings the fallen New Keys fighters stood up. They bled upon the docks, but showed no pain.

"What devilry is this?" a soldier in front of Quentin whispered.

The New Keys soldiers ran forward. They slammed against the shield wall. Axes, spears and swords pierced and hacked the attackers who did not fall back but pressed forward. The shield wall broke.

Quentin watched in horror. He turned to Bairne and yelled, "We have to leave! These are soldiers of the Terrestrial. He's making his move. We will not win here. You have to man the city walls. They won't be able to break through Chinchiplas's defenses, not with your large army here."

Bairne opened his mouth with a scowl, then he closed it again. He looked at the mad brawl down the docks. He saw soldiers fighting with their entrails trailing behind them. He saw children stabbing men. He nodded and turned to the city. He did not run. He walked briskly to the gates into the city surrounded by his guard. Quentin followed. As they approached the city, a horn sounded from the other side of Chinchiplas.

"Sir, the landward gate is under attack!" a soldier exclaimed.

"I know the signal, nitwit!" Bairne replied.

Two more blasts came from the landward gate. Bairne began running. They entered the city and Bairne ordered all of his men to the higher levels of the mound. Quentin quickly surmised that the two blasts signaled the gate had fallen.

Quentin ran up the spiraling slope that led up the mound city. He looked down and saw the city streets below him swarming with feathered men and women. The attackers were silent as they ran through the streets. They did not loot or burn any buildings. They simply ran forward, intent on destroying the city's inhabitants. Quentin shuddered.

'This', he thought, *'Was what Morsmani and Shangri had warned against. If only I had listened.'*

As Quentin approached the topmost level he was stopped by men behind a makeshift barricade.

"It's one of them!" A soldier shouted.

An arrow landed at Quentin's feet and Quentin shouted back, "No, no, don't shoot! I am one of you, not one of them. I am free! I am free!"

Another arrow whistled by Quentin. Quentin, figuring the soldiers would never believe him, and not blaming them for doing so, ducked into a tunnel leading into Chinchiplas. Inside the tunnel, Quentin leaned against the wall. Soldiers ran past the tunnel entrance. The city was alive again with terror.

"I have to get a weapon and get out of here," Quentin whispered as he tried to catch his breath.

He ran further into the tunnel and headed down into subterranean Chinchiplas. He was running to a place where he figured he could find some sort of weapon and armor, Lichtenfrumph's forge.

Quentin burst into the forge and ran to the empty weapons rack. The place had been ransacked. There were no weapons or armor here. Outside in the hallway Quentin heard footsteps coming closer. He peaked out the door and saw feathered silhouettes coming down the tunnel. He ducked back in and began barricading the door with the weapons rack and loose pieces of iron.

As he was pushing the anvil to the door's base someone behind Quentin said, "Quentin, don't hurt my anvil, please."

Quentin whirled around and threw a small piece of raw iron at the voice. A slight, ghostly figure dodged the projectile and threw his hands up in gesture of peace. The figure was Lichtenfrumph.

"Please leave my forge alone. You'll attract Bairne's men here with all that noise," the smith complained.

"What are you doing here?" Quentin asked. "I thought you would be spared, since Bairne is allied with the Tommy Knockers."

Lichtenfrumph shook his head. "I would be spared, yes," he explained. "But, I am the only person outside The Spine Mountains who knows how to make Knocker steel. I would be tortured until I revealed the secret, and I'm afraid I wouldn't last long under the torturer's knife. I would probably spill everything if Bairne just looked at me funny, you know? So, I hid in my secret room, where I keep my iron. Or, well, where I used to keep my iron until it was stolen by the brick makers. Now it's a big empty room. But, if I talk it echoes, so I can make whole conversations in there. The conversations are a little one sided at times, but they honestly are pretty similar to real conversations. It's not too bad."

"All your conversations are a little one sided, Lichtenfrumph," Quentin said. "The Terrestrial's army is here. They broke through the gates and are taking the city. We have to get out of here. Do you have any weapons or armor?"

Lichtenfrumph looked alarmed. He disappeared down a trap door and reappeared with two swords and two shields.

"These are what I've got. I was hoping to use both swords at the same time. It would look so cool as I battled my way out of here. I know it's a difficult technique to do well, but since I have no technique anyway, I might as well go for style. I won't make it either way. But, with you I might make it! I'll hide behind you as you attack, okay? How did Order's army get here? Did the silver folken lose already?"

Quentin answered, "The Terrestrial is using the people of New Keys. It looked like the entire kingdom is attacking us, even children."

"Children? Like, teenagers, because Tommy Knockers sometimes have teenagers join the gladiatorial contests to see their strength."

Quentin stared at the loquacious Tommy Knocker and said, "I saw a child of no more than five cut a man's achilles tendon. Order has even the babies fighting. Come on, let's go."

The man and the Tommy Knocker moved the barricade out of the way. They stood inside the door gathering their strength for the fight to come. Neither had much hope for survival. Quentin's face was set in determination, Lichtenfrumph was sweating. Outside, the corridor was quiet, but fighting could be heard far above them. They burst open the door and ran out of the tunnel, into the street. The sun blazed, reflected off the white walls of Chinchiplas.

The city was silent. Quentin looked around. The people of New Keys were everywhere. There were hundreds of them, both above and below Quentin. There was no escape. Quentin lunged at the nearest islander. The black skinned islander did not defend himself. Quentin's blade slid easily into the man, who slumped to the ground silently. Quentin raised his sword ready to strike when the man rose again. The man did not rise. None of the islanders attacked. Quentin looked around. The islanders stood silent and still. Their dark faces were blank. The few who had wounds slowly slumped and fell, succumbing to their hurts.

"What happened?" Lichtenfrumph asked.

Quentin shook his head. He did not know. Suddenly the followers of Order screamed in unison and dashed to the edge of this level of Chinchiplas. Quentin and Lichtenfrumph rushed to the edge of the level and looked down. Below them, above them, and throughout the entire city the army of Order was chaotically killing themselves. Thus, heralded the Age of Order.

*****

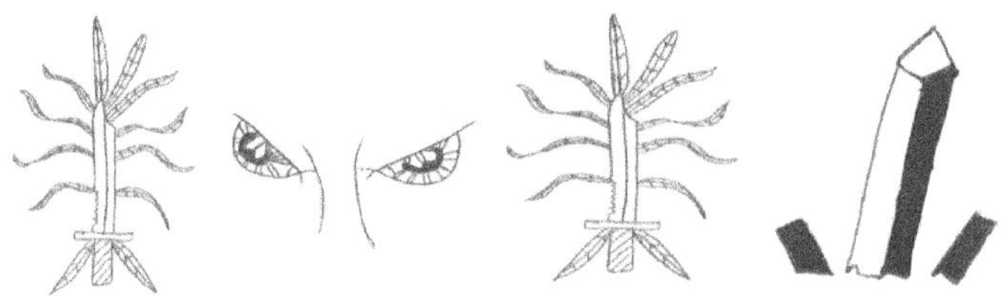

Chapter 25
Breaking of the Gods

At the bottom of the chasm that separated the lands of the Prometheans and the land of Order, ran a swift river. In the gloom of early morning the water rose. The white crests of the rushing rapids rose to form a dome, and then the head of Klart Bumble. The disembodied head, ten times larger than Klart's real head rose up through the chasm and perched, floating, in front of the armies of scags, humans, and silver folken.

The head opened its mouth, and Klart's voice boomed out as large in proportion to Klart's normal voice as the head was to Klart's normal head.

The head said, "Come Prometheans, and others of great power. Stand beside me and look upon the soldiers willing to fight for your cause. Look upon the men and women who are willing to die for your war, your fight. Without them, we are nothing but wandering ghosts. They are the world, and for them we wage this war."

Into the air rose the Prometheans and Amy. Azra fluttered next to Klart's head on wings of fire, Myco soared lazily as a pink cloud of spores, Shangri stood as firmly as ever far above the chasm floor, Amy and Shinigorath were lifted invisibly into the air by Klart. They floated in front of the armies. Behind them, the Terrestrial was gathering his men.

Klart continued, "Men, scagkin, and silver folken, gathered here in the greatest alliance since the Golden Council waged war against the demon, Red, look to the south. See the armies of Order and know there is no army. All but the tyrors you see there are one person, the Terrestrial. If we lose today, we will all be the Terrestrial. We fight today for our freedom, and the freedom of our families, our wives, husbands, and children. We fight for our friends, our neighbors, and those closest to our hearts. Will we disappoint them?"

The armies shouted back, "No!" They banged on shields and hollered at the procession of gods before them.

When the noise died, Klart continued, "This war is not a war of gods. This war is a war of the world. You will fight besides the gods and against the gods. Show us, you mortals, that you are worthy of standing beside us! Prove that you can protect this fragile world! Prove that you are each as strong as any god!"

The army screamed back. Shields were pounded, spear butts beat the dirt, buffscags pounded their chests with closed fists. Klart's head fell back to the river in a cascade. The Prometheans floated back to land. Across the chasm stood Order's army, silent, stoic. Not a sound came from them. The thralls stared across the bridge expressionless. Their silence quieted the northern armies and made them feel uneasy. In the early morning silence, fire tyrors stepped to the forefront of Order's thralls, each a burning soul amongst a singular sea of one mind and body. The tyrors growled. Their growling, like tumbling lava flowing from mountain peaks, swept over the chasm and sent shivers down the northerners' spines.

Then the thralls spoke in one voice, "Silence, my fiery servants. Come now, people of the north, why must we fight? You scags, join me and I will show you true equality, for none stands above another in my kingdom. And for you humans, I can grant you immortality, and the freedom from pain. And you silver folken, seekers of knowledge, I can show you the far reaches of the heavens. I can reveal to you the dark face of the sun, and you will see Usmer as a blue pebble in an inky infinity. Join me and you will all become as gods. Fight and you will die like moths to a flame."

A moment of silence. Then, from the war beast came the creaking of turning axles and hundreds of mechanical feet stamping upon the ground. The war beast moved to the front of the bridge and began making its way across. On the top of the moveable tower stood two beescag tribes, Korki's and another's. Their soldiers held up bows. Order's army began marching forward. The bridge fit five men shoulder to shoulder, and the war beast had been modified to fit the entire width of the bridge. As the army approached the beast, the beescags stopped pedaling. The war beast stood still, and then its feet were pulled up. The beast was now a tower in the middle of the bridge blocking any further movement of Order's army.

Order stood still, looking at the tower. Three fire tyrors burst forth from the ranks and sprinted at the war beast. Flames burst out in front of them in large gouts. The fire licked the beast and died in whisps of smoke. The metal sides of the tower resisted the flames. The beescags on the top of the tower peppered the tyrors with arrows. Two tyrors died at the base of the tower. The third turned and ran. Two arrows bit into his back and, as he reached Order's army, another tyror stepped forward and killed him with a blow to the head. Red light escaped the dying tyrors and dispersed into the remaining tyrors, making each that much more powerful.

Ladders and grappling hooks made their way to the front of Order's army. Then, Order moved forward. The thralls ran a steady pace toward their obstacle. Arrows rent the ranks, yet the thralls did not stop. They felt no pain and would fight through injuries until they bled out. The only thralls that fell and stayed fallen were the ones unlucky enough to have their skulls split and their brains spilled, or the ones who bled out and had no more energy. The ladders went up the walls. The grappling hooks arced over the parapets. The beescags repelled the ladders and cut the ropes. This continued for some time, until Order retreated.

The northern armies cheered. They had won the first clash. Nom, watching from Isen's Wall wondered what would happen next. They needed the Terrestrial to come out in order to win. Would the scags move forward?

Large planks and poles were now passed to the front lines of Order's army. Ropes and chains were tied to the ends of the poles. Order moved forward again. The thralls on the sides of the bridge ducked down and hung off the sides, over the abyss. The walls on either side of the bridge had long ago fallen into the river below. The thralls shimmied against the sides of the bridge. When they reached the war beast, the thralls on the bridge passed them the poles as they were shot full of arrows. The poles were inserted under the sides of the war beast. Once they were inserted securely the thralls quickly jumped onto the poles and ran to their ends. Once there, the thralls, using blunt weapons, pounded the poles further under the war beast. Many thralls fell. More poles were inserted until both sides of the war beast bristled. Thralls piled onto the poles and hung off them precariously. Scag and human archers stepped up behind the war beast and shot any thralls who attempted to use the poles as a way to circumnavigate the tower. The thralls on one side of the beast jumped on their poles. As they came down the other side jumped. Thralls began crawling down the ropes and chains which hung off the poles and began applying their weight in unison with the jumping. The war beast began to shudder and then tilt to the jumping.

Nom saw a bright light leap from the near side of the chasm into the air. Azra had given wing and was now shouting to the scags. The remaining beescags and the chocobscags took to the air behind Azra. Shangri soon followed. The flying defenders peppered the sides of Order's army and attempted to stop the thralls on the poles. But for every thrall that fell two more came forward. Myco, growing gargantuan mushroom stocks, created pathways from the chasm sides that allowed the northern army to attack the thralls from the sides in pincer moves. Fire tyrors lit the mushroom stocks on fire. Nom heard Myco screaming in pain as her mushrooms wilted and charred under the embroiling flames.

The war beast shook. It rattled from side to side. It swayed like a ship in tall waves. The thralls scrambled on the poles like ants climbing tree branches to find food. Then, with a shatter, the war beast tipped too far and tumbled into the chasm. The beescags on the war beast screamed as they fell. The thralls were silent in their deathly plummet, cast off like nail clippings by the Terrestrial. Most of the beescags took wing as they fell but were met on the ascent by the spears, arrows, and fire balls of Order's army. None made it back to the bridge alive. They met their end in the rapids far below. Nom shuddered, and tears appeared in his eyes as he watched Korki fall.

Order surged forward, his army running in silent unison across the bridge. The silver folken stepped forward for their turn in the fight. They lined the side of the chasm and raised their hands. As their hands rose, the wall underneath Nom shook. Nom looked down over the edge of the wall and his breath caught in his throat. The wall was moving. The statues of warriors carved into the side of the wall were moving. They twisted in the stone and broke free. For the first time since the Red Gold Conflict, the golem army of the silver folken marched into battle.

The stone golems ran toward the bridge. Shinigorath's Pet, the first golem and one of only two golems to ever gain sentience, led the army across the bridge to meet the coming army. The rushing thralls and thundering golems met in the middle. Pet kept the battle silent using his own magic and his hatred of noise. For the silver folken controlling their golems from the edge of the chasm, the fight was quiet. For those further away the magic was lost, and the battle was a tumult of shuddering stone. There were golems of all shapes and sizes, from golems the size squirrels, who incapacitated their foes by hamstringing and cutting heels, to golems thirty feet high and wielding stone clubs that weighed as much as a full grown buffscag. As the golems and Order clashed in the bridge's center, the flying scags and Prometheans continued their bombardment of the thralls. Order answered with archers of his own on the far chasm side. A few fire tyrors tossed balls of flame at the flyers.

The golems began to gain ground. The stone armor of their flesh ran down to their very cores and even the fine steel and tungsten weapons of the thralls could do no more than barely scratch the unfeeling golems. The thralls fell to the golems, but Order did not retreat this time. This time he stood his ground. The thralls died, crushed under foot as the golems moved forward. Then, like a flame of doom, a squadron of fire tyrors stepped forward to the front of the army.

The tyrors unleashed an onslaught of fire that would make even the strongest of dragons envious. The flames wrapped themselves about the golems. The bellowing flames sounded like hurricane winds blasting through the tropical branches of Nom's old home. They scorched the bridge and made the air waver like desert mirages about the fight. Pet, unable to hold back the deafening sound of roaring conflagration, let out a scream which pierced every watching heart with utter fear and terror. He ran from the fight. The small, white marble golem, only the height of a man, pushed his way through the golem army to the end of the bridge. There he sat down and made the world around him silent.

The remaining golems moved forward into the heat. Before they could reach the tyrors however, they began breaking. The great limbs of living stone hardened, crystalized, and cracked. The golem army fell to gravel and boulders. After a few minutes of struggling, all that remained of the silver folken's offensive was a short wall of loose stone in the center of the bridge. The fire tyrors moved forward.

Azra and Shangri alit on the bridge. The three artificers ran up behind their teacher and pointed crystaline staffs at the top of the rubble pile. The tyror's mounted the new wall and sent hellfire down upon the five defenders of freedom. Azra and Shangri, using the dragon's familiar stone which he had shown to Quentin, redirected the flames away from the artificers. The artificers raised their staffs. At the top of each staff was set blue diamonds, each taken from one of Backbone's krakens. Water spouted out of the staffs and struck the tyrors, who stumbled back.

The defender moved up the wall. The tyrors, their flames subdued and dying from the deluge of water, retreated. The slower tyrors were completely snuffed out by the water jets. The free people of the north cheered and rushed forward to help the artificers and The Incarnate. Nom flushed with pride and a little voice in his head whispered happily, *'I know her.'*

The armies of the north gained the wall of rubble. They hurled insults and blows down upon the thralls. The different races of Usmer had forgotten their pride and prejudice against one another in the heat of battle. Silver folken fought shoulder to shoulder with scags and humans. Order backed away again. Silence enveloped the battlefield.

"They have to move forward," Nom stated. "If they do not attack, the Terrestrial will give up the fight and we will lose our chance, right?"

Klart looked down at the boy and nodded. "Do not worry, King of Kings. Your mentor believes in this plan. Watch."

Nom looked back over the battlements and saw Morsmani pushing his way through the tightly packed army. He reached the top of the wall, the horns on his helmet glowing like rays of the sun. He lifted his tomahawk and brought it down upon his left palm. He put the tomahawk away on the belt of his red scale armor, placed his blood on his summoning tattoo, and took his hammer from its place upon his back. He held aloft the golden hammer with both hands.

"Come forth, Gold, god of war! Though you withered and died in far lands, saving your mountain kin from darkness, come back now for a final fight and a lasting sleep! Give in once more to your anger, to your fighting spirit, and join me! Take your hammer back from your friend and drive it through the chest of my enemies!"

The hammer crashed to ground and from it erupted golden light. Next to Morsmani stood a mountain of a man, his skin as golden as the silver folkens' was silver. He stood a head taller than all the army, save the buffscags. Gold beamed out at the bridge and let out a wild yell of jubilation. He lifted his own copy of the Golden Key and rushed down the rock pile. The army followed him screaming triumphantly.

Order fell to the onslaught. Thralls were swept like chaff upon the wind from the bridge. Morsmani, using the scythe side of his hammer cut through their ranks, a farmer harvesting his stock. Gold's hammer blew away the enemy army like the sudden mountain winds that fell entire forests. The few thralls that survived the gods were picked off by the following army. They reached the end of the bridge.

The army spilled over onto the other side where they were stopped. Here, on the far side of the bridge, Order's numbers finally counted. Thralls surrounded the attackers in a semi circle. Spears, swords, and arrows rained down from three sides and the northern army was quelled. The free folk lost ground, then hope, and then, finally, retreated to the bridge where they held strong. Morsmani and the shade of Gold were separated and tried to fight back to their army. Nom leaned forward gripping the wall. He hoped with all his heart that the army would surge forward again. It did not. The free folk lost more ground. They were pushed back to the top of the rubble wall, and then further. Their numbers were now reduced by three quarters and there seemed to be no hope left. Then from behind the thralls rushed Morsmani and Gold. They took back the top of the wall.

In the ebb of the battle which followed, Azra alit next to Morsmani. Her eyes and her markings glowing brilliantly white. She said something to Morsmani, who scanned the badly beaten army and nodded. He turned to the thralls and took out his tomahawk again. He slashed his chest. Blood erupted from him and as it fell like rain upon the remains of the golem army, shadows appeared amongst the rocks. Dark shades crawled from every crack and crevice.

The dead spirits rushed forward. The thralls answered. For every shade that fell two more arose. The shades had no weapons or armor. They tackled the thralls and took their weapons as their own. The sight was terrifying. The thralls fell back under the unceasing horde.

As the shades broke to the far side of the bridge, a blackness rose from the Terrestrial's Monolith. The blackness was not like the shades' shadows, but appeared like a bruise upon the air, virulent and wrong. Beneath it, the shades and thralls fought unaware. The blackness coalesced into a shape as tall as the war beast that now lay at the bottom of the chasm. From the shape's head sprung yellow white horns as tall as a man. Dark blue skin formed upon six arms and a bald head. Red and black armor protected the humanoid shape. Large turquoise earings, each the size of a carriage wheel, hung from its ears. Now the armies stopped fighting and looked upon the Terrestrial.

The Terrestrial spoke in a booming voice that was heard only in the minds of the onlookers. He said, "Shinigorath, we meet face to face at last. Pity it is as enemies. We could have joined together. Two great hiveminds to conquer the world. I could have helped you hone your powers, but instead you sided with them." The Terrestrial waved a dismissive hand at the northern armies.

"Now hear me!" the Terrestrial roared. "I am the Terrestrial. I fell to your planet from the far reaches of the heavens, where I was a conqueror. While your planet was a swirling mass of dust in the cosmos, I was creating armies. When your moon was blasted from the Earth's surface, I was destroying planets a hundred times more powerful than yours. My time here has been short and annoying, and I will not remain for long. Upon your backs I will ride my way to the stars again. So, come, weak mortals and short-lived gods. Come, Shinigorath, send in your army of a million shades. I will break them all, and in the end, you will serve me as all have."

Gold laughed up at Order and shouted to Shinigorath, "I love fighting arrogant bastards! There's a sense of righteousness in it. Let's get him!"

Shinigorath smiled and put up a hand to slow down Gold. Shinigorath looked up at the Terrestrial and said, "An army of a million shades? No, try saying that again, but this time with a b and an s, and not bs as in bullshit, but bs as in billions."

As Morsmani said "billions" the chasm walls exploded in writhing black shapes. Shades covered the entirety of the chasm and flooded the ground. They crawled on the Terrestrial like a fuzzy cloak of ants. The shades were so numerous and so tightly packed that they no longer rushed forward as an army but as a fluid. Their momentum crashed against Order like a tsunami. The Terrestrial stumbled back. The shades crawled up him. They clung to his hide, and two more layers of dead warriors clung to them. Under this great weight the Terrestrial fell to his knees, his head bowed. Gold burst through the throng and delivered a great blow with his hammer to the Terrestrial's brow. The shock of the strike could be heard over the battle all the way from where Nom stood. The Golden Key's copy shattered against the blue hide. Order lifted Gold into his hands as he stood again. Holding Gold above his head, the Terrestrial ripped the warrior god's head from his body.

Klart gasped. Nom looked over at the old man. Klart whispered to himself, "Not like him, not like him, not like him. Get him out of your head."

Nom looked back at the battle. The Terrestrial was sweeping away the shade army. More and more rushed forward, but they were all beaten back. Although they covered the ground and made it shake with their advance, they could do no harm to Order. Shades split into more shades. Shades crawled over one another to get at their enemy. Shades covered the earth and the air like a grotesque foam of human limbs and faces. They smothered the ground. The tramping of their feet was louder than thunder. The dust picked up by their movements was greater than The Sand Sea's dust storm. The earth was transformed into a writhing macabre mass. And that mass could do no harm to the Terrestrial.

The sea of shadows parted and Shinigorath walked to the feet of his enemy.

Shinigorath shouted into the minds of everyone present saying, "You have gone through a few million with your wild swings, Terrestrial. You were right. You will break them all if this continues. So, why don't we fight, you and I?"

Shinigorath raised the Great Star of Isen in his fist. The Terrestrial's scream echoed across the sky as a golden dome fell around the hiveminds. As the golden light descended, all the shades, save Amy, disappeared in black mist that fell away down into the chasm. The Terrestrial's thralls stood vacant and empty, staring into the air. The thralls who were injured in the fighting now showed their hurt and fell to the ground. Inside the dome, the Terrestrial and Shinigorath were transforming.

Morsmani shrunk to be even smaller than he already was. His red armor rusted, the gold leaf on his helmet cracked and fell off. He undid the clasps on his armor and let the rusting, ancient garment fall to the ground. He slowly took off his helmet and let it drop. The helmet split into its two pieces on impact. The horned crown with the fox face fell away from the mask. The mask rolled out of the dome of light. Outside the dome, the helmet returned to its lustrous red hue. A fire tyror picked up the helmet and was immediately killed by his companions. In the small scuffle for the helmet amongst the fire tyrors a runtish tyror grabbed the helm and slunk away.

The Terrestrial was shrinking as well. His blue skin melted revealing writhing black tentacles underneath. All that remained of the god of order was a mass, taller than two men, of a thousand tangled, thrashing tentacles, each with a barbed claw on their ends.

Morsmani, now stripped of Shini and Gorath, fell to his knees. His age was finally showing. The wrinkles on his face were as deep as the chasm he had crossed moments before. His white hair was brittle and sparse, like abandoned spider webs. He began screaming and pounding the dirt with his fists.

Nom gasped and wondered what Morsmani was doing.

"Gorath and Shini have returned to being a part of Morsmani. He placed them in his helmet and crown long ago to keep them away, as a way to control himself better. Isen's light takes away magic. So, they returned to him. That is how most of us knew Shinigorath long ago," Klart Bumble explained.

Nom looked at the screaming man and the massive monster. He closed his eyes and saw Korki falling from the bridge. He saw his childhood village in flames. He saw Azra burnt, broken, and depressed. Rage swelled in his chest. Nom opened his eyes and stepped off the wall. Air rushed by him as he fell. He felt no fear; a rare occurrence. His only concern was reaching the battle between the gods as quickly as he could. Before landing on the ground and breaking his ankles, he slowed down. He alit softly and thought, *'Thank you, God King.'*

Klart answered in his mind, "I will not save you again, Nom."

Nom nodded and rushed through the remaining army. Down at the bottom of the wall the battle was much more real. The air smelt of blood and sweat. The dust clogged Nom's throat. All around were wounded soldiers moaning and crying. Nom felt all the carnage and terror and wondered why anyone would ever want to start something that would end like this. Why would anyone wish for war? Nom ran across the bridge, his feathers billowing out like banners behind him. As he approached the dome of golden light, he unsheathed his sword and took out his knife. He entered Isen's light.

Shinigorath screamed at the mass of tentacles as he clutched his head. His scarred skin stretched tight against his thin skull. The Terrestrial, now in his true form, sat and pulsed. The tentacles constantly moving. They rubbed one another and rolled about like a pile of worms in a puddle after the rain. The Terrestrial was silent, there apparently was no mouth inside the tentacles.

Shinigorath stood. He hobbled, uncertain on his newfound ancient legs, toward the Terrestrial with his tomahawk raised. The Terrestrial ignored his approach. Shinigorath let out a shout of "I hate you!" as he weakly swung the axe down on a tentacle. The tomahawk bit flesh. Green blood gushed out. The mass writhed in response and lashed out in search of the cause of the pain. The tentacles touched Shinigorath who swatted them away, causing more damage. The monster shied away, bleeding. Then, the tentacles rushed forward and wrapped themselves around the god of madness. The claws cut deep into Shinigorath and he screamed out weakly. He cut a few more tentacles with the tomahawk and was released. Before he could stand, more tentacles came down upon him. The Terrestrial beat and cut him, pounding Shinigorath into the ground.

Nom could not watch this. He shouted, "Stop! Can you not see he is old? He is no match for you anymore. Please. Stop this."

The tentacles did not cease. They did not stutter. Nom wondered if the the Terrestrial was blind and deaf. He crept forward and pricked a tentacle with his sword. He jumped back as a tentacle swung to where his sword had been. The tentacle thrashed the air and then returned to beating Morsmani. Nom stepped forward and swung with all his strength at another appendage. The tentacle split under his sword and lay dead upon the ground. Nom scurried undignifiedly away. Tentacles rushed to where he had been. They searched the air and ground and found nothing. Nom again severed a tentacle, and again retreated. This dance continued for a time. Nom lead the Terrestrial on a merry chase about the dome of golden light, until he was grabbed.

A tentacle wrapped itself around Nom's leg. Nom tried to break free. He hacked at the appendage with his sword. As he attacked one tentacle more came and grabbed him. One grabbed the sword, bleeding in the process, and snapped the sword in two, the sword's black familiar stone powerless under Isen's gaze. Nom cried out in fear and anger. He struggled against his bonds. The tentacles were slippery with slime and hard with scales. They dragged Nom forward, toward the center of their great mass. The writhing limbs parted, and Nom saw in the center of the Terrestrial was a red, glowing orb. The tentacles all connected to the orb, but they did not protrude from the orb. At the base of each tentacle were rows of teeth as large as Nom's pointer finger that bit into the orb. Nom was dragged toward the pulsing orb at the center of the writhing mass.

The boy wriggled until the hand with his tungsten knife came free of his slimey bonds. He squinted forward and threw the knife at the orb. The knife sank into the orb up to its haft. The tentacles writhed in agony, dropping Nom. Nom leapt up and rushed to his knife. He pulled it out of the glowing orb and plunged it back in again and again. The Terrestrial began retreating. The tentacles dragged themselves backwards, away from the enraged boy. Nom slashed at the encroaching worms and cut at the orb. They approached the edge of the dome of light. The injured tentacles that left the light quickly began healing. Nom saw this and nervously thought, *'Can not let the orb leave. Can not let the orb leave.'*

Nom needed something large, something that could do more damage. He looked around. Lying on the ground was Shinigorath. He was bleeding and broken in a thousand places. He smiled and slid the Golden Key across the ground to Nom. Nom picked up the rusted war hammer, its weight now gone along with its magic and structural integrity.

The Terrestrial's orb was now out of Isen's light. It screamed into the minds of every living thing within a hundred miles. Its wound began healing and its armor began repairing. Nom rushed forward and raised the hammer above his head. He swung downwards at the orb. As the hammer arced forward its head left the light and returned to its golden hue. Along with the color, the magical weight of the hammer returned. Nom lost control of the hammer as it sped forward under its own momentum. The hammer slammed into the orb, splattering it like a tomato. The worms writhed and cut at themselves until they lay still, dying.

The Terrestrial was dead. The red orb turned to dark amber.

The dome of light lifted upwards and formed the dress of a beautiful woman. Isen's ethereal form floated down to Nom and kissed him upon his brow. A bright starburst that shone a golden white appeared on Nom's dark skin where she had kissed him. She disappeared back into her familiar stone, which flung itself far away into the chasm, never to be found again. The Golden Key, Nom's sword, Morsmani's armor, and crown began healing under the sun's natural rays. Nom rushed over to Morsmani.

The god of chaos lay in a great pool of crimson. His hair slowly returned to red and his wrinkles disappeared. His scarred face was strained, and his eyes were scared. He was still bleeding.

"Will you make it?" Nom asked.

Amy walked over and stood above Nom.

Nom looked up and asked, "Will he make it? He will not die, will he?"

Amy smiled sadly. Across the bridge, Pet cried diamond tears. Morsmani grabbed Nom's arm. Nom looked down.

"I died the moment I summoned my army. I died the moment I agreed to Klart's plan. In all the best scenarios, I died." Morsmani explained.

Nom let large tears roll down his cheeks. He could not say anything. He burst with questions but could ask none.

Morsmani continued, "Nom, take my crown, The Crown of Madness. It harbors Gorath, who may help you in whatever you do next. Oh! And also, take the Golden Key, it harbors Gold. Maybe with his help Klart won't be mocking you when he calls you king of kings. I'm sorry, Nom."

"For what?" Nom choked out.

"Your childhood. You were nearing its end and I took it… I took it. I stole what remained of it away by taking you to war."

Nom shook his head. Snot fell off his watery face.

"You did not take my childhood," Nom said. "My childhood ended when my father's village burned down. You saved me. I was so sad, and my life felt so grey. I was alone, so alone, until you and Amy came."

Mormsani smiled. His scars stretched gruesomely as he replied, "I'm glad. You will do great things, Nom." Then the god of chaos, death, and madness looked up at the Phoenix Goddess of Shadow and asked, "Amy, isn't it funny how the only good things I ever did were to help kill a monster, a monster with feelings, like me. Even my good deeds kill. Will you be there?"

Amy smiled. Her red eyes glistened with tears and she replied, "That's not true or funny. And yes, I'll be there. I will show you all the secret places between the burning pools and frozen plains. We will wander the eldritch halls together for all time."

Morsmani smiled, his eyes closed, and he turned to dust. Nom saw two smokey shapes leave the dust. One rushed to the crown of madness and one ran towards the south in search of a runtish fire tyror.

*****

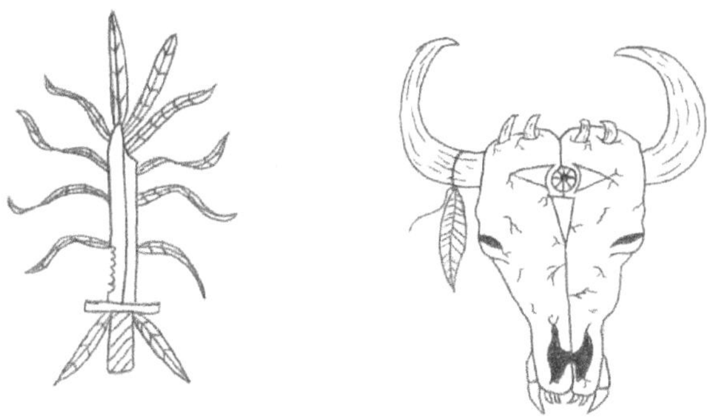

Chapter 26
A New Age

The scags celebrated the birth of Korki's son. Celebrations had gripped Urbe and Ghett for many days after the fall of the Terrestrial. The silver folken had a massive formal feast with such formidable entrees as swan, goose, and roast pig. The peasants of Ghett had frolicked in the streets, their beer glasses overflowing and spilling into the gutters. Now, however, the last of the celebrations was at hand. One of Korki's wives, Cormellan, had given birth to a boy beescag. All the scag tribes and scagfriendkin were outside Ghett, they were not allowed to celebrate such an occasion in the city.

A massive barbecue sat to the side of the gathering. Nom was in line for seconds. He had piled his bowl high with noodles, bell peppers, and buffkin meat. He watched the scags fawn over the larval beescag. The grey worm wriggled and lifted wet, translucent wings. The scags gasped in adoration. Nom looked away horrified.

He took his bowl from the chef and sat at the edge of the celebration, looking out at Urbe. Isen's Wall was no more. The towers stood in their green glass glory alone. They looked lost and forgotten already. Many silver folken had died in the battle and Nom had been told by Klart that the silver folken would soon be forced from their homes. Their numbers would dwindle over time, and eventually disappear. Nom knew they blamed Shinigorath for this fate. When a silver folken had seen Nom wearing the crown of madness on top of his feathers, they had glared and quickly walked away.

Azra sat down next to Nom and asked, "Why are you out here alone, Carver? Don't you want to join the celebration? Beatrice's embrace has allowed Korki's tribe to survive! It's a joyous occasion."

Nom shook his head. "There has been celebration every day since I… since the Terrestrial died. Everyone is so happy, but I feel so sad. How can people be happy after seeing battle? All I see when I close my eyes is that battlefield covered in blood. I see the shades swarming the ground. I feel the panic…"

Azra put an arm around Nom's shoulders and replied, "Part of the celebrations is to forget the pain and celebrate that we survived. This celebration, though, is to celebrate new life."

Nom nodded and leaned towards Azra.

Azra smiled and asked, "You don't like the baby, do you?"

Nom jerked away and looked at Azra shocked. He answered unconvincingly, "I do! The baby is cute."

Azra laughed. "It's fine. Beescag babies are… different." Azra leaned in and whispered, "And between you and me, beescags never really become cute. They just get less slimey and more scaley."

Nom laughed. He only felt happy when he was with Azra now. When Azra was gone all he could think about was the battle, Morsmani, and Amy. He remembered how he had banished Morsmani so coldly, but now that he was gone, Nom was filled with a sense of loss. Nom also wondered why Amy had not tried to save Morsmani by explaining that she would die when he died. Nom could have accidently ordered both of their executions in the trial. The thought made Nom shiver.

"So, what are you going to do now, Godsbane?" Azra asked Nom.

"What?" Nom asked.

"Well, now that the war is over and you completed your mission, what are you going to do? Are you going to go back to New Keys?"

"No, what did you call me?"

"Godsbane. That's what everyone in Ghett is calling you, seeing as how you killed a god. You're getting titles just like me, but you've earned yours. You are Nom Carver, Representative of New Keys, Last Apprentice of Shinigorath, Keeper of Gorath and Gold, Blessed by Isen, Godsbane, Scagfriendken. I left the best title for last. So! What are you going to do now?"

Nom looked into Azra's purple eyes. She seemed worried. Nom noticed she wasn't breathing while she waited for his answer.

He said, "I do not know. I am not going back to New Keys. There is nothing there for me and I really like it here. The mainland is exciting. Maybe I will wander around Usmer. Become a scholar like Morsmani. What are you going to do?"

Azra finally breathed, but she still looked worried. "I have to finish my incarnate training." Azra paused, bit her lip and looked south towards Ghett. Then she continued, her words running into each other as they rushed out of her mouth. "You could travel with me, I'll be going from totem to totem to see my past lives, all over Usmer, will you come with me?"

Azra stopped. Her face was beet red, and her eyes were watery. Nom finally understood why she was nervous. She was worried that she'd never see him again. He was flooded with warmth. Nom had always figured he would travel back the way he come and would be with Azra at least until Scagtower, so he was not worried about not seeing Azra again just yet.

He smiled, and all of the pain and sadness from the battle disappeared in an instant. He said, "I woud like that. I would love that, Azra. I was planning on staying with the scag tribes for as long as I could, because, well, because…" Nom took a deep breath and dived in saying, "Because you would be there."

Azra beamed. Her pale face lit up like the sun and her pearly canines shone between her red lips.

Before she could reply a small toadstool at their feet began banging on Azra's sandals.

Azra and Nom stared down at the mushroom. It had small protuberances around its stem which seemed to act like arms and legs, and four large eyes peered out at them from under the wide shelf of the red mushroom cap. The mushroom-like animal stared at Azra and Nom and began gesturing with his appendages. Nom and Azra had no idea what was happening. Nom wondered if it was trying to say something.

"Sorry, sorry. He ran away on me. How do you people keep track of your spores when they can think on their own?" Myco asked as she hurried towards them. She was in her pink spore swarm state today. She shimmered in the air like a dream of beauty. If Nom did not know that she was made of spores he would have thought she was a spirit of young beauty.

Azra asked, "Myco, is this your child?"

Myco nodded as she floated up to them. "Yes, yes," she answered. "One of my many children. I've never had kids. Never could, 'cause, you know, I was alone since leaving the Golden Council. But, I decided to try for some now. I realized after being with all of you how alone I had been. And I know you will all leave soon. After all you can't live in Mycostadur. So now I have a family to keep me company."

Nom asked, "Who is the father?"

Myco looked wistfully through the crowd and replied, "Oh, just someone who has a passion for mushrooms, like me."

Nom and Azra glanced at each other and tried to hide their smirks. Azra giggled slightly. Luckily Myco did not notice.

Myco picked up her lost son and sat cross legged on the ground.

"Nom," Myco said. "Will you help me?"

Nom looked from Azra to Myco and asked apprehensively, "With what?"

Myco stated, "I want to make a peace treaty with Hort. Hort, Gerud, Backbone and I have had a treaty where we each get our own lands and we stay in those lands. Although, Gerud seems to forget this quite often. I want to break that treaty. I want my family and myself to live in Hort's lands, closer to the humans and scags. I want you to broker this new treaty."

"Why me?" Nom asked.

Myco tilted her head to the side in confusion. "You've been blessed by Isen. That starburst on your head means you're something special. You carry a god's soul on your back, a god's soul on your forehead. You have stood in judgement of the gods, been trained by the gods, and killed the gods. You are something special, Nom, maybe even a god. I want you to broker an arrangement between my children and I, and Hort."

Nom looked at Azra in amazement. Azra smiled widely and laughed. She threw her arms around Nom and yelled, "Carver's not a human! Carver's not a human! Carver's a big beastie who talks to trees and shrooms!" Then Azra looked at Myco and quickly added, blushing, "No offense Myco. I was just poking fun at Nom."

Myco smiled. Her son stuck what looked like a tongue out of a hole below his eyes. Three more mushroom children peeked around Myco and did the same. Myco waved her hand in a gesture that said she understood.

Nom nodded. "Okay, I will help you. I would be glad to help."

Myco smiled and her children, clapping their appendages, climbed out from behind their mother and danced a strange bobbing dance. There were around a dozen of them, each with a different number of arms and legs and different colored mushroom caps. A few even had more than one cap.

Azra and Nom watched the dance smiling. Nom reached out and grabbed Azra's hand. She squeezed his hand in return. Nom wondered what may lay ahead for them in the north.

Glossary and Appendices

This section of the book is to provide a quick guide and reference to the world of Usmer for the reader.

Glossary of Terms

1. **Promethean:** Prometheans are magical beings created by the Forbear, the Maker. For more information see Appendix A: Prometheans

2. **Forbear:** The Forbears were an ancient people who ruled the world long ago. Many Forbears were rumored to be magical and many people consider the Forbears to be ancient gods.

3. **Scag:** Scags are a grouping of many different races that appear in Usmer. For more information on scags see Appendix B: Races of Usmer, Section 2

4. **Familiar Stone:** Familiar stones are magical stones that can be found in magical creatures and beings. They hold the souls and power of the creature they come from. Familiar stones are often used to enchant objects.

5. **The God Spring:** The God Spring is a legendary spring which fell from the heavens and is the source of magic in Usmer.

II

Appendix A: Prometheans

Prometheans are powerfully magical beings created by the forbear the Maker. The Maker took a select few humans and gave them magical abilities through his inhumane experiments. The Prometheans are generally considered the most powerful beings on Usmer and many have been given the titles of gods. Due to the reverence and power given to the Prometheans most have taken over some aspect of Usmer. Many have taken to protecting certain places of Usmer as their domains or have taken it upon themselves to protect the lesser races of Usmer. The immortal Prometheans generally are very unique in their powers and abilities.

In the time of *Forgiveness,* the term Promethean has been changed slightly to include any being with unique magical abilities whether they were granted their powers by the Maker or not. Notably, Ruhk, Amy, and Gold are all considered Prometheans, but they did not receive their magical powers from the Maker.

List of Prometheans appearing or mentioned in *Forgiveness*:

1. **Morsmani**
   a. Abilities: Telepathy/mindreading
      Great strength and speed
      Summoning of shades and the red tide
      Skin stealing
   b. Titles: Namer
   c. Description: Morsmani, also known as Namer, is a traveling Promethean. He claims to be a scholar. Not much is known about this promethean besides the fact that he works closely with Klart Bumble and Shangri, and that he hangs around undesirable parts of town. Few know why he is called Namer. He is the husband of Amy Milliken.

2. **Backbone**
   a. Abilities: Control of water
      Control of storms
      Control of sea creatures
   b. Titles: god of water
   c. Description: Backbone is the god of water. He was a member of The Golden Council during the Red Gold Conflict. Disgusted by the atrocities of war and vileness of humans he abandoned the world. He left Usmer near the end of the Red Gold Conflict to live alone in the ocean. His name was given to him mockingly by Shinigorath, who stated that Backbone was the moral backbone of The Golden Council.

3. **Shangri**
   a. Abilities: Great control over familiar stones
      Flight
   b. Titles: Collector and Keeper of Souls
      Supreme Artificer
   c. Description: Shangri is considered the wisest of the Prometheans. He was a member of The Golden Council and still stays in touch with the council's remaining members. He teaches his disciples, the artificers, the art of enchanting objects using familiar stones in his temple in eastern Usmer.

4. **Amy Milliken**
   a. Abilities: Control over shadows
      Resurrection
   b. Titles: Titaness of Shadow
      Phoenix Goddess
   c. Description: Amy Milliken is the granddaughter of the Maker and wife of Morsmani. She is one of the last of the Forbears, but most people in Usmer think of her as a Promethean. She is famous for her control over shadows, and many people who rely on the

night for business, like the Carrion Feeders, worship her, believing that she brings the shadow of night.

5. **Klart Bumble**
   a. Abilities: Telepathy/mindreading
      Telekinesis
      Foresight/the ability to see the future
   b. Titles: King of the gods
      Great Prophet
      Protector of Usmer
   c. Description: Klart Bumble is considered to be the most powerful being in Usmer. He is the king of the gods, though he does not claim this title. He was the leader of The Golden Council. He has the ability to see the future and spends his time advising and manipulating the people of Usmer so as to avoid great calamities. He works closely with Shangri, Morsmani, and many other powerful beings. He is the husband of Beatrice Bumble.

6. **Beatrice Bumble**
   a. Abilities: Control of fire
      Flight
      Reincarnation
      Beatrice's Embrace
   b. Titles: Queen of the gods
      The Incarnate
      Protector of Scags
      Mother of Dragons
      Mother of Scags
   c. Description: Beatrice Bumble, the wife of Klart Bumble, was the most powerful dragon. She was killed by her son, John, a buffscag, in the Battle of Fallen Arms. As she died, she gave her soul to the scags and is continuously reincarnated in a scag woman every generation. Her reincarnations are called Incarnates. The Incarnates have the body of

scags but can harness all of Beatrice's powers and can commune with all their past lives. She also granted the doomed scags with what they call Beatrice's Embrace. This power granted the scags the ability to reproduce, which was taken away by the Maker, and ensures that there is always a male scag in each tribe. As long as each scag tribe is still within Beatrice's embrace their tribe cannot die unless they are all killed at once.

7. **Shinigorath**
   a. Abilities: Mind reading/telepathy
      Skin stealing
      Great strength and speed
      Creation of thralls
      Summoning
   b. Titles: God of Death
      God of Madness
      God of Chaos
      Trickster
   c. Description: Shinigorath is the most reviled of all Prometheans. During the Red Gold Conflict Shinigorath was banished from the Golden Council for his crimes. After this he brought about the apocalypse which destroyed all of the Forbears, as well as most of the world. Shinigorath disappeared after the apocalypse, but most people believe he is still wandering the world, sowing discord.

8. **The Tormented**
   a. Abilities: Mind reading/telepathy
      Fear
      Shapeshifting
   b. Titles: God of fear
   c. Description: The Tormented, the oldest of the Prometheans, was the teacher of Klart Bumble during their time in the Maker's Palace, and a

member of the Golden Council. His uncontrollable mind reading ability allows himself to see the fears of everything around him. All who gaze upon the Tormented see their worst fears. Because of the pain inflicted on the Tormented and the things around him by his mindreading abilities, the Tormented has hidden himself away in his tower and allows no visitors to see him. He remains in contact through letters with many of the other Prometheans.

9. **The Lady**
   a. Abilities: Voice of Control
      Reincarnation
   b. Titles: Queen of the Tommy Knockers
   c. Description: The Lady is the queen of the Tommy Knocker nation. Unlike the other Prometheans she is not immortal and lives a human span of years. She is reincarnated each generation to continue leading her people. Her power, the voice of control, allows her to completely control all those who listen to her.

10. **Myco**
    a. Abilities: Control of fungi
    b. Titles: Goddess of mushrooms
    c. Description: Myco, the youngest of the original Prometheans, is the godess of mushrooms. She herself has become a fungal lifeform and controls all the fungi within her domain of Mycostadur. She is at war with Gerud, and is enemies with Hort.

11. **Gerud**
    a. Abilities: Control of Sand
    b. Titles: God of the Sand Sea
    c. Description: Not much is known about Gerud. After the Red Gold Conflict Gerud disappeared until the Sand Sea appeared in south eastern Usmer. No one has seen Gerud since the Sand Sea's appearance and

one theory is that Gerud is the Sand Sea. He is currently at war with Myco and Hort.

12. Red
- a.   Abilities: Telekinesis
- b.   Titles: None
- c.   Description: Red, son of the Tormented, was the Maker's assassin until the Prometheans' escape. After the Prometheans escaped the Maker's Palace, Red began leading the scags, the tyrors, and a few Prometheans and humans in an attempt to conquer the world and punish the Forebears. He was defeated by the Golden Council and died at The Battle of Fallen Arms.

13. Hort
- a.   Abilities: Control of Plants
- b.   Titles: God of plants
       First Ent
- c.   Description: Hort is a member of the Golden Council, and the Promethean in charge of his forest, Hort's Forest, which covers most of Usmer. Hort has become a tree whose roots and offshoots stretch throughout Usmer. He is in constant war with Gerud and Myco.

14. Gold
- a.   Abilities: Telekinesis
       Great Strength and Speed
- b.   Titles: God of war
       Leader of the Silver Folken
       Leader of the Golden Council
- c.   Description: Gold was not created by the Maker. After Klart released the God Spring many plants and animals gained special powers naturally. Gold was one of these. A troubled youth with anger problems, he gained superhuman strength and speed, golden

skin similar to the silver folken's silver skin, and telekinesis that was less powerful than Red's. He led the Golden Council in battle against Red. After defeating Red, Gold left Usmer to search for a Forbear artifact to help the Tommy Knockers survive, and to help the people of Usmer fight the fire tyror king when it will eventually attack Usmer in the far future. Gold died on the other side of the Sundering soon after finding the artifact he was searching for. All that came back to Usmer of his mission was the artifact and Gold's hammer, the Golden Key.

15. **The Terrestrial**
    a. Abilities: Telepathy
    b. Titles: God of order
    c. Description: The Terrestrial is a being who fell from the heavens with the tyrors, Isen and the God Spring. Little is known about the Terrestrial other than its ability to take control of other's minds and control their thoughts and actions.

16. **Isen**
    a. Abilities: Can banish magic
    b. Titles: Goddess of light
    c. Description: Isen fell from the heavens like the Terrestrial. However, she fell as a familiar stone, having already died. Nothing is known about Isen. She has never spoken or communicated with anyone. She is considered the protector of Usmer.

X

Appendix B: Races of Usmer

1. Humans

Humans are the most prolific race in Usmer. Most humans do not naturally have magical abilities, but some are born with magic. According to legend all of the sentient races of Usmer, including the Prometheans, can trace their ancestry back to humans.

2. Scags

The scags are a diverse group of races who came about by the Maker combining humans and animals. They sided with Red during the Red Gold Conflict and, due to this, the scags are hated, feared, and discriminated against by the other races of Usmer. Beatrice Bumble gave the scags the ability to reproduce and ensures that there is always one male for each tribe. Below is a list of the different scag races.

    i. <u>Kajscags</u>

The kajscags are a nomadic race of scags who come from a combination with cats. The kajscags have markings on their skins like cats and extra canine teeth. The males are completely covered in fur. Because of their cat ancestry the kajscags are faster and more agile than humans and can see in the dark. The kajscag tribes wander the plains of Usmer following the great herds of buffkin. They are known for their hunting prowess and their finely crafted tomahawks and string instruments.

    ii. <u>Beescags</u>

The beescags are a giant race of scags who come from a combination with beetles. They all have hard exoskeletons which are impervious to most weapons. They have wings which they use for communication and flight. Due to their size and their heavy armor the beescags are incredibly powerful and slow. Most of the beescag tribes live in the deserts of Usmer and help journeying scags across the more dangerous areas of these deserts. They have little contact with races other than the scags.

iii. <u>Chocobscags</u>

Chocobscags, humans combined with birds, are the most well liked amongst the nonscag races of Usmer. They appear human except for the large feathered wings which sprout from their shoulder blades. Many people from the other races are reminded of the angels which, according to legend, lived in the times before the Forbears. Because of this comparison the chocobscags are treated better than the other scag races. They are still discriminated against however. The chocobscags are known for their wind instruments, long staves and spears, and for flying across Usmer. The chocobscags prefer to live along tall cliff faces and in the tall trees of Hort's Forest. They act as the messengers for the scag races.

iv. <u>Buffscags</u>

Buffscags were created by the Maker to be the strongest and most warlike race. They were combined with many animals to become strong and fierce. After the fall of the Forbears the buffscags began believing that they came from the buffkin, a post-apocalyptic species of bison. This, however, is not true. Most their animal nature comes from the gorilla and they were named buffscags due to their large muscles, not their similarity to the buffalo. The buffscags are a warlike race of scag. They are tall, strong, and covered in thick hide and hair. They have horns, fangs, and claws which they use in battle in place of conventional weaponry.

v. <u>Gerudscags</u>

Gerudscags are a race of scag that lived in The Sand Sea. The fast evolution native to the scags caused the gerudscags' skulls to develop bone extrusions to protect their eyes from the wind and sand of the desert. These extrusions eventually became a single shelf of bone which covered their eyes and caused the race to go blind. In response the gerudscags' sense of smell and feel increased. They developed a second set of hands and thin cracks in their bone shelf to help utilize these senses. The gerudscags were wiped out by the Promethean Gerud.

vi. <u>Zorscags</u>

Zorscags are the most hated scag race after the buffscags. Unlike the buffscags, however, the zorscags are also disliked by the other scag races. They are a race of scag who come from frogs. Unlike the other scags the Maker gave frogs human DNA instead of giving humans frog DNA. The zorscags live in swamps, marshlands, and rivers throughout Usmer. Due to their habitat and their difficulty in traversing the Sand Sea to go to the yearly Scagmoots, the

Zorscags forsook Beatrice and began worshipping Backbone, the god of water. They now live outside Beatrice's embrace and are shunned by the other scag races.

3. Tommy Knockers

Tommy Knockers are a race of people who, after the fall of the Forbears, hid in safety shelters made in the mountains in ancient Usmer. They hid themselves away and were unaware for many years of what happened in the outside world. They tunneled from one shelter to another without going outside. They subsisted off mushrooms and gardens powered by the Forbear's artificial suns deep under the ground. The God Spring caused most people and animals in Usmer to evolve quicker than normal. This caused the Tommy Knockers to evolve to fit their subterranean lifestyles. They grew large eyes suited for low light, became short, lost most of their hair and pigment, and developed sensitive ears. Due to their reliance on Forbear technology and their hate and fear of magic the tommy knockers have become the last bastion for Forbear technology and the foremost leaders in smithing and machinery in Usmer. They are led by The Lady, a mortal Promethean who reincarnates every generation. The tommy knockers control every mountain range in Usmer and charge tolls to cross the mountains. Due to this and their disdain of other races they are not trusted and often referred to by their derogatory name, dwarrows.

4. Silver Folken

The silver folken are an immortal race of scholars living mostly in southern Usmer. They were created by the Maker as an experiment in what would happen to humans exposed slightly to the God Spring. The silver folken are extremely magical but less powerful than the

Prometheans. When they are not living near Isen's Wall watching the terror to the south they are wandering throughout Usmer conducting research on magic. They view the other races as barbaric and uncouth. Silver folken have silver skin and glow with a silver light.

5. **Dragons**

The first generation of dragons were created by the Maker by giving humans the essence of the God Spring. The first two generations of dragons can change from human to dragon form. Later generations remain in their lizard-like dragon form. Dragons born in the sixth generation and later lose their intelligence and humanity and are no more than beasts roaming the sky. Tommy knockers enjoy hunting these later dragons.

The earlier generations of dragons are considered by many in Usmer to be gods and are worshipped next to the Prometheans and spirit animals. Many of these dragons have used their strength and the people's worship to rule cities and kingdoms across the west of Usmer.

6. **Tyrors**

Tyrors are creatures not from Usmer. They fell from the heavens the same as the Terrestrial and the God Spring. They are the strangest race in Usmer. They do not reproduce, and appear to be made of either lava or ice and are extremely violent. When a tyror is killed their magical power is dispersed into all the other tyrors of the same type throughout the universe. If a tyror is killed by a tyror of the same type the killed tyror's magical power is given entirely to the killer.

During the Red Gold Conflict, the tyrors followed Red into battle. During the time of this story the tyrors follow the Terrestrial, their leader of old. The tyrors follow whoever is strongest, believing that the strongest being will be the one to throw down the current god and rebuild the universe in their image.

i. Fire tyrors

Fire tyrors are monsters of fire. They are creatures made from lava and volcanic stone. They are the most violent race on Usmer and have difficulty working with anyone, even other tyrors. They believe, through their knowledge of the heat death of the universe and how their power is transferred, that eventually everything will die. All the magic and energy of the universe will eventually become nothing but heat, which the god of this universe will absorb into himself. At this time there will only be their god and the last fire tyror, who has the combined power of all the fire tyrors. The last tyror and their god will battle, and eventually the fire tyror will defeat their god and take all of the magic and energy of the universe. This tyror will become the god of a new universe, which he will create, until the next final being of the new universe will defeat the final tyror.

ii. Ice tyrors

Ice tyrors are beasts of ice. They live in the far northern regions of Usmer on top of the Great Ice Shelf. They are violent and treacherous. Like the fire tyrors, the ice tyror's culture and temperament is greatly influenced by their religion which varies slightly from the fire tyror's. The ice tyrors believe that in the end there will be one being of this universe left, who will fight the being who created this universe from the ashes of the previous. Unlike the fire tyrors, however, the ice tyrors recognize that this being may not be an ice tyror. After all, the final being of the previous universe is most likely not a tyror. The ice tyrors see this as a sign that anyone strong enough could be the last being. Due to this belief the ice tyrors are much more willing to work with others and have created a society amongst themselves. This belief also has allowed the ice tyrors to not actively seek to be the final being. The fire tyrors fight and kill to become the last, the ice tyrors believe that eventually, with or without their help, there will be only one being left. In the ice tyrors' opinion there is no reason to hasten the end.

XVIII

Appendix C: Nations and Groups of Usmer

1. **New Keys**

   New Keys is an ancient kingdom in the tropical islands off the eastern coast of Usmer. The kingdom was founded by fugitives fleeing from mainland Usmer during the Red Gold Conflict. The fugitives integrated with the island natives and set up a new kingdom with strong isolationist and anti-magic policies. The natives, since they knew how to live on the islands, became the leaders of New Keys and their native tongue became the language of royalty while the fugitives' language became the common tongue for the island people. The island kingdom's main exports are sugar and rum.

2. **Chinchiplas**

   Chinchiplas is an eastern kingdom of Usmer. It is the most southerly human nation in eastern Usmer and lies next to Hort's Wall and the great coastal swamps of south eastern Usmer. The kingdom consists of the city of Chinchiplas, and the surrounding lands within three days travel. The city, Chinchiplas, is known as a mound city. It is a giant pyramid made of mounded earth and clay bricks. The people have been building Chinchiplas for hundreds of years by adding layer and layer to the mound. The people of Chinchiplas are great traders and merchants and enjoy peace. Chinchiplas has never gone to war, only been targets of war. The kingdom has relied on its great walls and the artificially created high ground of the city to defend its people. The main exports of Chinchiplas are chinchilla fur textiles, sake, beer, rice, and wheat.

3. **Scag Nation**

   The Scag Nation is a large group of scag tribes. All the scag tribes except the zorscag tribes belong to the Scag Nation. The only land the Scag Nation officially owns are small pueblos in western Usmer and the Scagtower in eastern Usmer. The nation is as diverse culturally as the tribes and races that comprise it. One common thread throughout the nation, however, is that all the scags are known to be warriors. Long, constant warring between the Scag Nation and all the other races of Usmer has caused the scag tribes to place great pride in their fighting ability.

4. **Silver Folken**

The dwindling silver folken nation lies along the southern border of Usmer. The nation consists of silver folken and the humans who live near Isen's Wall and stretches from the eastern to western coast of Usmer. The silver folken have settlements along Isen's Wall with Urbe being their capitol. The silver folken nation's goals are to protect Usmer from southern threats and research magic.

5. **Tommy Knockers**

The tommy knockers lay claim to every mountain range in Usmer. Their nation is led by the Lady from their capitol Mariah. Due to their control of the mountains the tommy knockers control trade from east to west in Usmer and exact tolls. This means that the tommy knockers are the richest nation in Usmer. This control on trade and the hoarding of ancient Forbear technology makes them the most powerful nation as well.

6. **North Eastern Tribes**

The humans living in north eastern Usmer consist of many tribes without any rigid structure to their kingdom. Most tribes are made of a single family or a landowner and his farmhands. There is little rule of law amongst the tribes. The closest thing the tribes have to law is a code of rules that is discussed and decided on once a year at a gathering called The Thing. These rules are not hard set and often are ignored entirely. The people of north eastern Usmer are hard, brutal, and honest. They trust no one but their family and are not afraid to fight. Most young people in the tribes spend their summers raiding and pillaging the surrounding lands, while the older folk farm. In the winter the tribespeople shelter themselves from the cold in their homes and tell stories to pass the time. In the time of this story the north eastern tribes had come together under one ruler for the first time in history. Bairne brought the tribes together and they have begun conquering eastern Usmer.

7. The Terrestrial

The Terrestrial is a hivemind who controls a vast nation of people south of Usmer. While the people in his nation have no free will and are no different than the Terrestrial there is a structure and culture. It takes time for someone to fully succumb to the Terrestrial, and to lose themselves completely. While the process of control is taking place, these people have some free will and can sometimes act on their own. These people are given menial tasks by the Terrestrial until they come fully under his control. The Terrestrial's nation also harbors the fire tyrors. Tyrors cannot be controlled. They are wild and strong. The Terrestrial cannot take control of their minds. However, the Terrestrial keeps the tyrors around since they give advice and allow his nation to be more mobile and autonomous.

8. Groups

i. Artificers

The artificers are a group of people led by Shangri. They study the art and science of enchanting objects using magic. They work closely with traveling silver folken and do odd jobs around Usmer.

ii. Carrion Feeders

The Carrion Feeders are a group of assassins led by the forbear Ruhk. They have set up hideouts in every major city in Usmer and are usually at the center of any major conflicts. The Carrion Feeders are split into four groups; ravens, crows, magpies, and vultures. The ravens, named after the intelligent carrion birds, perform difficult missions, like political assassinations, spy work, and kidnapping. The crows perform jobs which require less finesse. Their jobs range from inciting riots, extortion, jail breaks, all the way to simple murder. The magpies are the accountants of the Carrion Feeders. They handle contracts and payments. The vultures are the leaders of the Carrion Feeders. They give directions and orders to the crows and ravens and secure contracts with clients. These groups are further delineated into three levels, eye, claw, and beak, with beak being the highest rank and eye the lowest.

iii. Shipwrights

The shipwrights are a group of sailors intent on keeping alive the ancient sea faring technology of the Forbears. They maintain and sail the metal ships of the Forbears. Most shipwrights are merchants although some are mercenaries and place their ships for hire. They work closely with the tommy knockers who are the only people in Usmer who can provide adequate replacements to damaged parts on their ships.

Acknowledgements

Firstly, I would like to thank my readers. Thank you for picking up and reading *Forgiveness*, and I hope you all enjoyed it and will continue to read the rest of the series.

Secondly, I want to thank my editors, Will and Dakotah. Your inputs were extremely helpful in completing this work. Will, your help with sentence structure and word choice made the book more fluid, and your issue with Quentin Duluth was hopefully mitigated. Dakotah, your grammar critique and continuity advise was fantastic. Thank you both.

I would also like to thank my family for their support, as I write this on my mom's couch in her living room.

About the Author

Joseph J. R. Johnson is a young engineer working and living in Colorado. He is a graduate from Colorado State University with a bachelor's degree in mechanical engineering and a bachelor's degree in Biomedical Engineering. His hobbies include skiing in the winter, playing tennis, playing the drums, reading, and of course writing.

Other Works by Joseph J. R. Johnson

Rising Wrath